Angela's Battle

E. Martin Savilla

AmErica House
Baltimore

Copyright 2000 by E. Martin Savilla

All rights reserved. No part of this book may be reproduced in any form without written permission from the publishers, except by a reviewer who may quote brief passages in a review to be printed in a newspaper or magazine.

First printing

Cover design by Carolyn White

ISBN: 1-893162-56-7
PUBLISHED BY AMERICA HOUSE BOOK PUBLISHERS
www.publishamerica.com
Baltimore

Printed in the United States of America

Every writer no doubt has a person close to them who puts up with his strange hours and mood swings while he is trying to both earn a living and to put an idea into manuscript form. In my case that person was my wife, Betty. She has been most understanding and encouraging throughout the more than three years, part time, it has taken to write this novel. She has been the model for Angela Beaver's inner strength, courage, determination and yes, even softness and loving tenderness. To her I owe much.

Before she died, when I was nine, my mother had instilled in me a work ethic and an ambition to be all I could be. She was a hard worker for her family, and always had a meal for the hungry, no matter their race. I call her the Good Samaritan of the Desert. I believe that if called upon, she could have been Angela Beaver. I owe her much also.

My father, William "Willie" Savilla, was an accomplished bandsman and a Navy veteran. He and his Quechan mates once served as the Navy band on the USS California. He gave me his musical ability, but it is his story telling and description of ancient Quechan history, myths and customs that are now priceless to me.

I dedicate this book to these three in appreciation for what they have done for me, and what they have given me.

Chapter One

It was January 20, 1963. Angela Beaver, a 41-year-old Native American woman, was driving west on the North side of the Grand Canyon in a battered once-blue Ford pickup truck. She had been to Phoenix, Arizona attending a three-day meeting of Native Americans who were concerned about what was happening to the environment of Mother Earth. What she heard there had only added to her concerns for her part of the country. Now, almost fearfully, she was going home to the Southern Paiute Indian reservation in southern Utah.

The Paiute Indian lands were located in the mountains of southwestern Utah almost due east and downwind of the Nevada Nuclear Test Site. Since the testing of nuclear bombs had begun on the desert of Yucca Flats, changes in the mountain environment had taken place so gradual that no one had noticed until Angela recently brought it to their attention.

When the wind blew from the west towards the Paiute reservation there was more dust in the air than was usual. Trees on the western slopes and in the mountain valleys were dying from polluted rainwater runoff from higher elevations. What had alarmed Angela was that last spring she noticed that there were no birds returning to nest in the forest. Then last November, in a month when the squirrels were usually out in large numbers gathering food, there were none to be seen.

She had asked the elders if this had happened before. "Never," they said. They were shocked when they found that Angela was right. They hadn't noticed. There weren't any birds, rabbits, squirrels, or other small animals to be seen. In December, she learned of a meeting in Phoenix to discuss environmental problems. She decided to make the trip to Phoenix. "Someone there might be able to tell me what's happening," she reasoned.

At the meeting, Jason Storm Cloud, a Native American journalist from Washington, D.C., had told them of a new kind of World War, called a Cold War. He told of the government's new rush to develop strong weapons of mass destruction, and of the potential for nuclear warfare which could destroy cities and people around the world. His report had frightened Angela.

Then in a small discussion group Storm Cloud said, "I encourage you to tell us of unusual things that are happening locally which might be messages or warnings from Mother Earth to wake people up to the harm being done to Her. Everyone should begin documenting all of these things so we can better understand what she is trying to tell us."

It is not the Indian way to assume that everyone wants to hear what one has to say. Wisdom is gained by listening to others, it was believed, so no one wanted to be the first to talk. After a few minutes of polite silence, an elderly man from the Nez Perce people said, "The Earth is beginning to do strange things everywhere, so we must open our ears and our eyes. Tell us what you have seen and heard so we may know what to do."

Tradition had been recognized. The stories began.

A man from New Mexico's Pueblo of Taos said, "For months, in the silence of night we have heard strange thumps, never heard before, coming from the earth. Many have heard this strange sound, even the white people in Santa Fe have heard it. Maybe the Earth is hurting. I don't know."

Another man from the Yakama people in Washington State said, "Yes, we have heard it too. It has even been reported in the Sunday newspapers in Seattle and in Portland. No one knows what is causing it."

A Mescalero Apache woman whose tribal government was planning to put a U.S. nuclear storage facility on their reservation told them, "One day a sudden strong wind came to our reservation. It was a cold and chilling kind of wind. It had a strange howl, and lasted for several hours. Large trees were snapped in half like twigs and others were pulled from the ground by their roots. My mother has told me that this is an omen of bad things to come."

She continued, "The nuclear fuel rods and other dangerous material which would be stored on our lands are made of uranium which came from Mother Earth, and the way the government has used it is a violation of Her spiritual being. There is a supernatural power working here, something that Man cannot control. The results of violating Mother Earth will be tremendous and we need to understand what she is telling us."

This opened the floodgates and others began telling of strange things which they had noticed recently. But the most chilling story came from a Mojave woman who lived on the lower Colorado River, downstream from Hoover Dam.

She said, "One of the legends of our people is about a thing which is called, *hoof man*, or *goat man*. It is an evil thing whose upper body looks like a man, but its lower half is that of a goat with split hooves. It is rarely seen, but when it appears people die horrible deaths. The legend said that it was last seen many generations ago, and yet there are new stories that it has recently reappeared and is again killing people. I have not seen this thing, but there are too many rumors being circulated, and if it is true, I think it is related to the many underground explosions of those damn nuclear bombs at the test site. For some reason, Hoof Man is awake again and I blame the government for everything bad that is happening."

She hesitated, then, *"Nya na mumpk.* That's all I have to say for now."

When the stories ended, Storm Cloud, who was of the Quechan people, also on the Colorado River, told them to begin talking to their friends about these things. The conference ended in a concerned mood.

Yes, Angela was frightened, but she had no idea of how to go about stopping the environmental damage being done to the Earth. Now she was hurrying to get home before dark. She was upset and concerned that Nature could get angry if the indigenous native people were not willing to protect Her. All kinds of weird thoughts were crowding her mind. She wondered what the future would be like for the children. At that thought, she became anxious to get home to her two daughters.

Angela's husband, Earl, had died of lung cancer over two years ago. In 1945 he had insisted on going down to Navajo country to work in one of the new uranium mines to get in on the "good money" to be made there. For ten years he brought home that good money, and later, when he got sick he was dead within three years. Her two daughters were now her main concern. She was angry at herself for letting Earl work in the mines, and at the government for not warning them of the danger from uranium.

She was now deep in the Dixie Forest of Utah where the soft pine trees grew thick and tall. Her Southern Paiute reservation home was about two hours ahead of her.

Suddenly, she was jolted out of her thoughts when a large dark form skimmed the top of the truck and flew in front of her. She was surprised to see that it was an eagle, an unusually bold one. *He must be very hungry and is looking for road kill,* she thought. *He'll leave me pretty soon.*

There was a fork in the narrow road just ahead. The right fork would take her home. The left road went to a deserted part of the forest. Six years ago the road had been cut through to enable fire fighters to reach a large fire at Posey Lake. The dirt road ended there. There were no ranches or houses on that road.

The eagle had been flying in front of her, then suddenly it swooped up and came back to her. It took the left fork and seemed to wait there for her. She slowed and the bird looped again and flapped one wing, as if to signal her to turn in that direction. She was amazed. She had never seen anything like this, so she slowed more. The eagle sat on the roadway, again signaling her. Suddenly she felt as if she was in a dream, not really seeing this happening. Almost by itself, the truck turned and took the left road.

The eagle flew slowly in front of her, leading her up one mountain, then over another. At the upper end of a valley, just before the road headed up a steep hillside, the eagle flew off the road and over a level patch of ground. Then it stopped. Angela stopped the truck and turned off the engine. The eagle immediately flew up and towards a thick patch of underbrush. She got out of the truck to see if there was a way to safely turn around.

I was a fool to take this road, she thought.

Then she heard a faint chattering which sounded like people talking softly, so no one could hear them. The sound was coming from the thicket.

Angela quietly walked towards the sound. There was a large boulder at the edge of the thicket, so she climbed on it to look over the underbrush. What she saw caused her to almost fall. Now she felt as if she really was dreaming.

In a small clearing directly in front of her was a circle of ten eagles. In the center of the circle an extraordinarily large eagle had its wings outstretched as if he were talking to the others. The others would nod their heads and chatter as if to agree with the speaker. Seated on the ground next to the large eagle was an old man that she knew. He lived in her Paiute village and had been a good friend of her grandmother. Now he seemed to be part of this strange group. Not one of them looked at her, yet they knew she was there.

Finally the large eagle folded his wings and looked at each one in the circle. Then he looked up at the treetops where the one who had brought her here was perched like a lookout on guard. This one then circled down and stood alongside the large eagle. When all was quiet, the Indian man who she knew as Amos Turkey, turned to look at Angela. She was frozen in place by fear and wonder. Then a warm feeling came over her, and she felt suddenly comfortable with what was happening.

"This is crazy, it can't be," she said aloud.

Amos stood, then said to her, "Angela, this is *Teek-awis*, the leader of this Council of Eagles. His son, Whistler, brought you here. He went with you in spirit to your meeting and it was his words that told the Council that you were worthy of being the first human female to see the Council of Eagles. All here today," and he indicated the circle of eagles, "came from the far points of this land to discuss ways to deal with a great danger which may come as a result of Man's foolish tinkering with the laws which Nature herself has set down. There is also a greater danger which if it comes to pass, will rob all of us of the spiritual strength and life which the Great One has put into us."

"The native people of this country are the closest relatives of the eagle. If we die so will they from sorrow and spiritual weakness. All of our ancestors have honored the eagle through the centuries, and now they have chosen you to carry a very important message to all people in order to prevent the coming disaster. They cannot ask you whether you want to do this or not. The Great One has given you no choice in the matter. You have been honored by His selection of you, and He has the greatest trust in you."

Amos continued. "Whistler has been assigned to watch over you at all times. He will help you at those times when you may be threatened, and he will help you to restore your spiritual strength when you need it most. Listen to him, for he will go with you now and explain the details of the danger which all of us will soon face. If you need help, he will call his father. Please trust him as the Great One has trusted you. I will talk with you later."

The large eagle then put his huge wings around his son and spoke quietly to him.

Angela's memory strangely faded, and when she awoke she was in her truck, back on the main road to her home. The young eagle called Whistler looked at her, then asked, "Are you alright?"

She looked at him sitting on the passenger side of the truck's seat. She hesitated before answering. It seemed so strange to be talking to a bird....an eagle. She had been raised to believe that eagles were to be honored and respected, but this was unheard of.

"I understand your confusion," Whistler said, "but you will get used to this before long. I am speaking to you by what we call 'mind talk.' You can understand my thoughts, and I can understand your speech, so let me start by telling you about the coming trouble. Then you can ask questions." Angela could only nod her head.

Whistler began a narration. "A long time ago, when the ice melted in this land and the mountains were formed by earthquakes, many strange beings were released from deep within the ground. They were half-man and half-animal and were ruled by the horned outcast who you people call the Evil One, and others call Devil. The Devil gathered them together and taught them only one thing, and that was how to corrupt and steal the spirit away from humans so that their spiritual souls would be delivered to his world of fire and punishment."

"You, of course, know that the souls of our native people, after their bodily death, are returned to the rivers and lakes where they stay until once again the Great One assigns them another body. I have lived before in another body as you have also, although you have no memory of that."

"Today, we have two problems. First, Man has embarked in a direction that poses a serious threat to our very existence. They have developed what they call 'atomic bombs,' and now they're on the verge of exploding powerful new ones called 'H-bombs.' The life-giving substances given us by the Great One are being destroyed by Man without a thought to future generations. Time is short in which to stop them from producing dangerous products which can destroy all of us. If we cannot stop them, the Great One will reclaim all that Man has destroyed."

"The second danger is that our Great Circle of Life is now threatened by the goat men. The Devil is again sending his servants above ground to begin collecting souls for his underground kingdom. He believes that a catastrophe, the end of our world, would be to his advantage. He is influencing human leaders to continue on their path of destruction to make it easier for his servants to collect those souls. If they succeed, our Great Circle will end and the world will become overrun with sickening evil just before the end of the world, and many souls will be lost forever."

"This is why you have been selected to lead an effort to bring together those who have the power to prevent the end of the world, and to send the half-man half-animal beings back to the land of eternal fire. We must not fail."

Whistler looked closely at Angela, then continued, "I know you are concerned about the health of the air, water, and Mother Earth, and so are we. When the waters become so polluted that we cannot drink it our spirits can no longer live in the River of Souls, and it will be a serious matter for all of us. All of this has been considered, and it has been decided that these demon creatures must either be destroyed or sent back to where they came from before they claim many human souls. Without souls, all Mankind will be lost spiritually, and they will become like animals."

Two hours later Angela was on the verge of tears when she turned into the dirt road which led to her frame house which the Paiute Tribal Housing Program had built for her. Her mind was in turmoil. "How was she going to manage all they wanted her to do and still take care of her children?"

When she stopped the truck in front of her home Whistler told her, "We'll begin by visiting with Amos Turkey later tonight I will call for you." Then he flew up into the trees to wait for their night visit.

Chapter Two

Amos Turkey's ancestral home was in the southeast part of the country. He was a half-breed indigenous Native American man whose father was of the Choctaw people. In 1885 his father had rescued a young black woman from the clutches of two white men near a backwoods town in Alabama. He had taken care of her, and one day he took her for his wife. They raised a family in western Alabama, in the mountains of Talladega.

One evening in the summer of 1900, Amos had been out hunting a rabbit for supper and came home just at twilight. He was 11 years old. He had expected to hear girlish laughter from his three sisters playing in the yard, but instead he heard loud cursing and shouting, and the sound of dry branches being dragged across the ground.

He ran into the woods, then crept closer to see what was happening. He saw a horrific sight. A dozen white men were piling logs and dry brush up against the doors and windows of his family's wooden log house. He could hear his father hollering at the men, asking for mercy for his wife and children while the men outside laughed insanely, whooping and hollering.

Amos watched, horrified, frightened and helpless to do anything as the fire began burning. He could have shot at them, but his father had told him never to shoot at a person. "Never, my son," he said.

He heard the screams of his mother, and saw his father trying to break through the walls, the doors, and windows in a futile effort to save his family. Finally, the screams stopped, the fire died down and the men went away quietly, sobered by their inhuman deed. Amos shivered silently all night in the woods.

In the early morning light he found and removed the charred bodies of his father, mother, and three siblings from the ashes while tears smeared soot on his face. He lay them together in one common grave behind the small barn. After filling the grave with dirt, he cried loudly while reciting a prayer he had learned from his mother. He left the grave unmarked, fearing that the men would come back and find it. Then he took their one mule out of a small corral, fashioned a rope bridle and began a long ride to the West. He didn't know where he was going, but his father had once told him of relatives who lived somewhere West of the Mississippi River. In 1835 they had been forced from their homes and made to walk to a place called "Indian Country."

Living off the land he wandered slowly westward. He found many Indian tribes, but none knew his father, so he continued on. In 1940 he arrived in the mountains of southern Utah. He felt peaceful when he reached the Southern Paiute community and decided to stay here because it reminded him of his own home.

He explained to the Paiute Tribal Council who he was, and where he had came from. "I only ask for a small piece of ground on which I can build a log cabin to live out the rest of my life," he had said to them. So, in accordance with their teaching that the earth belongs to no one, and yet to everyone, they allowed him to choose his own homesite.

He chose a spot near Angela's grandparents, and they became close friends. It was they who introduced him to spiritual men of several tribes, and under their guidance he had studied and prayed for weeks and months at a time. Later, he walked to the village of Kaibito in northern Arizona to spend time with a Hopi spiritual man, a very wise man, who taught Amos many things of the soul and of the mind. After three years of study in Kaibito, he had ridden with a trucker to the railroad town of Gallup, New Mexico, and from there he walked to the small village of the Zuni people, where he sought out one of the most revered and respected holy men in the southwest region.

Here at Zuni, he subjected himself to poverty and hunger in order to learn the secrets of the Great One's universe. He learned to focus his mind, body, and thoughts at a high spiritual level in order to purify his entire being so that he could communicate with the spirits who commune with Nature's forces. Through further teachings he entered the path of the *Shi'wanni* and *Shi'wano-kia* who performed great things, not with their hands, but with their hearts and minds.

Later, he walked to Katzimo, the Enchanted Mesa inhabited by the sturdy Acoma natives. From there he crossed over desert and mountain to reach the wilderness of Keet Seel and Betatakin where a 90-year-old Navajo man showed him secrets of the old ones, the Anisazi people, who had once lived here and then had suddenly disappeared completely without a hint of where they had gone. The old Navajo man, *Kla-begatho*, had said he knew the secret of why they had disappeared, but he could not reveal that secret until the time was right.

For ten more years he wandered, consulting with and learning from those who had committed themselves to serving the Earth Mother, with the goal of becoming a worthy spiritual disciple.

After an absence of many years, he returned to his log home in the Paiute community. That very evening Amos prepared his sweat lodge for an all night prayer session where he asked the Great One for guidance in his quest for spiritual progress.

The next morning he went into the mountains for a period of fasting and vision questing. One month later, in spite of eating nothing but roots and berries, he came home much refreshed and clear minded of what he had to do. He was now past his 74th year of life, and because of his teachings he knew the Great One was about to require something of him. He felt ready for anything that might come.

One night, while in his sweat lodge, Amos prayed for enlightenment. He soon found himself slipping into a trance-like state. He felt he was flying through the sky at a high altitude and he could see the beauty of Earth far below. His companion, a Spirit whose face he could not see, said, "Amos, the Great One has said you must see for yourself the suffering and death which Man has brought on his own kind. I will show you things you have never dreamt possible, yet these are things that have happened, and some are things to come if Man's ways are not changed. Below us now is a land far from your own. It is Eastern Europe. In one country, leaders are ordering their people to work day and night to make what is called poisonous 'biological weapons of war.'"

"There," the Spirit said, pointing, "is a region called Chelyabinsk. Watch closely, you will see a tragedy that is yet to come."

He watched in horror as a bilious green-yellow cloud with tinges of black and red came out of several huge buildings. The cloud engulfed hundreds of houses where people were sleeping. They died coughing and writhing in terrible pain, unable to breathe, while their skin blistered.

"Half a million people will die on this night," the Spirit said. Amos watched as people ran out of houses only to fall dead in the streets.

After a few more minutes, they moved on.

"We are now over a place called Chernobyl in western Russia." As he watched, an ugly brown building exploded in horrifying flames and a huge cloud of black and brown dirty smoke rose thousands of feet toward him.

Frightened, Amos exclaimed, "What is that?"

The Spirit answered, "*That* is what happens when Man tampers with the laws of Nature. It is an explosion of a nuclear power plant. It will happen a few short years in the future, and will kill several thousand people. It will cause the deaths of thousands of small children, and its residue will help to poison the nearby sea water. Its dust will carry around the world, falling on tree and mountain, further poisoning our rivers and lakes of life. Yet they will not learn. This same kind of explosion will take place in the United States in the near future and the government will lie to the people of the danger which they face."

"Come, we go now to another man-made tragedy."

"Now I show you the continent called Africa, where devilish weapons made from insidious germs of disease, some of them produced by your country, will cause death and destruction. These green forests will hide natives crazed with fear, and they will turn to killing each other with weapons provided by your country's merchants of death." Amos knew that this was where one-half of his family roots were and he felt a great sadness.

The Spirit continued, "Greedy corporations from your country and others, covet the oil and minerals of these poor people and they will spend millions of their dollars to stir up trouble. They will send arms and ammunition to these natives to fight each other, all so the corporations can be the ones to pump their oil and mine their gold. Death is their real product."

As they flew further eastward, they neared the large body of sea water called the Pacific Ocean. Then ahead he saw a tremendous explosion, much, much larger that anything he had seen yet. It was fearful just to see it. They neared a huge bright mushroom-shaped cloud which rose up from an orange fireball. It almost obscured a ring of green tree-covered islands, and a huge plume of water and clouds rose to the heavens in a monstrous column of fire and smoke. The huge ball of fire was now obscenely colored with shades of red, orange, and gray, with black streaks. The very top of the swiftly rising mushroom-shaped cloud was blood red.

The Spirit explained, "This explosion happened only nine years ago, in 1954. Your country was responsible for this. They told the natives of these islands that this thermonuclear explosion was safe, yet they moved them off their island, but not far enough away. They told the natives that they could move back to their islands in a short while. This was a part of a long list of lies told in order to carry out this explosion and others like it, and they used these native people for test purposes. Look now."

Amos looked and saw a village of dark-skinned natives huddled in a clearing where a man, obviously their village leader, was speaking to them.

He said, "We were moved away from our home island so the United States could test some sort of terrible new bomb. The ash and smoke has come to us on the winds. Now many of us have tumors and cancers, and our babies are born either dead or hideously disfigured. We are all deathly sick, but U.S. officials have told me that there is no link between our sickness and their explosions."

In order to impress on them the seriousness of what they were facing, he held up a pitiful bundle of flesh. "As you know, these things we call 'jellyfish babies' are being born regularly to our women. Some have no eyes, no heads, and most of them do not resemble a human baby. They are twisted lumps of flesh that breathe for only a few minutes, and they die. We usually burn it quickly, because it would not be right to show the *thing*, the jellyfish baby, to its mother."

"We, the people of Rongelap, mean nothing to the people of the United States. We are victims of their wicked tests, and I have asked officials of the U.S. to please relocate us to another island far from the test site. I received their answer today. They have refused to move us, saying that it is safe here. Yet no one comes to see our jellyfish babies or to see how sick we all are. I think we must prepare to die."

The Spirit said to Amos, "They are victims of an unconcerned civilized country who has practiced the worst kind of genocide and torture on these people. They were used as guinea pigs, as test subjects, and the rest of the world is turning a blind eye to what has happened here."

They then left the area and flew eastward. Tears were flowing freely from Amos' eyes. He remembered when no one came to help his family as they were burned alive in their own home.

"Now we are nearing your own country where this terrible cycle of destruction began. The lands of your Sho-sho-ni brothers was taken from them to build underground test sites for even more powerful and devastating hydrogen bombs. What you see first is yet a few years in the future. Continued underground explosions in the place called Nevada will eventually contaminate all surrounding water supplies for 50 million people. Many will die of thirst, and many will move to other locations where water supplies cannot be sustained or regenerated by Nature's rainfall. But that is not the most urgent problem."

The Spirit explained, "Because of the drying up of the underground regions, huge cracks will develop in the already active geological faults deep within the Earth. The entire southwestern edge of your country will fall into the ocean and be covered with salt water up to the lowest levels of what is known as the Rocky Mountains. This will happen all because of Man's unwillingness to open their eyes to what they have created by their nuclear madness. Look there."

ANGELA'S BATTLE

Amos looked to where the Spirit pointed. He saw the West Coast from the Gulf of California to San Francisco Bay slowly disappearing beneath the waters of the Pacific Ocean. Soon all that he could see was the ocean's waters lapping at the lower elevations of the Rocky Mountains. Gone were the cities and towns and their millions of people. As they swooped low, Amos could see countless bodies floating on the still roiling water. The ocean had reclaimed the Great American Desert. He was shocked, and afraid.

"I will take you home now," the Spirit said. "Keep the images of what I have shown you forever in your mind, and you must tell others of what you have seen so they will have a choice of continuing the destruction or to stop and be saved. You must tell everybody that the production of dangerous nuclear things must stop immediately. That is the Great One's final word. The choice is theirs. Come now, you are home."

Amos awoke in a heavy sweat. He had strong feelings of trepidation and of sadness. He remembered none of the sensations of flying high in the sky, but he could vividly remember the suffering, pain, and destruction he had been shown. He placed more cedar on the smoldering coals and prayed for guidance from the Wise Ones who had taught him many things.

His thoughts reached them at Zuni, Katzimo, Keet Seel, Betatakin, and in the remoteness of Hopi country.

Then a few days later, a day in January of 1963, he was summoned to meet with the Council of Eagles. This was the meeting to which Angela had also been summoned.

Chapter Three

The goat-man creature's year of re-awakening was in the spring of 1960. It had no idea how long it had been in hibernation, but as always, its first feeling was of deep hunger. For what, it didn't really know. It had been called upon several times over past centuries, and it had gotten used to the feeling which was like a tickling yet painful sensation deep inside. It was something like an itch that couldn't be scratched, and which persisted until attention was focused on something else.

This creature had the upper body of a man, yet from the waist down the body structure was that of an animal, not unlike a goat. It could change its upper body appearance to that of a human female, but for several episodes now it had considered itself as being a male creature because of the freedom and anonymity enjoyed by males. It had found that females attracted too much attention, usually of a sexual nature.

Now he was fully awake, and he lay there comfortably while considering his next moves. He liked the feeling of first waking up in the pitch black darkness of a cliffside cave. He stirred himself into a standing position and checked things out. Yes, two legs, two arms, two of everything. Time to go. He walked surefooted up the steep incline of the cave, always able to see extremely well in the dark. Finally he emerged into the bright sunlight of what was a beautiful spring day.

Far below, he could see a ribbon of water flowing swiftly at the bottom of a rocky canyon. Overhead, several large birds were soaring on strong wings and warm winds, now and then swooping swiftly to grab an unsuspecting rodent or snake which had come out to sun themselves on a flat rock. He looked down at himself to take stock of his needs, because he always got rid of any clothing or garments before finding a cave to retire in. His animal legs and cloven hooves, which it had instead of human-type feet, would need covering and his upper body needed human clothes. He would also have to find what humans called a "head cover" to hide the two short horn-stubbles on his head. Until he found a human community he was satisfied to be naked, especially with the warmth of the sun and the coolness of the spring breeze covering his entire body. Later, leg coverings would be a necessity to hide his legs and hooves.

He hoped he would be lucky in finding clothing of the times. Until he met people he never knew where he was or what time period he was in.

He decided to climb down the canyon to the ribbon of water far below. He picked up a large tree trunk and took it with him down to the river. When he reached the river he threw the log in the water and it was swiftly carried downstream. He laughed, and ran nimbly, jumping from rock to rock and finally with a huge leap he landed squarely on the log where he balanced himself as it plunged through rapids and foaming water. The river did its best to throw him off the log, but he roared in enjoyment and challenged the river to do its worst.

About twenty miles downstream the river gave up trying to best the creature and slowed down, giving way to sand bars and shrub-covered banks. He left the log on the western bank of the river and walked to the top of a small plateau of desert sand. Not too far away he saw a small house made of wood and he walked in that direction, not forgetting that if anyone saw him they would run from him.

The small house was built of scraps of wood and anything else that was handy. Carefully, he slowly circled the shack looking for signs of someone inside. On the shady side of the shack a large brown dog was dozing underneath a rough wooden bench. When he approached, the dog woke up, took one look at him, and ran whimpering into the desert. He went to a window and looked inside. He saw only one room with a small table and one chair along one wall, a small single bed along another wall, and a black-iron wood stove in the center of the room. Luckily no one was home, so was able to find clothing and boots for himself.

He found a dirt path leading southward, parallel to the river. He was in no great hurry so as he went, he studied the desert shrubs and grasses that covered the desert. Several times small animals and desert lizards came near, only to flee in terror when they saw him. He had known this would happen because wherever he had gone in the past, animals and birds wanted no part of him. Only humans would come near him.

He suddenly felt uncomfortable from a warm spot on top of his head, and instinctively he looked skyward. There he saw an eagle flying high above him in a slow circle. He had seen these birds before, but this one seemed larger than most, and strangely, he knew it had an interest in him.

He finally reached a little town built a ways back from the river bank. It consisted of a row of storefronts on each side of a hard dirt road. It was late in the day, and people were shopping in the relative cool of the evening and gathering to talk in front of their favorite stores. He saw a large wooden bench in front of one store, so he sat down and waited to see what would happen. Women passing by glanced at him as they always did. His fair skin and long brown hair always attracted their attention.

ANGELA'S BATTLE

He had once wondered what his mission was supposed to be in places where humans lived. He knew that he was nothing like them. The answer had come to him slowly when he realized he only had to help them destroy themselves. Their souls would be delivered to his Master, the one who had placed him here without instructions of any kind.

It hadn't taken long to discover that he didn't have to seek out the susceptible ones. They sought him out. He just had to make himself available to their darker impulses and desires. He decided he would stay in this town for a few days. From his own experiences, he knew there would be no shortage of corruptible people here. Later, he would move on, gathering souls until he was recalled.

Chapter Four

Amos was not surprised when a knock on the door announced his visitors. He had been expecting them. He invited Angela to sit on a wooden chair that he had made from pine branches. He didn't know what to provide for the eagle. This was only the second time he had met Whistler.

The eagle spoke first. "As you know, my name is Whistler, the son of Teekawis, leader of the Council of Eagles. The Creator has said it is necessary for all of us to come together in spirit and strength to save the world from the evil that threatens our existence. We're here tonight to help begin making plans to save the earth and its people."

Whistler continued, "As we know, most Americans have a far different spiritual concept than we do of how to live. They know little of how each part of the earth depends on another for sustenance, and they seem unconcerned of the fact that our Mother, the Earth, is a living thing which depends on her children to heed her wishes so that we may all live good lives. They have belittled Her warnings as 'natural phenomena' and they think they can control nature through study, science, and analysis. They claim to live by reality, yet ignore the real truth. Our beliefs, yours and mine, they call pagan witchcraft, symbolism, or mysticism.

"So we are asked to do the most important and dangerous task the Creator has ever asked of us. My father has told me that whatever you say must be done, will be done. We are waiting for your words now."

Whistler shuffled to a spot on the floor near Angela's feet and waited expectantly. Amos nodded his head and rocked very slowly in his chair as his mind turned over all of the things he had seen and heard in the past two weeks.

They looked at each other until Angela broke the silence. "What do we do first?"

Amos spoke. "I will first tell you of a vision given to me. In my dream-vision I saw you, Angela, directing the activities of a large group of people of all races who looked to you for strength to carry on. Many were tired, hungry, and dust-covered, yet at your words they drew themselves up and carried on, renewed in strength and in spirit. Until now I didn't realize the meaning of the dream which the Great One had sent to me, and now that both of you are here, I know that you, Angela, are meant to be our leader. I also realize that the sum of all my experiences has been to prepare me for this time.

He spoke softly. "In my talks with the Hopi, Zuni, and Navajo spiritual men they discussed the many things which "the white man" was doing to Mother Earth. There were things such as the atom bomb, which they once witnessed exploding in the early morning skies to the East, and now that land is poisoned beyond recovery."

"Now we are told there is a new breed of bomb called a thermonuclear bomb, which has been recently exploded far away in the Pacific Ocean. It is planned to explode one of those powerful bombs soon in *Sho-sho-ni* country. If it is exploded it will cause much destruction and death here in the southwest. One of our tasks will be to prevent this explosion from destroying our world, and to alert the people of the dangers to come from the explosive power and radioactivity of their nuclear programs."

"This nuclear madness has spread throughout the world and even the smallest of countries is trying to build their own nuclear bomb. Kla-begatho, the Navajo man, received a vision that a message had to reach governments of the world that *'the making of these things must stop at once, or else the Earth would be consumed in fire at the end of this thousand-year period.'* "

"It is not the first time that Man has ignored Her warning, and now the Creator has become impatient and angry at Man's arrogance. Even if these nuclear birds of death are not exploded, their waste will soon foul our land, our water and our air making it impossible for us to live. They must be made to realize that it is not enough to store the droppings of the birds of death far beneath the ground."

Amos looked at each of them for a few seconds, seeking to find any trace of doubt or insecurity. Seeing none, he said, "I have been in mind contact with the shamans who are my mentors. They see the urgency of our mission and want first to meet for seven days with us and the Council of Eagles at a time and location to be named by Teek-awis. Soon after that they want to meet with holy men from the indigenous people of the America's. From these meetings we will know what we have to do to save our world."

"I suggest that we begin our meeting on the night of the next new moon, which is only ten days from now, so if your father will name the location the mentors can make preparations. When can we know his answer?"

"I'll talk with my father tonight," Whistler replied. "I will tell him what we have discussed here and by tomorrow you may be able to tell your mentors the time and location of the meeting. I'm excited about our coming work. Think of it, never before in our history has such an army taken the field against such a formidable foe.

It almost makes me want to be human again."

This caused a smile to appear on the faces of the other two. Amos cautioned, "Be careful of what you wish for, it may come true. I have sometimes wished to fly like the eagles and yet I have no idea of why. I am afraid of heights." Angela laughed at this while Whistler clacked his beak in what was taken to be laughter.

With that, Amos closed his eyes and began telling Angela and Whistler of what he had been shown in his travel with the Spirit. They too, were horrified at the destruction which Amos described.

When Amos finished his story, Angela and Whistler returned to her house. Whistler flew into a tree top near Angela's house to rest and to "mind talk" with his father. Angela went inside to be with her children who were wondering why she had left them alone. She didn't want to explain anything yet. How could she? She hardly knew the full story herself.

Chapter Five

Jason Storm Cloud was born in 1931 on the Quechan Indian Nation's homeland in southeastern California. The Quechan homeland was 180 miles west of Phoenix, Arizona and the same distance east of San Diego, California. Their biggest village was on the western side of the Colorado River, and directly across the river from them was the town of Yuma, Arizona.

His birth certificate had read Jason Celaya, Jr. Later, his own investigation had revealed that this name was given to his father in 1905 when he was forced to attend a school run by Catholic nuns. The nuns had been unable or unwilling to pronounce or to spell his real name, *Tsi-pi-ya-tho*, so they named him Celaya, without regard for Quechan customs and tradition.

Jason lived with the name until after his graduation from the University of Arizona in Tucson. Over the next three years, while at the University of Missouri's School of Journalism in St. Louis, he made it his own personal project to do research and a report on why it was that so many Native Americans had last names which were not their real family names. He discovered that many Indian families were saddled with non-Indian names like Jones, Smith, Kelly, Roosevelt, Lincoln, Miller, and even a Vanderbilt. In all cases, they were names given them when doctors, nurses, or other minor government officials refused to put an Indian name on birth certificates or other records. Jason concluded that Indians had been denied their heritage and had vowed to correct this wrong.

After meditation, he had his name legally changed to *Storm Cloud*, taken from an old Quechan legend of one who could bring on a rainstorm to wash away danger or uncover the wrongdoings of others. After completing his education in journalism, he set out to gain experience in the mainstream of American society. He was offered a job as a reporter in Washington, D.C. for a Tucson daily paper. He soon tired of covering the Washington scene. The more he saw of politicians and political appointees, he reasoned that more was wrong with the country than was right. He was considering a change to a line of work where he had a better chance of making a difference in daily lives.

One day, after his work day was finished, he stopped in a small place on Washington's upper Connecticut Avenue for a bite to eat. The restaurant was crowded. A young woman came in, and was looking around for an empty table. There were none. She saw Jason sitting alone at a table for two, so she came over and asked, "Hi, would you mind if I shared the table with you? Every table is taken."

He glanced up and said, "Please, sit down."

The young woman peeled off her coat and lay her rather large briefcase on a chair. "I hope you won't mind if I read. I won't bother you."

He had a mouthful of chicken fried steak so he just nodded at her in approval.

She took out a sheaf of papers and began reading, ignoring him. Twice she said quietly, "Damn. Damn those bastards." Jason looked up and saw a title of one paper she had on the table. It read "Atomic Energy Act of 1954."

"Is there a problem?" he asked.

She looked up. "Oh, I'm sorry. That just slipped out. I was just reading of how Congress is proposing to handle all of the radioactive waste that's going to be produced by their damn nuclear power plants and military bomb factories. It's unbelievable. And I'm sorry too that I didn't introduce myself when you were nice enough to let me sit here. My name's Diane Olson. I work for a citizens watchdog group that wants to make sure Congress does the right thing with nuclear waste."

He returned the self-introduction. "My name's Jason Storm Cloud. Call me Jay. I'm a newspaper reporter for the Tucson Advocate. I work here covering national news and matters of interest to Indian tribes in the southwest."

The waitress came and took Diane's order for a well-done hamburger and a Coke.

"Well," Diane said, "Your neighbor, New Mexico, is already knee deep in nuclear problems. You know they exploded the first atom bomb there, and now they're getting ready for a more powerful bomb. Besides that, there's all of these nuclear electric power plants that this country plans to build. Over 120 of them in the next 20 years. One of them is in Arizona. The problem is, nuclear power creates radioactive waste that can be deadly for 240,000 years or more."

"What made me angry awhile ago is that they have already dumped some of that waste in the Pacific and Atlantic oceans and they plan to dump more. They're poisoning our oceans. Damn, how dumb can they be. And did you know that the power companies are suggesting that the waste be stored underground in the Carlsbad Caverns? That ought to make you mad."

"I have to confess that I don't know about these nuclear things. I was hired right out of school in Missouri to work here. So I guess I'm green as a gourd," Jay said.

Her eyes flashed impatiently. "If you're really Native American you ought to be concerned. Where do you think all these nuclear things come from? The uranium that made it all possible is mined right out of Indian country. Doesn't that ring a bell with you?"

"I'm afraid not," Jay replied. "I've spent all my time in school learning how to speak the white man's language in order to write and report news stories. But I'm glad we met because I've been dissatisfied with what I'm doing. I didn't get an education just to melt into the white crowd. I've always wanted to help my people. Tell you what. If I can get some time off I'd like to hang around with you. Maybe I can learn something and help you at the same time. With my press pass I can get into some places that you can't. What do you say?"

Diane's eyes opened wide and she had a smile on her face. "Are you serious? You don't know how hard it is to get anyone interested in listening to me. No one believes that nuclear waste is dangerous to our future. They think that just because it's stored out of sight everything will be OK. Even the Congress is like an ostrich with its head in the sand."

She took a last bite of her hamburger and rinsed it down with the Coke, then reached into her briefcase which apparently served as her purse too, because she took out a business card and a five-dollar bill. She gave the card to Jay.

"If you're serious about what you said, give me a call when you're ready and I'll tell you where to catch up with me. I have to tell you, it's hard work and takes a lot of bouncing around from Congress to the Atomic Energy Commission and all points in between. Let me know. Gotta go to a meeting with other concerned groups now. I hope to see you soon."

She stopped, turned to Jay and said, "You know, you're the first American Indian I've ever been this close to. You don't still scalp people, do you?"

Jay frowned, but before he could think of a decent comeback, she was gone.

Over the next two days, he arranged to work three days a week for the next month. If they needed him, the office would call him to come in. On Wednesday morning he called Diane at 6:30 a.m. He woke her out of a sound sleep, he guessed. "I apologize for calling so early, but I didn't want to miss you. This is Jay. Remember, the Indian scalper?"

"Huh? Oh yeah. The guy who's gonna follow me around so I can teach him all I know. That might take all of ten minutes," Diane joked.

"I can work with you for the next three days plus the weekend, and each week if you want for the next month," he said. "How about it. Where do I meet you?"

"Give me a few minutes to get myself together. Are you at home? Give me your number and I'll call you back in just a few minutes." She wrote down the number and hung up. Jay sat down to wait for her call.

Ten minutes later Diane called. "We're going to attend a press conference at nine this morning so you're going to get broken in good. The Chairman of the Atomic Energy Commission is going to announce that electricity produced by atomic energy is too good for the people to pass up. Meet me at the National Press Club at eight-thirty. We'll use your press pass to get good seats up front. Don't be late."

At 8:25 he was in the Press Club lobby looking for Diane. At 8:30 sharp she came out of a telephone booth and hollered, "Jay, come on," as she headed for the elevator.

When they reached the press conference room, the news cameras were already setting up. Jay flashed his press pass, and with Diane right behind him, he found two seats directly in front of the podium. He asked for a press information packet which featured a glossy document titled "*Atomic Power: A Bright New Age For America.*"

He gave the document to Diane to read. She buried her nose in it, and occasionally she underlined parts that she would want to review later.

At nine o'clock the first man got up to the microphone and very pompously introduced, "The Honorable Henry Straub, the Chairman of the United States Atomic Energy Commission."

Smiling broadly, and looking directly into the cameras, he began his talk by telling of the tremendous advantages of being the world's leader in the development and use of atomic energy to produce electricity for commercial and home use.

Every so often when the chairman said something she didn't agree with, Diane would jab Jay in the ribs with her sharp elbow. Later, he found that every place in his notes where his writing was scribbled, this was a signal for one of Straub's comments to be checked out.

Thirty minutes later, the conference ended and Diane had only one thing to say. She loudly whispered to Jay, "This is what is called PPB. Propaganda, Promises, and Bullcrap." Chairman Straub shot her a wicked look and disappeared out the back door, leaving his assistant to answer the questions.

After the press conference, they went to a nearby Little White House sandwich shop, sat down for a cup of coffee, and discussed what they had heard.

Diane said, "Jay, I'm so glad you were there. You can learn more than I can teach you from this one meeting. If you take this book and check out those items that I've marked out for you, this will give you and your boss a good story of how Mr. Straub and company are hoodwinking the public into believing that atomic radiation is good for them. A follow up story can be done on some of the cruel and barbaric tests that have already taken place, and are taking place as we speak. They've been using radioactive substances on human beings just to find out how their bodies react to it. Jay, they're killing people just to find out how dangerous this stuff is. Wouldn't you think that our government would find out first before using it? Things like this keep me angry most of the time."

For all her impatience, Diane did a good job of teaching the ABC's of nuclear production processes to Jay. She was able to point him in the right directions to write about the field of atomic radiation and its uses, as well as its dangers. Three weeks later Jay had finished checking out most of the statements made by AEC Chairman Straub. He found that official government studies were pessimistic about the economics of atomic power, and that in order for nuclear power to be viable, commercial generating plants would have to be partly paid for by money appropriated for military uses of nuclear power. Jay discovered that the untold secret was that the military needed the plutonium produced by the commercial reactors and was therefore willing to significantly subsidize nuclear power plants.

For several more months Diane and Jay worked together pouring over documents submitted by nuclear power plant contractors and the government inspectors of the AEC who inspected and approved their work.

Diane explained her reasoning to Jay, "I want to build a record of complaints and problems of faulty construction methods and to see if the problems are fixed or merely written off as immaterial to the safety of the power plant. It's possible that the AEC officials are being paid off by the industry. We should begin building a case history for future use."

Jay was able to dig up earlier Atomic Energy Commission reports to Congress which warned against optimism in the use of nuclear power because there were just too many technical difficulties to overcome. This report was signed by at least two leading atomic scientists who had helped to develop the atomic bomb.

Particularly damaging to Straub's assertions was a statement by an official of the General Electric Corporation who said, "It is safe to say that atomic power is expensive power. It is not cheap power as the public has been led to believe."

Finally the story was ready.

With Diane's concurrence, he submitted the story to his editors and they were ecstatic. The theme of it was that the commercial nuclear industry was not being honest with the public about the dangers and the cost of nuclear generating plants. It was called a scandal. The story made headlines in mainstream newspapers and Jay Storm Cloud became known. He got a nice pay raise and also a new assignment to the Environmental Desk in Washington for his newspaper. He took Diane to a fine restaurant, the Seaport Inn, across the Potomac River in Alexandria, Virginia, to celebrate, then to a stage play at the Ford Theater in appreciation for "just being you," he told her.

During lunch one day, Diane said, "Jay, I can't help but notice a troubled look on your brown face. Is there someone else? Are we through? Is this the end?" She said this in a joking manner, but the questions were honest.

Jay smiled at her. "You're not only good-looking and smart, but you're extremely perceptive. There is something I wanted to talk to you about, but it has nothing to do with you personally. Selfishly, it's about me."

"Go ahead. The floor is yours," she said.

Jay took a deep breath, then began. "I think every Native American who has left their reservation for an education has at one time or another thought about making the choice of going back to help their communities grow and advance, or like me, do I leave that up to somebody else and make my mark in the mainstream of America. That's where I'm at, Diane, and I need to talk about this with somebody."

Diane tapped her spoon on the table and twisted her mouth into a thoughtful expression. "Hm-m-m," she said. "Ho-o-o-kay. Tell you what. Let's take a couple hours off. We'll stake a claim on a
private patch of grass in Farragut Square, and we'll talk about you. I'm better than just *somebody* to talk with."

Jay was grateful. He was beginning to really appreciate Diane's humor and directness. She didn't pull any punches and told you what you needed to know. They paid the bill and went to the Square, which was in the next block. There was a clean spot in the shade of a tree so they sat on the grass.

Diane smiled at him. "You begin, Indian, whatever you want to say, pal."

Jay pulled at a dandelion weed, trying to think of the right thing to say and how to say it. His college major had been Journalism with a minor in English. That was to be his profession, but was he in the right place? And why was he here in Washington, D.C. instead of out West somewhere?

He began, "I think that to get things in order of importance to me, I have to start way back, at home. I was only 10 when my father joined the Marines in 1942 and went to war. He loved this land and was willing to fight for it. He never came back, but I love the memories of him doing things with me when I was little. He showed me how all things that lived along the Colorado River depended on each other to keep things livable, if you know what I mean. I think we're all supposed to be like that, but it's not working out that way. Instead we have one group, for instance, making one thing for profit while others die because of it. It doesn't make sense to me."

"My father told me stories about legends and the old times, and they're priceless to me now. I remember he wrote a letter to my mother from a place called Tarawa. He said the thing that he kept dreaming of was to come back to our green river valley homeland. When he came back he would never leave it again, he said, because it was the most beautiful place on earth. That was his last letter."

"It's probably just as well that he didn't come back because while he was gone the U.S. government cut down every blessed green tree, bush, and twig that he loved. Because of that, all of the deer, quail, rabbits, and other animals which lived in the trees and brush disappeared. They said the trees used too much water and that we didn't need them anyway. Even the fish disappeared from the river after several dams were built."

"According to my mother, no one asked the people if they wanted the trees cut down. My father would have been disappointed and fighting mad to see how the land looked with every green thing gone. She told me that someday I could take his place in asking the government why they had to cut everything down. It may be time now, Diane. But I'm not sure. That's where I'm at."

For more than an hour he spoke, stopping now and then to gather his thoughts and words. "I used to listen as the older people talked about how life used to be, and how things began to change after the first visit by Europeans. Later, when gold was discovered in California, a bounty of $50 was placed on heads of Indians to keep them out of the gold country."

Diane listened attentively, her eyes glued on his face. Now and then a tear would roll down her cheek, but she did not brush it away. She had never before heard the Indian's side of the story of western settlement.

Finally, Jay stopped talking about the past and focused on his present. "I'm on the verge of quitting my job with the paper in order to do free-lance investigative stories of the environmental damage that government policies are doing to the country."

"I want to expose wrongful policies so that Indian people can deal with them before the fact instead of after the fact, as has always been done before. I need to know in my own mind if I'm way off base, and that I'm not acting out of emotion when I say I want to help my people, whatever that means. I've never considered working in Indian affairs before. You've opened my eyes to some of what's being done, and I admire and respect you for how you do your job and how you deal with the power structure."

Then he fell silent, put a blade of grass between his teeth and looked at Diane expectantly. He had never really appreciated how pretty she was, and now her big brown eyes were looking at him as if seeing him for the first time. He couldn't help but reach over and wipe what was left of a tear from her cheek with his finger and he noted how soft and smooth her cheek was. In fact, they spent a long minute just looking at each other.

Diane broke it off and got back to the subject matter. Women always seemed smarter than men in such things.

It was Diane's turn to speak. "I don't know a thing about Indian affairs, Jay, but when it comes to damage to the environment from nuclear waste, garbage, or water pollution, things can't be that much different than how it affects people in places like Anacostia, Detroit, Los Angeles, or your reservation. Smoke is smoke, and trash is trash, wherever it's at. Radioactivity will kill white folks just like it kills Indians, so I don't think you have as big a problem as you might think. It's just new to you, that's all."

"Everything's the same," she said, "and only the names have been changed to protect the guilty. I think you're on the right track and all you need to do is put your mind to the job ahead. Whether you're working for the betterment of New York City or the Sioux reservations, it's all the same."

"Now, I've never told you how I got into this business, but you and I are alike as peas in a pod, Jay. My father was in the military too. The Army. When the war was ended by the uranium bomb called Little Boy being dropped on Hiroshima, he was horrified. The Army told everyone that once the bomb exploded there was no danger to anyone. To prove it they marched his group through Hiroshima 'to look for survivors.' "

"In 1947, his company came home and they were assigned to stand close and watch while a nuclear bomb was exploded in Nevada at a place called Yucca Flat. After the blast the group was marched right up to ground zero to prove it wouldn't hurt them. It didn't hurt them, not right away, but within six years he was dead of brain cancer. My mother died broke, financially as well as from heartbreak. She could never prove that his cancer was caused from the radioactivity so the Army wouldn't pay her any compensation. All his insurance went to pay the hospital bills."

"So if you think you're the only one with a right to be mad at the government, think again. Ever since my father died, all I've wanted to do is expose the lying bastards who killed him and so many others." She wiped her own tears this time. "Wherever you go and whatever you do, if you're working against nuclear power, we're on the same side. Do it, Jay. Follow your instincts. If you want, I'll be right with you."

They sat there for another ten minutes, each thinking of what the other had said. After awhile they got up and walked towards the offices of the organization that Diane worked for. They had a lot of planning to do. For the first time since they met, their hands met in mid-stride and they crossed the street holding hands.

It was a strange sight they offered to the streets of Washington, D.C. One brown face and one white face, both wearing a silly grin. They looked like anything but a formidable team.

It was shortly after this that Jay was invited to speak to a Native American environmental conference in Phoenix.

Chapter Six

By noon the next day Whistler and Angela were on their way to see Amos with the news that the Council of Eagles had agreed to the time of the meeting with the tribal holy men. After Amos had shared his out-of-body vision of human suffering and disaster with them, they were clearly affected by the story. Now it was time to begin their work.

Amos was deep in meditation when they arrived and they waited until Amos acknowledged their presence. When Amos finally greeted them, Whistler said, "The Council will meet with your people on the first evening of the new moon. The place will be in what is called Canyon de Chelly in the eastern part of Navajo country. There are three fingers of this great canyon. The meeting will be held at the eastern reach of the middle canyon finger. It is isolated and hard to reach by outsiders. There is a huge cave in the southern side of the canyon. Here we can light our fires safely, and our young scouts will patrol continuously and warn us if intruders are nearby. You, Angela, and myself should plan to arrive at least two days early to make the place ready for everyone." The eagle was excited and anxious to get started.

Amos was satisfied. They now had a time and location, and all that was left was to notify *Apish'taya*, the spiritual leader of the Zuni, who would then notify everyone else, seven in all, who would come from the Hopi, Navajo, Chiricahua, Onondaga, Lakota-Dacotah-Nakotah people , and the Aztec Yaqui people. These old men were foremost in knowledge, wisdom and spiritual power of the ancients. Apish'taya by virtue of his attaining the age of 103 was the undisputed head of the holy men. These seven holy men served as teachers and mentors to more than three hundred other practicing neophytes throughout the country who were in varying degrees of spiritual growth, hoping and preparing for the day when they would join the respected circle of seven holy men.

Amos asked, "Is there any other news to share with us?"

Whistler spoke first. "We have had a definite sighting of one of the hoofed goat men on the Colorado River near the Mojave reservation. One of our scouts had gone to check out a report from an owl who had seen a strange creature in the rugged cliffs of a canyon several miles below Hoover Dam. This was verified when the scout saw a goat man creature walking towards an isolated shack near a small town on the banks of the river. While the scout watched from high in the sky, the goat man had dressed himself in humans clothing then walked towards a nearby town."

"This puts an urgency on our meeting so our plans can be finalized," Amos said.

Angela decided to tell what had been on her mind ever since her meeting with the eagles. "I'm unsure of why I'm here," she began. "I don't know what my role is here. I'm not an educated person nor am I an overly religious person, although I do worship our environment and all that lives within it. I'm willing to do what little I can, but I want to feel comfortable with what I do. I'm only a plain Indian woman with two children to take care of. I don't know if I can fit into such a grand and noble plan to save the world. I have never....."

Amos raised his hand and politely cut her off. "Angela, every army in history has had its person or persons like you who not only provides leadership, but also relays information and encouragement to those people who are not directly involved in the fighting. There are several million native people on this continent who must support what we are doing and in order to do so, they have to know the real stakes involved here and what the real dangers are if we fail."

"There is another aspect of all this. The mainstream American, the non-Indians, will have a hard time understanding what is happening not only in our world, but also in theirs. They may not be ready to understand, to believe, that their nuclear science and experiments pollute the world in violation of the Great One's natural laws. Your role will include the spread of this information to them and to lead the people in doing whatever it takes to stop their plans. It is a big job, and you would not have been given it if the Great One had any doubts about you. You, and each of us, must accept the responsibility given us without question. We must be grateful for having been chosen to do this work."

Angela was silent for awhile, then said, "I know what you say is true. I'll do the best I can to carry out this new responsibility. My mind is relieved and I will not wrestle with my doubts any longer."

Amos nodded approvingly, and reminded her, "The Great One has placed His faith in you and you will find that at the right time you will be given the necessary tools to do the particular job at hand." Angela was glad he said that because a lingering last doubt had crossed her mind, *How do I tell the rest of the world about their possible destruction?* She decided that this was not her worry. She would use the tools placed at her disposal.

The next morning Angela thought it was time to tell her two daughters just a small bit of why she would be very busy in the coming weeks. After their breakfast she said to the two girls, "Come outside and sit with me in the sunshine for awhile. I want to talk to you about something."

After they were comfortably seated she said, "I have a very important job to do for our Indian people, and because I'll be gone from home much of the time I'm sending you both to live with your aunt and uncle in Albuquerque for awhile. I know you don't want to go, but it's important to me that you do this. I'll make the arrangements in the next few days and send you there on the bus. So pack what clothes and things you want to take with you and be ready. You may be there for a good long time."

The sisters, Mina, 13, and Angela, 15, were actually pleased with the news. They were looking forward to the 'big city.' They had been to Las Vegas and to Phoenix twice and what they saw in their brief stays interested them and they wanted to see more. In two days time they were enroute via a Santa Fe Trailways bus to Albuquerque.

Angela hustled around her house making sure that things were secure in case she had to be away for a long period. She also wanted to see the Tribal Chairman, Ned Hatanami, but was unsure of how much to tell him. One day soon he would have to be made aware of the entire situation. She decided to tell Ned about her trip to Phoenix in January and what had been said, and maybe just a hint of what was really happening. The next morning she walked into the tribal office.

Maggie, the office secretary kidded her. "Hi Angela, haven't seen you for awhile. I thought maybe you found a rich young lover and moved away. Naw-w-w-w," she said in the manner they had both learned at the Indian school in Stewart, Nevada, class of 1939. The slang term *Naw-w-w* was shorthand for *I'm just kidding*. The longer-drawn-out the *a-w-w-w*, the heavier the kidding was intended. Angela was a year older than Maggie. They made small talk and traded local gossip for awhile.

Finally Maggie said seriously, "Is somebody sick, did somebody die? You look real worried."

Angela quickly put a smile on her face. "Nothing is seriously wrong. I just sent the girls to visit their aunt in Albuquerque and I miss them already. But I need to talk with Ned about something. Is he around?"

"Gosh, you just missed him. He went down to Mojave Valley for a wedding. He signed our paychecks then fired up his old Chevy. The old man couldn't wait to get out of here because he's probably going to stop in Las Vegas to see one of those tall showgirls. I bet, init?" They both laughed loudly at this.

They liked Ned. He was a real grassroots man who took his job as Tribal Leader very seriously. The 358 adults of the tribe elected him year after year because of his gift of talk. Like most other Indians of his generation, his education had been limited to basic English and arithmetic at Phoenix Indian School. There, an emphasis had been placed on vocational skills rather than on academic knowledge. They taught him to be a cement mason, but after he returned home he had never used a cement mason's trowel again.

For five years he had been bombarding the Bureau of Indian Affairs with letters asking them to stop teaching vocations at all their boarding schools, and instead, provide full time education in scholastic studies. Ned was sure that this would be better for Indian students than learning something which they would never use. He was frustrated because the stodgy bureaucracy refused to change. Now he was hoping to interest their intertribal association to join him in this effort. He was going to the wedding of Mojave Tribal Chairman Milford Haynes' daughter because it was a chance to talk with other tribal leaders.

Contrary to Maggie's joke, Ned drove through Las Vegas without stopping because he wanted to reach the Mojave reservation in time to have dinner with the others. After leaving Las Vegas, he was southbound on Highway 95. Ned turned left towards the Colorado River after passing through Searchlight, Nevada. A two-lane road ran South alongside the river and was a shortcut to the northern end of the Mojave reservation.

After passing through the small river town of Laughlin, he came upon a man walking downriver. He stopped and asked, "Want a lift?"

The man was white and looked like a laborer with his high boots and denim suspender overalls. "Sure, I'll ride with you for awhile. Thanks."

Ned noticed that he walked like the boots hurt his feet. "My name's Ned," he offered. "I'm going as far as Needles to meet with some friends. The daughter of one of them is getting married this weekend. He's the leader of the Indian tribe at Needles. Me and the rest of the men are also chairman of our tribes at home. I'm Paiute from Utah. Ever heard of them?"

"No. My name's John. I appreciate the ride. I'm not going anywhere special, just gonna keep walking 'til I find a job of some kind. I'm a mechanic. I haven't heard of the Paiutes. But let me ask you. I have heard that the white people here have really treated all you Indians pretty bad. Is that true?"

"Well, in some ways we were treated pretty shabby, but we're not holding a grudge, you know. We're just trying to make the best out of a bad deal and change things for the better. It'll take a while."

For another fifty minutes Ned told John the history of how the Paiutes came to be settled in their remote mountain reservation. John listened politely, yet remembered all he was told. He recognized a hint of resentment and dissatisfaction in Ned's tone of voice. *This man can be had*, he decided.

They passed a road sign which proclaimed **Boundary Of The Mojave Indian Reservation - No Guns Or Liquor Allowed.** Ned stopped at a side road. "This is where I turn, but the town is about four miles ahead straight down this road. Just a short walk. Good luck to you, maybe we'll meet again," he said.

John looked deep into Ned's eyes before he opened the door to get out of the car. "Ned, I know this might sound strange, but I may be able to help you to get real education for your people. Really. I'll contact you again soon and I'll tell you how I can help. In the meantime, have a good time at the wedding. Thanks for the ride."

It wasn't until after he drove off and left John that Ned wondered, *How in the heck did he know about the education thing? I didn't even mention it. But no matter*, he thought. *I'll never see the bum again.*

He checked into a nearby motel, took a cool shower, then headed for the home of Milford Haynes. Most of the other tribal leaders were not there yet, so Milford, Ned, and three others drove into Needles for dinner. It was a good time, with good food and lots of joke-telling, especially stories about each other. Ned didn't get a chance to talk about his education project, but this was okay. There would be time tomorrow, Saturday.

When they left the restaurant two hours later, they piled into Milford's station wagon. As they turned the corner Ned got a quick flash of someone leaning against a corner building. He thought, *That's John*, and turned around to see if it was indeed him. But there was no one there.

It was Saturday morning. Milford Haynes, Chairman of the Colorado River Mojave Indian Tribe had a lot of things to do today. His daughter was getting married on Sunday at the Valley Presbyterian Church and Haynes had to make the final arrangements and order the flowers, make sure the caterer and the band was ready for the reception after the wedding, and a hundred other things.

Milford Haynes was a popular man among the tribal leaders in the southwest, and

ANGELA'S BATTLE

he was hosting a dinner tonight for friends from Nevada, California, and Arizona, who represented 21 tribes. They all belonged to the Southwest Intertribal Association. His daughter Emily was marrying the son of Joe Gorman, another tribal chairman from central Arizona. If everything wasn't just right, he would be embarrassed.

He spent the day pestering the three Indian women who had been hired to cook for the dinner, and at six o'clock he was finally satisfied that everything would be a success. It was. After the dinner of native foods the women took over the kitchen and the dining room for cleanup purposes, and to talk with the bride to-be. The men, all tribal leaders, gathered outside on the back lawn. After lighting up cigarettes and then some small talk, Adam Feather, Chairman for the Tohono O'Odham people near Tucson, motioned for the others to come closer.

"I need to talk with you," he said softly. "I apologize for bringing this up at this happy time, but this past week I've had people from an outlying district come to me with strange stories of seeing images of their dead relatives. When they would try to approach them, the dead ones would move away but would also say to them, '*The evil ones are nearby. Warn your relatives.*' If it was only one person, I would ignore it, but there have been six families who have come to see me. And just before dinner tonight, I had a telephone call at my motel saying that two more families have reported this same thing. I have to take this seriously and I need your advice."

"Has anything like this happened in the past?" Haynes asked.

"No," Adam Feather said. "But the district where those families live has always been considered sacred land because years ago, sometime before 1600, an old man was crossing the hot desert and he suddenly came across a beautiful Indian woman dressed in glowing blue robes. She told the man that a church must be built on that spot. It was down near Sonoyta. As you know, there were no borders in those days and our people lived all over the area. This man had recently been baptized into the Catholic church. He went to see the bishop in Tucson and told him of what he had seen and what he had been told to do."

"The bishop was interested, but did not believe him and asked for proof, some kind of sign. When the man returned to the desert spot there was a spring flowing cool, clear water. The woman again appeared and gave him a robe exactly like the one she was wearing and said, 'Take this robe to your bishop. This is the sign he asks for.' The Indian man took the robe to the bishop, and when he opened up the robe, fresh red roses fell out of it. The bishop believed and the church was built."

"So the ground where these people live is said to be consecrated holy ground. But why they would see images of their dead relatives is the mystery. And what does the message mean?"

The men were silent as they thought on what they had heard. They dealt with business affairs, not spiritual matters. This strange information needed explanation in a way they could understand.

Milford Haynes was troubled by this story, but he decided to do nothing until he knew more about it. He told the others, "This is a strong message here for all of us. But I think we need to bring this to the attention of our tribal holy men. It is not a matter for the white churches. They would call us pagans. You should each consult with your own holy man as soon as possible after the wedding and I will call a special meeting soon after. In the meantime let's not spoil this weekend. Our wives would be very unhappy."

"Wait," the Tohono O'odham man insisted. "There's something more I have to tell you that may be a clue. It may be important for your holy man to hear. Long ago, after the church was built in honor of the Lady of Guadalupe, they held a great fiesta. On the last night of celebration there was much native dancing and happy songs."

"Near midnight just before the final mass was to begin, a pretty young lady was dancing with a strange man who looked like a Spaniard. Suddenly she screamed and pointed at the man's feet. *'La cabra, la cabra*, a goat, a goat,' she hollered. The stranger's feet sticking out from below his peasants trousers were like a goat's. Split hooves. The man laughed like a madman, and before anyone could move he grabbed the young lady by the arm and threw her high in the air. She landed on her head and broke her neck. The man, or goat man, ran into the darkness and disappeared. From somewhere in the darkness he shouted, *"I will return for all of you."*

"How do I know this? It's a story we pass down from generation to generation, but we never talk of it in public. I have not, until now. I know this sounds like witchcraft, but I live way out in the country far from my neighbors. It scares me."

"All the more reason not to alarm anybody until we learn more about this." said Milford Haynes. "I ask you to make this your priority next week."

Emily's wedding went off without a hitch. Milford Haynes was relieved and happy. But he was worried. There was a reception and a dance at the Community Hall. He instructed the tribal security police to admit no one they did not know. If there was a doubt, they must call for him immediately. Milford Haynes wanted assurance that there were no strangers at this party.

Later that evening, from a perch in a nearby willow tree, John watched the festivities and said aloud, "I am nothing if not patient. I will wait. I have plenty of time."

But did he have plenty of time? Certain forces were being separately assembled. Old knowledge and old ways were slowly moving towards a union with others who were younger but just as determined. The Great One was gathering her forces. The Council of Eagles was keeping track of where all the players were and on this night they were satisfied with the progress.

Chapter Seven

Two days after his last meeting with Angela and Whistler, Amos placed his pipe, flute, sage and native tobacco, and a few other things, in the back of Angela's pickup truck which now had a camper-type shell covering over it. Maggie had generously loaned the camper shell to Angela. In the early morning darkness, Amos climbed in and sat on an old brown-colored U.S. Army blanket, ready to begin the trip to Canyon de Chelly. Earlier he had tied a stout tree branch across the bed of the truck which now served as a perch for the eagle. Whistler waddled into the bed of the truck and perched on the tree branch. He too, was ready to go.

Angela closed the door of the camper shell, then climbed into the drivers seat and looked around for a minute. Two months ago she had only wanted to do her little bit for the environment. The birds and squirrels had disappeared, trees were dying, and now she was involved in a grand plan to save everyone and everything. *Unbelievable*, she thought.

She was worried about Whistler. If any state or federal official should spot the eagle, they would be in deep trouble. The possession, hunting, or trapping of eagles was a federal offense, and she didn't know how she would explain Whistler to anybody. She couldn't say he was a pet, yet if she said he was a good friend--- well, it just wouldn't work. She was glad when Amos had insisted on sitting in the back with the eagle. "We have a lot to talk about, he and I," he said.

Angela planned to cross into Arizona just north of Fredonia by noon and reach Tuba City before nightfall. They would camp somewhere near *Moenkopi* alongside one of the many small streams and enjoy the night sky. The next morning they would pass through Hopi country near the old villages of *Oraibi, Kykotsmovi, Polacca*, and *Jadito* before going back into Navajo country. They would camp one more night then reach Canyon de Chelly before noon. Then would come the hardest part of the trip. They would have to hike down into the canyon then walk about twenty miles to the remote cave site. She had never done this kind of rough outdoor living before. Angela marveled at herself. In years past her husband had made all necessary plans and now she felt comfortable doing it. It was like she was reborn as someone else. She felt good.

In the back of the truck Amos and Whistler were having a lively discussion about the attitudes and beliefs of the Americans and how to convince them to stop their pollution of the world. The young eagle had never had a chance to get into deep discussions with a human in this lifetime and he was amazed at the intelligence of this grassroots mountain Indian. He knew he would learn a lot from him.

When they neared the Utah and Arizona border Angela drove off the road to a secluded spot. She got out of the truck and looked around to make sure they were alone, then she opened the door of the camper shell.

"Whistler, when we cross the state border the inspection people will look in here to see what we're carrying so you'll have to leave us now. Fly overhead and meet us farther down the highway. We have another seventy or eighty miles to go before we stop for the night, then we can heat some canned soup for supper."

This was a welcome break for Whistler. Being cooped up in the camper was not to his liking. With a great flapping of wings and a clacking of his beak, the eagle flew straight up into the sky and circled overhead.

They reached Tuba City about four in the afternoon. An hour later, near the Indian town of Moenkopi, Angela crossed over a small stream, turned onto a dirt road and parked under a friendly-looking willow tree. As soon as she had built a small fire, Whistler swooped down with two rabbits in his talons. He dropped them by the fire. "Here's something to go with your soup. I'll go find another one for my own supper."

After supper they relaxed by the fire. Angela felt like singing. She remembered her childhood and sang songs in the Paiute language which her mother had taught her as a child. They were songs of the four seasons and the blessings that they brought to the people. Whistler was enchanted by her singing and the beauty of nature they described. Amos too, was appreciative of her songs. These were the kind of things which his father had not had time to teach him and he longed to hear more, but Angela choked with emotion on remembering her mother and could sing no more.

Amos lit his pipe. When the tobacco was burning evenly, he spoke. "I want to tell you two, my close friends, how and why I came to be in the mountains of Paiute country. Up until now my life has seemed to be a constant search for some way to live with the horrors I have seen and the spiritual strength to forgive those who wronged my family."

He then described his early life in Alabama's Taladega Mountains, and remembered many small details he thought he had forgotten.

"On cold winter nights," he told them, "our family would sit around the wood stove and sing spiritual songs my mother had learned on southern plantations, and during the cold days my father worked at a nearby saw mill. He taught me hunting skills and how to provide for a family." He hesitated before telling of how the family died in the fire.

When he finished, he said, "That scene still haunts me. Sometimes I think that I could have done something to save them, but what? I try to flush the memories out of my life because it poisons my heart with hatred and my mind with thoughts of revenge. That is why I sought out the holy ones who could put forgiveness into my heart. It has been a difficult struggle, but I am near that goal, I know."

Then it was the eagle's turn. "There is little I can tell you about my life," he said. "Up until the time I was assigned to bring Angela to the Council of Eagles I trained with the others to be a scout for the Council, and to hunt for food. We also learned to avoid contact with white faced humans because whenever they would see one of us, they would reach for a gun. One of my brothers was killed by a bullet and when the man came to pick his body up, he brutally pulled my brother's tail feathers out, tossed his body to the ground and squashed him with his heavy boot. They are the ones who I have learned to avoid. It's strange. Now we are being asked to save them too. I guess I have much to learn yet. I'm tired now, so I'll sleep in the top of this tree, and I'll wake you early in the morning." Then he was gone to find a comfortable tree limb.

Angela cleared pebbles away from a small area and put a blanket on the soft ground near the fire. She lay down, said goodnight to Amos, and was soon asleep.

Amos put a small piece of wood on the fire, then sat puffing slowly on his pipe, and thought of the coming days. The Great One had saved him to be used in this fight and he felt ready. Life was good.

From a nearby hilltop, a coyote saw their small fire and sang his song of loneliness. There was no answer from any direction so it moved on.

Just before daybreak Whistler woke the others and told them he was going to fly ahead to look around. "I'll catch up with you later," he said. He wanted to stay alert for their protection. "Trust your instincts," his father had said, "but rely on your eyesight." So he flew high and surveyed the countryside for any sign of unusual things.

By the time the sun showed over the distant mountains, the pickup truck was back on the highway rolling towards the East, through Hopi country. This evening they would be back into Navajo country. They would camp one more night somewhere near Ganado, then the next morning they would turn North towards the town of Chinlee, very near Canyon de Chelly.

ANGELA'S BATTLE

The next day, they reached Chinlee about mid-morning. They still had about fifteen miles to go before they could think about finding a place to leave the truck. She left it to Whistler to determine where a path would lead down into the canyon. They drove for another half hour, then Whistler swooped down on them from above. Angela stopped the truck and the three of them climbed into the camper shell where they could talk without being seen.

Whistler said, "About six miles ahead there's a Navajo hogan a mile off the road and it is close to a place where you can climb down into the canyon. Let's get moving and I can show you." Now they were all encouraged and anxious.

The hogan was well hidden from road traffic. Angela parked the truck near a narrow trail leading downwards. Some of the lighter burlap sacks holding their supplies were left on the canyon rim. Whistler said he would fly them down to the canyon floor, one at a time. Amos and Angela strapped the heavier sacks holding the rest of their supplies on their backs, and began the slow trip down to the floor of the canyon. Moving slow, they reached the bottom in an hour. Then they began their long walk to the cave.

Once they safely reached the bottom of the canyon Whistler left them to find the eagles who had arrived earlier. They would provide security and protection for the meeting.

Amos and Angela said very little to each other as they trudged through sand and rock. Each was lost in their own thoughts. Amos recalled the history of this canyon and others like it. The "Ancient Ones" called *Anasazi* by the Navajo, lived in these canyons centuries before the coming of the Europeans, and had long ago suddenly disappeared without a trace. It was they who had built the apartment-like dwellings made of rock and clay mortar called a pueblo, meaning *village*, by the Spanish, and now almost all of the Indians living in central New Mexico were known as being of the Pueblo Tribe.

Especially of interest to Amos was the fact that some of these pueblos were built in huge caves at the bottom of these canyons. Amos wondered, *Why here?* Why did they leave their sunlit places on the plateaus and come here? Could it have been for some kind of self-defense purposes, and if so, defense against who, or what? Even more wonder, some of these pueblos had an outer wall, a perimeter, built as if to protect the pueblo. The question kept coming back to him. Protect them from what? Other tribes? Maybe, but it was apparent that during daylight hours the Anasazi worked and played outside in the sun. Why did they have to barricade themselves only at night?

So many questions, and now they were going to stay in one of those caves for the next week. Maybe some of the answers would be given to him in this ancient canyon..

In the depths of the canyon the sun disappeared early. At six p.m. Amos estimated they were about two-thirds of the way to the cave. He stopped and looked back at Angela who was about one hundred yards behind him. *What a brave woman,* he thought.

Surprisingly, Angela was in high spirits. She was tired, yes, and she knew her legs would ache tomorrow, but she vowed that she wouldn't complain to anyone. She was able to wear the good work shoes that her husband had left. He always bought the best shoes he could afford because as he had told her, "Cover your head and your rear end, take care of your feet, and you'll always come home from the mines."

By the time she caught up to Amos he had cleared a space where they could camp for the night, and he had a fire going. "For an old man, you're really something," she said. Amos only chuckled and poured water from the canvas water bag into a scarred-up blue enamel coffee pot and hung it over the fire on a tripod made from tree branches.

"We're going to have beef jerky and oatmeal for supper. If you want anything fancier you'll have to go back to the restaurant in Chinlee," he told Angela. She laughed and said, "Hey, oatmeal sounds good to me. I just want to take my clodhoppers off and cool my toes."

Twenty minutes later Whistler flew in from the eastern end of the canyon. "Good news, friends. You're only about five miles from the cave. In the morning you can be there in no time. I've been to the cave, and it looks like people lived there long ago. It's like a small village. It's dusty and run down, but it's sheltered from the sun and the night air. And that's not all, there's a spring for fresh water about 300 feet from the cave and there's a grove of trees, too. We're going to have a good time." Then he turned serious.

"The young scouts have been there since yesterday. They flew the entire length of all three canyons and scouted the rims and plateaus for ten miles around. There's no sign of danger anywhere, but last night they saw a figure of a man sitting beside a small fire by the spring. He stayed there all night singing and shaking a rattle which appeared to be made from a turtle shell. He was not there this morning, although none of the scouts saw him leave. They think he was a friendly spirit."

Amos was very interested in this news, and he said to the eagle, "I am going away from the camp tonight for meditation, so I would like you to stay here with Angela until morning. For now, please go and tell the scouts that I thank them for their alert work, and that I would like them to stay on the rims near the cave tonight, and tomorrow they can report what they see, if anything." The eagle flew away, but returned within a half-hour.

They were all hungry after this days work. They heartily enjoyed their sparse meal, and the coffee was excellent. Afterwards, they sat around the fire and reviewed the events of the past few days. Things were progressing so fast, it seemed. A week ago, they would not have dreamed they would be camping in a lonesome canyon on this night.

Amos smoked one pipe of tobacco while he listened to Whistler tell of his experiences since they had left their mountain homes. Then he stood up and went into his medicine bag and put a handful of sage into a depression on a small rock, lit it, and when it was smoldering smoke, he circled Angela and the eagle while singing a Zuni prayer. He made sure the smoke drifted down over their heads and down their bodies to cleanse them of any evil directed at them. Then he circled their camp ground, blowing smoke all the while and singing his prayer.

Angela raised her head for her own prayer. When she lowered her head and opened her eyes Amos was gone and the canyon was silent. The only sound was the occasional snap and pop of the small branches in the fire.

The next morning Angela was up before daylight. Amos was there, curled up in his brown Army blanket. When the coffee was ready he got up.

After coffee and wheat crackers, they began the last leg of their trip to the cave. The eagle flew off to check on his scouts, saying that he would meet them at the cave.

Two hours later, Whistler flew to meet them. "Hello, travelers. The hotel is just around this next big rock. Welcome."

When they rounded the huge boulder Amos and Angela stopped and gasped in wonder. The cave opening was huge, about seventy-five feet high and two hundred feet wide. It looked tremendous. As they walked toward it, the inside of the cave became clearer to them. They stood amazed at the stark beauty of small dwelling houses stacked on top of each other, like apartments, and extending more than one-hundred-fifty feet to the rear of the cave.

Angela marveled, "What a wonderful place this must have been, with adults doing their chores and many children running around playing."

Even now, the clay plaster which covered walls and ceilings was cool to the touch and as smooth as a modern brick. At the top of the dwelling sidewalls, wood poles which supported the ceilings and the apartments above protruded out, evenly spaced about two feet apart. Clay ovens, shaped like bee hives, seemingly in good condition, were lined up in two rows extending West from outside the cave entrance. Angela counted thirty of them.

Along the bottom of the opposite canyon wall a small stream was flowing westward away from a spring. *What a sight this must have been in its day*, she thought. Angela marveled at it all. She went to the spring head to fill the canvas water bags. She drank the water and it was sweet tasting and cold. Just a few yards from the spring head there was a grove of willow trees which reached their top branches 100 feet high towards the sunshine.

She heard a familiar crooning bird call and jerked her head up. This was the first bird that she had seen close up in a long, long time. There were two grey doves busily putting a nest together in the fork of two stout branches. "How wonderful," she said.

When she went back to where Amos was, she was humming a tune. Amos looked at her with a grin on his stubbly face and went back to his own work.

After their backpacks and supplies were stored, Amos called the other two to meet with him. "Tomorrow night is the first night of the new moon. Everyone will be here and we must prepare for a fire which will burn all day and night. It must not be permitted to die out until the meeting is over." He looked at Whistler, "Please have the scouts come down now."

The eagle's eyes shown with pride. He proudly strutted a few steps before rising to the plateau above to round up the scouts. One by one they arrived and stood in a half-circle in front of Amos who was seated on a rock alongside the stream. Whistler flew in and reported, "They are all here and they are at your service." Then he assumed a position of leadership in front of the scouts.

Amos looked at all twenty scouts for a full minute, then cleared his throat. "My good friends, he began, "all of us are here on a mission which we did not ask for, but one which our Creator has mandated that we do. It is the beginning of a united fight to prevent a tragedy which would affect every living thing on our Mother Earth."

"All of you scouts have a very important job to do which will help the success of the conference which will take place here. The ones who will be meeting here are very important to our world, and each of you should be prepared to protect them at all costs. With your life, if necessary."

Amos then instructed them on what he would expect from them in the coming days and nights. They listened attentively. Amos finished by saying, "Your future is at stake as well as ours, so be watchful. You are all brave hearts. You have my respect."

Whistler then led them up to the sky above where he would assign them to their duties.

Angela was amazed at the scene. A few weeks ago, in her wildest dreams, she could never have imagined she would see a sight like this. After a few moments Amos and Angela turned to the task of preparing for the arrival of the holy men and the Council of Eagles.

Chapter Eight

Night darkness came to the deep canyon around seven p.m. There were two stacks of wood ready to be lit. One stack was just outside the cave where all would meet before filing into the *kiva*. Another fire would be in the *kiva* itself, to give dim light and heat for those meeting inside.

Amos had located the ancient *kiva* where hundreds of years ago the holy men and the elders of the village had met to offer prayers and to commune with the Great One. It was also the storing place for their holy symbols used on special days of giving thanks, like the annual Corn Dance and Deer Dance, in which prayers for good crops, rainfall, and good hunting were offered.

On other special days, *Kachinas*, who represented the Great One, would be honored by special songs and dances. Images of these lesser gods were worn by selected men who would represent them at these colorful celebrations. Those images and paraphernalia were stored here in this sacred place. The kiva was the symbolic spiritual and sacred *sipapu*, the opening from which their ancestors had emerged eons ago from the body of Mother Earth. It was the place of emergence. Amos had spent the afternoon preparing the *kiva* to receive its guests.

After they had a simple meal, Whistler came with news. "The Council of Eagles will be here within an hour. One of the scouts flying ahead of them has arrived. I can't hardly wait for things to begin. Just think, my friends, this will be the first meeting of this kind in over a hundred years. We will make history here this week."

In his excitement he hopped about with a great flapping of his powerful wings. Then in a more serious tone, he said "The scouts saw no unusual activity last night anywhere, and they are prepared to give close inspection from now on to everything. They will fly in pairs. Even if a coyote approaches, one will fly down to verify that it is a coyote and it will be warned to stay away. Believe me, these scouts are the best there is, anywhere."

"I agree," Amos said. "Everything is as ready as it can be. You've done a great job as has Angela. Our team is the best there is, anywhere." Then in a sudden impulse, he reached down and put his hand on the young eagle's head. Amos lifted his voice and offered a prayer to the Creator that they be made strong, that they be given the courage to carry out the will of the Creator, whatever it was. "*A-ho!*" They all felt better after this.

It was now pitch dark. Amos lit the first of the fires. He asked Angela to light the smaller fire in the kiva. When she returned, they stood at the cave entrance and waited.

Suddenly Amos raised his right arm and motioned to the East and said loudly, "Welcome, Apish'taya, of the Zuni; U'yuyewi of the Yaqui; Karahkwa of the Onondaga; Kla-begatho of the Navajo, the Din'e; Sunka Wakan Wicasa of the Lakotah, Dakota, and Nakota people; Ga-a-moo of the Chiricahua Tind-eh; and Monong-hovi of the Hopi. Welcome all."

Angela was startled. She hadn't heard or seen anything in that direction, yet as she watched awe struck, an old man in Zuni trappings came out of the darkness walking slowly, leading a group of other holy men who were the mentors of the many Native American spiritual groups. Each was plainly dressed in their own tribal way. Some in white cotton trousers and blouse, some in buckskin, but none were wearing the flashy trappings which the younger generation had begun to affect.

The group filed by in front of Amos and Angela, saying a word of greeting to them, each in their own language. To her surprise Angela understood every word they said, and she nodded in acknowledgment.

Amos raised his arm again and said, "Welcome to you, Teek-awis, and the great Council of Eagles, messengers of the Great One. Come, join us."

From the darkness to the West, Teek-awis, looking huge, handsome, and regal led his Council towards the fire. When the Council was gathered, Teek-awis motioned to the mentors with his right wing and said, "Holy ones, we are honored to meet here with all of you. Apish'taya, the last time the Council of Eagles met with the seven mentors, it was your father who led your group. I am happy that you have followed in his footsteps."

"It is good to be with you to talk of important matters. We hope to conclude our meeting before the seven day period ends so that activity coming from our plans can begin as soon as possible. We know we do not have much time before Mother Earth begins to object strongly to the insults upon her body. I offer my thanks to Amos Turkey, Angela Beaver, and my son, Whistler, for their work here and in the past few weeks. We elders may have the easiest task of developing strategy, but these three will have to see that those plans are carried out."

"If you should see the need for another meeting with us, you are to contact Amos Turkey and he will make the arrangements. Amos has achieved a spiritual level which the Great One has recognized. Amos and Angela will see that our plans are carried out by those who are ready and willing to believe that what we say is true. Now, let us begin our talk."

Angela had placed a candle at each turn in the path leading back to the kiva. Now she walked ahead as the procession, led by Teek-awis and Apish'taya, filed into the circular kiva where the Council of Eagles seated themselves on one side of the room, and the tribal holy ones, the shamans, on the other side. Angela placed two small logs on the fire, providing just enough light to see by, yet not enough to be uncomfortably warm or smoky. The heat and smoke escaped through an opening in the ceiling.

Teek-awis made sure all were comfortably seated, then he asked Apish'taya to bless the meeting place and everyone in it.

And so it was that the historic meeting began. It was an impressive sight. Apish'taya and his group were now seated on the dirt floor with blankets over their shoulders and some had a sprig of evergreen spruce braided into their long hair.

They listened as Teek-awis addressed the group.

"The Council of Eagles deliberately wanted to meet in this place. Many years ago, our people, the Anasazi as they are now called, lived in happiness and harmony in their villages on the flat plateaus above the canyon. Their fields were productive and no one went hungry. Yes, as humans will always do, they had disagreements with their neighbors and they sometimes stole the young women of other villages, but by this means they also propagated their race by intermarriage with other blood lines, and life was good for them. Then suddenly, they and their relatives disappeared as if the wind had blown them from the face of the Earth. Today there is little trace of them. We who knew the truth of what happened were sworn to secrecy and until now, we could not tell this truth. We can now tell you this story." There was a brief buzz of excitement.

When all was quiet, Teek-awis continued. "One day a handsome stranger came to their main village. His skin was dark and his hair was like lambs wool. He wore clothing like that of an old man, with feet wrapped in animal skins bound with leather thongs. The Anasazi had never seen a person like this and they thought he was an incarnation of the black warrior god, a Kachina."

"They treated him as a Kachina. They gave him presents of food and clothing. He received these presents and stayed in their village until one day it was noticed that several of the young unmarried women seemed to be with child. They questioned the village men, thinking that one of them had impregnated the women.

All denied having done so. Surely, the Anasazi leaders said, the black warrior would not have did this. A representative of the Creator would have no use for laying with human women."

"*Nah-vathoo'* was the spiritual leader of the village. He suggested that while the black warrior was resting one of them should creep up to him and quickly cut him on the arm to see if blood would flow like that of a common man. If blood did not flow, he was indeed a god and should be allowed to have his way."

"That night, the elder women were told to cook a favorite meal for the black warrior. After the meal, the black warrior lay back to sleep and the Anasazi leaders watched as Nah-vathoo' crept up to the black warrior and quickly ran a sharp flint blade across his arm. Red blood spurted out and splashed everything around him. Nah-vathoo' cried out, *This is not a god. He is a common man and must be put to death for having deceived us and taking our young women.*"

"Members of the Anasazi warrior society immediately grabbed him. One grabbed his legs and the leather wrappings fell off his feet. What they saw was the legs of a goat and when they pulled on his robe they saw the body of a man who from the waist down had the body of a male goat. The covering on his head fell off, revealing two short horns. This creature became enraged and was so strong that he killed every one of the warrior society, then he ran off into the night. He shouted, *Nah-vathoo', I will deliver you to the Devil, beware!*"

"A few nights later, the black goat-man returned with several others of different colors, some were brown and some white faced. They grabbed Nah-vathoo' and made off with him. The next morning his body was found torn limb from limb and scattered to the four directions. A runner was dispatched to other villages to warn them of what had happened. In two weeks time the runner returned with the news that several villages were empty of people and that in three other villages the people were preparing to leave immediately. They all had similar stories to tell: a goat man had taken advantage of them and when found out, many people were killed and the goat men promised to return for the rest of them."

"Some of the Anasazi leaders were convinced that these creatures would be back for all of them and they decided not to leave the area, but to move here, to this canyon, and they built this village and kiva that we now occupy, thinking that they could protect themselves by being well prepared. There were only two ways into this canyon and they placed warrior guards there."

"The end of their story is known only by chance. A wandering eagle was hunting one day and saw ten strange creatures who resembled a man, yet did not look like a man. He followed these creatures to this canyon, then from the canyon rim he watched as the creatures came down the rough canyon walls, jumping from rock to rock. They leaped over the barricade wall, the remains of the wall which you may have seen outside. They went into this village where we are now and began killing everyone here while they slept. The Anasazi were butchered into pieces then placed on top of log piles which were then set on fire. The eagle remembered one creature crying out loudly, *These are all for you, Master."*

"That is how the Anasazi disappeared. The others who fled the area split into small groups to hide better and they scattered into the lands and mountains to the North and to the East. They never spoke of the disaster again, so today even their second seventh generation descendants know nothing of the truth."

After a slight pause, he said softly, "A similar fate was suffered by the Hohokam, our cousins to the South."

"You were asked to meet here at the scene of their death so that each of you would know the kind of danger which we are faced with. Today, more of these goat creatures were sighted in several places. The Great One advises us that they are from the land of fire and perpetual punishment."

"The Devil, as he is called, has sent them to collect souls for his own use. He thinks it will be easy to collect many souls at this time because a great catastrophe is about to happen which will frighten the billions of people now living. Many humans, when they believe their world is about to end, become carefree and forget their teachings of spirituality, religion and morality, making them easy prey for the Devil."

"This catastrophe will be caused by those who have made things which are slowly destroying the world in which we all live, and the Creator of all things has given them only a short time in which to realize the truth, otherwise we will all be destroyed."

"The Creator has sent warning after warning to them and they still will not listen. It was prophesied by you and your disciples that certain things would happen as signs that they should stop their destructive ways. Even as I speak to you, there is a strong, cold wind sweeping across this country. Unusual storms have covered many areas and soon floods will begin. Earthquakes will increasing in number and intensity. The signs are there for them to see, but they do not see."

"The Creator sent a bright star tinged with the colors of death to move across the night sky as another warning. The people only marveled at its brilliance and bright plumage while scholars pretended to know its origin and even its age. They are unwilling to admit their ignorance."

"Our task then, is to prevent the destruction of the world by powerful explosions, and the second task is to prevent souls from being delivered to the Devil. The two tasks are separate, yet actually one large one. Let us now begin our plans."

The two groups buzzed with excitement. Teek-awis allowed the two groups to talk among themselves for ten minutes, then he said, "We are going to talk first about the threat to our sacred Circle of Life. Each of you may speak as long as you like on the subject of the evil ones, the ones called goat men. Then when we have all spoken on that subject, we will then talk about the white man's mis-use of the natural elements and which has poisoned our mother Earth. When we have fully discussed both subjects, we will hear each of your thoughts on what must be done. Only then will we assemble the final strategy. *'Ee wit tsu'*. Let it begin."

For four nights and three days the discussion continued non-stop. Once every few hours, Angela would offer them water, but none asked for food. They were well used to fasting and to them, the business ahead was too important to stop.

Every four hours, Whistler would come to report to Amos. He told him that the scouts were extremely alert and efficient. They were taking their responsibility for the safety of this honorable group very seriously.

In the early morning darkness of the third day, Whistler called urgently to Amos. "The scouts flying over the South canyon spotted what looked like a goat climbing down the canyon wall. When they flew down to look at it, it jumped under a large rock overhang and is there now. More scouts are on their way. One of them will go into the overhang for a close look. The others will stand by to rescue him if necessary. We are not certain what it is yet, but I will return as soon as we know, but be prepared. Wish us luck." Then he was gone.

Amos immediately told Angela of the possible danger. She stiffened, then said, "Just tell me what to do, Amos. I'm ready."

"Thank you, dear one. Nothing is sure yet, but we can't take chances. I have to tell Teek-awis just in case we have to take immediate action. Keep a watch by the fire outside." Angela flashed him a smile, then went to put more wood on the fire.

When Teek-awis was told of the possible sighting, he merely nodded and resumed listening to the speaker.

ANGELA'S BATTLE

The southern-most finger of the giant Canyon de Chelly extended slightly parallel to the others, but in a more southeasterly direction. It was eight miles from the one in which the meeting was taking place. When Whistler reached the spot where something had been spotted, he saw a v-shaped formation of the eagles slowly circling above the canyon. Six others were perched on top of the huge rock where the thing was hiding.

One of those eagles, Sharp Eye, flew up to meet Whistler. "Ho-go-ton is heading the formation above us. He has told us to wait for your signal, then I will approach the hiding place for a look at the thing. Whirl Wind and his group will stay on the top of the rock in case I need help. Everything is planned. We were waiting for you."

Whistler was pleased that the scouts were ready to act. "Good work," he said. "We will wait ten minutes." Then he flew up to see Ho-ga-ton and asked him to fly just below the canyon rim in order to be closer to Sharp Eye if he was attacked. All was ready, and he noted how calm everyone was, but he knew they were as excited as he was.

When it was time, Whistler signaled to Sharp Eye to move in. Sharp Eye began a slow flight level with the bottom of the huge rock, reaching the rock he swerved in close and looked towards the rear of the cavity underneath the rock. Suddenly he increased his speed and flew up to where Whistler was waiting. "There's another smaller cave in the back. Whatever is in there has the tail and legs of a goat. I couldn't see the upper body, so I'll have to go in for a close look. Be quick if I need help," and he was gone to begin his close inspection.

Sharp Eye landed on the edge of the opening and looked inside. The lower part of the thing was visible, but the upper body was hidden by a rock protrusion. He took a step forward, then another. The thing had not moved at all. From where he stood he let out a screech, and the thing flinched, but did not move. He took two more steps, watching for any leg movements which would indicate a gathering of strength for an attack. Now he was only a step away from being able to touch the legs which were now quivering slightly.

He looked all around and saw nothing else which presented a danger to him, so he decided it was time to move decisively. He took that one step and clamped his strong beak down hard on one of the legs in front of him. The thing let out a loud noise and charged swiftly out of the hole. A hand holding a piece of sharp flint rock reached out and hit Sharp Eye. Then the thing lowered its head and ran to the outside. Sharp Eye had only time to screech out a warning to Whirl Wind who was waiting outside. In this sudden mad rush, Sharp Eye was flung straight out the cave opening where he fell a few yards down the canyon wall before he regained the power of flight.

The thing quickly stopped, changed directions, and started to run up the canyon wall. Whirl Wind's group was prepared. They hit it from the two sides, knocking it rolling. It had only time to get back on its feet when Ho-ga-ton, swooping down swiftly, hit it again with his talons tearing into the flesh of its face. It got up slowly, trying to focus on what had hit it. Twice, in close succession the six other scouts in the formation swooped down and raked their talons across the back, neck and head of the thing. It fell, rolled a few feet, and lay still. It didn't get up. There was no further movement. Whistler called off the attack, then flew down to personally inspect the body.

It was barely light when he met the others on the canyon rim where they sat telling each other how they had moved in on the creature. They were excited and chattering, as young warriors do. Only Sharp Eye was silent. He felt strange, as never before. He was lightheaded and he seemed to be dropping blood on the flat rock where he sat.

He said nothing as Whistler stood before them and asked for silence. "The thing below us is one of the evil goat men. This is the first time any of us has seen such a creature. Now we know they are real and can be stopped. It may have wandered here by accident, or it could have been sent to find the meeting place. We must assume there are others nearby. Ho-go-ton, double the patrols immediately and tell the scouts what happened here. With real danger a possibility, we cannot take a chance that there are not more goat men nearby."

Suddenly, Whirl Wind said loudly, "Sharp Eye, what's wrong? Are you alright?" Everyone gathered around Sharp Eye, who was now lying on his side. A small pool of blood was forming around his neck.

Sharp Eye looked up at his friends. "I know I am going to see the Great One today, then I will go to the Lake of Souls. I am happy to go, and I hope you will be happy for me. A flint rock ripped my neck when the beast charged into me and my life blood is flowing out of me now."

His eyes closed for a time, then slowly opened once more. "It has been a good life, living with all of you. I will see you again, I know, in another lifetime."

"I have only one request of you, Whistler. My tail feathers have been said to be the finest ever seen on an eagle." He tried to smile. "Please take two of my tail feathers and present one of them to Amos Turkey and the other to Angela Beaver as a gift from me, Sharp Eye, the bravest of the scouts. They will need much bravery in the near future." Sharp Eye breathed his last breath, the blood stopped flowing, and he was gone to the other place where his relatives were already waiting for him.

Everyone was silent for a moment. Whistler motioned to one of the scouts and sent him back to tell Amos what had happened, and that he would be there shortly. "In the meantime," he said, "we'll place Sharp Eye on the big rock nearby where he died. Then the other scouts can come to say goodbye to him."

Amos had not yet told Teek-awis of what had happened, and stood waiting for Whistler to arrive. Together, Amos and Whistler entered the kiva and told Teek-awis of Sharp Eye's death. He was saddened, and interrupted the meeting. He asked Whistler to tell them what had happened.

Apish'taya rose to speak. "The clan of the eagles has always been revered by we humans. We have always admired your strength and courage and we fall short when we strive to attain your level of bravery and spiritual progress. Now we pause in the matter of our own survival to pay honor to Sharp Eye, the first to fall in this new battle to perpetuate our existence. Sharp Eye did his duty without hesitation and with courage. We can all be thankful for his time with us."

Teek-awis said, "I have known Sharp Eye since his first flight. He has always been one to be in the forefront of activity. We are extremely proud of him." Then he asked Amos to once again cleanse the kiva of any evil that may have wandered in with Death.

Later, outside, Whistler told Amos of the gift from Sharp Eye. Amos and Angela gratefully accepted the feathers and said a prayer of thanks for the dead eagle.

The meeting of tribal shamans and the Council of Eagles ended two hours before dawn on the morning of the fifth day without further incident Ho-go-ton had reported that the eagles had not sighted any further signs of goat men.

The participants had met day and night without pause. Everyone of the shamans had spoken their mind on the topics of the goat men and on the nuclear dangers to the world.

Sometime after midnight on that fifth day the talking stopped, and after a period of silence and thought, Apish'taya prayed for the blessings of the Creator.

Then it was over. The historic meeting ended as it had begun, with a minimum of ceremony.

Teek-awis asked Amos and Angela to meet with the Council of Eagles to learn of the plans that had been made. He told them, "The best of our ideas have been sorted out. Now we can sit down with you and finish our business here."

When they emerged from the kiva four hours later the morning sun was rising in the East and shining into the length of the canyon. The several shades of red and brown on the rocky canyon walls seemed brilliant in the light, and the stream which flowed westward along the northern side of the canyon shone like silver in the sunlight. The shrubs and grass alongside the stream and the tall willow tree were a pleasant sight. The entire scene was etched in Angela's memory. It would be a beautiful memory.

High overhead the entire group of scouts had assembled and was flying in a large lazy circle, waiting for a signal to begin the trip home. Ho-go-ton, the scout leader flew apart from the main body ready to give his commands.

As Amos had expected, the tribal holy men had departed as they came and were nowhere to be seen. Soon the Council of Eagles came out into the sunlight.

Teek-awis said goodby to Amos and Angela. "You two are on your own now to begin carrying out the plan. If you need help at anytime, call to me, and someone will be there. Whistler will stay with you always."

Then he spoke softly to Whistler. "Son, you are my pride and my joy. I will miss you, but it is necessary that you stay close to Angela. Protect her at all times and if you must, do not hesitate to give your life for her. I must go now, but when the war is done we will all meet again."

To the Council of Eagles he said, "Let us go now." They rose up into the sky and with the scouts leading the way they were soon out of sight. They were going home.

When they were gone, Angela asked, "Whistler, did you teach the eagles to do the military formations and activities?"

Whistler laughed. "No. They learned to do the formations and tricks by watching the war planes that train in the desert. Ho-go-ton then organized them into flights. They can now do everything, and more, that the Air Force pilots can do, except carry bombs, but who knows? One day they may be able to do that too. They are good. They learned by copying."

They spent the next few hours cleaning up the kiva and the part of the canyon they had used. Amos wanted to leave everything as they had found it. Angela went to the tree where the doves had built their nest and sat down in its shade. When she first saw them a few days ago the large male dove seemed to speak to her when he crooned, "Hello-oh-oh-oh." She had heard the dove call many times before, but this was the first time she could figure out what it sounded like. It was so peaceful here that she didn't really want to leave. Now it crooned, "Good bye-bye-bye."

Early the next morning Amos woke Angela. "We'll be leaving soon. We need to travel fast today. We'll stop once to rest and have something to eat, but we need to be out of the canyon before dark." Angela wondered about the urgency to leave, but kept her silence.

Soon they were on their way. Angela looked back only once for a last look at her *dove tree*. *I only hope that someday I can return here*, she thought. Then she bent to the task ahead. With short, quick strides she followed Amos through the bottom sand of the canyon. The afternoon sun was about an hour above the western horizon when the two tired travelers reached the canyon rim where they had entered one week before.

A short time later, after passing through Chinlee, at Amos' direction they turned North, heading towards the wilds of Skeleton Mesa in the north-central part of the Navajo reservation. They soon found a suitable camp site.

After their supper, they sat around the small fire and reviewed the events of the past week. Each took a turn to talk about what they had learned from the meeting in Canyon de Chelly. Finally, Amos laid out their next moves.

"Tomorrow we meet with the tribal holy men at Betatakin. We will review our plans with them, then it will be necessary that we split up for awhile to carry out our own part in the strategy. This will be the start of your job, Angela. Whistler will travel with you, always. After tomorrow, we will know more of the details so for now, let's give thanks to the Creator for this day, then we'll get a good nights rest. I feel like I haven't slept in a month."

That same night, back in Canyon de Chelly in the dim light of a quarter-moon, a strange figure arrived at the eastern end of the canyon where the conference had been held. It nimbly descended down the canyon wall and then ran to the West where it had been told it would find one of its own kind. Together, they were to find a man named Amos. Amos was to be killed. It arrived at the cave where the meeting had been held and found no trace of anyone. It was too late, he was gone, everyone was gone, so it retraced its steps back to where it had come from in the darkest reaches of a place called Canyon del Muerto, the Canyon of Death, to the northeast. This was the reason for Amos' haste to be gone from the canyon.

Chapter Nine

The next day, they reached the hogan of Kla-begatho just before six p.m. The seven holy men were already there, and were well rested. They were getting ready to enjoy a meal of mutton roasted over hot coals as only the Navajo could do, along with the rare blue corn bread. The bread was a delicacy of the Hopi people. Kernels of blue corn were first ground into a flour on stone grinders, then mixed with water to form a paste which was then spread by hand on the surface of a smooth hot rock which had been heated in an open fire. The paper thin layers were then folded over several times, making a crisp delicacy with a special flavor. It was much sought after.

Two elderly women, one a Navajo and the other a Hopi, were the cooks for the group. They were longtime trusted friends of Kla-begatho. The coffee was brewed in a large, old enameled pot hung over a fire of juniper wood. Angela thought she had never tasted finer coffee.

The meal was eaten Indian style, without spoons or forks. "Fingers were made before forks and it's better this way," Amos said. Without a self-conscious thought, Angela noisily licked the mutton grease off her fingers.

"Heck," she told Amos, "This is like dessert. The best part of the meal." Amos smiled indulgently.

After dark, the two elderly women lay hand-made wool blankets on the ground around the fire and everyone found a comfortable spot to sit. For awhile all was quiet. When the night sounds started and the night birds came out to inspect the group, the holy man of the Lakota-Dakota-Nakota people unwrapped his flute made of northern cedar and began to play a tune that was old long before the time of the Spaniards arrival. While he breathed through the flute another holy man lit his pipe using his own mixture of desert sage, herbs, and mountain grasses, and presented the smoke to the four sacred directions, then passed the pipe to the others in the circled group.

When all was silent again the Zuni, Apish'taya, began to talk softly. "Tomorrow, we elders will go to our homes safe from the dangers which are to come. You two," motioning to Amos and Angela, "will go to face those dangers for us. You will be our warriors. We will always be only a thought away from you, but you are to call us only in the case of the most extreme emergency, that which is at the limits of human abilities."

"For a time, your work will be done separately. Angela, you will begin a campaign among the people of all races to enlist them in the effort to stop the explosions in Nevada. The people do not yet know the damage and destruction that will come from it, and they must be told."

"Amos will go to the indigenous people for help in ridding the world of these monsters of evil, the ones that we call goat men. None of we shamans have ever seen one of these creatures because they only appear among the common people, the working people. He will have to identify them and try to persuade them to return to Hell, from where they came. The one we call the Devil may not want to lose what he sees as a great opportunity to steal the souls of living humans, and he may order the goat men to stay and fight. In that case they will have to be destroyed. That would be the greatest task."

"Both of you have a difficult job, and it would be impossible to say which one is more difficult. Angela, you must remain strong. There are those in the land that are as concerned for the health of the world as we are, but they don't yet know how close to the end they are. You will find them, or they will find you. Either way, there may be enough of them to make a difference. Look for them, tell them the truth. The world must be made to listen."

With that, all was silent. Each was deep in their own thoughts.

There was only one more thing spoken. Karahkwa, the Onondaga, said, "There is one person who I think would want to help you, Angela. His name is Jay Storm Cloud. He comes from the warrior tribe called the Quechan in the southwest. He is now working somewhere in the East. Washington, D.C., I think. He would be an asset to you if you can persuade him to help you. He is a newspaper man."

Angela sat up quickly. "I know that man. I heard him speak to a gathering of Indian people just a few months ago in Phoenix. Yes, I will speak to him. Thank you for reminding me. There must be a hundred others who will help. I'm ready to go to work." The seated shamans nodded their heads in approval of her spunky spirit.

The flute began to sing its song again, and everyone lay on the blankets provided and soon were sound asleep. During the night the only movement was that of the two old women who would occasionally rise to put wood on the fire. Although days were warm at this time of year, the nights could become quite chilly.

All night, the camp was under the watchful eyes of Whistler and Ho-go-ton who sat unseen on the very top of a nearby juniper tree.

Angela woke the next morning to find that except for the Navajo and Hopi women, she was the only one left at the hogan of Kla-begatho, All of the shamans were gone, as was Amos. Whistler was nowhere to be seen. She wondered why they had left without telling her.

They'll be back soon, she hoped.

The Hopi woman brought her a washpan and a small bucket of water. While she performed her ablutions they cooked a breakfast for her. She suddenly felt all alone and unsure of how to begin the big task that she had undertaken.

While she ate the breakfast they had prepared for her, the two women came to sit with her beside the fire. The sun had just risen above the horizon so the morning air was still cool. This was the first opportunity the two had to speak to Angela and they politely waited for Angela to speak first. It was obvious that they had a great respect for her, and this was because for as long as they could remember, no woman had ever been allowed to work so closely with the shamans.

After drinking some of the strong coffee, Angela broke the silence. In English she said, "My name is Angela Beaver, a Southern Paiute from Utah." The two women smiled self-consciously. Angela guessed them to be at least 70 years old. Almost a generation older than she. The larger woman, smiling broadly, simply said "Fawn. Navajo."

Encouraged, the other said quickly, "Star. Hopi."

Angela discovered that the women spoke only a little English, but like all Indian women before them, they communicated through hand-signing and the use of dialect words. Soon they were sharing breakfast and laughing together as they told stories of life and Indian men. Angela was thoroughly enjoying these moments, especially noting how Fawn seemed to shake all over when she laughed.

After the laughter and talk died down, Star very seriously asked "How are you going to work with the holy ones?"

As best she could, Angela explained the situation, briefly telling all that was happening to the Earth and its environment and how the goat men fit into the picture. The women were horrified. They had worked for Kla-begatho for thirty years and had never heard anything like this. After a long pause, Star asked, "What can we do, how can we help? If women are to be involved in this fight we would like to help."

"I don't really know what you can do. I don't even know what I'm going to do. I have to go home and figure out how to get started. I have so much to do, with traveling and all, and I don't know how I'm going to pay for it. Maybe, my tribal council will lend me some money."

Fawn spoke. "We are old, yet we are still useful. We are strong in body and strong in spirit, and we have been taught some things by the shamans. For over fifty years we have weaved our rugs and sold them to white people. We have sold them turquoise nuggets. We have had no use for the money, so we have wrapped it in sheepskins and stored it away in a cave nearby. We don't know how much it is, but if it will help you to do this task, it is yours to use."

Angela was shocked at the offer and was silent. Fawn and Star looked at each other, wondering if they had insulted Angela by offering her the money.

Star cleared her throat and spoke. "We would like to go with you."

Angela sat back astonished. She wished she could talk to Amos about this turn of events. *What would Amos do*, she wondered. Then she remembered what Amos had once said. "There are no coincidences. Things happen for a reason." Yesterday she had wondered how she could travel the country without money, and now these women had come to her. She saw this as a good sign. She could have no better companions that these women who had already dedicated their lives to serving the Indian cause.

"I am going to need a lot of help," she told them. "I will be happy to have you with me, but we would have to leave soon. You should know that this will be a hard job and possibly dangerous. Do you still want to come?" Star quickly looked at Fawn, then smiles appeared on their broad faces. They were going.

"We will get our things together and be ready soon," Fawn said. In a joyful mood, she added, "Indian time. *A-wah.*" They all had a good laugh. This was an Indian inside joke. Indians had always laughed at the white man's insistence on punctuality, so if they would tell them, "I'll be there in an hour," they would quietly add *Indian time*, and then they would take their own sweet time. This never failed to exasperate the waiting white man.

Angela was putting her things in the truck when suddenly Whistler swooped down. "Hey, sleepy head. We've got to move soon," he said.

"Where have you been? I thought you all had deserted me. We're almost ready, so where's Amos?" she asked. "The two women are going with us. They volunteered to help so I said they could come."

"That's fine with me. Amos won't be back. He said he had to go start rounding up tribal people and organize them into teams. He'll contact you later, and we are to go ahead and organize the environmentalists."

Angela checked the water and oil levels of the truck, cleaned the windshield, and puttered around until the two women came out of the hogan with their belongings in an old weathered leather suitcase. Star said, "I thought I would never use this. Got it in Phoenix long time 'go."

Angela introduced Whistler. "Ladies, this is Whistler. The Council of Eagles has told him to stay with me. He is able to speak to us, and he is a good friend and has a brave heart. Whistler, this is Fawn, and this is Star. They will go with us."

Fawn handed Angela a briefcase-sized bag made out of sheepskin. "This is for you."

Angela said, "We had better count the money so we'll all know how much it is." She emptied the bag's contents on the ground as they gathered around. It took a while to count the fifty-year accumulation of bills, but finally Angela looked at them in amazement and said, "There's a little over eighty-five thousand dollars here. You ladies were very rich and didn't know it. Now we can go to work, and thank you very much."

The morning sun was shining bright upon the beautiful hills and mountains as the pickup truck slowly bounced over the dirt road towards the paved asphalt highway. Looking into the rear view mirror Angela could see their trail marked by a long cloud of dust. Fawn and Star were in the back, inside the camper shell, happily looking forward to their new adventure.

Up front, Whistler was asking Angela what their first move would be. Where would they go? Her mind was trying to sort things out, yet tend to her driving. A thought came to her. Something her husband had once said. "Do anything. It's better than just standing still."

When the truck reached the highway, she hesitated for a full minute before deciding to turn South, towards Kayenta. Angela shifted through the gears and was soon cruising at forty miles an hour. Her mind was clear now. She knew where she was going and what she would do.

Angela knew that to reach Jay Storm Cloud and others, that she would have to have access to telephones as well as some office equipment. Flagstaff might be an ideal place to begin. It was in the center of Arizona's Indian Country. There was plenty of transportation to bring people in if necessary. There was a small airport with service to Phoenix. Route 66 highway and the Santa Fe Railroad ran directly through the center of town and there was plenty of camping grounds nearby. She said to Whistler, "Yes, Flagstaff. That's where we're heading."

Around noontime they reached Tuba City, near the western edge of the Hopi reservation. Angela stopped at a roadside grocery store and bought lunch supplies, sliced bologna, two boxes of soda crackers, and several bottles of red strawberry soda. She knew that most older Indians loved this kind of treat. They called it "baloney." Most would choose baloney over steak anytime.

Ahead, Whistler appeared and before they reached the little town of Cameron, he directed them to turn right. They had lunch in a spot which was in the shade of several huge boulders and some cottonwood trees.

"Good job, Whistler," Angela said, "I hope you like what we have to eat." When she spread the meat and crackers out on one of Star's blankets there were smiles all around. Fawn said, "A long time since we had this. It's good." Star shook her head in agreement. After Whistler had his first taste of baloney, he too agreed.

While they ate, Angela laid out a tentative plan to them. "We'll find a tourist cabin or even an old house near the pine forest camp grounds. We can camp and eat our meals outdoors, then use the house for baths and as an office. There will be a lot of telephone calls coming and going and other people will need the office too. We may have to move somewhere else later."

An hour later they were again on their way. At sunset they located a camping spot for the night.

Early the next morning they reached Route 66 highway and turned West towards Flagstaff. There were numerous roadside signs advertising *Genuine Navajo turquoise jewelry and wool rugs.* Fawn and Star were glued to the windows taking in all the wonders of the town. It had been years since either of them had been here.

West of the downtown area, Angela turned right when a road sign with an arrow pointing towards *San Francisco Forest* appeared. Angela found a dirt road leading into the forest and turned again at another side road. It was isolated enough to be shielded from curious tourists. The women quickly set up a camp, gathered stones for a fireplace, and began rounding up fallen tree limbs for firewood. It was mid-morning before the campsite was up to the standards of Fawn and Star.

Angela then gathered them together. "I'm going to find a nearby cabin or house that we can use for our headquarters and make arrangements for telephones and other things that we're going to need." From experience she knew that summer afternoon showers were normal so they would need a tent for shelter. "I'll try and be back before it rains and we can set up our tents. I want to have one for you two women and a larger one that we can use for meetings and for our guests. In the meantime, Whistler, you can patrol the area and become familiar with what's normal here. I'll be back as soon as I can."

Back on the highway Angela drove around the nearby area searching for a suitable tourist cabin. Most of them were too small for the group that she was expecting to meet with her. Disappointed, she parked curbside to think. Just ahead at the intersection, there was a small hand printed sign timidly announcing *House For Rent*.

She quickly put the truck in motion and turned the corner looking for another sign. She found it at the very end of a dead-end street where there was a weathered frame house that looked perfect to her. "Oh, I hope the owner will let us have it," she said to herself.

She parked in the driveway and scrutinized the place. Neighbors were not too close by. There was a large barren back yard with no cover for intruders yet it was rimmed with tall trees that could serve as lookout points for Whistler.

Her knees were weak as she knocked on the solid oak front door. An elderly white man answered her knock. He wore high-top laced boots of the kind worn by white men who walked the hills and deserts. He had thinning grey hair that ponytailed in the back. A neatly-trimmed moustache and small beard framed his jutting chin. His brown eyes twinkled just a bit when he saw Angela standing on his front porch.

"Yes ma'am," he said in a strong voice.

Summoning her courage, she said, "I saw your *For Rent* sign and I want to ask about the house. Can I ask you a few questions?" In all her life Angela had never rented a house, and now she was surprised at her own confidence in going about it. It never entered her mind that some town people might not rent to Indians. She had heard about signs that read, "Indians and dogs not welcome."

The man was courteous. "Why, yes, lady. Come on in out of the hot sun and we'll talk about it." The living room had furniture made in wagon-wheel design, not new, but nice. There was a large Navajo rug laying on the wood floor in front of a large cast iron wood stove.

The man asked, "What's your name, ma'am. I know you're not from one of the Arizona tribes, so where are you from?"

"My name is Angela Beaver and I'm a Southern Paiute. I'm here with some friends who will be camping out in the forest, but we're expecting others who will be coming to see us and they'll need a place like this to stay. We would need to have at least two telephones installed so they can keep contact with others." She stopped, unsure of how much she should tell this man.

The man seemed to sense her confusion and tried to ease her fear. He got up, went to the kitchen and got Angela a bottle of Coca Cola. Then he quickly and expertly put her at ease.

"Let me tell you about myself, Angela. My name is Hamilton Gardner, everyone calls me Ham. I'm an engineer, a surveyor of land. Me and my wife came to Arizona some thirty years ago to work for mining companies and geologists. I know your people were here first, but I've come to love the land as if it was my own. My wife used to go with me on trips but then she got sick and died five years ago this coming September."

Angela sipped at her soda, surprised that this white man was taking the time to tell her his story.

"I've come to know almost every part of your desert country and I have seen the changes that progress has visited on even your most remote areas. For instance, the proposed Glen Canyon Dam is going to affect the environment clear down to where the river empties into the Gulf of Mexico. Power plants and power lines will someday ruin your clear desert skies. I regret that some of my work helped to bring this about and now there's nothing I can do about it."

"One of the last things my wife said to me was that she loved this land as much as I did. She said she hated to leave it in this condition. 'We're supposed to leave things better than we found it, and we haven't done that', she said to me. Then she asked me to do what I could to keep the desert clean. I promised her I would, and that's what I do nowadays. I try to spread the word to anybody who'll listen. Then as a form of apology I try to help Indian people when I can. So yes, I'll rent you the place for however long you want. The rent is Fifty Dollars a month and you pay for your own electricity and telephones. If there's any damage to the place, you'll have to pay for it. Is that fair enough?"

Angela was amazed at this man. He talked so much different than other white men. He seemed to understand the environmental dangers and wanted to do something about it, and he didn't even ask for payment in advance.

"All right," Angela said, handing him one hundred dollars. "This is for two months. I'll have the telephones put in my name and me and my friends will be in and out of here until others get here. I have to go buy two tents for our

ANGELA'S BATTLE

campground."

Ham quickly said, "I have two tents that I'll loan you. Tell me where to bring it and I'll deliver them and put them up for you."

Later that afternoon, Ham showed up at the campsite and Angela introduced him to the Indian women. He treated them with such politeness and courtesy that they were taken with him. They pitched in and helped him to erect the two tents, one large, one smaller. They were as perfect as if they had picked them themselves.

Angela introduced him as Hamilton Gardner. When he quickly told them to call him Ham, they said the name a few times. Fawn, the Navajo said *Ham* perfectly. Star, the Hopi, had trouble and could only pronounce it as *Hem*. "Hem, Hem, Hem," she repeated several times, and it sounded all right to her. Ham only smiled and said, "That's right." The two women tried to suppress a smile and looked down at the ground. Fawn spoke for them. "*Aw-w-w Keh*," she said in her Navajo dialect. Her body shook as both women giggled at her boldness.

Angela looked up and saw Whistler in the tree top. She thought of calling him down to meet their new friend, Ham. No, she would wait. *Ham might not be ready for that*. Before he left, Ham told them he would drop by now and then to see if they needed anything and to fill their water jugs.

Next morning Angela went to the house to meet the telephone man. Two new telephones were installed, and now she could begin her work. As she sat thinking of how to begin, she wondered about Ham. She was going to need all the help she could get from knowledgeable people, but could she trust him? After their evening meal at the camp, she would discuss this with Whistler and the two women.

Their supper was canned corned beef hash, biscuit bread, strong coffee and a special treat of canned cling peaches. Whistler said, "This is good. You Indians really know how to live." Star, who rarely joked said, "*A-wah*. If you married me you'd eat good every day." There was a lot of laughter at this, and again, Fawn shook like a bowl of jelly.

After the fire had died down a bit, Angela talked to them about Ham, who seemed to be their friend. "Should we trust this man," she asked them. "He talks like he's on our side. He knows the land and he knows our people. Most of all he knows how to talk to other people like scientists who might be able to help us. I want to trust him, but I wanted to ask you first. Tell me what you think."

There was silence while they thought. Then Star, the quiet one, said "I have not met many white men. Only the ones who wanted to cheat me when they bought my rugs and turquoise. I know that many talk from both sides of their mouth with many lies. This man, Hem, is different from that kind in looks, the way he acts, and the way he talks to us. A man can talk good and tell lies at the same time. The difference is in their eyes and in their heart. If his skin was darker he would look like an Indian man. I think this man can be trusted. That's what I say. *Ah-uh.*"

Fawn said, "Star speaks for me."

"Me too," Whistler agreed.

"That settles it I guess. I wanted to trust him, but sometimes other opinions are good. I'll invite him to have supper with us tomorrow night and we'll talk to him," Angela said.

Chapter Ten

The next day, Angela went to the house, made a pot of coffee and sat down to think. She knew who she wanted to reach but how to go about it? In the big city of Washington, D.C. how could she locate one Indian man? She remembered that Storm Cloud had said he was from the Quechan tribe near Yuma. She called the telephone operator and soon she was talking to a secretary in the tribal office of the Quechan tribe.

When she asked if they knew how to contact Jay, the woman said, "Yes, Jay Storm Cloud is a member of this tribe. We don't have a current address or telephone number for him, but he works for the Tucson Advocate newspaper in Washington, D.C. If you call information there they can probably find him for you."

Within three minutes she could hear the telephone ringing in the newspaper's office. She couldn't help but wonder, Are things always this easy?

In Washington, D.C. it was three in the afternoon on one of the first hot and humid days of the summer. The date was Monday, June 25, 1963. It was one of those days when things seem to shut down and the concrete buildings conspire with the asphalt streets to throw waves of heavy damp heat at those foolish enough to be out and about.

The Washington office of the Tucson Advocate was located near Union Station close to the center of national news, Capitol Hill and the halls of Congress. Jay was sitting at his desk trying to make a story out of nothing. Usually pleasant and informative contacts had been unusually short and untalkative today. His shirt was damp and stained around the collar and in the armpits. He had called Diane and she too was out of sorts.

He fiddled at his typewriter and was almost finished with a 1200 word article on how the Bay of Pigs fiasco was affecting the Congress when the phone rang.

"Jay speaking," he said, not realizing he had reached another turning point in his life and in his career.

After a short silence a soft voice asked, "Is this Jay Storm Cloud?"

"Yes ma'am, it is. What can I do for you."

The soft voice said, "My name is Angela Beaver of the Southern Paiute tribe of Utah. I hope you remember me. I met you at the environmental conference in Phoenix. I heard you speak about the dangers to the earth and damage being done by bombs. Something very important has come up and I have no one else to turn to. I have to talk to you soon and tell you the full story. The future of our Indian land

and the people is in real danger. I can't tell you all of it right now, but I want to set up a time when we can talk maybe tomorrow night. It must be real soon. It is that important. Can we set a time?"

Jay responded, "Give me your telephone number and I'll call you back. I'll do my best to talk with you tomorrow. Can you give me some idea of what we'll talk about?"

"Right now all I will say is that something very dangerous to all of us is happening. It involves not only nuclear explosions, but also the spiritual lives of Indian people."

"All right," Jay said. "Tell me where you're at and I'll call you at nine o'clock your time tomorrow morning. What's your number?"

Jay wasn't immediately impressed. After he hung up, Jay wondered if this was one of the crackpot calls that newspapers frequently get. If he stayed in town tomorrow night it would upset his plan to go to the sea shore. "I'll talk with Diane and see what she thinks."

That evening when he told Diane about the call she could hardly contain her curiosity. "If it's about nuclear things that's my territory, Buster, and don't you forget it. It's worth our time to talk to her and then decide if she's a crackpot. What if she's not? If we miss this opportunity we'll always be sorry we didn't listen. Tell her to call us at my place tomorrow night. We'll have dinner in, then hear what she has to say. In the meantime I'll call a friend of mine and have him put an extension on my phone, that way we can both listen."

It was settled. Tomorrow morning Jay would call Angela and arrange for her to call Diane's apartment at seven p.m., four o'clock Flagstaff time.

Meanwhile, in Flagstaff, Angela had asked Ham to have supper with the group at the campground. She only told him that they wanted to thank him for his friendship.

Fawn had asked Whistler to find several rabbits for their special supper. Whistler flew off, happy to be able to contribute. By sundown everything was under the control of Fawn and Star. They were ready for their special guest with a tasty rabbit stew and fry bread as only Navajo's can make it. Hot tea instead of coffee would be their beverage.

"Fry bread" was another delicacy to southwest Indians. Fried in hot lard much like doughnuts are, the difference is in the flour and other ingredients mixed to make the dough. Most Indian women had their own recipe for the mixture and kept that secret to themselves. When it was sold commercially at pow wow's and other gatherings there would be long lines of people waiting to get theirs.

Just before dark, Ham showed up at the camp and brought a keg of water for them and a large frosted chocolate cake for dessert. He knew that Hopi's would "walk a mile" for chocolate cake. After supper and chocolate cake, everyone was happy, especially Star. While the water was heating for the dishes, Angela decided it was time to tell their story to Ham.

Angela and Fawn sat on one side of Ham, and Star maneuvered to be alone on the other side of him. Star drew up her courage and said to him, "Hem, you want more tea?" Hem smiled at her and said innocently, "Yes, thank you, dear." Star's eyes sparkled. No one had ever called her *Dear*.

Angela pretended not to notice and began her story. In a tree top Whistler listened and watched. For over an hour she told him about events beginning with the environmental conference in Phoenix and up to the present time. Ham listened in amazement. He had never heard such an intriguing story, but it had to be *just a story*, an Indian legend, he thought. What he was being told was just unbelievable. Things like goat men and Council's of Eagles were just incomprehensible to the white scientific mind.

He chose his words carefully when Angela finished her story. "Would these two ladies, Fawn and Star, would they vouch for your story?"

"Yes. More than that. They are part of the story."

Ham asked, "And in what way could I have some sort of proof? I'm sorry to be so skeptical, but to be suddenly told about this takes some getting used to. Do you understand?"

"I understand perfectly," Angela said. "I went through the same doubts myself in the beginning." Then she raised her arm and called, "Whistler." Ham seemed a little frightened when the eagle swooped down and sat near Star. Ham's eyes opened wide and his jaw dropped when the eagle addressed him.

"Ham, my name is Whistler, the son of Teek-awis who is the leader of the Council of Eagles. Everything that Angela has told you is true. My father has sent me to protect Angela in her work. Only yesterday I received word that the most powerful bomb ever to be exploded underground is being readied at the Nevada Test Site. It will be so large that my father fears it may be the one that fractures the underground layers of rock and causes massive flooding of the western countryside. That is why our mission is so critical and we cannot wait to begin our work. We are all hoping that you will join with us."

All was quiet as Ham digested not only his supper, but also the information which had been given to him over the past hour.

From a distant hollow an owl called to his mate, ready to begin their nocturnal hunt for food. From another quarter the wailing of a coyote resulted in an answer. In the dark of the night the world seemed to be all right. But within her heart, Angela knew all was not well. Everyone was silent while Ham pondered what he had heard.

After a time, fears and doubts began to creep into Angela's mind. With shrug of her broad shoulders she shook off the negative feelings and broke the silence.

"Ham, we took a chance and have been honest with you. We told you our story, and of our mission. We need help from people like you, people who understands us and our ways. Will you help?"

She disliked being so blunt, but time was short. They had to know who their friends were.

Ham looked around him, then said, "My skin is not the same color as yours, but my heart beats in the same cadence as yours and my mind thinks as you do. You have spiritual skills which I do not have, yet I have knowledge of other things that you do not have. If we are to save the people and our world we must work together. I'm yours to command. That's all I have to say."

Whistlers beak clacked in approval while the women's faces beamed. Hugs were exchanged all around, and truth be told, Ham thought that Star had hugged him much stronger than the other women.

So what, he thought. He hadn't felt this alive since his wife had died. Now he had a direction to go and a new purpose in life. He suddenly felt like Superman or Tarzan might have felt when faced with a crisis. He could handle it. He was glad these Indians had come into his life. Before tonight he had seriously considered selling his house and moving back to Pennsylvania.

Before parting, Ham had agreed to be with them tomorrow when Angela talked to Jay Storm Cloud. There were many people to call and many things to do in the meantime.

At exactly twelve noon the next day, Jay dialed Angela's number. Ham and Angela were waiting for the phone's ring. They both jumped when it did. "Hello, this is Angela Beaver," she said.

"Hi, Angela. This is Jay Storm Cloud. What little you told me yesterday has really got me interested. After the Phoenix conference I hadn't heard from anybody. I was beginning to think the trip was a waste of time and money. But let me ask you. Are you sure there is an immediate environmental danger, and is it really a crisis? After all, you know, somebody's always saying the world's going to end on Friday."

Ham was sharing the receiver with Angela so he spoke up and said, "Son, my name is Ham Gardner. I'm an engineer and a scientist. I assure you this is no joke. When you learn the full story it will blow your mind. Now, we want to talk to you tonight for as long as you want. You can ask all the questions you want but I must tell you that we don't have a lot of answers yet. That's why we need you and others to get involved. It will help us if you know someone who knows about radioactive contamination to join us tonight, because we here don't know the first thing about radioactivity and how it behaves. Do you know someone?"

It was a few seconds before Jay answered. "You know what, from my end, this is so strange. Too many coincidences all at once. Yes, I know someone who knows about radioactivity and she has already planned to be in on our conversation. Since Angela's first call yesterday, I've looked through some back issues of our paper and noticed that a Hamilton Gardner several years ago had warned Arizonans that their plans for nuclear power plants were far more dangerous than anyone realized. Are you that Hamilton Gardner?"

"That's me, son. Guilty as charged. But I have to tell you that I was ready to give up the fight until I met Angela and her friends. After our talk tonight, if we convince you we're right, we would want you to come out here to Flagstaff and work directly with us. Would you be able to do that? It would be hard work, though."

"You can't scare me with your hard work. If you can convince me, I think I can arrange to come out. Wow, what kind of magic are you using. Just talking with you two, I'm already enthused. I've talked with my friend, Diane, who is a nuclear radioactivity expert, and what we'd like you to do is call her number tonight at 7 p.m. our time. I guess that would be 4 p.m. your time. Is that all right with you two?"

Angela answered. "Yes, that's fine. I'm so glad that you're willing to listen to us. All I can say is that our story is so bizarre that few people would believe it. Please don't tell anyone else about this. We wouldn't want to be called crazy. After we talk, we would want you then to tell the world about it. We'll call you tonight at seven. Thanks, and goodbye."

Ham arranged to have an extension installed on one of the telephones so they could both talk and listen tonight. Angela called the Arizona Intertribal Council offices in Phoenix for a list of people and organizations who had attended the environmental conference last year and then began calling each of the organizations to see if they could round up their members to attend another meeting which might be held within thirty days.

It was tedious work because it was difficult to find the directors of organizations in their offices. By two-thirty she had spoken to two out of the fifteen organizations. She began to appreciate how hard it was to schedule these kind of conferences.

At three p.m. Angela drove to the camp to pick up the two women and Whistler. It was ten minutes to four by the time she returned. While they waited, Ham showed Star how to make coffee in the electric pot. After that it was her job to periodically check the pot and make sure there was enough there for everyone. Star was elated that he had chosen her for the job.

At exactly four p.m. Angela picked up the phone, called the long distance operator then gave her Diane's number. Jay answered. "You're very punctual for an Indian," he said. When Angela hesitated, he quickly added, "I was only joking. Everyone has heard the stories about *Indian time*. Forgive me, I'm Indian too, you know."

"My friend Diane is here with me. I have told her about our previous talks and she's ready to hear all about this situation. She is a technical specialist on radioactive materials with an organization who keeps their eye on power plants and other places that uses nuclear power. They try to point out the dangers of radioactivity to the public. Ham told me to find a knowledgeable person. She's it. I guess it's okay for her to listen?"

"Yes," Angela said. "And I'd like to introduce you to the people that are here with me. First, there's Ham, whom you've already talked with. There's Fawn, a Navajo woman, and Star, a Hopi woman. Both have been a great help and comfort to me. Last but not least, and the most unbelievable, is Whistler, who is an eagle. Really. His father, Teek-awis, is the leader of what is called the Council of Eagles, and he has assigned Whistler to work with us."

In Diane's apartment there was an exchange of confused looks between Jay and Diane. This sounded so crazy. Maybe these people *were* kooks.

Angela sensed their confusion. Ham quickly assured them that he had felt the same when he first met them and he was now convinced these people were real, even the eagle.

Jay kept his silence, then said, "We'll assume you're all real and sincere for now. But we'd like to hear the rest of your story before we say anything else."

Angela said, "Fair enough."

Then she launched into her story once again, as she had done for Ham. Once in a while, Jay the reporter would stop her and ask a pertinent question. Diane had a perpetual look of shock on her face while she listened.

It took almost an hour and a half for Angela to tell the story and answer the questions. When it was all done, there was silence again.

Angela said, "There's no way you can verify anything I've said unless you come out here. We want you to be convinced so you can join in our decisions and plans on how to go about organizing and carrying out our so-called battle plan."

Ham joined in. "This effort is of such magnitude that there is no way a small group of dedicated people can carry it out. We need help from many sources. Jay, I implore you and Diane, if you only half believe us and want to be convinced of the truth, please, we need you to come out here and meet with all of us. Come see the things Angela is talking about. Then if you still don't believe, we can say goodbye, no hard feelings. Say yes, you'll come out, and we'll send you the money for your train tickets. Please."

Jay promised that on tomorrow, Wednesday, he and Diane would try to find out from their bosses if they could get away for awhile. If things were worked out they would be on a train West very soon. "I'll call you just as soon as we know for sure," he told Angela.

It wasn't as hard to get leave from their jobs as he had thought. News is scarce in Washington during summer months. Congress goes home for a week on the first of July and again for three weeks in August and over Labor Day, and the wheels of government turn slowly. For newsmen, they almost have to invent the news. For Diane, her organization's director was happy to let her go when she explained that she would be doing "research on the effects of radioactivity on Indian people."

On the following Sunday morning, July 1, they boarded a passenger train to Atlanta, Georgia, then traveled across the southern states. Four and a half days later on Thursday, July 5, they arrived at the Atcheson, Topeka, and Santa Fe Railroad depot in Flagstaff. Excited, they looked out the window and saw three dark-skinned

Indian women standing on the platform with a brown-skinned white man. "Grab the bags and let's start our new adventure," Diane said.

When the conductor opened the door Diane ran to where the women were standing and asked, "Angela?"

Jay was still struggling with the bags so Ham went to help. After everyone was introduced they all trooped inside the station and sat down to get acquainted. Diane had never been out of the eastern states in her life, but she was immediately attracted to Fawn and Star.

Angela had bought a heavier truck and it too had a camper body on the back. Fifteen minutes later they were all packed into the truck and on their way to the rented house. Like all new visitors Diane couldn't help but notice the many Indian men and women on the streets. The women dressed attractively in their bright velvet dresses trimmed with turquoise and silver. The men all looking like cowboys with their big Stetson hats, boots, and blue Levi pants.

At the house, Jay kept breathing deeply of the clean air and repeated several times, "God, it's good to be back, it's good to be here."

Angela and Ham looked at each other, sharing the knowledge that things would change for all of them, real soon. Angela wisely postponed Jay and Diane meeting Whistler until that night at the camp. After they were rested Fawn announced that a lunch was ready, so everyone enjoyed iced tea and sandwiches.

After getting acquainted with downtown Flagstaff in the afternoon, Jay and Diane returned to the rented house where the others were waiting. Fawn and Star had been taken back to the camp to prepare supper and for the meeting later. Diane was still excited about having seen "real live Indians."

Angela told them, "When you're ready, we're going to the campground for supper, then we'll sit around and get better acquainted with each other. I imagine you two have more questions, and so do we. It's important that we all understand the seriousness of what we're going to do before we make any more plans. So take your showers and get settled. There are three bedrooms here so take your pick. Choose your own bedroom."

Jay spoke firmly. "We've already discussed our situation, so if you don't mind we're going to begin by getting used to camping out because we'll probably have to do it many times. We bought two sleeping bags so we'll stay at the camp like everyone else."

"That's fine." Angela said.

After dinner that evening, they all got comfortable in front of the larger tent. While Fawn and Star cleaned up the supper dishes and utensils, the others sat deep in their own thoughts. In the twilight the stars were just beginning to show and the western sky was slowly turning from pale blue to a darker shade. There was no moon yet.

Diane got up and walked a short way into the forest. She loved the smell of the pine trees. Back home there were no pine tree forests. She was used to the sugar maples and oaks of Lebanon, New Hampshire. In all her twenty-eight years she had never experienced anything like this. Tonight this scene of Indians, the campfire and forest were vaguely familiar because she had seen similar scenes in one of the many Hollywood Western movies which her father had taken her to.

A tear came to her eye when she remembered her father going off to war. She had been only six years old when he left, never to come back. Now here she was, getting into something she knew nothing about and instead of going back to a comfortable home, she and her new friends were talking about saving the world. Was this real? When had all the fun and happiness disappeared from her life? Her work in Washington had left her no time to really enjoy life. She was always rushing from one meeting to another. Even on those infrequent short visits home, it was rush home, rush back. Was she in the right place?

She suddenly realized that she was feeling sorry for herself, something which she rarely allowed herself to do. She wiped the tears away, took a deep breath and returned to the camp. She sat down next to Jay and put one arm on his shoulder.

When Star and Fawn finished their chores and joined them, she quickly got down to business. Angela called for Whistler to come down from the treetop to join them.

Jay and Diane were startled when Whistler swooped down and joined their circle but they remained silent and wide-eyed. Diane squeezed Jay's arm tightly until Angela spoke again. She introduced Whistler to the newcomers and explained his role in all that was going on. As expected, Jay and Diane were flabbergasted at meeting an eagle who could talk. Diane's mouth was stuck open, so Jay managed to say for both of them, "We're very happy to meet you."

"I'm glad to see both of you," Whistler said. "We need your help very much. Thanks for coming."

Ham saw the look on their faces, so he said, "Get over it as soon as you can. The shock will wear off faster if you talk to him like you talk to me. He's for real."

ANGELA'S BATTLE

Whistler first informed everyone that he had brought in two of the scouts, Fast Wing and Mud Eye, to join him for security purposes. Beginning tonight, one of them would be on lookout duty 'round the clock.

For the benefit of all but herself and Whistler, Angela began by telling of the events beginning from the time that she had first noticed a change in the forest three years ago. She left nothing out, shocking them when telling of the activities of the goat men and the revelations shown to Amos on his night trip with the Spirit. By the time she finished her story of the Canyon de Chelly conference and the last meeting at Kaibito, everyone was as fully informed as she was.

Ham had not heard this full story, and he was as amazed as were Jay and Diane. They had not even dreamed that they would face a two-headed danger, nuclear destruction and spiritual annihilation. A week ago it would have been incomprehensible, unbelievable, but here tonight, the newcomers, Ham, Jay, and Diane were beginning to understand the nature of what they were going up against. They sat silent, with a look of concern on their faces. Diane's eyes were open wide and she sat dumbfounded. Angela left them alone in their thoughts.

After several minutes, Jay broke the silence. "When I was a young kid, we boys used to scare each other at the night dances by naming one boy as the goat, not knowing where the game came from. The goat would chase the others and if he caught you, you were dead. Later, there were other stories told that goat man was always around looking for someone to take."

"I remember one time at a tribal celebration, *Mattic-whit*, our medicine man, our spiritual shaman, was challenged to a wrestling match by a tall stranger. The shaman, an elderly man called Red Weed, didn't agree to the match until he had studied the newcomer for a long time. He sat playing a flute while studying the man and when he had finished he got up, went to the stranger and slapped him hard across the face."

"They began to wrestle. Although the shaman was many years older, the stranger could hardly move him. They stood locked head to head for over an hour before the people realized they were seeing something extraordinary, something supernatural. The clan head-man quickly sent for a Yaqui shaman who had been living with the nearby Cocopah people. When he arrived, the Quechan shaman was drenched in sweat and trembling, still locked in combat. The stranger was hardly damp."

ANGELA'S BATTLE

"The Yaqui shaman watched the wrestling for awhile. He then filled a small clay bowl with a substance and put a match to it. A large white smoke cloud formed and drifted slowly towards the wrestlers. Then when Red Weed appeared to almost stumble, the smoke swirled and covered him completely. The smoke disappeared and Red Weed quickly picked up the stranger and threw him a distance of about thirty feet where he landed at the feet of the crowd. One old woman standing nearby where the stranger fell, screamed "*Inawee-ka*, it's him. The goat man!"

"The stranger got up quickly and ran through the crowd towards the forest along the river. From time to time, someone would say they had seen him, especially at the dances where he would mingle with the crowd. Shortly after this the eldest son of the Quechan head-man disappeared and was never seen again. There was speculation that the goat man had taken him. The stories soon died down. Now, from what you've told me, the stories may have been true. If I hadn't witnessed that wrestling match myself I probably wouldn't believe you. But I can make a connection now and I believe."

Diane couldn't contain herself any longer. "Okay, so there is something to the stories of goat man, as you call him. I'm a realist, a white realist who believes in science and things that can be worked out on a blackboard with equations and formulas. I know the fundamentals of nuclear power and the dangers of radioactivity. These are things governed by laws of science. I have no way to deal with your myths and legends, so where do I fit in here?"

Ham listened with great interest and had nothing to say yet. He understood well the questions Diane had raised, yet his years spent with various tribal groups had left him open to all sorts of possibilities, like talking eagles, for instance. He knew that in Indian country anything was possible.

Fawn remembered much of what had been said at meetings between Klabegatho and the other shamans. She looked inquiringly at Angela who then nodded to her. Fawn looked directly at Diane and said, "It might be that you have been trained and educated more than our Indian people. For many years I have served our Indian shamans and I have heard our shamans who have never been to a white man's school say that all things come from our Creator."

"They have talked about your radioactive uranium and they said it is a natural thing which comes from the earth, and your people took it out of our land. So they said the evil is not in the uranium which the Creator has placed here. The evil is in how your people misused the gift."

"It seems to me that if you can understand Nature's laws through your writing and study, you can see the harm and evil of a bomb. You can also understand that the presence of the evil ones is real and that they are part of the Creators plan. Maybe even *they* can be helpful and maybe they can do evil only if we let them. For one thing, they have helped to bring us together to plan how to get rid of dangerous things."

Everyone was surprised at this lecture. Fawn herself, most of all. Diane marveled at such wisdom. What she had failed to take into account was that education is subject to interpretation. Fawn had received an education in nature and the occult from the best teachers in the world. She could only bring herself to say, "Yes, you may be right."

Jay could feel her discomfort, so he asked rightly, "Exactly what is our task in this issue? As I understand it, your man Amos is gathering native shamans to work with the Council of Eagles to fight the spiritual threat, so if you could explain what you have in mind for us it would help to form a plan."

Angela quickly picked up this thread. "Our task most of all is to prevent the catastrophe that was shown to Amos by preventing the U.S. from exploding two powerful bombs underground at the Nevada Test Site. Our justification for stopping the explosions is that it would fracture underground layers of rock, draining surrounding water tables for hundreds of miles around into even deeper levels. Amos was told that the drying up of the rock layers would create huge cracks in the earth. Earthquakes would follow, causing the earth to sink and allowing the oceans to bring catastrophic floods. Somehow, we must tell this story and get people to believe it."

"The other thing we must do is to convince the people that if their government continues with their nuclear programs for weapons and for power plants, they will soon run out of places to store their dangerous radioactive waste products. We have been told that there is no really safe place to store this dangerous waste. We have to convince them somehow that nuclear power and its radioactive waste will eventually poison every corner of the land."

"All of this seems like too much of a job for our small group, and that's where you, Jay and Diane, come in. Diane, you know the right people that we need to help us, and Jay, you know how to go about telling them. The lives of everyone depends on how we go about this task. If you can't commit your efforts to this task, you should tell us now. We will understand if you can't do this. Ham is already given his promise of commitment. What do each of you say?"

It only took a minute for the two to make their commitment. "I'm in," Jay said.

"Me too," Diane said. The others breathed sighs of relief. Their basic team was complete and they could begin on the larger plan of action. It was early morning, and the eastern horizon was just getting light when Angela called it a night. She yawned, then said, "All right, our first moves are planned. We may have to break up from time to time to carry out our individual jobs, but we will meet regularly to review our progress and see if we have to make any changes. It's Sunday, so it will be hard to contact anyone today. Let's get some rest, then this evening we'll review what we've said so far."

Chapter Eleven

Jay woke Diane just after twelve noon. "C'mon, sleepy head, wake up. We've got a lot of work to do." The others were still sleeping in the large tent. Taking the older pickup truck they drove to the rented house, stopping along the way to pick up bacon and egg sandwiches for their breakfast. Diane put on a pot of coffee, then joined Jay, who was furiously scribbling notes on a yellow pad at the kitchen table.

"I've got a ton of phone calls to make," he told Diane. "I need you to give me a rundown on the dangers of nuclear power and all the horror stories associated with it. For instance, there are rumors of many secret experiments with humans and animals. We've never printed them because we couldn't verify them. We need to know the downright dirty truth about the nuclear industry and their military weapons. You can point us in the right direction."

"Us?" Diane asked.

"Yeah, the media. If we're going to do a bang-up publicity job we have to use the entire media, which means the big national newspapers, radio networks, and most of all the new teevee networks. They'll love this stuff. It's what sells newspapers, if you know what I mean. I'm going to start with my editor, Fuzzy Williams, in the main office in Tucson. He was always urging me to 'bring me the big mean story, son,' while he waved his stinky cigar around. This story is big and mean."

In Tucson, Fuzzy Williams had just returned home from a round of golf with three buddies from the local Veteran's of Foreign Wars post. They were schoolmates in high school, and had all gone to war in 1942. Fuzzy, whose real name was William T. Williams, had been the national news editor at the Tucson Advocate for sixteen years. He had hired Jay at the recommendation of an old pal at the Missouri School of Journalism in St. Louis.

He was in the shower when the phone rang. His wife, Aimee, answered the call then called to Fuzzy, "It's for you, a Jay Storm Cloud. He says he works for Gene and he needs to talk to you, that it's very important."

Fuzzy was not pleased. "For cripes sake, he's in Washington. Nothing is important in Washington on Sunday. Tell him I'll call him back tomorrow."

"Honey, he heard you. He says he's not in Washington and that this is the most important story you'll ever get except that of the second coming of you-know-who. He says he needs to talk to you now. He'll call you back in five minutes."

"Damn kid," Fuzzy griped. "Gave him a good job, made him famous, and now he thinks he's my boss." He nevertheless toweled off and quickly got dressed, then sat by the living room phone and waited---and waited.

Jay had also placed a call to Gene, his immediate boss in D.C. He wanted to ask for expense money for this story. There would be a lot of phone calls to make and a lot of traveling to do. Gene and his wife Jenifer, usually spent Sundays at a boat dock in Deale, Maryland, on Chesapeake Bay where they had a 40-foot cabin cruiser. When Jay placed his calls, three of them, Gene and Jenifer were on their way home and wouldn't be there for another hour. Jay was now impatient to talk to somebody. Eight minutes had passed before he was able to call Fuzzy again.

"What do you want, kid. I've got company," Fuzzy lied, "so hurry up and tell me what's so damn important."

Jay had only met Fuzzy twice. Fuzzy made infrequent visits to D.C. to evaluate the office. He knew he was imposing on his main boss, but he reasoned that if Fuzzy fired him the Arizona Republic or the Albuquerque Tribune would want this story.

"I apologize for bothering you today but I wanted to alert you to a story that I've run across. It ties in directly with the big story we did last year on nuclear power plants. It has all the elements that you would want, Indians of the Southwest who are going to wage a fight against the nuclear establishment and, get this, supernatural forces. What could be better than that? It'll knock your socks off. I swear it's a true story and I can prove it. Do you want to hear it?"

Fuzzy grumbled, "Go ahead, but make it short."

For several minutes, Jay ran through the basic story, emphasizing the part of the nuclear bomb tests which was the most believable. "It'll be a big story, Mr. Williams. Meet with us and let us show you some proof. Please believe me, Mr. Williams, you won't be sorry."

With the sixth sense of a good reporter, Fuzzy almost believed Jay but he wanted to hear more before making a commitment.

"All right, kid. I'll be in Phoenix for a meeting on Wednesday. I'll meet with you and your friends on either Tuesday or Thursday. Take your pick."

Jay quickly said, "Make it Tuesday, but we'll have to meet at our hotel because we'll have something very unusual to show you. If you agree, I can call you at your hotel on Tuesday and tell you where to meet us. Okay?"

"All right," Fuzzy said. "But you better not lead me on a wild goose chase. The only reason I'm meeting you is because I'm still paying you, so you better not

ANGELA'S BATTLE

be wasting my time and money. Got that?"

"Yes sir. Where will you be staying? I'll call you there at three p.m. Tuesday."

"Call me at the Adams Hotel. It's right downtown, and don't be late with your call. I may have better things to do."

Jay quickly said, "No sir. I won't be late--and sir, you won't be sorry. I promise you."

Fuzzy quickly hung up. Jay sat there still holding the phone with a huge smile on his brown face. Diane could feel his enthusiasm as she looked at him. He said, "There's work to be done, fields to be plowed and cows to be milked. Let's get at it."

Jay told Diane what Fuzzy had said. Then, "I've got to write a plan of action by tonight, so what I'd like you to do is go back to the camp and ask them to meet us here at six o'clock or sooner. I've still got to reach Gene at home, so I'll be busy for a couple of hours."

"What I'll need from you is a summary of worst-case nuclear problems from both bombs and power plants and how they can affect the public, then I'd like a realistic scenario of how an underground nuclear explosion could create the kind of disaster that Amos guy described to Angela. Call some of the experts that you know and ask them to help you put it together. Ham is a geologist, he can help do that. We've got to have a pretty good case by the time we meet with Fuzzy Williams. And ask Angela to come here as soon as possible. I need her."

Diane started to go out the door. She hesitated, as if waiting for a kinder word instead of just a string of orders. Jay suddenly stopped what he was doing, like he had remembered something important. He turned towards the back door and said softly, "Diane, I need you too." That was all she needed to hear and she bounced out the door.

Two hours later the whole group arrived. Diane's good mood had infected them all and they knew good things were going to happen now. They stood in a circle around the kitchen table where Jay was still writing.

He suddenly stopped. "Let's all go into the living room and sit down. I want to tell you what's happening. We need to be in Phoenix as soon as we can." Then he told them about events of the afternoon and what was going to happen now. "So that we don't have any blank spots between now and then, I propose that we leave for Phoenix first thing in the morning."

"If it's okay with you, Angela, Diane is going to finish a report for me because on Tuesday we'll meet with Fuzzy Williams, who is my big boss at the paper. He can be our key to getting great coverage nationwide because he is this years President of the Newspaper Editors of America. If we convince him, we can convince the others."

"I'm hoping that we can get a large group of Indians and environmental groups to meet in Phoenix on Wednesday on an emergency basis. Diane's material will be very important to all of us. By Tuesday noon you should know about how many people will be there on Wednesday. We have to be ready to convince them of the crisis."

"When we meet with Fuzzy Williams, Amos and Whistler will be a very important part of our story. Angela, please ask Amos to be here for that meeting. If Whistler and Amos can't convince old Fuzzy Wuzzy, nothing can."

With a tentative plan in place the team split up. Jay continued his writing with the help of Whistler. Ham and Diane worked on underground geological anomalies and nuclear explosions. Fawn and Star joined Angela in formulating a list of people to call to attend the conference on Wednesday. Nature was indeed gathering her forces.

Jay finally reached Gene at his home in Bethesda, Maryland. He filled him in on his talk with Fuzzy Williams, and in spite of Gene's pleading, would not tell him more about the story until after he had talked with Fuzzy. With the promise of something big to come, Gene agreed to send expense money to Jay.

Angela was busy on the other telephone. She first called her own tribal chairman, Ned Hatanami, and told him where she was. She was careful not to say anything to alarm him but she did want to impress him with how important her work was to the future of the Paiute people, especially those who were downwind of the Nevada Test Site.

"Ned, it's important that we get as many Indian leaders and those interested in the environment to an emergency meeting that will be held in Phoenix on this next Wednesday. I promise you that this is a really serious matter and I want to ask you to call all the other chairmen in your Intertribal group to be there. Will you do that?"

"Gosh, Angela," Ned said, "something important has come up here too. I went down to Mojave country a couple weeks ago for the wedding of Milford's daughter. Something strange happened there that I can't tell you about, but now all the leaders are scheduled to meet with Amos Turkey on Thursday at the Papago reservation, near Tucson. This is also called an emergency meeting. What the heck is going on? Enough has happened already to scare the hell out of me."

Angela thought for a moment, then said, "Forget what I asked you to do. Go ahead with the planned meeting with Amos and the others on Thursday. But will you please send at least a few people to our meeting on Wednesday? This could be the most important meeting in their lifetime. I will only tell you that it's about damage to the environment, our homeland, from all those damn nuclear bombs they're exploding in Nevada."

"All right. I'll ask Marge to pick a few people and get them down there. Where will the meeting be?"

"Gosh, I don't know yet. Things are moving so fast that we haven't got a place yet, probably one of the bigger motels on Van Buren street. We'll be in Phoenix tomorrow and I'll call Marge to tell her where we'll be. Thanks Ned. I hope to see you soon."

Now that she knew Amos was having a meeting in Tucson, she wanted to think past the Wednesday meeting. She thought it important to have Amos there, but she didn't want to have a conflict with Amos' plan. Maybe Whistler could reach Amos tonight.

She got up and called to Whistler, "Let's go outside for a minute. I need some cool air."

Whistler joined her. It was dark in the back yard, and she could hear the night birds calling and squeaking as they chased the bugs and moths. Before she could frame her question, Whistler said softly, "Amos is already here. He wants to talk to you about his upcoming meeting."

Surprised, Angela looked around but could see no one. At the rear of the lot there was a fallen tree trunk and as they walked toward it she saw a dark shape sitting on the log. It soon took form and she recognized that it was Amos. He stood to greet her.

She ran towards him and hugged him tightly. "It's so good to see you. I've missed you so much. I hope you're all right," she said.

"I'm fine, and you? Sit with me and we'll talk, the three of us."

Amos first told her of what had happened and his progress up to now.

"The eagles report sightings of goat men at several locations. We've planned a gathering of Indian leaders and their shamans to be held at the San Xavier Mission on next Thursday. It's a very sacred place, so we'll be safe there. Milford Haynes is worried because strange things have been happening near where our meeting is going to be held. It seems that our two tasks have now become one, so I would like you and your group to be there also. You will be a great help in uniting the people. But I must warn you. It may be dangerous there, especially in the surrounding countryside. I will not meet with your friends tonight, but I will be at your meeting on Wednesday for a short time in the afternoon. Then I'll see all of you later in Tucson. After your meeting is finished the battle will begin. Please have Whistler call me whenever you think it necessary. I will be there for you. Be very careful. I must go now, but I'll see you again soon." Amos touched her hand tenderly, then he walked into the darkness and was gone.

Angela was quiet as they walked back to the house. Whistler knew he could say nothing that would comfort her at this time. His intuition told him that only Amos could do that.

She gathered the group together and told them some of what Amos had said. Jay made some mental notes and after Angela said goodnight he returned to his writing, furiously penciling new notes and plans. By the time they got to Phoenix he wanted to have his plans pretty well completed. Then he would review Diane's writing.

The next morning Angela woke them all at four a.m. "We'll leave right after breakfast," she told them. "I want to be there before ten and get settled. We have a lot of work to do before Wednesday." The highway south through Oak Creek Canyon had little traffic and by ten-thirty their new Ford pickup truck was turning into the Desert Inn Motel/Hotel on East Van Buren street. It was only about a mile from the Adams Hotel.

Angela thought this would be a perfect place for them. After checking in and while the others were unloading the truck, Angela sought out the manager and told him of their plans for the meeting on Wednesday. She asked him to provide typewriters for their use, then she headed for the telephone. She promised herself, "This is going to be one heck of a good meeting."

She called Milford Haynes and secured his permission for the Intertribal office to begin calling the network contacts for environmental groups in New Mexico, California, Nevada, Colorado and Utah, asking them to attend. The groups had a network by which they could call each other to share information. By two p.m. she had promises from most of the tribes in Arizona that representatives would attend the meeting on Wednesday. Things were working out great.

She was mentally tallying up the numbers of possible attendees when she suddenly shouted, "Darn it. I forgot St. George!"

St. George was a small town in western Utah which was directly in the windborne path of hot radioactive fallout from nuclear explosions at the Nevada Test Site. North from St. George to Cedar City, there were several dozen smaller communities in that fallout path. In the past few years people had begun to die from various types of cancer, mainly thyroid and brain cancers in the very young and in the very old.

The people had formed a coalition, calling themselves the St. George Downwinders. They brought the illnesses to the attention of the state and federal governments, asking if the radioactive fallout might be the cause. They were assured that the fallout was not the cause, yet the deaths continued, as did the bomb explosions. It was impossible for them to fight the federal government, just as it had been impossible to get the government to admit that Indian uranium miners were getting sick from breathing uranium dust.

"The Downwinders need to be here. How could I forget them. They're right in my back yard." She could now kill two birds with one stone. She called Marge at the Paiute Tribal Office and told her of the date, time, and location of the Wednesday meeting.

"If you come in on Tuesday evening, I'll have rooms waiting for you. Will you please call Abner Cranshaw in St. George for me and tell him about the meeting. Tell him I said it is very important. I think we can finally do something about the fallout problem."

Marge said, "Ned already told us about the meeting early today, so four of us are leaving in about two hours. We'll stop in Tuba City, then leave early for Phoenix. We should be there by early evening. We'll see you then, and don't worry, I'll call Abner right now and he'll have plenty of time to drive to Las Vegas and catch a plane directly to Phoenix. 'Bye."

Now that people were coming to the meeting, Angela needed a place to put them. "One more thing to do, and that's to get a meeting room that will hold a lot of people."

The motel had an ancillary building next door which they called The Conference Center. It was made to order for the meeting. The manager was happy to make it available to them. He told her, "Since you're going to have so many people here, you can have the conference room at no charge and we'll even set up five hundred chairs. We aim to please because we want your business."

The meeting arrangements were all set. Now they just had to put the program presentations together.

She went to Jay's room and found him on the telephone. "Denver Post," he whispered.

When he hung up he smiled broadly at Angela. "All the biggies are going to be here. New York Times, Philadelphia Inquirer, Atlanta Journal, Chicago Tribune, St. Louis Journal, Los Angeles Times, San Diego Union, all the big papers. The television networks and local stations have been notified. I've got to call Fuzzy now and ask him to meet us tomorrow at three p.m. With all this media attention I've got to let him have the exclusive on the story. He'll be madder'n heck if he gets scooped by the other papers."

Fuzzy wasn't too happy about changing his schedule but when he heard about the possibility of getting scooped he quickly agreed to meet with Angela's group privately on the next afternoon.

"Oh man, this is shaping up great. Ol' Fuzzy's going to be proud of me. Hot dog! Now all we've got to do is make it worth their time and the trip," Jay told Angela.

"That's exactly what I want to talk about," she said. "Let's get together with the others for dinner at five o'clock in the restaurant downstairs, then afterwards we'll gather in my room to see where we're at."

Diane had been in her room all afternoon with the door locked. She too, had been busy on the telephone and writing on her yellow pad. The phone rang. It was Jay.

"How are you doing?" he asked.

"I'm working like a dad-burn slave," she said. "What do you want?"

"I'm going to knock on your door in one hour, then we'll go join the others for dinner. That's it, goodbye." He appreciated the way she had dived into her work. He just needed to leave her alone until she was ready to unlock the door.

By six-thirty they were through with dinner. Angela announced, "All right, everyone. Let that apple pie dessert settle down, then come to my room ready to go to work at seven. We only have one more day to get everything planned and ready." She knew they had accomplished a lot in the space of just a few days, but they couldn't let up now. She had to keep the momentum going.

ANGELA'S BATTLE

Angela returned to her room to find Whistler impatient and restless. "Angela, we may have a problem tomorrow. While you were gone Amos talked to me. He said that he is sure that two of the goat men have been sent to see what's happening here. Because of that he is going to try and get here earlier than he had planned. Because I won't be able to roam freely yet, he wants you to confide in Star and Fawn. Apparently Kla-begatho gave them specific instructions of how to identify the goat men and how to deal with them. I feel helpless being cooped up in this room. I'll be glad when Wednesday comes."

Just before seven o'clock the others began to drift into Angela's room. When they were seated comfortably Angela said, "We have some disturbing news from Amos. I'll let Whistler tell you about it." Whistler repeated what he had previously told Angela. When he finished, Angela asked Jay to conduct the meeting on Wednesday. "You know best how to get the attention of the media. It will be important to keep them interested until Amos gets here."

"The general idea will be to lay out the specific dangers and consequences of the nuclear explosions. We'll tell them the truth, and then try to convince them of it. Diane and Ham can lay out the technical stuff to the media and the environmental groups. Right after a break for lunch I'll talk to them, then prepare them for what comes next, Amos and Whistler."

"If any of them have any doubts about what we're telling them, that will help to convince them. After that, it will be up to all of us to lay out a plan of action for the people to get involved. We can work that out together later. In the meantime, Amos has cautioned us to be careful of strangers who might be a goat man. It will be hard to screen everybody we don't know, so I want Fawn and Star to mingle with the crowd, walk around, and see if you can detect any danger. Just don't forget, they can look male or female and be of any race. I don't know what to do if we recognize one of them, but I think that if we expose them it will help convince everyone of the danger we face. Just be careful. I have heard Whistler's father, Teek-awis, describe how they killed some of the Anasazi."

"Let's take a break now. Whistler is going outside to look around. So when he gets back we can start laying out our plan of action."

Whistler made several flights around the area before returning to his friends. Angela was just beginning the planning session. "Everything seems to be all right outside," he reported.

ANGELA'S BATTLE

It was two a.m. Tuesday morning when Angela said, "Well, we seem to have everything covered. Jay, will you write up what we've said tonight? The action plan needs to be understandable to everyone, then we'll need maybe a thousand copies of the information sheets made so we can pass it out to everyone."

"Jay has arranged for an interview with his boss at three p.m. today so everyone needs to be here in my room before three. By six p.m. tomorrow, people will begin arriving and they'll want to know what this is all about, but let's not tell them anything about the danger or our plans until we talk to them at the meeting. I don't want anybody to decide beforehand that we're crazy. Just be sociable, and if they ask about the meeting, just tell them to wait, that it'll be worth it. I think we're all set now and I feel great. Now let's try to get some sleep."

Chapter Twelve

Fuzzy Williams and his wife left their home in Tucson at ten-thirty Tuesday morning, and stopped to pick up his local reporter, Jim Tanner, who would write the story for the morning headlines in Washington and Tucson. Then he headed for Highway 19, enroute to Phoenix. Just outside of the city he stopped for gas at the first Texaco station he saw and told the attendant to "Fill it up." He got out of the car and went to the rest room so he wouldn't have to stop anywhere.

When he came out he saw a young man leaning against a wall. "Howdy, son," he offered. The man smiled back at him, then asked, "Would you be going into Phoenix? If you are I would certainly appreciate a ride. My wife called me early this morning and said our little girl is sick, so I've got to get there soon. I was going to drive up there this morning, but my car wouldn't start My name is John Barnes. I work nearby for a plumbing shop. Can you help me?"

Fuzzy looked at the man. He looked working class respectable and he spoke very well. Fuzzy was cautious.

"Can't be too careful," he thought. "Wait a minute. I'll ask my wife. We're kind of in a rush, but I'll see what she says."

Aimee listened to the man's story and her heart went out to him. "We can't refuse a simple request for help. The poor man, he must be worried sick. Tell him to come on."

A few minutes later Fuzzy and his passengers were on their way. That was the last anyone saw of Fuzzy, Aimee, and the reporter alive.

They had driven about thirty miles when Jim Tanner attempted to make small talk with the man who called himself John Barnes. Jim had been trying to size him up because he had noticed that John didn't have the usual hands of a plumber. Then too, he didn't take his hat off when he got into the car. Plumbers, he knew, didn't usually wear hats because of the close spaces they often had to work in.

"Do you get out into the desert much?" he asked.

John said, "No, I don't." He sensed Jim's suspicious and prying attitude and not one to waste time he calmly, almost nonchalantly, reached over and grabbed Jim's neck with one hand and squeezed it hard. There was a crunching sound and Jim went limp.

Aimee was reading the latest Look Magazine and didn't notice or hear anything amiss. Fuzzy noticed something happening through the rear view mirror. He glanced around and saw Jim sitting upright, but something was very wrong.

Jim's head was completely turned around facing the rear window.

"Good God. What's happened to Jim?" he said excitedly.

John said calmly, "God had nothing to do with this."

Aimee looked up and John immediately grabbed her head in his hands. He said, "Fuzzy, take the next side road or Aimee will join Jim right now."

For a moment Fuzzy thought of quickly stopping and throwing this young man out of the car. John began to turn Aimee's head a little. The look of horror and fear on her face was too much for Fuzzy.

"All right," he said to John. "Don't hurt her. I'll stop, then you can take the car and all our money. Just don't hurt her, please."

Three miles further he took a side road to the left. Fuzzy was driving fast, wanting John to release his hold on Aimee's head. He had gone less than a mile on the dirt side road when he heard the sickening sound of Aimee's neck bones cracking. He looked over and saw Aimee's head also turned backwards. He let go of the steering wheel and reached for John. He had time only to say, "You no good sonofa....," then he too died in the same grotesque way. The car ran off the road and became stuck in the sand.

Two hours later, a grizzled ranch hand was driving down the dirt road towards the main Tucson to Phoenix highway when he noticed a plume of black smoke rising from behind a small hill up ahead. "Somebody's burning old tires again. There oughta be a law against that. Too much smoke already," he said aloud to himself. He stopped his old truck when he neared the smoke plume and walked towards the fire. He was alarmed when he saw it was an automobile.

"Godamighty," he shouted and ran towards the car.

The fire had died down and he got close enough to see what had to be three bodies that were blackened and charred from the flames. "What the hell? I've got to find a highway patrolman right away."

He raced his old truck as fast as he could towards the main highway and headed South, hoping to run into a patrolman. He was in luck. A motorist on the highway had noticed the smoke and had called the highway patrol at the nearest telephone. The ranch hand saw the patrol car coming with its red light flashing. He waved it to a stop and told the officer of his grisly find. The officer immediately radioed for a fire truck and an ambulance. He instructed the ranch hand to wait at the turn off and direct the emergency crew to the burned car, then he raced off with his red lights on and siren blaring.

ANGELA'S BATTLE

It was almost an hour before the emergency crews arrived at the scene. By this time the fire had burned itself out. The car was sprayed with water and when the car had cooled down enough to touch, a fireman opened a door and looked inside. What he saw made him sick. The reporter's body was in the back seat folded up at the waist. Fuzzy and Aimee were still in the front seat. All had their heads twisted around from their body so they were looking backwards! All three had their necks completely broken.

It was another two hours before the County Coroner arrived and found the bodies burned beyond recognition. The highway patrol was able to trace the car's ownership from the license plate, and the main office of the Tucson Advocate was notified. A reporter and photographer were immediately dispatched to the scene. It was some time before officers could piece together the reasons for Fuzzy to be on that highway and what his destination had been. Fuzzy had told his news editor of his three p.m. meeting with Jay Storm Cloud and the Phoenix police were alerted. Detectives were sent to confirm the meeting and Jay's whereabouts.

By two p.m. both Diane and Jay had finished typing their press releases on the special mimeograph paper, then they took them down to the motel offices to have copies made. At three p.m. everyone was waiting for Fuzzy to show up. And they waited. After a half hour Jay called Fuzzy's office and was told that he had left at eleven o'clock. Jay wasn't worried yet. All kinds of things might have happened. The car might have broken down, or had a flat tire. Maybe he was still checking into the Adams Hotel. He called the Adams Hotel and was told that "Mr. Williams has not arrived yet, but we expect him to be here soon. He's never late."

It was nearing five o'clock and they were thinking of going down to dinner while waiting for Fuzzy to show. There was a knock on the door.

"There he is, finally," Jay said. He opened the door to find two well dressed men standing there.

"Jay Storm Cloud?" one asked.

"Yes. What is it?"

"We're detectives from the Phoenix Police Department. Can we come in? It's important," one detective said.

"Sure, come on in," Jay said. The two came into the room and introduced themselves.

The younger of the detectives said, "We need to ask, have you been in

Phoenix all day? If you have been here, can these people vouch for you?"

He nodded towards Ham and Diane. Ham couldn't help but notice the inference that only the white persons present would be believable.

Ham quickly replied, "Of course he has, all of us can vouch for that. Why, what's the matter?"

Speaking directly to Ham, the detective said, "We have bad news for you. Do you know a man called Fuzzy Williams?"

Ham deliberately said, "No, I don't know him."

Jay quickly replied, "Yes, I know him. He's my boss."

The two detectives quickly looked at each other knowingly. They had heard their share of stories about quick tempered Indians with chips on their shoulders. They just knew they had a suspect here.

"Well, he and two others, a woman and another man, were found dead in their car along the road. All we want to do is to verify that none of you had anything to do with it. So, you can all swear that you were here all day, is that right?"

"Absolutely," Ham answered for them.

The officers left after getting names and addresses. When the door closed, Jay slapped his hand to his forehead.

"Wow," he exclaimed. "I wonder what happened."

Fawn quietly said, "I think they were killed by a goat man. It's the beginning of the fight. It's started. This is meant as a warning to all of us, *Ah uh*."

Jay called the paper's Tucson office and spoke to Steve Gunther, the assistant editor. He verified that Fuzzy had left town with Aimee and the reporter. He described how they had died and how their bodies had been twisted and burned. Jay was horrified, but more than ever, he knew this story had to get out.

"Look, I'm going to telegraph a story to you that Fuzzy was coming up to get. You've got to run this story in a special edition, an extra edition, tomorrow morning or you're going to get scooped on a very important national story. You should teletype the story to Gene in D.C. as soon as you can so that he can place the story in tomorrow's Washington papers. This is a big story, believe me. If you can, send another reporter and your best photographer up here right away so he can get a first-hand story of this whole thing. I promise you, Steve, Fuzzy would have wanted this. Listen, he and the others were murdered and it's directly because of what's happening here. We'll be at the Desert Inn on East Van Buren. Be there or you'll be sorry. Your choice." Then he hung up.

ANGELA'S BATTLE

Angela said, "This is very serious. We have to prepare for tomorrow. Fawn and Star, mingle with the people that are coming in tonight. Find at least a half dozen Indian men that you trust, then bring them to me here. They'll have to be our security force because if we went to the police they'd laugh at us."

Diane was frightened. She had trouble comprehending the deadly danger she and the others were now faced with. What did Mr. William's murder have to do with what they were doing? Nothing added up. In Washington, her life had been virtually danger-free. All she had to worry about was the evening rush hour traffic on Connecticut Avenue. Now three people were dead and possibly more to come.

Ham saw her situation and went to comfort and assure her that everything would be fine. But inside himself, he was also worried. In his years of roaming the desert and the mountain canyons he had never encountered anything that scared him as much as this news today.

It was ten p.m. before Fawn and Star returned with not six, but nine broad shouldered, husky Indian men whom they had convinced that they were needed as never before. Once inside Angela's room, she and the two other Indian women told them enough of the story that they wanted to help, but were not sure of how they could help. They didn't want to appear to be fools.

Angela called to Whistler to come in. Within fifteen minutes the Indian men were believers and swore to Fawn that they would protect them. They had all heard of the power of Kla-begatho and respected those who worked with him.

The night passed without incident. Next morning at seven o'clock Angela and her entire group, minus Whistler, went to the huge meeting room to prepare for the eight-thirty start of their historic meeting. Television film crews were setting up their equipment. Some local news anchor men tried to get any one of the group to speak with them, but Angela had laid down a strict rule: No one would talk with the media until they had cleared it with Jay, and Jay did not want to give them an early story in fear that they would pull off the coverage when they got the gist of the story, thinking that it was just another crazy bunch of Indians telling a superstitious tale of legends and witchcraft.

The motel manager had prepared everything in grand fashion. A raised podium had been set up with a speakers stand. Floor microphones and speakers had been set up, and the backdrop curtain Angela had asked for was there. It was her plan to have Amos and Whistler behind the curtain, which would be dropped at her signal. Everything seemed ready.

ANGELA'S BATTLE

The hundreds of grassroots Indians, environmentalists and newsmen who had arrived during the night, began to fill the auditorium. Since yesterday all kinds of rumors had been flying around town. The murder of Fuzzy Williams, the rumors said, were closely tied to this meeting. But exactly how, no one knew yet.

Usually, the back rows of seats at any meeting would always fill up first, but today was different. The Indians had heard a little of what was happening, so they all wanted a front row seat. Television cameras were already rolling and newsmen were talking with anyone who would stop for a minute. Excitement was in the air. The media could sense this, and they wished they knew just what was going to happen.

Unnoticed by anyone, Star had placed four of the Indian security men near the front entrances of the building where they casually scrutinized the arrivals in a way they had been instructed to do by Fawn and Star. In the rear of the building Fawn and four of the men stood out of sight watching those who came out of parking lots next door. Angela had asked that one of the men be placed in a front row seat inside, so to be near the podium in case of a disruption. In that case, two men from each team would rush in to help.

Because of the publicity generated by the meeting, and coupled with the recent killings, the Phoenix Police Department had detailed a dozen officers to be on hand. The commander of the police detail, Sergeant Hayes, was a Pima Indian from the nearby Gila River Indian reservation.

Angela was satisfied. Then it was time. At 8:15 Angela called her group together and quickly reviewed their agenda for the morning. Jay tested the microphones, and noted that every seat was already filled. He asked the manager to place a loudspeaker outdoors so those who could not get in could hear what was being said. He was happy to comply with the request, "At no extra charge," he said. He just knew corporate headquarters would smile on him this day.

Chapter Thirteen

At exactly eight-thirty Jay turned on the microphone and said loudly and firmly, "Good morning, everybody." The excited chatter immediately subsided and one could hear the hum as the cameras began rolling. There was an immediate explosion of light from the dozens of newspaper cameras.

"My name is Jay Storm Cloud. I am a member of the mighty Quechan Nation of Fort Yuma. I am also a Washington D.C.-based reporter for the Tucson Advocate."

"As you all know, yesterday the paper's chief editor, Fuzzy Williams, his wife, and another reporter were brutally murdered while on their way to meet with myself and this group of people you see here." He indicated the others who were seated behind him.

"Those murders are only a part of the true story that we're going to tell you about today. So if you will all be patient and listen to what we have to tell you, I promise that you will hear and see things you once thought to be impossible. But I assure you, *they are true*," his emphasis was on the last words.

The crowd buzzed, and reporters scribbled furiously. Jay described the meeting in January when Native Americans had met to discuss environmental dangers. He outlined for them the ways in which the United States had gone ahead with development of nuclear weapons and commercial power plants, all without an inkling of the monster that was created, and without a thought of how to handle the tons of dangerous waste that was being excreted on the world.

"That nuclear monster is unmanageable and uncontrollable and it is going to destroy our world," he almost shouted.

He quickly realized he was being too impassioned and cautioned himself to slow down. Let the others tell their story and the people would make up their own minds.

A man in a dark suit walked up to one of the microphones placed on the floor. "Can you tell us more about what this nuclear monster that you mentioned looks like?"

Jay paused. He knew the man wanted to make him appear to be a misguided environmentalist, a crazy kook. The man wanted him to describe a nuclear *being*.

"The nuclear monster I referred to is only a metaphor for the nuclear industry which is blindly continuing to create something which present technology cannot really control. But I would ask that you wait and direct any questions to our expert speakers at the proper time. I am merely giving this audience an overview of what will come. I'll tell you one more thing before we begin the presentations by our speakers."

Jay looked around the room and saw as many brown faces there as there were white faces. A crowd was beginning to form outdoors. The room was full and there was an overflow. It was time for him to hit them on the head with a two-by-four to get everyone's full attention.

"There are two disasters waiting to happen, and they will happen soon if you and the people of the United States fail to believe us. After you hear what those two disasters are, we will spend the rest of the day giving you real facts. Ask any questions you like later, and I guarantee you we will have an answer for you. It will not take a technical mind or knowledge to understand what we'll tell you. The facts are there and can be seen."

"Listen carefully to the first threat. The continued worldwide use of increasingly larger enhanced nuclear bombs for test purposes will create the first disaster. Tests of first and second-generation thermonuclear bombs have been made on a regular basis at ground level and at high altitudes. These have already poisoned the atmosphere and the combined fallout from all tests has polluted our rivers and streams as well as having killed thousands of unsuspecting innocent people. You know this to be a fact already, so it shouldn't be too hard to believe what I tell you next."

"Underground tests of third-generation nuclear explosions are ready to begin. It is planned to begin thermonuclear explosions which are millions of times more powerful than the original atomic bombs which were dropped on Japan in 1945. If you will recall, scientists who built the first atomic bomb didn't have the slightest idea of how powerful their bomb would be. The same is true today. All they are sure of is that thermonuclear bombs are more powerful that atomic bombs. They know that much, but they don't know its real power. That's why they're going to test it on us."

"The first test is planned to take place in just a few weeks. We know the thermonuclear explosion will fracture underground geological plates and the deep underground aquifer will drain out. This in turn will cause huge earthquakes, and these quakes will then cause the states of California, Arizona, Utah, New Mexico, and Nevada to completely disappear and be covered with sea water. *Phoenix will be covered by waters of the Gulf of California and the Pacific Ocean!*"

Again, he almost shouted his last words.

An eruption of shouts and talk took place. Some of the crowd began shouting "Stop the tests. Stop the tests." Television cameras were swinging around to catch the crowd's reaction. Reporters were running from person to person getting statements.

The excitement quickly spread to those outside the building. A Catholic priest called for everyone to kneel in prayer, but no one was listening.

Reporters were frantically trying to locate a telephone. What they needed was more reporters. This story was going to be too big for one person to cover. Jay had succeeded in getting their attention more than he had hoped.

During the excitement Diane came to whisper in Jay's ear. "The man in the dark suit who asked you to describe the 'monster' is from the Nuclear Institute which runs the public relations duties for the nuclear industry. He'll probably come back to ask more questions. He wants to make you out to be a nut case, so be careful."

"I will, and I'm not going to let him do that." Diane squeezed his hand, then sat down.

Fawn was uneasy and she and her group of security men were a little worried. Their job was made harder because Whistler couldn't bring in any of his scouts for surveillance just yet.

There was an alley that ran the length of the block behind the motel. One of the Indian men, Aaron, had noticed a tall man turn into the alley and begin walking towards them. When he saw the Indian man looking at him he had quickly stopped and went back to the side street. Aaron described him to Fawn as having a light complexion and seemed to have a large brown spot on the left side of his face. He was wearing a straw hat like Mexican farmers wear. Fawn sent Aaron to the front of the building to report this to Star.

Star was having her own problems. The crowd had grown so large that she had trouble keeping track of where her four men were. She went looking for them to have two of them stay on the perimeter of the crowd so they could see newcomers. She then brought the other two to stand near the front doors. She wanted to be able to keep suspicious persons out of the building.

There were city policemen around but they were staying discreetly back and away from the crowd. Sergeant Frank Hayes had introduced himself to Star and told her they were there in case the crowd got out of hand. He wouldn't interfere with their meeting unless needed.

When Aaron told Star of the man he had seen, she asked him to stand near the door with her in order to be able to point him out if he appeared.

"We won't tell the others yet. No need to alarm them. We'll just keep a close watch here."

Sergeant Hayes came out and headed for his car. He was going to need more men if this crowd became unruly. Using his car radio, he told his captain, "There's an overflow crowd here and some guy is telling them things that you wouldn't believe. The crowd is kind of excited, inside and outside the building. I've only got twelve men here and I'm going to need at least twelve more if anything happens."

Captain Morris asked, "What kind of a crowd is it? I was told it would be an Indian meeting, and they're usually pretty peaceful unless they've got something to drink."

Sergeant Hayes winced at the inference.

"Well, Captain, you've never seen anything like this. The crowd is all colors. Maybe two thousand people, and more are arriving. Most of them are from out of town. There's more television cameras and newsmen here than I've ever seen before in Phoenix. Then there's this Indian guy from Yuma that's feeding them all kinds of stuff about the world going to end if the country doesn't quit exploding nuclear bombs. I tell you, Captain, the crowd is what could explode."

"Okay, Sarge, I get the picture. A bunch of religious nuts or something, right? I'll send you ten men right away, but you stay in touch with me. We'll get in trouble if we hurt any of those nuts, but we can't let them get out of control. All right? You find this Indian lady, Angela Beaver. She set up the meeting. Tell her we don't want any trouble or we'll have to shut down her meeting. If you have to call me again, I'm going to come down there myself. Got it? I'm going to send someone from OCR down there too."

"Gotcha, Captain. Don't worry. I'll take care of it."

As soon as he hung up, Captain Morris called the newly established Office of Community Relations which had been set up to keep problems from developing between citizens and the Police Department. The director was Sgt. Sandra Cummings, "a real sweet looker," as the Captain described her to his friends. He regularly used any excuse to get her into his office to talk with her.

He always referred to her as Sandra, never as Sergeant Cummings. He told Sandra what was happening and said, "Go down there and keep an eye on what's going on? I don't want my guys to start busting heads if something happens. Sergeant Hayes will use more sense if he sees you hanging around."

Sandra Cummings answered simply, "Yes, sir. I'm on my way." She stood up and walked away, fully aware that the captain's eyes were following her. He did this to all females. She disliked being around the captain, because it seemed his eyes were constantly moving, roaming over her body, and he seemed always on the verge of putting a hand on her. He was a real "letch," she knew and she had made it a point to never get in an elevator alone with him or to socialize with him at department functions.

She had promised herself, *Six more months, then I'm asking for a transfer*. She could handle herself, but sometimes men like Captain Morris would not take "No" for an answer. If she angered him he had the power to get her fired. She was happy to leave the building on this assignment.

Meanwhile, the two Catholic priests were telling people, "Settle down, settle down. Let's hear the rest of this preposterous story." It was clear that the priests didn't want the crowd to believe what they considered to be blasphemy. Several minutes went by before the crowd inside got over their initial excitement. They clearly wanted to hear more.

Jay asked for silence, then said, "I know I got your attention with my last remarks, but I want to emphasize that every word is true. The west coast will drop into the sea if the thermonuclear explosions take place. Those of us who know this for a fact are here today to give you convincing proof that what we say is true."

"Now I'm not a scientist. I'm a hard nosed journalist trained not to believe everything I hear. A couple of years ago, Diane Olson and I uncovered and exposed many lies and devious methods used by the nuclear industry to hoodwink the country into accepting nuclear power. The things I have learned over the past few months have convinced me that you and I are in big trouble. We have some experts in their own fields who will tell you about what we've learned. As I said before, if you are not convinced this morning, by the end of this meeting I promise you, you will believe."

"At the end of the day we're going to ask that all of you join a national movement to shut down the production of all nuclear weapons, and after that, to close the nuclear electric generating plants. That will be the only way that any of us will live to see our grandchildren grow up. We may have to force our government to shut these things down if they refuse to listen to us."

"We're going to begin at the beginning. We'll tell you how an Indian woman first became aware that Nature, our environment, was in big trouble, and how this information was manifested by events most of us a few weeks ago would have considered as silly fiction. Please listen, then make your own decisions. Our first speaker is Angela Beaver."

Before Angela could begin her story the man in the black suit again spoke from the floor microphone. "Are you saying you called us here today to listen to an Indian fairy tale? There are some of us who are bonafide scientists that know all about nuclear power and the benefits that come from it. Either give us clear scientific proof or shut this meeting down. Now."

Cameras whirred and flash bulbs lit up the room. The man stood there with arms folded across his chest as if waiting impatiently.

Angela looked out at the crowded room, unsure of how to proceed. Jay sat down next to Diane and she was tugging at his arm with fire in her eyes. "That sanctimonious industry s.o.b."

Angela looked directly at the man from the Nuclear Institute, then she began, softly, "My name is Angela Beaver. My people live in the mountains of Utah directly East of the Nevada Test Site. For over ten years we've been exposed to radioactive fallout. My own husband, Earl, was a victim of your industry, Mister whatever your name is. Please, tell us your name and who you represent. We don't want you to leave. We want you to please stay and at least listen to us."

She stared at him until he shuffled uncomfortably.

It was his turn to speak softly, barely audible. "I'm with the Nuclear Institute, a consortium of power generators. My name is," and he hesitated a moment, "Earl. Earl Jemison."

"Well, Earl," Angela said, "It's been a long time since I spoke that name. Not since my husband died from uranium poisoning. Earl is a great name. With a name like that I know you're not a bad person. If you will listen to us, I promise we will listen to you later today." She gave him a sweet, friendly smile and extended the palm of her hand towards him.

This was so effective that the audience murmured, "Sit down, sit down." By now his chubby face was turning red, and he felt hot and sweaty, so he quickly sat and was quiet. One point for Angela.

She then described the high points of events over the past six months, leaving out only direct references to the Council of Eagles, Amos Turkey, and the Indian holy ones, the shamans. When the time came, she would let Whistler and Amos speak for themselves. If necessary, she would ask Amos to call on Kla-begatho.

By the end of her forty-five minute talk, the audience was mesmerized by her descriptions. That is, except for the cynical newspaper men. The reporter from the Los Angeles Times said to another reporter, "If she can prove any of this, it'll be the biggest story ever, but so far it's not even a B movie."

The other said, "Yeah, Central Park is loaded with men from Mars, and others who have the exact date when the world will go up in flames. I came because Storm Cloud promised proof. He'd better hurry and give us the proof. I have a four p.m. flight out of here."

Now another man was at the floor microphone.

"My name is Abner Cranshaw from St. George, Utah. I live downwind from the Nevada Test Site. I've known Angela for a good many years, and I know she's telling you the truth. People in St. George have been dying from cancer ever since those damn clouds of fallout have been raining on us. The government has lied to us about the danger. They have never told us the truth about nuclear radiation. I know this for a fact. I know the Indian people and they wouldn't come up with a story like this unless it was true."

He sat down, and Angela quietly said, "Thank you, Abner."

In front of the building five police cars had arrived, and the ten officers went to report to Sgt. Hayes. After Star was told of the man who had been seen in the alley, she had requested Sgt. Hayes to have one of his policemen to stand near the doors with her, and she advised him of the Indian security men who were nearby.

Sgt. Hayes told her, "We'll work with you. Let me know what you need. I'll also send one man to the back to stay with your friends."

Sgt. Hayes thought Star reminded him of his own grandmother. She too had been a feisty one until the day she decided to accept her own death at the age of ninety-three. He still missed her. He was seven when his mother had died in a Phoenix jail, drunk and out of her mind. In those years alcoholism was a disgrace and not known as a deadly disease, one that you could recover from. She was quietly buried on the Gila River reservation and never mentioned again. His grandmother had taken him and his two sisters into her home, and raised them in a traditional way.

His grandmother would occasionally caution him about the dangers of "drinking booze and becoming just another drunkard." She would mention his cousin, Ira Hayes, who she said had been a good boy until he joined the U.S. Marines to fight in World War Two. She reminded him that Ira had been called a hero, "getting his picture in all the newspapers just for putting a flag on top of a mountain during one of the battles."

"But when he came back, instead of letting him come home they took him on trips all over the country to show him off," she said. "This was not good for him. He had no experience for living in the white man's world and others got him to drinking, and as you know, after he came home he died drunk on a dirt road, trying to find his way to his mother's house. I don't want you to end up that way."

Afterwards he had tried to fashion his life in a way he thought would please her. After high school he had taken a job with the local Bureau of Indian Affairs reservation police and attended night classes in law enforcement at Tempe Junior College. He then put in an application with the Phoenix police department. He was accepted and had worked his way up to the rank of sergeant.

After Angela finished her talk, Jay introduced Fawn and Star to the crowd. Neither one really wanted to talk to such a large group. They had never done anything like this before, but Fawn knew that it would be necessary in order to help assure the many Indians there that this was not another wild *white man's* scheme. She knew she would have to speak in the white man's language so everyone could know what she was saying. She didn't really want to do this.

Fawn bravely went to the microphone and surprised herself when she said in a strong voice, "I am Navajo and my friend Star, here, is Hopi. We've only been off the reservation a few times in our long life. We have seen many things that white people think is strange, but you know, some Indians with certain power are able to talk with things and see things others can not see. Star and me, we have served those kind a long, long time. Our Indian friends, Jay and Angela, and the others who are helping them, know the truth about Indian power, and that is why the holy man named Kla-begatho, told us to come be with them and to help them."

"You Indian people know me and Star are here because we believe what these people say. Others have seen the visions about the future, and what will happen if nobody believes. I ask all Indian people from all tribes to join together in this thing. Help us to save our seventh generation of people. That is what I say. *Ah uh.*"

Almost as one, the large group of Indians rose up with loud shouts and yells and showed their support for the things that Fawn had spoke of. This was an Indian version of a standing ovation.

Chapter Fourteen

After the din died down, Jay introduced Diane with just a short history of her work in the field of anti-nuclear activities.

Now it was Diane's turn to begin her talk. "In 1945 the atomic scientists were in such a hurry to build an operational bomb that no one thought about study and research on exactly what happens when an atomic bomb explodes and how to control the effects of the explosion. Even nuclear physicists Enrico Fermi and J. Robert Oppenheimer were willing to bet government officials that the first Trinity atomic bomb would wipe out all life on earth. The scientists had a betting pool and their guesses of the power of the Trinity bomb ranged from 12,000 to 45,000 tons of TNT."

"After the Trinity bomb exploded, with all of their combined knowledge, they estimated the power of the explosion at equal to 20,000 tons of TNT, but even this estimate was wrong. This was only half of what most of them had expected, but the heat of that explosion was 10,000 times hotter than the surface of the sun. Every living thing within one mile disappeared. In seconds, the mushroom cloud rose up to 40,000 feet."

For many reporters, this was the first description they had heard of the Trinity explosion. The information had been withheld for reasons of national security.

Then pausing for effect, she said, "Not one of those distinguished scientists knew exactly what would happen, and they gambled with our world and our lives from the start, and they are still gambling they can harness the atom. But everyone of them knows that if they make one serious mistake--we all lose."

"The government first developed the uranium bomb, then the plutonium bomb. They have not completely controlled either one, and they are still learning from the high altitude and ground explosions in the Pacific and at the Nevada Test Site."

"They have discovered that by combining tritium with hydrogen they can create a more terrible explosion. They call this a thermonuclear bomb, but again, they have not learned how to control the explosion. They know it will be larger than the first hydrogen bomb, but how much larger they have no real idea. That's why they are planning to explode two thermonuclear bombs deep underground at Yucca Flat soon."

"Remember, they have no idea of the size of the first explosion. If it doesn't fracture the rock mantle deep underground it will at least weaken it enough that the larger second bomb will break through the layers of rock and cause the catastrophic flood that Jay Storm Cloud told you about."

"I'm not a physicist or a geologist, but one doesn't have to be, to see the evidence of damage that has already been done to our world and its people by nuclear scientists who are out of control and answerable to no one except their military masters."

Outside, the crowd began to renew its chant of, "Ban the bomb. Ban the bomb." Inside and outside, an air of fear was gradually growing among the crowd. People looked at each other questioningly. More than one person asked, "Has our government been lying to us?"

Then one of the Indian security men came to Star and said he had spotted the man with the straw hat. "He has a large brown spot on the left side of his face."

She said, "Take Wallace with you. Find that man, then have Wallace come get me while you keep your eyes on him. Don't lose him in the crowd. Don't get too close, if he is one of them he will be very strong. Keep your hand on your medicine pouch at all times. Go quick."

Star quickly went inside and told Fawn what had happened, then she went out to join Aaron and the others at the front door. She had to find out if this threat was real, or not.

Inside, it was Ham's turn to tell his story. "I'm sure none of you know who I am. I've never done anything real important in my life---until now. My name is Hamilton Gardner. I am a rock scientist by trade, a geologist and an engineer. I've walked and climbed almost every hill, mountain and valley of Arizona over the past fifty years. Now I'm involved in the most important project that I've ever been a part of."

"When I first heard the stories which has brought all of you here today, I was also a skeptic. Science and fairy tales really don't mix, and you know that. What Angela and the others have told you, and what I will tell you, is not a fairy tale, I assure you. I joined their team only after I was completely convinced that somehow they have been given a divine knowledge of the catastrophe to come if we are not able to convince our government that what we say is true."

"We will share some of the most important facts that I and other scientists, geological experts in their own right, have discovered recently. I want you to believe these facts, but for the unbelievers I promise you that later today, you will believe."

He pounded the speakers stand to emphasize his last three words, "You - will - believe."

"Because I'm not a famous geologist, and because I am so close to Jay and Angela's team, I've chosen not to present these facts to you myself. Over the past few weeks I have consulted with two of the best known experts in the field of tectonic plate movements. These two men together have a total of 120 years in the study of our underground world. First, I call on Dr. Charles Lyell of the University of California at Berkeley. Dr. Lyell has thoroughly studied seismic events in the western states and in Mexico. Please welcome him." There was a polite round of applause.

The press knew of Dr. Lyell. He had become well known when he had predicted the eruption of several volcanoes. Recently he had been saying that Mt. Shasta in northern California and Mt. St. Helens in Washington state would be the next major eruptions in the U.S., and if they triggered major earthquakes and underground movements along major tectonic faults in California and Nevada, the entire West Coast would sink and the western side of the Rocky Mountains would become virtual ocean front property.

A reporter from the local Phoenix paper, the Arizona Republic, whispered to his colleague, "What a set-up. This guy's the perfect nut to put a stamp on this hokey story."

Dr. Lyell was now 84 years old and was always prepared for criticism of his theories. He shuffled up to the mike and adjusted it for his height. He was a tall man with thinning white hair which was always in need of a combing. Surprisingly, he did not wear glasses, and his sparkling hazel eyes looked out at the gathered media, almost defiantly. He had always attracted attention for his habit of wildly flailing his scrawny arms to emphasize his words.

He began, "In my long work career, I've often been wrong," he hesitated for three seconds for effect, then he continued "and I have more often been right. Today, I stand before you convinced by my over sixty years of work that the catastrophe these people speak of is entirely possible. In my opinion, the earth movement they speak of is overdue. It has been merely waiting for the catalyst, the straw that would break the camel's back." His arms waved the air frantically. "Two thermonuclear explosions of a high yield could be that straw. Here is why."

"The western U.S. is really very young in terms of volcanic activity. The deep rock faults underlying the West are still moving. As a matter of world history this specific region that we're talking about today has been under water more often than not. Let's start at from about 400 million years ago. At that time, what is now your desert was under water. Then about 50 million years ago the Rocky Mountains were pushed up in their present location, and the sea withdrew to about 1,000 miles West. When the land masses dried out, volcanic action filled in many low spots."

"So, we know that over the past few hundred million years or so, the western states have dried out then been covered with water about fifteen different times. It could happen again under the right conditions. And while such an event would be a catastrophe to you, it would only be a continuing function of the earth's evolution. The earth's crust is in constant motion and this causes from 400 to 900 earthquakes in the United States each year. These quakes occur along faults where rock layers have separated and are moving in different directions."

"The principal reason why my colleagues and I have concluded that a thermonuclear explosion could cause a catastrophe is, the entire length of the Sierra Nevada Range, which is nearby the Test Site, is one gigantic fault. On the East side, the surface has moved downward and formed Death Valley, which is the lowest point in North America. The rock layers have been dry for so long that water will help to soften them, causing the surface to sink even lower."

"Even without the bomb's effect, some time in the future the tectonic shifting could by itself trigger the calamity. What is not well known or advertised, is that the tens of thousands of years of movement has created a large pocket underneath the tectonic rock layer that is slowly but surely moving eastward. That tectonic layer is slowly climbing on top of the plate on which the Rocky Mountains sit." Again, there was a buzz of comments from the crowd. A reporter went to a mike to ask a question.

"Dr. Lyell, in all due respect, if what you say is true, wouldn't the climbing only serve to support the plate underneath the West Coast?"

"Yes it would, but for only a short while until the weight and pressure from above caused the short ledge on which it rests to break off and drop the western plate down into the empty pocket. Son, we are talking of a tremendous change not seen since the early formation of this continent."

He paused for a moment.

"Please understand that at one time eons ago, this continent was located near what is now the South Pole, and it has slowly drifted to its present site. It has always been in a state of flux. North America is not yet solidly in place and may not be for another hundred million years, if we last that long. That's the bad news, and there is really no good news. By preventing the powerful thermonuclear explosions, you could possibly delay the catastrophe for perhaps five to ten thousand years."

"My distinguished colleague, Dr. P. C. Badgely," who he indicated by a wave of his hand, "and I agree and recommend that all tests of thermonuclear explosions be stopped immediately. The results, if the nuclear scientists are wrong, are too grave to ignore. We join the others here in saying that our government must stop the nuclear nonsense."

Dr. Badgely rose and joined hands with Dr. Lyell and Ham. They raised their arms in an upraised gesture. "Stop the bomb tests," they shouted in unison.

This caused another loud commotion from the crowd inside and outside the building.

The commotion was making it difficult for Star to survey the crowd, and it surged closer to the entrance doors. The people were visibly upset by all they had heard and many wanted to get inside to have their say. Star quickly sent Aaron to locate Sgt. Hayes. When Hayes forced his way through the crowd, she asked him, "Can you have your men come to the front and move the people back. We need more room."

Then she told him of the man they were looking for: "A tall man wearing a Mexican straw hat, light brown skin, with a big brown spot on the left side of his face."

Sgt. Hayes was puzzled, but didn't ask any questions. Using his radio he called for the men in reserve to come quickly. When they arrived, Sgt. Hayes began slowly moving the crowd back and away from the concrete steps leading to the entrance.

The City Fire Marshal came to Sgt. Hayes and said, "I was just about to ask you to clear the entrances. If the crowd gets any bigger we may have a problem. In case of a fire inside our firemen wouldn't be able to get through. We may have to close down their meeting."

Sgt. Hayes didn't want to do that.

"Don't do it. We'll start moving them back a little at a time. Anyway, the meeting inside will be breaking for lunch in less than an hour. Let's just wait. Okay?"

The Fire Marshal agreed. He had dealt with crowds before and he didn't want this one to become mean.

In the meantime Star had sent Aaron to ask Fawn and two of the men to come to join her. Star's instincts were sending warning signals. As soon as Fawn arrived, Star sent Aaron to check with the other security men who were scanning the crowd trying to locate the man with the brown spot on his face.

She introduced Fawn to Sgt. Hayes and the three held a quick talk to update the situation.

Sgt. Hayes asked, "So you're trying to find this man. Why do you want to find him? What has he done? If he's a danger to anyone I need to know that."

The two women exchanged glances, not knowing whether or not to tell this city policeman the truth. Star could hear Kla-begatho saying, as he had before, "When faced with a decision, choose the path which will harm the fewest people."

In the Navajo language Star quickly told Fawn that they had no choice but to take this man into their confidence. He was Indian and would understand. Fawn agreed.

Fawn told Sgt. Hayes quickly about the legend of the goat man, and how they had discovered that the story was true, and that one of them could be here today to learn what was being said.

"We must be very careful if we see him. First we have to find out if he is one of them, and if he is, he must be chased away. There are too many people here and some might be hurt. He is very strong and powerful. A dangerous creature."

Sgt. Hayes' jaw dropped in wonder. "I can remember my grandmother telling me the goat man story. I can see you're both serious so tell me what you want me to do. I don't want anyone to get hurt either."

Fawn said, "When the man is located one of our men will come get me. I will then go to him and see if he is one of them. If he is, I will ask him to leave peacefully, that there is nothing here for him today. I will say that Kla-begatho has said this. I think he will go when he hears the name of Kla-begatho. If he does not go, I will have to deal with him, and you and your policemen should move the crowd away or it will be dangerous for everyone."

"Alright," the sergeant said, "but if trouble starts I'll have to move in and try to stop him."

"You must do what you must do, but that would be a mistake," said Fawn. "Bullets might not kill a goat man. They are already dead."

Sgt. Hayes was beginning to worry. These old Indian women were actually starting to scare him. He remembered how scared he was as a small child when he was locked out of the house one dark night. His sister was shouting at him, "The ghosts will get you. Look out for the ghosts."

He had to pull himself together. He told himself, "This is Phoenix, for Chris'sakes, in the middle of civilization, and not a remote reservation with all its superstitions." But he still felt an ache in his gut.

Inside, the crowd was almost going wild after the statements of Dr. Lyell, Dr. Badgely, and Ham, and their exhortation to "Stop the bomb tests."

Jay let them carry on for a minute, then stepped up and asked them to be calm. Sgt. Hayes quickly sent in six of his policemen to stand three on each side of the large room, hoping the sight of them would help to quiet the crowd. But it was only when Angela stepped to the microphone that they began to sit and be quiet once again.

Angela stood there reassuringly, while Jay proceeded to lay out the next presentation. He glanced quickly at his wristwatch. It was 11:45, almost time for their lunch break. He decided it was time to prepare them for the shock of seeing Whistler and Amos for the first time. But before he could begin, a colleague, Ron Holt, a reporter for the Native American News, quickly stepped up to the floor microphone and waved at Jay for his attention. He had heard the rumblings among the media people and hoped to impart to Jay that they were getting impatient.

Jay asked the crowd for silence, then said to the reporter, "Yes, Ron. Do you have a question?"

"Yes, I do, Storm Cloud, and so does every one else in this room. We have a lot of questions. In all respect to you, Angela and the good doctors, the things you're predicting are only just that: predictions. Here in the West we have earthquakes almost every day, and unless you or someone can give us something we can see or understand that makes sense, and clearly demonstrates the danger you say we're in, this is not news. It's science fiction, and the media doesn't print fiction, as you know. You've got to give us proof."

Jay realized the truth in what Holt said, so he asked the media and the crowd to give them one minute. Then he quickly called his group to a huddle in the back of the platform.

Diane was surprised to see a smile on Jay's face. She had expected him to be worried after the reporters ultimatum.

"This is great," Jay told them. "They're doubtful, but they're willing to stay. A good reporter can sense a big story, and if they really thought this was science fiction they'd be gone by now. They're nibbling and interested, now its up to us to set the hook, hard. When we come back we should have Whistler and Amos here, and hopefully Kla-begatho or one of the holy ones to tell them about what's led to this conference."

"We need to impress the media, especially the national TV and newspaper people if we hope to convince the country that what we say is true. Angela, we only have this one day to talk to the country through the media and we've got to make the most of this great opportunity. I say we pull out all the stops. What do you say? I even wish we had a goat man to show them."

Angela gasped. "I wish you hadn't said that."

Ham spoke first. "I'll go along with Jay. When one speaks to doubters one has to hit them hard to erase the doubt."

Diane said, "I agree."

"All right," Angela said. Someone has to find Fawn and tell her about our plans so she can contact Kla-begatho and as many of the holy men as she can, to be here on short notice. Jay, you must tell her how important it is for them to be here. We may even want to try and convince Whistler's father to be here. Now go find Fawn and tell her these things while I talk to the crowd. Hurry."

While Angela went to the podium, Jay went out the back door and ran quickly to the front of the building. He found Fawn busily searching for the strange face in the crowd. He told her of what Angela had said.

Sgt. Hayes thought he should know more about what was going on. He asked, "Is everything all right, Jay?"

Jay replied, "It's a bit frantic right now, but we'll break for lunch soon and let things settle down.. Thanks for all your help."

"That's my job. Let me know if I can do more. I'm on your side, you know."

Back in the conference room, the reporters and television crews were tired and hungry. They hadn't had a break since they started filming at eight-thirty. Several of them left their cameras running on automatic and stretched their legs. Two of them went outside to try and grab a smoke. They saw the restless crowd and quickly came back inside.

"There's an ugly crowd outside," one of them told the others.

Angela was pausing to decide how much more to tell them.

She announced, "Before we break for our lunch, I want to mention one other matter that will sound more than anything before like science fiction, but it too is something we can prove. It is about strange and mysterious creatures which until a few weeks ago we ourselves believed were only an Indian legend. Pure fiction, we thought. Some of you older people who have been around Indian people for awhile may recall the stories about a thing called Goat Man. We have discovered that those legends are factual. They appear on earth at times when people are under great stress and under threats of destruction. At times like that, people tend to lose their inhibitions and do bad things."

Loud gasps came from the crowd, and from the back of the room one voice loudly said, "Now you've really lost it. You're all nuts. Unless you can prove any of this, now, we're leaving. Listen to yourself. What you're asking us to believe is crazy. It's time to put up or shut up."

Angela squared her shoulders and looked directly at the young man who had now stood up, waiting for her answer. Angela was getting angry at the closed-minded ignorance and attitudes of young Americans who looked with disdain at anything that didn't fit neatly into their view of here and now, which they called Reality. They had no room in their minds for anything they could not see, hear, feel, or smell. If it didn't meet that test, it didn't exist. No ifs, ands, or buts. It did not exist.

Her eyes flashed angrily and she felt a shiver running up and down her spine. Her anger peaked and her face slowly returned to its original softness. For a moment she was afraid to speak in fear that it would show her feelings.

She smiled sweetly at the young man in the back row and said, "I understand completely what you're saying and we are ready to give you some proof of what we've said. The catastrophe to be caused by the thermonuclear bombs cannot be proven by any display or drawings, and must be taken from experience and history. One of your own has wisely said, 'If one fails to learn the lessons from history, one is doomed to repeat his mistakes.' This applies to your learned scientists, as well. Now, you already know the damage, the loss of human life, and the pain and suffering that the nuclear bomb has caused. Why is it so difficult to admit that it's at least possible that the nuclear scientists are wrong and misguided?"

"It's impossible to prove that Phoenix will disappear under the ocean, all we're asking you to do is to at least believe it's possible that we're right. When it does happen it will be useless for us to say, 'I told you so.' You reporters, if you will write of what we've said, and let your newspapers and your television networks tell the people of the world of what we've said, that's all we ask. If you will carry our words, the people can then decide for themselves if they believe it or not. They don't need our proof. It's already there to see."

"The matter of the legend of Goat Man being real, yes, that is so *very* hard to believe. A large part of the world's population believes in a God they have never seen, yet they pray daily. Most of the world believes without proof."

"We Indians also believe in a God, which we call our Creator. We look around each day and we can see what our Creator has given us. The sky, the trees, birds, animals, and so forth. Yet you demand further proof."

She paused, thinking that she was talking too much. She said, "Let's have lunch now. We'll come back at one-thirty and we'll show you........."

Suddenly she was interrupted by a loud disturbance and shouting at the front door. Everyone turned to see what was happening.

There was a struggle going on between several people, then came a horrifying sight. A man's body flew through the now open front doors and landed just behind the TV cameras. It was Aaron's body.

A goat man had come out of the thick crowd near the front doors. With head down, the creature had charged the doors in a direct line with Star. Star saw him first. She pointed her right hand at him and shouted, "*Kawilk-nyah, Mah-ly imm.*" Stop now, bad one.

Star was hit hard, head-on, by the fast moving creature and thrown into the line of police officers. Three of them, along with Sgt. Hayes, went down in a heap with her. Star was not moving. Aaron and his five friends had moved quickly, but not quick enough to stop the charge.

One of the men threw a body block, football style, at the creature and slowed it only briefly. Aaron grabbed for its head, reaching for the short horns. Aaron had bulldogged many a steer at rodeos and had been able to bring down huge bulls. This time, no matter his strength, he could not twist the creature's body aside. He felt himself being carried inside the building, then he was lifted into the air and hurled twenty feet. He lay unconscious on the hardwood floor.

Chapter Fifteen

Just one day ago, the creature Fawn and Star had been searching for was awakened from his slumber in a dark cave about 100 miles east of Phoenix. The cave was halfway up a steep canyon wall in the rocky and primitive Salt River Canyon.

For this creature it had been a place of refuge for 100 years since it last walked this land in 1862. Posing as Hernando, a wandering Mexican miner, he agreed to serve the U.S. Army as a scout in its effort to force the native Indians into submission. He served both General James Carleton and General Joseph West by guiding them to large groups of Indians who were hidden in the canyons, and he had encouraged them to take no prisoners.

"It's easier and cheaper," he had advised. He told them this would assure the Army officers of "a place in history," but he neglected to say that it also assured them a place in Hell.

His greatest joy had been in January of 1863 when he persuaded General West to ignore the white flag of truce carried by the Apache chief, Mangas Colorado. Mangas was captured, tied up, tortured with hot bayonets, shot several times and scalped. His head was cut off and boiled so that the skull could be sold. The headless body was then dumped into a ravine. The official Army report said that Mangas had been shot while trying to escape. General West earned a special place in Satan's house for that one.

The creature had been awakened and instructed to make its way to a place called Phoenix where a group of native Indians were going to tell the world about the existence of creatures such as he and others like him.

He made his way up the canyon wall, then looked for a high peak where he could survey the countryside. Far to the west he could make out the brown, parched desert hills which stretched southward from the rock cliffs of the Mogollon Rim. He vaguely remembered that his mountain canyon hideaway had been somewhere East of the last killing of the Army's Indian prisoners on the banks of the Verde River.

He knew where he had to go, but the immediate problem was how to get there. He had no clothes or boots to hide his frightfully weird body. Five hundred feet below him, and on the other side of the canyon, he saw what seemed to be a road covered with a ribbon of black which wound through the prehistoric canyon, sometimes in close tight curves as it followed the rough contours formed by earth movements eons ago. He decided he would go to the other side of the canyon. A road meant humans were nearby. The wonder and beauty of canyon country was now going to play a big role in the activities being planned in Phoenix.

It was still early on Tuesday morning and two men were in a vintage auto which was now slowly making its way up the steep western grade. Catholic Fathers Ignatius Felix and John Boland were taking a well deserved outing after completing their weekend duties in Phoenix. It was good to be away from the confines of their city parishes. They planned to have lunch at the small town of Show Low, which was at the top of the White Mountain range, then drive leisurely back to Phoenix arriving home in time for dinner.

As their Ford car labored uphill and slowed for one of the famous hair-pin curves, Father Felix noted that the engine's temperature gauge was near the boiling point.

"There's an off-road viewpoint just up ahead. We'll stop awhile and let the car cool off while we enjoy the view provided for us by our Lord."

He had made this drive several times before and knew where the cooling off stops were located. He turned the car off the main road and stopped in the parking space afforded for visitors. The two priests got out of the car and stretched their aging legs and arms in exaggerated movements.

They moved close to the cliff edge for a better look at Natures beauty. There was no guard rail to prevent sightseers, or automobiles from falling off the edge. Father Felix said in awe, "Isn't it wonderful what God has made?"

Before Father Boland could agree, he was hit by a hard blow to his back and hurled to his death, landing on rocks one thousand feet below. Father Felix had no time to protect himself from the creatures next move. The priest's head was twisted to one side until his neck snapped, and he died instantly. The creature stripped off all the priest's clothing, then threw the nude body into the canyon. Dressed in the dead priests clothing and black hat, he decided to wait there until some kind soul would take him into Phoenix. When he saw a car coming downhill towards him, he waved it to a stop.

An elderly couple were in the car. The creature said, "My vehicle has broken down. Can you give me a ride towards Phoenix? If I can get there someone can come back to get the car."

The driver said, "Get in, Father, we'll be happy to take you into Phoenix. We just happen to be going on to California, so we'll be going right through the middle of Phoenix. Let me know where to let you off."

When they reached a small town outside the city, he said, "I'll get out here. I have friends here who can help me. I thank you for your kindness."

The man responded, "Glad to be of help to you, Father."

Later, he found more suitable clothing provided by a luckless Mexican farm laborer who had been irrigating a large alfalfa farm on the outskirts of the city. He stayed near the field until after dark, then it was a short walk into the city proper.

Early this morning he had found the place where the Indians were holding their meeting. He almost walked into a small group of Indian men at the back of the building, but had retreated and then approached the building under cover of a large crowd gathered in front. Now he sat in their midst waiting for a plan. He now knew that others were aware of his presence.

Thoughts were coming into his mind. "Find the female Indian who is a danger to the creatures. Angela is her name. Without her the meeting will fall apart."

But there were men who were searching for him. Somehow they knew he was near. He had to get inside the building to find this Angela. If he knew what she looked like he could wait for an opportunity to kill her, then quickly leave the area until he was called on again. It seemed to be a simple plan. The confusion and fear in the air masked any sense of danger to him.

Fawn came to check on the security measures and was standing with Star and the police sergeant.

Keeping low to the ground, the creature slowly pushed his way through the crowd moving in the direction of the large front doors. He finally got close enough to see that there were two women and two men standing in front of the doors. The elderly Indian women seemed to be no threat. From his position he could not see the two groups of policemen which Sgt. Hayes had placed to the sides of the doors, near enough to react if the crowd rushed the doors, yet back out of sight.

"If I move fast," the creature thought, "I can get past them, run inside and get a look at Angela. Then I can quickly leave and hide somewhere until night time." His plan was made. Be quick and keep it simple. He edged closer. But his plan was already flawed. He knew nothing of who or what was inside. He assumed that there would only be a large group of Indian people inside, and he couldn't have known that the nation's media would be there to record the entire action.

Directed by Star, the Indian security men were slowly closing a circle in the crowd, trying to catch a glimpse of the creature, while Star's senses were ringing alarm bells in her mind. She knew danger was close by, but where?

They were unable to see him because he was hunkered down on his haunches in the middle of the restless crowd. He sensed that someone, something, was stalking him. He had to stay out of sight until the right moment. Then something happened that caused him to move sooner that he had planned.

Fawn suddenly had a strong feeling of extreme danger nearby. "Star, Aaron, be quick," she ordered. Call the other men to join you here. Something is wrong. I have to go to Angela," then she was gone.

Using a quail call and sign language, Aaron signaled to his friends to gather quickly. Sgt. Hayes saw the new activity and immediately called for five of his own men to join him behind the line formed by Star and the big Indian men.

There was extreme excitement in the air, and it was growing. Inside, Fawn had reached the platform and placed herself directly in front of the raised podium.

Something happened suddenly that caused the goat man to move sooner than he had planned. Directly in front of him there were two large white women, hot and sweaty, and uncomfortable. They were fanning themselves and constantly shifting their massive weight from one foot to the other. He edged closer. When he attempted to move around them, one woman who held her fan in one hand and rosary beads in the other suddenly moved against him and the rosary cross burned his neck. There was an audible hiss from the burn. He jerked away and the straw hat was knocked off his head.

The woman looked down at him, started to say, "Excuse me," then saw his strange looking head. She gasped and said loudly, "What the hell?"

There were two things resembling goat horns about three inches long on the top of his head. Attention was quickly drawn to him.

He had to move fast, now! He stood, lowered his head and charged towards the doors.

The commotion alerted Fawn and those on the stage. At the first shouts the two closest cameras had swung around to the doors and were now filming the frightening activity. The crowd, stunned at first, now was beginning to react. Women screamed, and men were trying to move away from the aisle where the creature had made his appearance. Fearful of pandemonium setting in, Ham ran to the microphone and told the crowd, "Please stay calm and get on the floor. Get on the floor. Everything will be all right."

Fawn told the group on the stage to bundle together to protect Angela. Jay asked Ham to call the four men from outside the back door to come quickly, then he smashed a wooden chair and handed one of the legs to Diane, Angela, and Ham.

"Use these. It's Angela they want, so circle around her."

Fawn positioned herself directly in front of the huddled group. The three men from outside came to join her and they stood in a line with Fawn. They watched in horror as the creature stood for just a moment over Aaron's still body. The crowd was now strangely silent, frozen in fear. They had no idea of what they were seeing.

Then suddenly, as Ham had feared, pandemonium set in and the crowd instinctively pushed towards the side walls. Women began to scream in terror.

The creature quickly looked around, then focused on an Indian woman standing in front of the stage. It assumed this was Angela. Then it charged down the aisle, sending some of the crowd flying through the air. The target of its charge was Fawn.

The four Indian men immediately made their own charge towards the aisle to head the creature off. Just when it seemed the men would collide head on with the fast moving creature, it leaped into the air and over the heads of the Indian men. It landed no more than ten feet from where Fawn was standing.

At that instant Fawn had no idea of how she would stop this abomination. She instinctively did what Kla-begatho had always told her to do. "If faced with danger to your life, call on me," he had said.

She faced the creature, and shouted in her Navajo language, "Stop. We have the power to destroy you. Go back to where you came from."

Her mind kept calling, *"Kla-begatho. Kla-begatho. I need you."*

The creature stopped and looked straight into her eyes, expecting to see them filled with fear. Humans always had that look when they saw him. He was puzzled. This one looked unafraid, courageous, powerful, and determined.

Fawn extended her left arm towards him, pointing at him with all five fingers. In Indian society, the pointing of even one finger directly at a person was a sign of disrespect. Five fingers indicated an utter disrespect.

Fawn said firmly, "You have no power here. We are protected by the power of Kla-begatho. Kla-begatho warns you to return to Hell. He knows you are one of those who murdered his ancestors in their canyon homes. Leave now, or he will have his revenge."

The creature didn't move.

He was puzzled. "How could this Kla-begatho know that he was one of those who descended the canyon walls and had torn the 'ancient ones' limb from limb almost seven hundred years ago?" *What should he do now?* The goat man decided to test this woman's power.

It raised its right arm in a striking position and advanced towards Fawn. It was immediately hit by an invisible force which knocked it to its knees. The goat man tried to get up, and was immediately hit again. It was dazed and unable to move.

Fawn called to the Indian men, "Quick. Tear off his shirt and pants."

After several loud ripping sounds the creature's entire body was exposed for the world to see in all its ugliness. The creature's existence was exposed on national television as a *Goat Man. An old Indian myth was turned into reality for all to see.* How could people now not believe?

Instead of accomplishing his task as directed, the creature had failed miserably, and by its failure had helped Angela prove that such creatures existed. It would be in disgrace when it returned to his Master. But its Master had already decided to destroy this obscenity.

The goat man fell to the floor. As the crowd watched, and the cameras recorded, its body and features returned to a human form, the form it had possessed at a time long ago when it had lived as a man in a place called Gomorrah in the biblical Valley of Siddim.

The crowd was silent and horrified, not believing what had happened before their very eyes. Fawn broke the silence and called to Ham. "Go quickly. Go to Star at the front door. She needs you."

Ham ran as fast as he could, forcing his way through the excited crowd to the front doors. When he reached them he saw Sgt. Hayes kneeling beside Star who was lying prone on the concrete landing at the top of the steps. He immediately cradled her in his arms. Blood was slowly flowing from her mouth.

He whispered, "Star. Star. It's Ham. Can you hear me?"

Sgt. Hayes said softly, "I'm afraid she's gone. I've sent for an ambulance and a doctor. We'll take her to the hospital. Maybe they can save her, but she hasn't breathed or moved since that damned thing hit her. It hit her hard. What in the hell was that thing."

There was the sound of a siren in the distance. Sgt.Hayes quickly directed his officers to begin clearing the crowd away from the entrance.

Ham held Star's hand tightly and tears were streaming down his face. "Hang on Star. You've got to live. Do you hear me?"

There was no indication of life from Star. When she was finally lifted into the ambulance, the attendants at first refused to let Ham ride with her.

"Rules, you know." they said.

Sgt. Hayes said, "The hell with your rules. Let him go with her!"

A second ambulance arrived, and Sgt. Hayes directed them to Aaron's body. Brave Aaron was dead. The Yavapai man had lived through World War II and the Korean War, winning a Silver Star and a Bronze Star for bravery. He had fought for his country, and now he had given his life for his Indian people.

Sergeant Sandra Cummings, the Community Relations officer, had arrived just when the pandemonium had begun. She quickly ran into the motel lobby looking for a telephone and saw the officers in reserve just standing there. She flashed her badge at them and hollered, "Get your asses out there right now and give your sergeant a hand. Now! Move it." Then she grabbed a telephone and called Captain Morris.

"All hell is breaking loose down here. I don't know what happened, but it looks like there may be a riot inside the building. I haven't seen Sgt. Hayes anywhere, so maybe he's involved inside. There's a couple of thousand people running around outside, and maybe half that many more inside. I suggest you get some help down here quick."

Captain Morris said, "I'm coming right down with two squads. Be right there." To himself he said, "Damn Indians. I knew they'd start some kind of trouble. We should crack some heads to teach them a lesson."

Jay again took charge of the meeting. As soon as he got the crowd to quiet down he announced that because of what had happened there would be a two-hour break to give them time to reorganize.

"Our group is going to meet now and evaluate the situation. One of our group is dead and another is on the way to a hospital. As soon as we know the details we will have a press conference. In the meantime, you know as much as we do. We were honest with you this morning and told you exactly what we had found out, so for now I suggest the media call your offices and tell them what has happened and that there's more information to come. We'll see you in two hours."

Sgt. Hayes gathered his men outside and detailed some to close Van Buren Avenue, and reroute the traffic. If he was going to clear the area this large crowd would need someplace to go. The officers directed the crowd into the now empty street. Another group of officers were moving the crowd away from the doors.

By the time Captain Morris arrived, Sgt. Hayes had things pretty well under control and the crowd was breaking up in an orderly way.

Within fifteen minutes local radio and TV stations were breaking into their regular programs to announce that "a large disturbance" had taken place in downtown Phoenix and that several people had been killed by an insane man. This was not the kind of publicity that Jay had been looking for. It was wrong information and misleading, so he decided that his first priority must be to frame a press release quickly.

He assessed his position. Star was in the hospital and Ham was with her. He had to establish contact with Ham. Aaron was dead and arrangements must be made to notify his family. The other Indian men had to be told and reassigned to keep them busy. He would have one of them call Aaron's people and make arrangements for them to come and take him home. Fawn was shaken, but she was tough, and would be able to carry on. Angela was all right and ready to continue. Diane hadn't said three words since the incident. She seemed frightened and on the verge of running.

Jay slapped his forehead. *Whistler*. God, he had forgotten all about Whistler. He must be going nuts, seeing all the excitement outside and not knowing what was going on. He decided to send everyone up to Angela's room to calm down. Things had fallen apart and now he had to be the strong one and brings things back together.

"Get moving," he told himself. "You only have two hours to get organized."

Diane and Fawn were sent to the hospital to be with Star. "When you get there call the motel office and leave a message with a phone number where I can reach you or Ham. If Star is alive and conscious, tell her--tell her we love her and we'll see her soon."

Chapter Sixteen

At the hospital, Star was in the intensive care unit of Grace Memorial Hospital. Doctors and nurses were gathered around her. Tubes and needles were stuck into both arms, and she was hooked up to a heart monitor. Only a faint pulse was showing on the screen.

Diane and Fawn walked in and saw Ham standing at the foot of her bed waiting for the doctors to finish their examination so he could talk to her and let her know he was there. When he saw them, he came to them and the three hugged each other.

Ham told them what little he knew so far. "Star suffered severe internal injuries from the force of getting hit by the goat man. They don't know yet where the bleeding is coming from but said a broken rib may have punctured the heart or lungs. She went without breathing for several minutes before the ambulance got to her so she may have brain damage from the lack of oxygen while her heart was stopped. Her heart beat is very weak now."

He told them that the doctors had said to be prepared for the worst. "It doesn't look good for Star," he said as his voice shook.

When the doctors finished their preliminary examination, they told the visitors, "You can have ten minutes with her, then we've got more work to do on her."

Ham quickly grabbed her right hand and whispered, "It's Ham. I'm here with you." There was no sign of recognition from Star.

The monitor was showing only a very faint heart beat. Suddenly, Star's heart stopped beating. The oxygen mask hissed uselessly. She had stopped breathing.

Ham ran out the door to find a doctor.

Star opened her eyes and saw Fawn and her mother standing near the bed. Her mother was dressed Hopi-style as she had last seen her sixty years ago. She had a black wool sleeveless dress over a white cotton shirt and a dark red shawl over her head. There was a colorful braided Hopi sash around her waist. On her feet were the traditional deer hide moccasins and soft, white buckskin leg wrappings. Now, as she stood there she seemed to have a white light around her.

Fawn spoke to her in the Hopi language. "You must be strong at this time. I know you would like to be with your relatives. It's peaceful there where you're going, and you will no longer feel pain. You have not seen your aunts and uncles for many years, but you must tell them that your work here is not yet done. I need you beside me in this important work. Our new friends need you. The man we call Ham, I know you have a feeling for him. He is a good man, almost Indian, *A-wah*. He needs you too. Kla-begatho will see you soon and will also say this. Tell your relatives to let you come back for a little while. We will wait for you."

Her mother spoke. "Little one, it's been a long time since I left our home at Shipolovi. I didn't want to go then and leave you alone, but the Creator said I had to. I have missed you, and now I have come to take you with me to see all your other relatives. They will be glad. Come."

When she rose from the bed she looked back and saw herself lying there motionless, with strange things sticking into her arms, nose and mouth. A man was holding one of her hands. She knew him, she thought. She said, "*Hem.* It's *Hem. I do know him. He's a good man. I want to talk to him.*"

"No, you can't," her mother said firmly. "It's time to come with me now." The hospital room disappeared from her sight.

Star sat with her long gone relatives. They had been glad to see her, but they had not expected to see her so soon. They sat inside a Hopi adobe house. Although there was only one window and an open eastern door the room was brightly lit. She had never seen such a light. It was shiny bright, yet it didn't hurt one's eyes like bright sunlight did. Her paternal grandfather was sitting by the eastern door singing an ancient song, one that she last heard when she was but a child.

She had been thirteen years old when her mother had left her. She then lived with her grandparents until, one by one, they had also left her. Her aunts and uncles had taken care of her until they too passed away. Now the relatives, many of whom she didn't recognize, were here in this Hopi house to welcome her to this new place. There were gifts for her.

Her grandfather sang a new song just for her while everyone picked at morsels of antelope meat and Hopi bread provided by her father. Other relatives had brought fresh corn, melons and squash. Her maternal grandfather, *Numtewa*, waited until everyone had eaten their fill, then he made a welcoming speech for Star.

"We are all happy that you have joined us at last. It is always hard to leave that other world. Sometimes we leave because of the doings of others, or perhaps our own wrongdoings. But once you get here it is nothing like you had been told. Here we live much the same as before, but we all know that the spiritual ways taught us by the Creator is the best way to live. It is a good way to be, and we wait here until we are ready to go back into the River of Life."

Star told them all, "I am happy to see all of you once again, but I am not ready yet to leave that other place. I have been very busy in my time there, serving and helping those holy men who try to keep evil away from the people. For over fifty years I served the holy man, Kla-begatho, and I am here today just because one of those evils, a goat man, hit me while I was trying to protect others. We are not yet through with what we have to do. I have to go back soon."

Her father said, "We have heard that goat men were again roaming our homeland. They killed many people long ago. We know you were doing an important job, but when the Creator calls for you, you must listen. You cannot return." Her mother and the other relatives shook their heads in agreement.

Star didn't know what to say.

After a long silence, her grandfather alerted them that someone was coming, and he began singing an honoring song, a song for a Head Man. Then someone appeared at the eastern door. It was a tall, big man. It was Kla-begatho himself. Star immediately went to stand before him with her head bowed.

He reached out to touch her head and said, "Sit, dear one."

Everyone waited for him to speak. They knew who he was and he was greatly respected.

"My relatives," he began. "I have come only to ask your permission to allow this one, Star, to return to us. She is a great help to all who are now trying to save our land from destruction by those who are ignorant of the Creator's laws. Your relatives are also in danger from one you know well. Because of the coming destruction, the Evil One has again sent the half-man, half-goat people to kill us and steal our souls."

"Star can help to defeat them. Where in your day, you had no way to fight against them, today we have a power given us by the holy men of many tribes, and we can now overcome them. It is important that Star be there with us. But I have been told that only with your permission, and well-wishes, can she return to us. I now ask you for that permission."

As is usual at Indian gatherings, a long silence was afforded Kla-begatho to make sure he had finished speaking.

Star's father stood in respect for Kla-begatho, then said, "We never got the chance to really know what kind of person she was before we left her. I myself had to leave when she was only four years old, and her mother left soon after. I am happy to know that she has done very important work for others. We have heard that things are more mixed up than they used to be when we were there. It is good to know that she is strong in the old ways. So many lose their way."

"Now unless someone here has something to say, I will say that it is good that she returns to your world, and we will wait to see her another time. I have said this and it is my words. Thank you for coming to see us, Kla-begatho."

He sat down and waited to see if anyone else wanted to speak.

The heart monitor hooked up to Star's body had actually stopped recording any heart beat for about a full minute. Ham had quickly called for a doctor, and by the time he arrived her heart had begun a normal rhythm with a stronger beat.

Ham could hardly believe his eyes. The doctor looked at the others and said, "It sure looks like she's past a crisis point. She seems to be coming back. This is a minor miracle. An injured heart almost never re-starts on its own after it stops."

Ham squeezed both her hands and whispered, "Thank you, Lord." Diane could hold back tears no longer. A few months ago she had no idea that she could get so attached to an Indian woman. Now her joy was released into a flood of tears.

She rushed to find a telephone and leave word for Jay and Angela.

Fawn softly sang a Navajo healing song which had been taught to her at her mother's knee.

The doctor cautioned them that the crisis might not be over yet. They would want to keep her for at least three days to make sure her injuries would heal and that no major organs were damaged.

Star had not yet become conscious, but she was now breathing with only a slight gurgle.

"From the fluids in her lungs," the doctor explained. "She may be awake some time tonight."

Diane told Ham and Fawn, "I'll stay here with Star if you two want to go back and help the others. This afternoon's program will be very important. I'll call if something changes here. I know all of you will be here as soon as you can tonight. Go on, Star will be okay now."

After they were gone the doctor cautioned Diane, "Look, if her organs are severely damaged or if chest bones are fractured or broken it could complicate things. Now that she's breathing somewhat normal we need to take x-rays before we can tell you if she's going to make it or not. Please don't get your hopes, or that of the others, up too high until we know more. Apparently she was hit by this person with the force of a small truck. It's incredible that she lived through it. So

ANGELA'S BATTLE

while we take her to the x-ray lab why don't you get some lunch. There's a nice cafeteria downstairs."

Diane suddenly realized how hungry she was. They had eaten an early breakfast and since then she hadn't had as much as a cup of coffee. She took coffee and a sandwich out onto a patio and sat under a large tree. This was the first chance she'd had all day to put her thoughts together, so she closed her eyes and leaned back in her chair and let her mind wander.

She couldn't get the sight of the goat man getting hit by the unseen force out of her mind. What if it had gotten by Fawn and reached Angela? She shuddered, and tried to get the thought out of her mind.

Chapter Seventeen

By 2:15 Sgt. Hayes had the crowd under control, and Aaron's body was removed to the City Morgue. He had given a brief report to Captain Morris and Sandra Cummings. This was the first time he had met Cummings, and he thought she was an efficient and business-like person. He liked her, but then so did Captain Morris, for different reasons.

Sandra Cummings summed it up for Capt. Morris. "Apparently there was only one of these creatures. The damage could have been worse considering there was a couple thousand people being scared out of their gourds. Without some kind of down-to-earth explanation from the Indian people of where this thing came from and why it was here, our reports are going to look kind of crazy. We'll need statements from this Storm Cloud guy and Angela Beaver, at least. We're lucky in a way. The television cameras got most of what happened on film and the evening news across the country will be showing the whole story. That'll make our reports much easier for the upstairs brass to accept."

Capt. Morris had hoped he could get her away from this place soon. The captain had a one-track mind and right now he was fantasizing about Sandra.

Sgt. Hayes spoiled the captains dream. "You know, I heard about this goat man story a long time ago when I was growing up on the Gila River Indian reservation. There's a lot of things that have happened that can maybe be explained, now that we know he's for real. Later, I intend to talk to this Fawn lady and learn more about it."

Sandra Cummings' eyes narrowed as she took a closer look at Sgt. Hayes.

"So you're an Indian. I've always been fascinated by the Indian culture. Would you mind taking me with you when you talk to this Indian lady? I can go with you even if it's after regular hours. How about it?"

Capt. Morris' face fell a foot-and-a-half.

With what he had been through today, this was the best news Sgt. Hayes had heard all day. "Sure, if you want to stick around, or maybe even go inside to hear the rest of their story it might help you to understand what happened. Then, if you want, after work we can have coffee and talk. How's that?"

Sandra quickly said, "That's fine with me. I'll go inside, then meet you after the meeting breaks up."

She liked this sergeant. He talked straight from the shoulder, not like Capt. Morris. Capt. Morris could hardly conceal his disappointment. But then, Sgt. Hayes didn't have a wife at home like he did, so he simply said, "I'll see you both back at the station later."

At 2:35 p.m. Jay announced the start of the afternoon program. He noticed that none of the media had left. They were all ordered back after they talked with their editors and were told to stay as long as the story lasted. There would be more than a few missed flights today.

Sgt. Hayes had arranged for an orderly seating of the crowd. He now had a hundred officers on hand, stationed inside and outside. Because of what happened, there were hundreds more people trying to get into the building. With Van Buren Street closed it was easier to keep the crowd away from the building's entrance. Everything was looking good.

Just before the session started, Sgt. Hayes took Sandra Cummings inside to meet Jay and Angela. Sandra told them, "I'm sorry I wasn't here earlier, but I hadn't realized how important this meeting was going to be. I'm extremely interested in our environment, and anything that I may be able to do to help the cause, please let me know."

Jay promised to do so. Sgt. Hayes put her in a front row seat, then left to do his duties.

Angela had a brief meeting with Jay and decided that the meeting should not continue. She told him, "We have publicity for our cause now and to go on too long may be counter-productive. Let's close the program with an explanation of our reasons. With Aaron dead and Star seriously hurt we should not risk any more lives. If more goat men appear many more people may be hurt. We'll have more opportunities to get our message out later. Then too, Amos wants us to be in Tucson tomorrow, so we need time to shut this meeting down and tend to Aaron and Star. Please tell the crowd that we'll announce later, where and when the next meeting will be held."

Jay made the announcement. There were some objections, but with urging from Sgt. Hayes' policemen the crowd begin to disburse. Outside, there was a huge crowd, attracted by the local news reports, clamoring for information of what had happened. Several individuals were surrounded by those willing to listen to their version of events. After listening to them the crowd took up the chant again. "Stop the tests. Stop the tests," they were shouting. The news media was having a field day. Since the news about the trouble this morning, additional news crews had descended on the meeting and many TV stations were providing live coverage.

Thousands of people had since come to hear more about a catastrophic disaster and especially about a weird creature who had terrorized the meeting. The streets were crowded for many blocks around the Desert Inn Motel/Hotel.

Born to a wealthy family near Dallas, Texas, Sandra Cummings was never far from the circles of high society, although she like to mingle with other people. At Southern Methodist University she associated mainly with the daughters and sons of cattle barons and oil tycoons, so before coming to the Phoenix Police Department had led a fairly sheltered life. This thing today was the most bizarre scene she had ever heard of. There was a "goat man creature" involved somehow.

The break in the meeting gave her a chance to get acquainted. Not one to be bashful she moved right in with her hand stuck out to Angela. Make friends with the woman first, her father had always cautioned her.

"Hi, my name is Sandra Cummings. I'm with the Phoenix Police Department, but this is not official business. I wasn't able to be here this morning, so I'm still in the dark about what happened. Sergeant Hayes has told me a little bit about what this meeting is all about, but I would like to learn more for my own personal knowledge."

Angela said, "I'm happy to meet you. I'm sorry we don't have much time now to talk, but later we'd be happy to sit down and tell you all about it. But let me introduce you to everybody. One of our ladies is missing for now. She's the one that they took to the hospital. Her name is Star."

Just then Ham came rushing in from the hospital. "Good news, friends. Star seems to be getting stronger. She's still unconscious, but she's breathing on her own now, and her heart is beating almost regular. The doctor said it's too soon to tell for sure how bad she's hurt. They're taking x-rays and checking her out real good. Diane is still with her."

They hugged, and assured each other, "She's gonna be okay."

Angela introduced Ham to Sandra. Ham asked innocently, "And what part of the country are you from? You don't look like the typical Arizonan."

When she said she had been raised in Dallas, Ham said "I did a surveying job for a 'Butch' Cummings a long time ago outside of Dallas. He was trying to find oil on his land."

Surprised at this, Sandra said, "That could have been my dad. Everybody called him Butch. He bought a thousand acres of jackrabbit land in 1935 and started drilling. After a dozen dry holes he finally hit a gusher, just in time for the war effort. He got rich, got married, and then got me. In that order, I'm happy to say."

Ham was really impressed by this coincidence. "When you talk to him next, please give him my regards. I remember him like it was yesterday. Nice fellow."

"Oh, I'm sorry to tell you that he died almost ten years ago," Sandra told him. "My mother died of loneliness, I think, five years ago, just before I graduated from SMU."

Ham said, "I'm sorry to hear that." Then, "Come on, you have to meet our eagle friend, Whistler."

Whistler was in a serious talk with Jay when Ham took Sandra over to meet him. Sandra had an eerie feeling as she walked towards them. This was definitely a different circle of people for her to associate with, but she didn't feel afraid or threatened as she did when she worked with other civilian groups. There was a certain calmness and friendly vibrations from each one of these people.

Ham moved to the eagle. "I want you to meet a very important person to all of us. This is Whistler. Whistler is our guardian, our protector, and good friend. Whistler, this is Sandra. She's interested in what we're doing and wants to know more. When you get time, you should talk more with Whistler. He is a fountain of knowledge."

Sandra couldn't help but be fascinated with Whistler. She tried hard to not stare at him, and she had an urge to reach out and touch the eagle to see if he was really, well, *real*. She felt a tingle as Whistler spoke to her. "I would be happy to talk with you later when there is time. I hope we can convince you that what you've heard and seen is very real."

Sandra responded, "I've got an open mind on the subject. We'll see. Your name is unusual. Just why do they call you Whistler?"

Whistler chuckled, "That's from my younger days when I would dive from a great height. The wind made a whistling sound if I held one wing in a certain way. There's more to the story, but it can wait. We have more important things to talk of now. If you're still around we can talk later when the others are at the hospital. They won't let me in, you know."

She felt a little strange, being asked to suddenly accept the fact this was a *real* eagle that could talk. A few days ago she would have labeled anyone as a nut if they had introduced her to a bird. She realized that these people thought of Whistler as an equal. She was trained as a psychologist with a minor in Criminology. There was nothing in the text books which came near explaining the oddity of this situation.

This was not a case of fantasizing. They *knew* he was an eagle, yet they *thought* of him in human terms. More than ever, she wanted to get close, be friends even, with these people.

Then looking at Angela she said, "I hope to see all of you later. Sergeant Hayes and I will make our own plans for tonight and maybe see all of you at the hospital, if you wouldn't mind us coming over."

"No. That would be alright, I guess," Angela said. "But remember, we can't promise you any of our time until we know more about Star. She's very dear to us."

Before they left, Sandra Cummings looked at Sgt. Hayes. "I don't want to go on calling you Sergeant forever. I only met you this morning, so tell me, what is your first name?"

He grinned, "Now don't laugh. It's Franklin. Franklin Delano Hayes. Please, just call me Frank. My mother, bless her soul, was a fan of President Franklin Roosevelt, so she named me for him."

Chapter Eighteen

It was Wednesday, July 19 in Washington, D.C. White House and congressional phone lines were being deluged with concerned calls from constituents across the nation. The time was six p.m. Newspaper headlines and television announcements about what happened in Phoenix had alarmed people and they were seeking assurance that there was no immediate danger.

There was no widespread pandemonium as yet, but as a precaution the president called a special meeting of his cabinet and called in the chairman of the Atomic Energy Commission to discuss the information being carried by network television stations.

When the entire group was assembled in the Oval Office the president told them, "I know all of you have seen the TV newscasts of what took place in Phoenix. We don't have much time, so I'll be brief. I want to hear right now if there's any truth in what is being said out there."

When he looked around the conference table, all the cabinet secretaries expressed no knowledge about the information from Phoenix.

The president looked directly at the one man who should have known if there were any serious problems with the H-bombs, the chairman of the AEC, Henry Straub.

"Do you have something to tell us, Henry?"

"No sir, Mr. President," Straub replied.

The president's eyes flashed angrily. "Dammit. Don't I have enough to worry about with Kruschev trying to put nuclear rockets on our doorstep in Cuba? You've got to help me out here."

"How about you, Mr. Secretary?" he asked Hugh Jennings, the Secretary of the Department of Interior. The U.S. Geological Service which kept tabs on earthquakes and other geological anomalies was a part of the Interior Department.

"Mr. President, as soon as we heard of these allegations I asked USGS to do a hurry up analysis of the situation. They're working on it now on a priority basis. It may be a day or two before they can come up with something definitive," Secretary Jennings said.

The president was impatient with them. As an ex-Navy officer he was used to things being done yesterday.

"What the hell do I have all of you on board for? Just so you can tell me you don't know what's going on? Do you mean to tell me those Indian people know more about geology and nuclear bombs than you smart guys do? Damn! And don't give me that two days stuff. I want a report by nine tonight. If we don't have an official statement by ten o'clock this evening the morning papers will have headlines that none of us will like."

He threw a stack of news photos from Phoenix on the table. "I don't like what I've heard, and that creature that attacked the Indian lady right there in front of everybody, I want to know what the hell it was. Was it for real? And why was it there?"

"I want to hear your responses," pointing a finger at George MacAdams, the Secretary of Defense, and Henry Straub, "to the charges that our H-bomb program is going to sink the entire West Coast, and I want it quick. Do you understand me? You'd better not let me down on this, do you hear me? If I'm forced to shut down our nuclear program I swear your jobs will be shut down too."

"Now hear this. I'm calling a press conference for ten o'clock tonight. All of you be back here by nine with some solid information so Harold can work up a believable statement."

Harold Buchanan was the White House spokesman to the media. He didn't have a clue on how to get started on this story. With all that had happened recently he was wishing that he had stayed in Boston.

"Harold, you get with these guys at nine. I want a statement ready by nine thirty with all the background information you can assemble. Now all of you get the hell out of here and get me some facts, quick. Go on now."

"Wait," the president hollered. "Do I have to do all your thinking for you? Get some people from the FBI and NSA out there quick to get a first-hand report for me from those Indians who started this whole damn mess. I want that report inside of twenty four hours. Get on it!"

Angela held a short meeting to make tentative plans. She included Abner Cranshaw, sergeants Hayes and Cummings, and Aaron's friend, Michael Roan Horse. Then she said, "Amos thinks that because of all that happened here we should be at the tribal meeting on Thursday night in Tucson, so that's where our small group will go from here. It seems that because the goat men have targeted us, the two parts of our battle have now become one. Also, Amos doesn't want anything said about the meetings in Tucson. He says the meeting place is secret, and he'll tell us where to go when we get there."

"We'll go to see Star, and tell her of our plans. Someone will have to stay with her and we can pick them up on our way back. We will hope to go to Aaron's funeral before we return to Flagstaff. Then I want to set up our headquarters in Las Vegas within the next few weeks. There we can gather environmental groups and concerned community organizations to stop the bomb explosions."

Abner Cranshaw, the "downwinder" from St. George was delighted at that announcement. He volunteered that he and his group would search out a good location for their headquarters.

Roan Horse told them that Aaron's funeral would be held in a few days. He would be buried in Prescott Valley, along the banks of Granite Creek.

Sandra said, "Frank and I will catch up with you sometime this evening at the hospital. Then we'll figure out some way to talk more with you. Don't worry about us. We'll just fit into your schedule. See you all later."

After saying goodbye to everyone, they went to see Star.

Star was still in the Intensive Care Unit in spite of her regaining consciousness. The x-rays had shown that there was no serious bone damage. The doctors were amazed. "Not one broken bone, not even a hairline fracture anywhere. This woman is Superwoman. Anyone else getting hit like she apparently did, they'd be in the morgue now."

The doctors agreed there was no apparent damage to her internal organs, but only time and close observation would prove that. Her major problem might be internal and external bruises and sore muscles. They wanted to move her to a room near a nurses station so the nurses could closely monitor her condition. She was in the process of being moved when Angela and the others arrived, expecting to see her still in ICU. In fact, Diane and Star were in an elevator going down to her new room while the others were going up.

When they arrived at the ICU nurses station they were told, "She's no longer here."

Everyone gasped. Angela said, "Oh, no!" They had wrongly assumed that Star had passed away.

The nurse quickly realized this and corrected them. "No, no. She's fine. She's recovered so well that they've moved her down to the third floor. Your friend Diane insisted that she be put into a private room instead of in a ward. So she's down there now."

By the time they made their way to the third floor Star was in a comfortable bed, and Diane had raised her to a more upright position. When the others came into the room Diane was combing Star's hair and telling her how well she looked. She was, in fact, glowing compared to how she had looked when they had last seen her. "It's about time you got here," Diane scolded.

Ham was the first to reach Star. He reached down and took her small hand in his. Star smiled broadly, and said softly, almost in a whisper, "Hem. I'm glad you came back."

In a choked voice Ham replied, "I told you I'd be back. You were sleeping then, but I know you heard me."

Diane had tears in her eyes as she said, "Angela, Jay. Let's go out and find the doctor so he can tell you about her condition." Ham and Star were left alone to say what they had to say.

In the hall, Diane was excitedly telling the others of the miracle that had brought Star back from sure death. "The doctors can hardly believe it. This is so great, and I'm so happy. It's good to see you again, Jay." She put her arms around him and hugged him tightly.

The doctor rounded the corner and came to them. "Well, folks. Nothing but good news. This is nothing like any of us had expected. Somehow she came through that experience without any apparent serious physical damage, and we think she's going to be fine in a day or two. We'd like to keep her here for awhile, just to make sure we didn't miss anything."

Angela said, "I know you'll be good to her. Someone will stay with her until we get back on Saturday. We have to leave town until then. Thanks for everything."

"Fine, my name is Doctor Jim Sanders. Ask for me if you want to call for an update. I'll expect to see you on Saturday. By then we should know if there are any complications."

They went back to see Star. Angela told Ham and Star what the doctor had said.

"I'll stay here with her, of course," Ham said. "There's no need for me to go with you to Tucson. Besides, I really want to stay here," and he quickly glanced at Star.

Try as she might, Star couldn't erase the smile off her face. She wanted to, but it seemed to be stuck there. *There is serious business to talk about. Be serious,* she told herself. But it was still there. She wondered, *Would Kla-begatho be ashamed of me?*

"Whistler sends his love," Jay said. "He wants to see you, but he knew he couldn't come in, so he's talking with the Indian security men before they begin their trip home with...," he suddenly realized that Star still hadn't been told about Aaron's death.

Angela was looking at him trying to tell him, "This is not the time. It will be much better if Fawn tells her."

He quickly finished his sentence with, "Well anyway, they're having a good time together before they all go home." Angela breathed a sigh of relief.

They had been with Star an hour when Sandra and Frank poked their heads in the door.

"Anybody home?" Sandra asked.

Frank immediately went to Star's side and squeezed her hand. "I'm sure glad you're feeling all right. We talked to the nurse and she told us about how well you were doing. We won't stay too long. We just wanted to make sure you were okay, and to bring you some flowers to brighten up the place." The nurse had placed the bouquet in a vase, and now she placed it on the small table next to Star's bed.

He introduced Sandra. "Star, I want you to meet Sandra Cummings. She's also with the police department. Sandra, this is Star, the lady who was so brave in standing up to that creature before it got inside the building."

Sandra went to shake Star's hand. She was surprised to see how small and soft her hand was. Frank said quietly to Angela. "We're going to wait out in the hall for you guys. When you get ready to leave we'll go back to the motel with you. We need to talk with you before you all leave town. I'm sorry to make it official, but with one man dead, and Star being attacked, there are questions that need to be answered."

"All right," Angela said. "We won't be too long. The doctor asked us to let Star get some rest. Two of us are going to stay a little longer and tell her the bad news. Then we'll be with you."

Ham told Star he would be back in the morning, then he left with Jay and Diane.

Fawn went to one side of the bed and Angela stood on the other side. From the serious look on their faces Star knew she was going to hear some bad news. As soon as the door closed, she looked up at Fawn. "Tell me, what is it?"

Fawn spoke to her in the Navajo language and spared none of the details of what had happened. She described how the power of Kla-begatho had destroyed the goat man creature. When she finished telling the story, Star asked to be alone with

ANGELA'S BATTLE

Fawn.

Angela said, "Of course. Before I go I have to tell you that the rest of us will be going to Tucson tomorrow to meet with Amos and the tribal leaders. We'll be back on Saturday to get you. We'll go to Aaron's funeral, then back to Flagstaff. Ham will stay with you here. Goodbye until then."

When they were alone, Fawn and Star sang their own song of sorrow for Aaron. When they had finished the song Fawn quietly left the room. There was nothing more to be said. Star lay still for a long time deep in her own thoughts.

She decided that she would get healed quickly, then she would dedicate the rest of her life to protecting Earth and the lives of the Creators children. She could do no less, she knew. The Creator had allowed her to come back to this life because she still had work to do. She made up her mind that she would be ready to leave on Saturday.

After leaving the hospital everyone gathered at a nearby coffee shop to answer the two sergeants questions for their report. Angela told them about their plans to go to Tucson in the morning.

"We'll be coming back on Saturday to pick up Star and Ham. Ham will stay here to keep Star company. Then we'll drive up to Prescott for Aaron's funeral. If you want to ask us more about what we're doing, do it tonight, but it's a long story and will take more than an hour to cover it all. If you don't know the background, some of the answers to your questions may not make much sense."

Diane chimed in, "It's true. It will take a long time before the whole story will make sense to you. From the time Jay and I first spoke to Angela over the telephone it was several weeks before I realized the full extent of what we were trying to do."

Sandra said, "I've got an idea. What if Frank and I take a couple of days off and go with you folks to Tucson. It will give us a lot of time to get acquainted and hear your story. Think that'll work, Frank? If you want to do that, I can fix the time off with Captain Morris."

Frank said, "That sounds good to me. What do you say, Angela. Would that be okay with you? When we get to Tucson you guys can take care of your business, and we'll wait for you at a motel. Besides, I want to learn more about your environmental work. I'm interested in helping in any way I can."

Sandra volunteered, "I can get a big station wagon that will carry all of us, and we can leave the pickup truck here for Ham so he can go back and forth to the hospital.

Angela was slow to respond. "Well, I don't know. We don't want to impose on you people, besides we hardly know you yet."

Sandra quickly jumped on the remark. "That's exactly the point. We both want to know more about your work, and this would be a great chance to learn straight from the horse's mouth, in a manner of speaking. We'll pay for the rental car and all of our own expenses. Please say yes. Who knows, I just might want to join your group."

Angela was almost ready to say "Yes," but she had to ask the others first. "Jay, you're the mastermind of this operation. What do you think?"

"I say yes. In this tough project we need all the help we can get and willing volunteers to help us. Well, we need to take advantage of these people." Jay turned. What do you say, "Diane?"

"I agree," Diane said. "We need to involve as many people as possible beginning now. There are almost no secrets left to hide, except for Amos' Thursday meeting, but I'm sure after that's over there will be no secrets at all. The world will need to hear every bit of information that we can give them. I vote yes." Angela turned to Fawn.

Fawn turned and offered a handshake to Frank and Sandra. "All right," she said. She had wanted to feel the touch of their hands and to note how they shook her hand. Their warm yet firm handshake was genuinely friendly. She smiled and approved. Angela saw and smiled too. "Ham," what do you say?" she asked.

"I think you already know my answer," Ham said. "When I first heard your story I knew less about what's happening than they do now. This project has become so important that I couldn't leave without feeling guilty, and besides I think all of you know how fond I am of Star. I need to be around to help her. If others want to get involved more power to them and to us."

"Well then. It seems to be settled. As soon as I get back to the motel I'll tell Whistler and I'm sure he'll agree too. Now, what time shall we meet tomorrow?"

Sandra's mind had already worked out a schedule. "Frank and I will meet with Captain Morris at eight in the morning. By ten o'clock we'll have the station wagon rented and be on our way to pick you up. Then we're off to see the world. Is that okay with everybody?"

Jay said, "Let's do it."

By the time they got back to the motel the Indian men had gone to bed. They had an early morning meeting with the Coroners Office to complete the paperwork so that Aaron's body could be released to them. Then they would travel in a caravan to Aaron's family home in Prescott Valley.

Whistler was sitting on the rooftop waiting for them to return. He flew down to the truck in the parking lot. He was happy to hear about Star's apparent recovery, but then he brought them back to reality.

"I'm going to stay outside tonight to keep a watch just in case another goat man is around. Two of the Indian men are going to stay with me, then they'll leave with the others early in the morning. You know, those men are great. They would do anything for you, Angela. I'm sure sorry I didn't get to know Aaron, but I'll meet him one day."

Fawn said, "Yes. We will see him again. It will be good."

"Oh, one more thing," Whistler said. "I brought one of the scouts here from Tucson. Ho-go-ton is up on the roof. You met him in the canyon, Angela. Say hello, everyone."

They all looked up at the rooftop and waved at him. Ho-go-ton flapped one wing at them.

"We'll both fly overhead on your drive to Tucson. One ahead of you and one behind."

Two husky Indian men came out of the shadows to greet them. They shook hands all around then went back to resume their all night watch.

The next morning, they were up early. Angela had suggested that they have breakfast with the Indian men before they left. The men were pleased to share a table with these leaders. After an hour they left to get Aaron's body. This time handshakes seemed not enough. The two days of sharing exceptional experiences had bonded them together forever. It was especially touching for two persons.

Ham had always had an affinity for Indian people, and now he felt like one of them. He understood their personal relation with the Earth and everything on it. He loved this land as they did. "I've walked every mountain, every valley, and desert of this region. Most Indians can't say that. I've seen their most remote and hidden ceremonial and burial grounds and caves and I've always respected their secrets. Yes," he had decided, "I'm going to be one of them whether they like it or not. The only difference between me and the Indians is the color of our skin."

Diane couldn't quite understand her own feelings yet. She was raised almost 3,000 miles to the East among people who never gave a thought about the natives of this country, and worse, didn't care. Her history books had told her that Indians were a savage people, yet she had found them to be deeply emotional and sincere in their beliefs and caring for others. She knew now that if anyone was savage, it would be those non-Indians who would stop at nothing to gain a profit from the resources of Mother Earth.

Her outlook on everything she had known and had believed in was slowly changing. She had never before felt anything like her feelings for Jay Storm Cloud, although she hadn't told him this yet. When she hugged these men she couldn't stop the tears from flowing. She suddenly felt as if she had made some sort of commitment to these Indian people.

Frank Hayes and Sandra Cummings soon arrived in a shiny, new nine-passenger station wagon. They tied their bags and suitcases in the rack on top, said goodbye to Ham, and they were on their way. Whistler and Ho-go-ton were circling high overhead.

Chapter Nineteen

It would be a two-and-a-half hour drive to Tucson. The motel manager had called to make room reservations for them at one of their motels which was located near the Papago reservation. Amos would contact them there.

Diane had volunteered to drive the car so that the others could begin the education of Sandra and Frank. From time to time she looked into the rear view mirror and saw looks of astonishment and disbelief on Sandra's face. She knew why.

I wonder if I had that same stupid look on my face when I first heard this story. I'll bet I did. She couldn't help but smile at Sandra's wide-eyed face.

Being a policeman, Frank had many questions, and would stop them to make sure he understood what they were saying. Sandra didn't want to waste time asking questions now. She just wanted "more facts, please." She knew her father would have loved to be here. This was the kind of adventure he would have jumped into head first.

Fawn had just told them of her spiritual work with Kla-begatho when Whistler circled in front of them and they slowed to a stop.

"The spot where your friend was killed is just ahead. Do you want to see it?" he asked Jay.

Jay turned to Angela. "If you don't mind, I would like to see it. Sometimes in violent deaths a spirit may be unable to leave. A prayer may be able to help them."

Fawn agreed.

"Yes, it will be good," said Angela. "They were coming to help us and they were the first to die. We need to stop."

A few minutes later they turned off the highway towards the site where Fuzzy Williams and the two others were killed. When they saw the charred, burned-out car, they fell silent. They stood beside the car each deep in their own thoughts.

After a few minutes of meditation, Fawn told the others, "The younger man who was in the back seat is still here. He is lost and confused. Your friend and his wife went regularly to a church and so were able to move on. The young man is alone and afraid. We can try to release him." She looked skyward and saw the two eagles circling lazily against the bright blue sky.

Fawn asked Jay to start a small fire, using the dry twigs from nearby sage brush, while she got some items out of her suitcase. When she returned, the fire was burning, and she broke off a few branches from a green bush and put the branches on the fire, extinguishing the flames but allowing the hot embers to create a cloud of pungent smoke. While the others watched, Fawn reached into her bag of herbs and "medicine" and sprinkled something on the embers which flashed a blue light. She did this four times while singing an ancient song. Kla-begatho had taught her this song and ritual because, "You will someday have to use it."

She was still sprinkling the embers and singing, when to the astonishment of the others, a breeze came up which slowly increased in intensity. The breeze wafted over the burnt car, then moved onto the hot desert sand in the form of a whirlwind, commonly called a *dust devil*. The whirlwind circled them four times, then slowly moved off to the South and disappeared over a dune.

Fawn said not a word, then knelt and with her hands she picked up sand and covered the small fire with it. After a few more words in the ancient language, she arose and dusted off her skirt. "*A-hawt. Va-thuts e-yemsh*," she said. "It's good. He's gone."

After seeing this strange ritual, no one could find the proper words to ask what it was they had witnessed. Sometimes a soul may not be prepared to leave the body to go to another plane. This was common when death would strike without warning and the soul did not have spiritual education or preparation. The soul, suddenly forced out of its earthly body would not know where to go and in its confusion would remain near the place of release. Fawn had reassured it that it could now go on to another place and she had provided directions of how to get there.

Jay thought of how it must have been for Fuzzy, his wife and the young reporter. Seeing this evidence of the brutality that the goat men were capable of it worried him that they were all just as likely to be killed in this way. After what had happened yesterday, it struck him that this wasn't just "us against the nuclear industry." It was much more than that and he had been too busy to see the total picture. This was a deadly game involving things that he didn't fully understand.

Everyone else was quietly mulling over their own thoughts of what they had seen. Diane was once again behind the wheel, seemingly concentrating on the road ahead. Frank Hayes was remembering old stories of *goat man*, once used to frighten him into being "a good boy."

Sandra was quietly excited. She had no idea of what this was all about, but she was determined to know the full story. She wanted to be a part of it. She decided that before they got back to Phoenix she would learn all she could, then offer her help to Angela. She hadn't been told, but her intuition said that Angela was the driving force behind this effort.

She nudged Frank with her elbow. "What say we explore the Old Town of Tucson this evening, just you and me? We'll have dinner then walk around Old Town as if we were eastern tourists. We should have a good time while we can. I have a hunch that things may change soon. Okay?"

"That's a good idea. While the others go to take care of their business with this guy Amos, we can talk about other things. It's a date."

Jay said, "Sandra, I hope you don't get the idea that we're all crazy. Really, we're offering a compliment to you. We've only known you for a day and here we are telling you the wildest kinds of stories you've ever heard and trusting you'll believe us."

Sandra laughed a soft tinkling laugh that made Frank's heart flip over. He'd already taken serious note of her gray eyes. She said, "The only place I have ever heard things like this is when I was a kid, my father used to take me to his favorite Frankenstein monster horror movies. I was scared then, but now I know the difference between movies and reality."

Angela answered, "Lord, I hope so."

Before they reached their motel, Angela stuck her head out the window to check on Whistler. The two eagles were now flying one on each side of the car at a good height in order to see more. To acknowledge Angela the two eagles swooped low, criss-crossing in front of the car, and quickly resumed their positions. Everything was looking good.

They soon reached the Tucson Desert Inn and a short distance away they could see the spires of old San Xavier del Bac Mission. Turning into the parking lot they saw many cars and vans belonging to newspaper and television companies.

Sandra spoke up. "If a newcomer can say something, I'd like to help here. While you people go on up to your rooms and get freshened up for the press conference, let me handle the press guys. Before I graduated from college I was doing public affairs work for my daddy. I'll get them settled down until you're ready to see them."

Sandra explained, "My daddy was rich and famous. Famous in Texas anyway. He couldn't go anywhere without somebody trying to follow him, trying to pry into his private life. In my junior year he talked to me about this, and I was able to turn it into a class project. It was called, 'How To Be Famous And Still Have A Private

Life.' You all have a similar problem."

"My education cost Daddy a lot of money and I just know he'd be pretty angry with me if I didn't put it to good use. I'm offering my help to you, no charge." She smiled disarmingly. Her gray eyes twinkled in a most charming way.

She was trying to slow them down a bit, and from the start it seemed to work. They seemed to relax, happy to just listen instead of think. *Psychology 101*, she thought. She looked at their faces and thought she saw frowns disappear, and some relief.

Jay smiled and said, "We're all ears. Go ahead."

She explained that she would handle the reporters until everyone had a chance to freshen up and have something to eat. Frank would get everybody checked into their rooms and order lunch. The press conference would begin in an hour. Everyone agreed.

When they stopped in front of the motel the reporters recognized Angela and started towards her. Sandra immediately took over. She had always known that she could influence people and win friends by being a friendly friend.

"Okay, fellas. My name is Sandra, and I'm handling the press duties today. Don't expect answers to your questions just yet. They're tired, and they need something to eat. So in just one hour from now we'll have a press conference inside, then they're all yours for as long as you want."

She knew the media was waiting to meet Whistler. They'd heard of the talking eagle and they wanted to meet him. She walked to the back door of the station wagon and everyone followed her. She opened the door and Whistler stepped. The media crowded around him.

"This is Whistler, the eagle you've all heard about. He's a very important part of the story. You can talk with him for 15 minutes, then he's got to leave."

She whispered to him, "Frank will come get you in a few minutes." She stroked his head twice then she ducked out of the way and went inside to join Frank. The others were already in their rooms.

As in Phoenix, the manager was delighted to have them as guests, even for overnight. Sandra arranged for a side room for the press conference, then she told the manager to set up a buffet of lunch meats and cold drinks for the press in the room where they would meet with them. She knew that reporters seldom got to eat while covering a story. This would soften their mood, making for friendlier coverage. She also arranged for soup and sandwiches to be brought to Angela's extra room.

"Good work, Frank," she said. "One last thing, go bring Whistler up here, and tell the press that there's food for them in the conference room. We'll go freshen up then we'll talk with the others while we have some lunch."

In exactly twelve minutes Sandra knocked on Frank's door. "Let's go, hot shot cop. We've got things to do."

As they walked down the hall, she put one arm around Frank's shoulder and told him, "You know, I haven't been this enthused in a long, long time. Tonight after dinner I'd like to talk to you about something, but it can wait for now." Frank was curious and wanted to talk about *it*, now, whatever *it* was, but she smiled her sweetest smile at him and he melted.

"It'll wait," she said.

Soon they were all seated and happily having their lunch. After a few minutes Jay looked questioningly at Angela. "Go ahead," Angela said.

He began, "Okay, while we eat I'll run over a few things, then Angela can clue us in on what's happening tonight. First, I'll mention our visit to Fuzzy Williams' death car. It won't hurt to give the public something, or somebody, to hate. Diane, lay it on heavy when you talk about the Nuclear Institute or the Atomic Energy Commission. People have to know who's to blame for these problems. The reason is that we've only got maybe six weeks to build a nationwide base of opposition to nuclear power."

After their agenda was set, Angela said, "Whistler, we should contact Amos before the press conference starts, then we'll know for sure where we're going."

Angela and Whistler went into the other room and closed the door. Amos was already there and had been waiting for them.

Amos said, "The Council is going to move the site of tonight's meeting because Whirl Wind's scouts have reported what they say are many goat men coming this way from the South. If there is trouble we don't want to place anyone in this small village in danger. The Council is pleased with your team, including the newcomers, Sandra and Frank. Teek-awis thinks the whole team should be at the meeting. When you are ready to leave, Whirl Wind will lead you to the meeting site."

"The Devil himself has said he will come to this meeting. We think we have a way to convince him to withdraw his goat men. So tonight, the Devil himself will face the Indian people, the holy men, and the Council of Eagles. It will be a great

ANGELA'S BATTLE

thing to see. It should be an exciting time. Tell the others that I'll talk with them after your press conference."

When they went into the outer room everyone was listening to Frank as he told his story of growing up on what was now called the Gila River reservation. Jay and Frank found they had something in common.

Angela looked at her watch. "Let's go do the press conference, then we'll come right back here. Our friend Amos will talk with us."

They trooped to the room where the press conference would be held. The media people were relaxed and in a good mood. Frank had spoken to the manager earlier and arranged for him to ask for police protection. Now a dozen officers were moving in and out of the building in pairs, eyes open for anything out of the ordinary. Frank joined Sheriff Jim Stafford, and quickly briefed him on what his men should be looking for, then he stationed himself near Angela's group. Needless to say, Sheriff Stafford was a little hesitant, but Frank reminded him of what had happened in Phoenix.

It was a little after three p.m. when the press conference ended. Today was a big difference in how this group of media persons reacted to their remarks. Yesterday there had been open disbelief, and today there was not a sign of it. So much had happened, and there were eye witness accounts. Now they recorded every word without comment or question.

There was a short period of reporter's questions and interviews, then it was over. Angela was in a hurry to see Amos, so she motioned to Whistler and they left the room. Sandra thanked everyone for coming and she promised another press conference in the near future. Then they went up to Angela's room to meet Amos.

Amos was seated on a straight-backed chair. When he saw them he stood and hugged Angela, then put his arm around Whistler's broad back.

"Sit down, Amos," Angela said. "It's so good to see you. I'll get us some coffee then we can hear what you have to say." She called room service and ordered several pots of coffee sent up. She had no idea of how long their talk with Amos would go on, but she wanted to be prepared.

She began by introducing Frank and asked him tell a little of his background. When this was done to Frank's satisfaction, she said, "Amos, this is Sandra Cummings. Like Frank, she works for the Phoenix Police Department. She helped a lot at our meeting and with today's press conference. Sandra, meet Amos Turkey. Amos is very important to the work we're doing. He's a liaison between the Indian people and the Council of Eagles."

Sandra put her hand out towards Amos. He took it and held it gently. Her gray eyes didn't waiver or shift as he looked deep into her eyes with a twinkle in his own. He liked her immediately. Even before he took her hand he sensed the warm vibrations emanating from her, and he also sensed a spirit of honesty about her which was unusual in many of the white women he had met over the years. He knew his scraggly appearance did not encourage warmth or friendliness from others if they had negative feelings of any kind.

Sandra looked at Amos, and saw not a scraggly old Indian man with a wrinkled brown face and long hair, but instead, she saw an interesting and likable person whose white hair and lined face spoke of his life's experiences. His eyes revealed compassion and care for others. She had once read about such a man and had hoped to one day meet him. She thought, *If this is not him, surely he's someone like him.*

She said, "It seems like I've already met you somewhere before, maybe it's because everyone here speaks so highly of you. I'm very pleased to meet you and I look forward to talking more with you, but I know this is not the time. It's so good to see you. I hope we can all be friends and work together." There was no need to say more. They *were* friends.

They made small talk for a minute, then Amos turned serious.

"I want to talk about the meeting tonight," he said. "It will be a very dangerous time for all of us, and before we ask the newcomers, Sandra and Frank, to join us they must know what they're up against."

"The Council met today with all of the holy men and tribal leaders. They discussed our situation thoroughly, and they heard reports that goat men have been seen recently in every corner of the country. Men, women, and even children are being coerced into committing unspeakable acts on each other, yet government officials are not alarmed. They call these things merely *criminal acts* and do not see them as unnatural acts. Just this morning three boys, only twelve years old, turned on a younger boy and beat him to death, then burned his body. There have been many other similar happenings among adults as well as the young. People who have known each other for years are killing each other. These reports mean we have no time to lose."

"First, Teek-awis and his Council have been meeting for two days at a remote spot in the desert West of the Mission. The scouts in northern Arizona, Utah, western New Mexico, and below the Mexican border have already reported that strange men are heading this way across the deserts, and they have apparently been called to disrupt our meeting."

"There are leaders from over three hundred tribes who are with Teek-awis now, in addition to the seven shamans and the entire Council of Eagles. The moon will rise at eight-twenty-five tonight, and the shamans will begin their strategy then. Sandra, Frank, you have not yet committed yourselves to our cause, but you're here for a reason that only you know and there is so little time. You have to decide if you want to get involved in our fight against the Devil and his demons.

"Jay and Diane, you have been with us since the beginning, but you also must make a choice. Understand, once you get to the meeting place there will be no turning back. We have to arrive at the meeting place before the sun sets. Ho-go-ton, Whirl Wind, and their scout patrols will provide protection for us while we travel to the meeting place. Once there we'll be well protected by the shamans, but on the road our well-being is in the hands of the eagles. Does anyone *not* want to go?"

Jay leaned over and whispered to Diane, "We're going, right?" Diane said nothing, but shook her head in agreement. "We're in," Jay told Amos. Frank looked at Sandra and saw the excitement in her eyes. He knew her answer without hearing it. As for himself, Frank knew that he had to be there. His ancestors had once faced this same danger and lost their lives. He realized he wanted revenge. "Sandra and I are going with you," he said firmly. "You're not going to leave us behind. If we're fighting the Devil, we want to be there."

"Good then, it's settled," Amos said. "I'll be traveling with you. We should leave within an hour. The road is dusty and rough in many spots so we have to allow some extra time to get through."

Sandra said, "We'll be better off in a large pickup truck, so Frank and I will go rent one and we'll be back as quick as we can. Jay, while we're gone would you see about getting water bags to take with us, and get some sandwiches. We'll eat on the road. Flashlights would be good to have, too." Whistler told Amos that he and Ho-go-ton would now go to confer with Whirl Wind to have scouts stationed and patrolling along their route.

"I'll then go on to see my father and to prepare for tonight's security. Ho-go-ton will return here with a group of scouts to accompany you on the trip to the meeting place. This will be a very important night. Good luck to us all." Soon Whistler and Ho-go-ton were flying swiftly to the west.

Chapter Twenty

Luck seemed to be with them. When Frank and Sandra got down to the motel lobby there was a sheriff's vehicle parked in the driveway. It had all they would need. Heavy duty tires, water bags hanging on the front hood, plenty of room for three in the front, and a sturdy shell on the truck bed. Even the truck bed was comfortable, with bench seats lining both sides. Importantly, it had a radio in case they needed outside help.

Frank said, "I'm going to find this guy and see if we can borrow the truck."

He found them seated at a corner table in the motel restaurant. "Sheriff, I need your help real bad. I want to borrow your deputies truck until tomorrow for a very important reason."

The deputy sipped his coffee while looking sideways at the Sheriff.

Sheriff Stafford said, "Frank, you know as well as I do that it's against the rules to let anyone use our vehicles. Liability, insurance and all, you know. I just couldn't do it. If something happened to the truck would Phoenix P.D. pay for it? I don't think so."

Frank drew up a chair. Sandra stood behind him.

"Sheriff, this may be the most important thing you will ever do to help people in your county. I don't have time to give you a long song and dance about why we need the truck. I'll just give you a short true story. First of all, I hope you saw the TV pictures of yesterday's meeting in Phoenix when that ugly creature showed up."

The Sheriff nodded his head, "Saw it."

"Well, tonight there's a big meeting of powerful Indian people out in the desert. Several hundred Indians and their holy men are going to try to destroy those goat men and their boss tonight, right here in your jurisdiction. Our people here are important to that effort. We need to be able to drive straight through the desert hills to the meeting spot, and a truck like yours is the only way we'll get through. Our rented station wagon would never make it. I hate to use this cliché, but *the future of mankind* depends on what happens tonight. Will you do it?"

The Sheriff knew he was in a tough spot. For a second he wished he had stayed home, but rules were rules.

"I know this is a serious matter," he said, "and after seeing what happened in Phoenix I want to help as much as I can, but I've got a responsibility to the people of this county. If there's going to be trouble you should tell me and I'll let my deputies handle it. No. I can't let anyone use our official vehicles for personal business."

Sandra had been listening to the discussion. She introduced herself to the Sheriff and showed him her badge.

"I'm Sandra Cummings, also with the Phoenix P.D. It's a fact, this is not for personal business, and we need your vehicle real bad. You do have a responsibility to the people of this county and to the state. Where we're going tonight there's going to be more of those creatures like the one that killed Fuzzy Williams and the others. We need to get there and your truck is our only way to get there safely."

She continued, "Let's see if we can handle it this way. Let your deputy here, if he's willing, drive us to tonight's meeting, and he can stand by in case of trouble. But he can't get involved in what happens unless Frank or I ask him to do it. That way your interests are served and you help the people of the state and county at the same time. If the deputy decides he needs help, he can use his radio to call you. How about it? Do this for us."

The Sheriff quickly glanced up at her face. She was looking directly into his eyes, and he had to say, "Yes." The deputy would be doing his duty, and, his own butt was covered.

Sheriff Stafford smiled back at her. "You can have the deputy and his truck, but he's got to be back tomorrow evening by five o'clock or we'll come looking for him."

"Sam," he said, turning to the deputy, "You be sure and contact me if you need help. Call me when you get there, then call in once every four hours. Got it?" Sam had a mouthful of coffee, so he just grunted, "Uh huh."

Turning to Frank, he said, "The truck and Sam are all yours until tomorrow evening. Take good care of both of them."

"Thanks, Sheriff," Frank said. "This means a lot to us."

Sandra went to tell Angela the good news while Frank filled the two in on what might happen tonight. When he was through, Sam said "Wow, I'm sure glad the wife and I went to church last Sunday. I might need all the spiritual help I can get. Wow." Then he went to call his wife to tell her he would be working all night and tomorrow, but "not to worry."

When Sam was gone, Sheriff Stafford told Frank, "Sam is a good man. A church-going family man. He and his wife, Eunice, have two kids, the cutest little girls you'll ever see. He needs the overtime, but he doesn't need to be put in unnecessary danger, if you know what I mean. Bring him back in good shape."

The Sheriff put on his white Stetson hat, started to leave, then hesitated. "You owe me one, Frank. *Hasta la vista*."

Angela took time to call Ham to tell him what was happening tonight. She would let him decide how much to tell Star. Then she hung up quickly so that Ham wouldn't ask too many questions.

A half-hour later, Sam was wheeling the truck towards San Xavier Mission. In front were Sam, Amos, and Angela. Frank had noticed that in addition to his sidearm, Sam had a ten-gauge shotgun and a 30-30 rifle in a locked rack. He mentioned this to Sandra. "Good firepower in case we need it," she said. Frank wore a .38 revolver in a shoulder holster, and Sandra had a small pistol in her bag.

In the rear of the truck, Fawn, Sandra, Frank, Jay, and Diane got as comfortable as possible and prepared for a hot, dusty, and bumpy ride. Everyone was in good spirits, and satisfied that they were doing the right thing.

At Amos' direction, the deputy drove into the small village near the Mission, then headed towards a one-lane dirt road which led into the barren desert hills. When they had gone less than a mile Amos asked Sam to stop for a minute. Amos got out and waved to Ho-go-ton who had been waiting for a station wagon to appear and wasn't sure of who was in this truck.

Ho-go-ton swooped down to where Amos stood. He was told of why they were using this truck, then he was introduced to Sam, the deputy. Sam was almost overcome with wonder and awe at being introduced to this talking eagle. What a story he would have to tell his kids when he got back.

Ho-go-ton motioned upward where Sam and Amos saw a group of eagles, twenty in all, who were slowly circling, waiting for their leader. "They'll keep watch for you on this trip," he told them. Sam was excited. He suspected he was going to be part of something important.

When the truck got under way again the group of eagles fanned out in all directions and provided an escort while Ho-go-ton flew directly over the truck, ready to act in case of a threat.

Sam said, "You know, this story would make a good movie."

Amos and Angela looked at each other and smiled. Amos looked at Sam. "I hope it has a good ending," he said.

Sunset was still an hour-and-a-half away and they had covered only about five miles when Ho-go-ton flew down alongside the truck and told Sam, "If we can, we need to speed up a little. The scouts to the South report ten men are running across the desert towards us from Sonora. They're about twenty miles away, but they're moving fast." Then he was gone to send two scouts in that direction.

Sam increased his speed to forty miles an hour. It made for a bumpier ride as the truck slid on loose sand then straightened out when the big tires hit more solid ground.

Amos then told Sam and Angela exactly where they were going. "There's a large natural amphitheatre at the northern foot of Mount Devine. It is about forty miles from the Mission village, so we have a ways to go yet. Maybe thirty miles. Mount Devine is the highest mountain in what is called the Comobabi Range. It's almost five thousand feet high so we should be able to see it in another fifteen or twenty miles. We'll have to turn off to the North side of the mountain, then we'll be able to see all the trucks of the Indians who have gathered there. Once there, we'll have to actually climb down into the amphitheatre where the shamans and the Council of Eagles are gathered."

"Sam, you will be one of the few white people to ever see such a gathering, but we've got to get there first, so don't be afraid to step on the gas. The road bumps are better than being caught out in the open by twenty of those goat men."

Sam looked at Amos with a look of concern on his face and his foot pressed further down on the accelerator. He laughed and said, "My momma didn't raise no dummy."

Ho-go-ton looked down, and was pleased when he saw the plume of dust increase with the speed.

Twenty miles farther on, Ho-go-ton reported that the goat men running through the desert had turned to the northwest and were heading towards Mount Devine, so there was no further doubt about who they were. They were headed towards the meeting place.

A few miles further brought them to a obscure spot in the road where an almost invisible trail ran towards the North side of the mountain which they could now see in the distance. When they were less than five miles from the mountain, Whistler flew down in front of the truck to welcome them. While Whirl Wind's scouts patrolled the whole mountain, Whistler guided them to the meeting place. There was still a half-hour left before sunset. Sam had made good time

Frank requested that Sam be allowed to park the truck on the side of a small hill from which the amphitheatre would be visible to him. Amos agreed, but said "It may be dangerous for him to be out here all alone. He may be safer with us. We don't know if his bullets can hurt the goat men and we don't want to find out too late that they have no effect. Invite him to come with us, but he's got to make his own decision just as the rest of us have."

When Frank relayed this information to Sam, he elected to stay with his truck and his weapons. "I'll stay here until I'm sure there's no real danger to any of us. I'll come down to you then. In the meantime, I have to call Sheriff Stafford and tell him we got here okay. You guys go ahead without me and I'll see you later."

When Frank was gone Sam checked his weapons and made sure they were loaded, "Just in case," he said. Sam didn't know it, but Ho-go-ton had placed one of his scouts on top of the truck. If a goat man came his way, Sam would need all the help he could get.

Amos and the others walked downhill to the floor of a huge depression which, as Amos had said, formed a natural amphitheatre for the site of tonight's meeting. Some of the Indian men had already built a fire in the center of the depression which would give light and warmth against the cool desert night. The sun was just beginning to dip below the western horizon, and the moon was expected to rise in another half-hour, but its light wouldn't reach them for an hour after that.

The first brown bats were emerging from their mountain hiding places, and their squeaks could be heard all around them as they chased insects attracted by the roaring bonfire. Amos asked Teek-awis if he would give the newcomers a briefing on what was going to happen tonight. Teek-awis stood in front of them as the group sat on the warm ground or on rocks. Milford Haynes, Adam Feather, and Ned Hatanami had been asked to join them.

After warm greetings and new introductions, Teek-awis began, "After two days of talks the Council, the shamans, and the tribal leaders have agreed on a plan of action and it is this. If we wait for the goat men to come to us one at a time or several at a time, it would take many months to send them all back to Hell. In the meantime many of our people would die. Many others throughout the country, Indians as well as whites, would yield to temptation and thereby give their souls up to the Devil. This way would be too time consuming and too costly. Therefore the group decided to go straight to their leader, the Devil himself."

He continued, "The shamans challenged the Devil to appear here tonight and discuss the merits of a plan, a compromise, in which Satan will hopefully agree to wait for the outcome of Angela's efforts to stop the nuclear explosions. It is no longer just this country that is engaged in "nuclear madness" as you have described it, Jay. The madness has infected almost every country in the world and they're now in a race to develop nuclear weapons for use against each other. If this group fails to convince this country to stop its tests we know what will happen. The Creator showed this to Amos for a good reason."

"The research and spiritual study by the shamans has provided us with a means to destroy these demons as you saw in Phoenix. That *means* must remain a secret for now. Only a chosen few know of it."

"So the stakes are high for us as well as for the Devil. If we fail, there will be millions of souls available for his underground kingdom. If we succeed, the world will be spared from not only a fiery nuclear holocaust, but the western part of this country, Indian Country, will not be drowned in the waters of the Pacific Ocean. The Devil will have to wait for another future time when Mankind finds other foolish means to threaten his own existence. We think the Devil will be willing to wait. If nothing else, he has the patience to wait an eternity."

"These are the points that will be argued to Satan. He will of course argue his own points. We think it is best to negotiate some kind of agreement with him instead of fighting a long drawn out battle. This will gain more time for Angela and her environmentalists to sway the national leaders. They must save themselves or destroy themselves. The choice is theirs."

"Angela, you are the means by which they can save themselves. We here, the Council and the holy ones, can only help you to do that job. We cannot do it for you. That is why it so important that we be able to stop Satan and his demons from interfering in your work. If they are able to kill you or stop you, it will mean the beginning of a series of manmade catastrophes worse than those that were shown to Amos."

"It can be done, Angela. You can convince the people that they have to save themselves. They may pray and make offerings, but there will be no divine help. Only self-help will work. That is why this night is so important to all of us. Your group did well in Phoenix. You opened the eyes and ears of many people. Even now, the president of this country has sent his own agents to find you and talk with you. The Council of Eagles is very proud of all of you."

"When the arguments begin, Amos has been selected to speak on our behalf. Then later, if you see it as necessary, you may join in the discussion. We must all remember, though, that the Devil is a trickster. He will tell any lie or make any promise to fool you, and he has a purpose in being. That purpose is to tempt people into following him. He cannot take any soul without the consent of the body. His demons may kill for his sake, but the soul is safe unless the body has yielded to his temptations."

"Our purpose tonight is to convince Satan we now have the power to destroy his demons and therefore we want his agreement to withdraw the goat men until the will of the people either stops the production of nuclear things, or they allow it to continue. Of course, if it continues, their destruction is assured and Satan can then unleash his demons without our interference. That is our position."

The full impact of what their activities meant to the world was made clear to the small group. Jay and Diane were quietly assessing what Teek-awis had said, but Sandra was extremely excited by what she had heard. It was like a continuation of her teachings in Sunday school, only this time she was being offered proof of God's existence. She was going to be part of His good works. What great news this was. She would be a part of *His* good works.

She asked, "Is there a time set for the meeting with Satan?"

Teek-awis turned to look at her and quickly appraised her sincerity. Whistler had praised her work in the short time she had been with Angela.

"The Zuni elder shaman, Apish'taya, and the Navajo, Kla-begatho, have been in contact with Satan, as your people call him, and he has said that he would come here tonight after moonrise, although he would set no hour for his arrival. Because we agreed to a time limit of four hours for arguments, it is almost certain he must be here before midnight in order that we finish before dawns first light. It has to be noted though, that there are now several hundred of his demons already here waiting in the darkness. The eagles saw them arriving from every direction this evening. Apparently they have been summoned to intimidate us before the Devil arrives."

"Until he gets here, I would suggest that all of you get something to eat and then try to get some rest. I know you've had a very busy day. When he arrives you will know it."

Then to Frank, he said, "Ask your white friend, the deputy sheriff, to please come down and join us. He is welcome. If he remains on the hillside out of our sight the goat men will be tempted to approach him."

"I asked him once, and I'll ask again. He doesn't yet realize the danger he may be in. I'll try to bring him here. Thank you for caring," Frank replied.

Sandra said, "If you're going up to the truck I'll go with you. We ought to get

Sam out of harm's way. We can also bring the sandwiches down here."

"C'mon," Frank said. They grabbed two flashlights and made their way up to the truck. When they got there Sam was nowhere around.

"Sam, where are you?" Frank shouted, thinking that Sam may have gone into the shadows to answer Nature's call. He remembered that Sam had several cups of coffee before they had left the motel, and it had been a long tiring drive.

"Sam, come here," Sandra called.

Sam did not answer their calls. They went into the rear of the truck and took out the sandwiches, then picked up two of the canvas water bags. Frank looked into the cab of the truck and saw that the two firearms were still there, locked up, and the radio was still on. So wherever Sam was he was not far away. Frank reached in and turned the radio off and locked the doors. Sam would have the keys with him and they needed to preserve the truck's battery. Then they went back to the meeting place.

In the darkness they could hear movement that caused rocks to roll downhill, and they quickened their pace. They reported to Amos that Sam was not around. He seemed not worried, but as soon as he could get away Amos alerted Whistler to that fact. If the scout who had been stationed at the truck was missing also, it would mean that danger was nearby.

Whistler flew off to find Ho-go-ton. He had an uneasy feeling, something was wrong.

Whistler swiftly flew up to where Ho-go-ton, Whirl Wind, and their scouts were patrolling. There was a total of 600 young eagles on duty this night. They had expected that the goat men would be approaching from the rocky heights of the mountain. Whirl Wind's eagles were patrolling the area South of the amphitheatre and to the East. Ho-go-ton's group was on the West and North sides. Whistler informed them that Stone, the eagle left with Sam, and Sam himself, were missing. The scouts were to begin flying at lower elevations to look for them.

The moon was just beginning to appear over the mountain ridge. Soon it would bathe the meeting place in its pale, dim light. It was a half-moon so it would give off little light to see by. Teek-awis passed word that all should begin assembling to await the Devil.

Amos reflected that never before had there been such an assembled group as those who were now finding their way to the floor of the amphitheatre to wait for someone, or something that they had always known existed, but which few had ever seen. In keeping with the importance of this meeting the large crowd was strangely subdued. Only the shuffling of their feet through the sandy bottom could be heard, interspersed with the squeaks of the unconcerned bats and night birds.

The Council of Eagles, led by Teek-awis, occupied space which looked directly to the South where they could see the moon rising slowly above the mountain. The Indian shamans led by old Apish'taya and followed by Kla-begatho, Monong'hovi, Sunka Wacan Wicasa, Ga-a-moo, Karahkwa, and Tind-eh, placed themselves to the immediate right of the Council. Amos, Angela and her group were asked to sit to the left of the Council.

Behind and to either side of them, sat the tribal leaders. Since morning, the number of leaders present had grown to four hundred and eighty three, the most ever gathered in one spot for over a century. Several leaders from the state of Montana had brought a ceremonial drum with them and they now began to sing an honoring song for the benefit of those sitting in the front row. When this was done and properly acknowledged by the honorees, they began singing of days gone by and songs of remembrance of the sweetness of life in those days when the rivers flowed unimpeded by dams and the fish and game had been plentiful.

The thump of the drum and their high-pitched singing reached out and drifted into the canyons and crevices and covered the mountain with memories of days long gone. All who heard remembered, and their hearts were full with appreciation and they gave thanks to the Creator. With the exception of course, of the demons who waited in the shadows.

The singing continued for some time and occasionally someone would come down from their place to join in. The crowd listened, and waited patiently.

When the moon was almost half-way up in the sky, a cold wind suddenly swirled its way down to the fire from the western side. Smoke, hot coals, and ashes were carried up thirty feet or more then showered down on the watchers. Then a figure suddenly appeared in the shadow of a large boulder which lay on the southern edge of the amphitheatre.

The figure in the shadow of the boulder raised one hand in a greeting and a voice said, "Greetings, to all of you. I hope I have surprised you by my entrance. My name is Sam and I have been delegated to speak for the truly great one whom you call Satan. You begged him to meet with you to ask for his mercy."

The singers quickly picked up their drum and retired to watch and listen. While the figure came forward into the light of the dimming fire, two Indian men quickly put more logs on the fire.

No one was more surprised at this sudden turn of events than Frank and Sandra. "My God, he's one of them," Frank exclaimed.

Sandra answered, "No. Let's wait and see. Maybe this is not really Sam. Remember, Satan is a trickster and a cheat."

Sam then walked out of the shadows, still dressed in his deputy sheriff's clothing, and wearing his pistol. "I'm ready to listen to your pleas."

Then looking around at the seated crowd he asked, "Which one of you killed the Master's disciple in Phoenix?"

No answer was given. Kla-begatho sat still and was silent. Apish'taya had explained earlier that the devil might try to divert attention away from the topic of discussion. This seemed to be such a tactic.

When there was no response, Sam thundered, "So, do you expect me to stay and speak with cowards? I have much greater things to do than to waste my time talking to old women who pretend to be men. Speak up! Which one of you killed Satan's disciple?"

There was still no response. In reality no one had yet acknowledged his presence. It was as if he was invisible. The Devil was getting angry at such disrespect.

Others were also angry, but they kept their silence. Teek-awis had an urge to challenge the Devil on the spot. Likewise Kla-begatho.

Sandra was not fearful at all, and wanted to tell him what she thought of him and his evil power. From her church's teachings she knew he could have no power over her at all unless she allowed it. Although she was seething she also kept her silence. Amos and then Angela received a thought from Apish'taya to remain silent, that their time for talk would come.

Now Sam swaggered to not more than ten feet in front of Apish'taya. "Tell me, old man. Tell me that you will come home with me tonight. You will have a large following there. And much riches. Look at you now, you are so poor that your clothes are ragged and you have no shoes on your dirty feet. No one in this land seems to care about you."

Then in a softer, more conciliatory tone, "This can change. I will take good care of you always, and even give you your youth back if you will come with me. Forsake these cowards, liars, and hypocrites, and come live with us. Anyone here that will come with me shall have riches like you've never known. Has anyone else made such a generous offer? No, I thought not."

Amos was on his feet now. He walked slowly towards the Devil, who was using Sam's body. Amos understood now that this was what he had been schooled and trained for, for these many long years. He felt confident, and spiritually stronger than at any time in the past.

He strode to within six feet of Satan, and said, firmly, "We've politely listened to your lies and your boasting. We know who you are. You are the Devil, and everyone here knows of your forked tongue. We have asked you to come here tonight hoping that you might have at least a shred of decency left to listen to our arguments. You have said you like to make bargains with us humans who still possess souls. All right then, what will you say when I, Amos Turkey, tell you that we want to make a bargain with you. Isn't that to your liking?"

Satan studied Amos' face closely, looking for any sign of weakness.

Amos went on, "If you will recall, a long time ago I was the young boy whose father, mother, and sisters were burned alive by men who listened to you. This should serve to prove something to you. My instinct is to hate you for killing my family, but now for the sake of others I am willing to talk man-to-man with you and to strike a bargain. I am willing to do this. Are you willing to listen? If not, be gone."

Satan looked hard at Amos, then laughed loudly. "Yes, I remember you. You hid in the dark, and cried like a baby while your mother called to you for help. You failed her, as you will fail those here tonight who have placed their trust in you. How can a cry baby like you expect to bargain with me?"

His voice increasing in intensity, Satan roared, "You know who I am. Kneel to me! I am Lucifer. I am Satan, the King of the underworld kingdom. And you, *you...are...nothing!* You are an old, ragged, and dirty half-breed black man who tries to act like a native of this country. Go back to sleep, old man, and send me someone more worthy to speak with me."

The Devil was trying very hard to cause Amos to lose his temper, to become angry enough to threaten him, or to challenge him in any way. Angry men are not wise men.

Unafraid, Amos moved a step closer.

"You are correct, Satan. I did hide in the dark while my family burned. I was but a boy then, and I was afraid. I didn't know you then. Today I am a grown man and I know you well. I am no longer afraid."

"But consider this. By hiding in that body called Sam, you are also afraid. You are the coward. You are afraid for us to see you as you are...a fallen angel. You are ashamed of that. Are you also ashamed of your appearance? If not, why do you use Sam?"

Now Amos was warming to his task. "You called me a coward, a black half-breed and a dirty old man. What are you then, if not a coward, and worse? You boast of being a King. Do King's hide behind others? Come out of Sam's body and let us see you as you are. I may be talking with one of the demons instead of with a King. We will not talk with you unless we know who we are talking to. If you yourself are not a coward, show yourself! *Show yourself now!*" Amos spoke these last words in a loud and firm voice which was without a hint of fear.

It was clear to Satan now that he had nothing to gain from using Sam's body any longer. His theatrics would do no good tonight. He would shed this human body, then find the one who possessed the power to destroy his demons. Sam turned and slowly walked back to the rock shadow from where he had come.

A buzz of whispers and hushed comments rose from the crowd watching this awesome sight

Chapter Twenty-One

As Sam disappeared from sight, a commotion arose on the eastern side of the amphitheatre. The body of Stone was hurled into the firelight where it fell on the ground near the fire. It lay still, feathers ruffled in death. The assembled crowd watched in horror as the eagle's body was followed by a black goat man wearing no clothing who walked swiftly to where Amos was still standing, waiting for the Devil to return. The demon tilted its head, then circled around, looking at Amos from one angle, then another.

Seemingly satisfied that it was Amos, the goat man said, "Amos, I looked for you at Canyon de Chelly. I wanted to kill you then, and I want to kill you now. For a thousand years, native people like yourself have been my favorite prey. You must come with me now, or I will kill you on this spot in front of all your friends."

Alarmed by what was happening, Frank reached for the pistol in his shoulder holster. He told Sandra, "If it makes a move towards Amos we'll find out what a bullet can do to a demon."

Angela saw, and said, "Wait. Amos is safe."

Amos calmly ignored the words of the black goat man and hurled a challenge back at the Devil. "Satan, come out and talk with us as you promised you would, or are you never to be believed. Come out now or we will destroy this demon of yours. He is an abomination who has killed one of our eagle friends and he must pay now or later. It will please us to do it now."

Fawn got up and went over to Stone and gently picked up his dead body and carried him to where the Council was seated. Then she went to stand next to Amos, facing the demon. Now Satan was deliberately delaying his reappearance, waiting to see what would happen next. Amos silently counted off ten seconds, then he said to Fawn, "Now."

Fawn stood up and pointed at the black demon, and shouted, "You will be destroyed and returned to Hell."

As had happened in Phoenix, the demon was suddenly hit by a terrific blow from an unseen mighty force. Its head was snapped backwards with such force that the crack of its neck breaking was clearly heard by everyone. The unseen force picked up the body and flung it hard at the boulder behind which Satan was hiding, exactly as Stone's body was thrown. The black demon was stuck to the boulder with arms outflung while its head seemed crushed from hitting the huge rock.

After a few minutes Satan walked from the shadows, stopped and looked at the demon's body. He shrugged. "They're a dime a dozen, you know," he said. Then he turned and walked towards Amos.

Sandra noted that the Devil's body was exactly as shown in old drawings she had seen at the church library. He was tall and slender with a reddish-colored and almost-human body, except in three places. He had a tail about two feet long which had a definite barbed point at the tip. While his head and face had sharp, angular human features, there were two curved horns on top, and he had no discernable male sexual parts. She knew she would never forget this scene. Her skin felt prickly, and she shuddered in disgust.

Satan finally said, "All right, let's talk. I want to hear about your proposed bargain." He gestured and a rock slid towards him over the sand. He sat, making himself comfortable. Then he said, "By the way, where did you find that power to destroy my demons? Is it the woman who has the power? Let's talk about that."

"No." Amos said. "First, I want to talk about a catastrophe that you and I believe is going to happen. I talk of the devastating earthquake and flood which will kill millions of people. Because people will believe all is lost, and with encouragement from your demons, they may turn to committing evil things which will then condemn their souls to your so-called kingdom. We want a chance to prevent that catastrophic event. We want to bargain for your promise that you will withdraw all of your demons until such time as the catastrophe actually happens. Will you bargain in good faith with us?"

"Now why would I want to do that?" the Devil said, laughing. "You know that in the scheme of things, regardless of what happens, I win. You can destroy one hundred or one thousand times one hundred of my demons. I don't care. I have at my disposal a great number of them and the supply is always growing. You can cry, whine, beg, as you all do when your time on earth is up, and it won't do you any good. All sinners are mine. You know that, or are you now senile? There will be no agreement. Not in your lifetime, which in your case, may be only a short time away."

The Devil let out a laugh which would have curdled the blood of ordinary men, and it echoed throughout the valleys and ridges, bouncing off huge boulders and into the darkness of the surrounding desert.

Amos reckoned that Satan had by now made his strongest arguments and was assuming Amos would now rebut with pleas based on moral arguments and cries for mercy. He figured right. Satan thought he had convinced Amos that there were so many thousands of his goat men, and he didn't care if he lost a few because they were so easily replaceable.

He sat back down on his rock. "Amos, you are out of your league if you want to bargain with me. You haven't got a thing to bargain with except your own soul. What a joke you are."

Amos continued to play the part.

"Satan. It's my turn to tell you why you must agree to our bargain. First of all, we don't want to waste time fighting against your demons. There are too many of them, as you say. It would take us forever to kill them one at a time, and we wouldn't have time to prevent the catastrophe. You may be right. Why should you bargain with us?"

Satan smiled. "Just as I thought. Now all that's left is for you to beg and cry. But why haven't I heard from your vaunted elders, the tribal shamans, the holy ones who spend all their time in poverty, in meditation, and studying things which I have forgotten long ago? And how about your talking eagles, who sit at the right hand of your Creator on behalf of Indian people? Has old Teek-awis lost his gift of gab?" he asked with a chuckle. "For one who thinks he's so smart, why has he let a dummy like you speak for him? It's no wonder that the Creator believes Mankind is a lost cause."

"Well," Amos asked, "What if a mere woman, an Indian woman, could destroy your demons just as fast as you could recruit them. Would that make a difference to you? It would save us a lot of time, and I think after they saw what was happening many of them might even turn against you. Didn't you yourself turn against your creator?"

He spoke louder. "After all, what would they have to lose now? They're already damned for eternity. What more could you do to them? Some of them might just be willing to help their living relatives if they thought the Creator would take this into account. They just might be willing to listen to us as we explained this to them. What do you think?"

The sound of voices murmuring came from among the rocks.

Satan looked closely at Amos' face. It had the look of innocence, like a child asking a simple question. He couldn't fathom this face. Was Amos really asking a foolish question of him? Did he really think he could be fooled?

Satan jerked upright on his rock seat. "What are you saying, old man. Don't play with me or I just might get angry, and destroy all of you as you sit here. Don't you know that your Mother Nature has been fooling with you, telling you Indians that you are at one with her? She doesn't care one whit for you or your precious seventh generation. I'm going to leave and get on with what I should have done long ago. With my help, people are going to enjoy killing themselves even if they know they're going to Hell in a hand basket." His obscene laughter again filled the night air and caused nearby owls and other night birds to flee for their lives.

When his laughter stopped, Amos said to him in a very authoritative tone of voice, "Very well. You leave us no choice."

Amos told the Indian men to put many logs on the fire, then he took off his neck scarf and waved it in the air. Immediately there was a great sound of air rushing over the wings of hundreds of eagles as they swiftly descended from a great height. Ho-go-ton had formed the eagles into squadrons which descended on the goat men. Their huge wings fanned the air all round the amphitheatre.

Soon these sounds were joined by the sound of hooves running on broken rock and of smaller rocks spilling from the ridges which rimmed the meeting place. The noise of hundreds of flapping wings were joined by the battle screeches of many eagles as they dived, scratched, and pecked at the several hundred demons who had been summoned to this place by Satan.

The demons were being forced out into the firelight by the eagles. They were supposed to have killed these people at Satan's signal. Instead the tables were being turned on them. They were being herded into the amphitheatre by hundreds of eagles who had been trained in a military manner by Whirl Wind and Ho-go-ton.

As Satan watched in stunned confusion, in a matter of only ten minutes the eagles had flushed all the goat men out of the hills and into the amphitheatre. They stood still, almost covering the floor of the amphitheatre, wondering what to do, waiting for some sort of word from Satan.

Whirl Wind flew down to where Amos stood and reported, "They're all here. There are no more in the mountains." Then he was gone to join the others as they hovered over the demons making sure that none tried to escape.

Amos motioned once again and this time Angela stood, raised her arm, and swung it towards all of the demons. Then she spoke loudly to them, "You will all return to Hell."

As a giant wind fells huge trees, the unseen force moved from one end of the line to the other, and as it moved, the demons heads were crushed as if between two large rocks. The crunching sound of breaking bone could be heard throughout the amphitheatre.

The Devil watched in disbelief as they all fell, destroyed.

Turning towards Satan, Amos said loudly, "Listen to me, Satan, this is not a fluke happening, and neither is it a trick. All your demons are destroyed, as they would be even if they numbered in the thousands. Each of the holy men, whom you insulted just a while ago, possess this power as do I, as do the two women who you saw destroy your demons. If you do not listen to my words, we shall soon pass this power on to the assembled tribal leaders seated behind the Council of Eagles. Satan, we are no longer in fear of your demons. Your only power over us is that which you will have if we ourselves commit evil things. We know your limitations."

"Yet we are willing, as I said before, to bargain with you in good faith that you will not send more demons to the surface unless we fail to stop the nuclear explosions and the catastrophe we have described, happens. Unless you make this agreement with us we will continue to destroy your demons in great numbers."

"It is possible that some of them may repent and be allowed back into the Kingdom of Heaven. Then you will be faced with disgrace. I may be an old fool and an ignorant man, as you have said. But I think you must bargain with me now. What say you?"

Satan replied, "Some of what you say makes a little sense, but only a very little. Without my demons my work will go much slower. People will still be inclined to commit the mortal sin which will deliver themselves to me."

"So, Amos. I am not a coward, but I am a sensible creature. I choose to *leave and fight another day*, if you will forgive the bad metaphor. I have nothing to lose, or for that matter, nothing to gain by being obstinate in this matter. It makes no difference to me if I have to wait six months, six years, or six thousand years for the tarnished souls of sinners. It's all the same to me."

"In my line of work, time is irrelevant. I agree to your bargain, in front of all you as witnesses," he said as he motioned towards the entire group, "that from this moment I will not release even a single demon on the world until such time as the foolish scientists use their huge bombs to disturb my underground world. I feel certain that it will be soon, because they, the scientists, do not have the morals and compassion in their whole society, that you do in your little finger, Amos."

"Anyway, with or without my demons, people will always sin, so they will come to me sooner or later. I don't care when."

"I wish I had known you when I was a *good* angel, Amos. We could have been friends. You are a gifted speaker, and an intelligent man. If you agree to it, I would like to come and visit with you from time to time, just to talk. You are an interesting fellow. All right?"

Amos chuckled. He knew that the Devil could not enter his house unless he was invited. "You almost convince me that I am a great fellow, and that your only interest is in my great mind. But I think you will continue to try and find ways to discover what our secret power is and where it derives from. No, I think it much better that we never talk face to face again in my lifetime. But be warned also from this night forward, that we will destroy any or all demons which threaten Mankind."

"Agreed," Satan said. He simply disappeared in a puff of smoke.

Chapter Twenty-Two

The first thing that Frank did when the spell of the Devil's visit was over, was to rush to the rock where Sam was last seen. He found Sam just sitting on the ground there, in a daze and unable to talk. He couldn't remember a thing, but he felt something terrible had happened and he was shaking. He looked at Frank, and began to cry softly.

Sandra had followed Frank, so she sat down beside Sam and held him in her arms, soothing him until his crying stopped. She called to Frank, "Give me a hand here. Let's take him back to the truck and lay him down in the back until he recovers. I think he's been in something like a hypnotic trance. Sometimes on an unwilling subject who eventually goes under, the effects can linger for a long time. Grab hold of him and let's go."

After they had him back at the truck, Sandra tried to get him to drink some water. She didn't have to try real hard. He guzzled water like a dry camel. She then said to Frank, "I'm going to stay here with him until he can walk and talk. You go on and be with the others, they probably could use your help."

Then she gripped his arm tightly and Frank squeezed her hand. Then he went to see the others. Teek-awis was explaining the details of their bargain with Satan to the tribal leaders.

"I don't think we can trust him for long, but if we fail to stop the nuclear tests we can be sure that he will flood the countrysides with the goat men. In the meantime, you must tell your people back home about all that has happened here tonight, and have them keep their eyes open for any sign of the demons returning. If they return, notify Amos immediately, and he can arrange for someone to come and destroy them. If really necessary, you will be told about the secret, but it must remain a secret within you, and with us. It is too powerful, and it could be dangerous in the wrong hands. Call us first."

One of the tribal leaders spoke up. "The bodies of the goat men have returned to a human form. Some of them may have been ancient relatives. Before we leave we should give them a burial and leave a prayer with them. We can bury them under sand, gravel, and rocks. It's the only decent thing to do."

The shamans and Teek-awis agreed, and the tribal leaders retrieved shovels from their pickup trucks and began digging a large hole in the desert sands away from the amphitheatre. When that was done, the 150 bodies were laid side by side, then covered with a layer of sand, then one of gravel. The mass grave was then covered with larger rocks to protect the bodies from predators and buzzards.

In the meantime, Angela and her group was meeting with Amos, the Council of Eagles, and the Indian shamans. It was settled that Angela would set up a headquarters immediately. Angela and her core group would focus on stopping the nuclear tests using any means necessary.

It was sunrise before the burial work was done and their meeting over. Whistler would fly home with his father and the scouts, then he would meet Angela's group on Saturday in Prescott Valley for Aaron's funeral. Finally, everything seemed to be taken care of, and hugs and handshakes were exchanged, then all began their long trek home.

Sam was walking around and talking with Sandra when the group returned to the truck. "I'm still a little shaky, friends, so will one of you drive us back to the motel? But first, I gotta call the Sheriff and check in to tell him we're all right. I haven't talked to him since we got here and I'll bet he's fit to be tied."

Jay was elected to do the driving. Sheriff Stafford was waiting for them when they arrived at the motel three-and-one-half hours later. In deference to Sam, Jay had driven slow and sensibly. The sheriff and Sam were given a full report on what had happened at Mount Devine.

The sheriff said, "I don't dare make a report of what you've told me. They'd lock me in the loony bin. I truly believe what you've told me is true, because of what I've already seen, but its gonna take a little while longer for everybody else to believe. You still owe me, Frank, but if you ever need my help in my county again, it's yours. I appreciate your returning Sam in one piece after what you told me. Jeez. I'm glad I'm retiring soon. I'm gonna move to the other side of the Rocky Mountains, to Denver maybe, just in case."

When the Sheriff and Sam were gone, Angela said, "Okay, it's now eleven-thirty. Let's get some rest until about three, then we'll head to Phoenix. I can't wait to see Star and Ham. I'll bet they're worried stiff about us. Anyway, we'll have some good news for them. See you in the lobby at three."

Sandra said, "Frank, before another minute goes by, let's have our little talk. I think its important to our future, mine anyway."

Frank said, "Okay, let's order up a pot of coffee and we can talk in your room. How's that?"

"You got it, pal," she said.

When they were comfortably settled, Sandra began by saying, "I want to quit the Phoenix P.D. and join Angela's fight against the nuclear bombs. I want to know if you would go with me. I feel pretty close to you, partly because of all we've been through, and partly because I've never met a man like you. You've treated me like a lady. You haven't talked raunchy to me or made any moves on me. In short, you've been a gentleman, and I appreciate that kind of a man. My daddy would have liked you."

"Now this thing with the nuclear bombs and radioactive stuff, I've always wished someone would stop the country from making the stuff. It's more important to me now, and I think to everyone, than ever before. I think anyone worth their salt should want to help Angela. Her heart's in the right place and all, but she still needs people like you and me, people who know the system and can help her get things done. I'm suggesting that we both join her. What say?"

Frank needed no convincing. "I'm ready. Ever since I found out that the goat man stories were real I've thought about leaving the P.D. and helping the Indian cause, mainly just because they're my people. I feel just like Jay does and I think that's good. And what I know now about the damage that's being done by the nuclear industry makes me sick. I'll go with you, no strings attached."

"Good. Let's both do it on Monday. We can put in for any leave or vacation time we have coming then submit our resignations. It sounds like a winner to me."

Frank said, "There's only one thing. Angela hasn't got much money to pay for living and operating expenses, and after our vacation money is gone we'll need some way to make living expenses. I don't want to mooch off of Angela, so we'll have to really hustle to begin a fundraising campaign for the Las Vegas headquarters."

"Well, if all that's bothering you, forget it," Sandra said. "I haven't told this to anyone yet, but when my daddy died he left everything to me in a trust fund. So I'm worth a few million. As long as the oil wells keep pumping all I have to do is collect the money. I'd like to use it to help fund Angela's project, the start of it anyway. We can easily get a fundraising operation going for Angela, and she shouldn't have to worry. I tell you Frank, I want to get involved in this fight."

"Me too," Frank said.

"Fine. It's settled. We'll take care of the details when we get back to Phoenix. For now, let's get something to eat, then we can snooze in the soft chairs in the lobby until we're ready to leave. She brought her face close to his and looked into his eyes. "Frank, seriously, would you mind if I told you I like you a lot? I hope not. I've never said that to anybody in my whole life. Really."

They were dozing side by side on a lobby couch, like old friends, when the others came down. Sandra paid the motel bill, then they were off to Phoenix, and points West, to new adventures.

The trip back to Phoenix was uneventful. Angela had called the hospital and Star had answered the phone. Angela only told her that their trip was a success and that they were on the way back. They would see her tonight and tell her all about it. Star was happy.

Back in Phoenix , the group checked in again at the Desert Inn Motel. They had an early dinner, then while the others went to visit Star, Frank and Sandra went to make their own arrangements to leave town next week. One of the first things Sandra wanted to do was to return the rented car, and then buy a truck of their own. That took the rest of the evening, and by the time Angela and the others returned to the motel, Sandra was the proud owner of a Ford three-quarter-ton red pickup truck with a custom-made camper body on the back.

"When we get to Las Vegas, we're going to have fun in this baby," she told Frank. "Have you ever seen Hoover Dam or Lake Mead, or the Colorado River, or the Grand Canyon?"

Frank said, "No. I've lived around here all of my life and never have been to any of those places."

"Well neither have I. From now on, every chance we get we're going to see one of those places. It'll be great, Frank. You're lucky you met me."

Frank smiled and said, "I know."

The following morning they met the others at 7:00 for breakfast. Then they all drove to the hospital to get Star. Before they got there, Star was up and ready to leave. The doctor was trying to caution her to be careful of any strenuous exercise.

Star's doctor and the nurses came to see her off. Ham pushed her out of the hospital in a wheelchair over her objections. By the time she was placed in the back of Angela's truck with Ham and Fawn there was a small crowd of well-wishers and members of the media there to say goodbye to her. As they drove away they all waved until she was out of sight. Then they were on their way to Prescott Valley to attend Aaron's funeral. After the funeral, all but Sandra and Frank would go on to Flagstaff to prepare their new plans. Sandra and Frank would return to Phoenix. After their papers were signed and they were officially released from the police department, they would drive to Flagstaff to join the others.

Chapter Twenty-Three

Michael Roan Horse had delivered Aaron's casket and body to a local Prescott undertaker on Thursday, then he went to explain to the family what had caused Aaron's death. He told them Aaron had given his life for all the world in a new kind of battle.

Aaron's parents didn't own a television set, and had read little of what had happened in Phoenix, so they didn't understand what Roan Horse was talking about, although they had heard rumors from people who had come to see them.

He spent two hours in explaining as best he could, the events in Phoenix, and why they and the others had become involved. When he finished his story they were shocked, yet proud of what their Aaron had done.

"We will give him the honors of a great warrior chief," Aaron's mother said.

"If this is so," Roan Horse said, "will you wait until the evening of Saturday for his burial? This will give time for all of his friends everywhere to arrive. I would like some time also to arrange for a military group to be here. Aaron would like that. We must send notices of the time to everyone." The burial was scheduled for five p.m. on Saturday.

Angela and her friends arrived from Phoenix just after 12:30 p.m. and they immediately went to Aaron's family to grieve with them. Diane and Sandra were at first unsure of how to express their grief to the relatives, but they were embraced by them, and quickly felt like family relatives as their own tears fell along with those of the family.

All afternoon, Indian and non-Indian friends arrived. The Mayor of the City of Prescott came to praise Aaron as a hero of America. Members of American Legion and V.F.W. posts arrived in a body to pay tribute. A bugler, color guard, and a firing squad from the Prescott National Guard were there.

At the appointed time of 5 p.m. the famous Yuma Indian Band, all Quechan tribal members, began playing military marches as veterans, military units and their color guards paraded in a final *Pass In Review* parade for Aaron. Military color guards led the way with flags of the United States, the State of Arizona, the Arizona National Guard, the U.S. Army, the American Legion and the V.F.W., all proudly flying and flapping in the warm summer breeze.

When the military procession had placed themselves to one side of the burial site, a colorful procession of mourners began a slow walk to the grave site led by the Yavapai holy man. Aaron's body was carried by relatives in their traditional ceremonial dress. Mourners of several races followed behind the body.

A Methodist minister delivered the eulogy while the band softly played "Nearer My God, To Thee." Then the tribal holy man blessed Aaron and committed him to his relatives who had gone before him. After the color guard's rifle volley, the bugler, at a distance, began the somber notes of "Taps."

Then came an unexpected tribute from the Council of Eagles. From the northern part of the river valley there was a single loud cry of an eagle. All eyes turned and saw a flight of one hundred eagles in a military flight pattern swooping low towards them. When they passed directly overhead they gave their battle cry, and split into two rows, rising swiftly to a great height where they formed into a single line, and circled the burial site once, then flew away as quickly as they had come. Whistler, Whirl Wind, and Ho-go-ton returned for a slow flight over the group.

Aaron's family knew that it was always good to see an eagle at a time like this, but one hundred? They knew then that Aaron was considered a special person in the eyes of the Creator.

After Aaron was buried and everyone else had departed, Angela had one more meeting with the others.

Frank told them, "Sandra and I will go back to Phoenix to cut our ties to the police department, then we'll drive up to meet you in Flagstaff. While you take care of your business in Flagstaff we'd like to go ahead and get together with Abner Cranshaw in Las Vegas. By the time you get to there, we'll have everything waiting for you. How's that?"

"You don't know how relieved I am," Angela said. "I'm really happy that you'll be with us, and I was wondering how to begin this phase of our work. Thanks to you, I can concentrate on getting other things done. I have some concerns yet, so why don't we all meet in Flagstaff at Ham's house in a few days to discuss our plans. Can we meet on next Wednesday?"

"I'm sure we can. If we have any problems we can call you," Sandra said.

Ham gave Frank the telephone numbers and the address of his house in Flagstaff, and hugs were shared by everyone. Then they were off to their respective destinations.

On Monday morning, everything went better than Sandra had hoped, except where Captain Morris was concerned. He had tried to persuade her to change her mind and stay with the police department.

ANGELA'S BATTLE

Morris said, "I have great plans for you, Sandra. If you stay with the department you can be a great asset to me and who knows, in a short time you could move up to being my assistant here. Why don't we go to dinner together tonight and I can tell you what to expect if you stay."

Sandra already had a good idea of what he had planned for her, and what to expect from him. She wanted no part of it.

By Tuesday noon both Frank and Sandra had completed their paperwork and with final checks in hand they went to Sandra's bank, then with cash in their pockets they began their pleasant drive North on Highway 17 to Flagstaff. From a pay phone out of the city, Sandra called Angela and told her she and Frank would be into Flagstaff on Wednesday afternoon.

They made one stop along the way at the ruins of Montezuma's Castle, near the Yavapai-Apache reservation at Camp Verde. The ruins were a group of cliff dwellings once inhabited by native Indians who disappeared around 1300 A.D.

They alone, among the tourists who were viewing the ruins, knew the real story behind the mystery of their disappearance. Something they had not known was that Camp Verde had been where the Apache and Yavapai Indians were held as prisoners by the U.S. Army in the 1860s. Many of them were killed here.

Camp Verde was also the place where the goat man of 1863 had persuaded General James Carleton and General West that it was better to kill the Indians than to feed and house them. Besides being a place of great beauty, this part of the Verde Valley was also a place stained with the blood of native people.

Before they left Montezuma's Castle they shared a prayer of thanks for their own recent deliverance from Satan and his demonic goat men. It was no coincidence, then, that as they drove away, a large whirlwind formed on top of the cliffs and dropped to the canyon floor in front of them, dancing back and forth a few times, then slowly moved towards the ruins and disappeared inside. The ancient ones had greeted them and wished them "good hunting."

That evening they stopped in the heart of "red rock country" in the town of Sedona. Frank located a motel away from the main highway and they checked into separate rooms. After a fine dinner, they sat outdoors on a long wooden porch and watched the stars appear. It was a pleasant evening, and they enjoyed the beauty of Nature.

Then on the horizon to the southeast a bright orange glow slowly appeared, looking as if there were a giant fire burning beyond the range of mountains.

"What the heck is that?" Frank asked.

Sandra answered, "Don't you recognize a full moon when you see it?"

"Gosh, it's been a long time since I've had the time or inclination to look at the moon," Frank said. It began to rise over the horizon, and it was a wondrous sight. He made the most of it. He put his arm around Sandra's shoulder, and she rested her head on his.

The moon had risen an hour into the sky when they said goodnight to each other with a hug, and went to their separate rooms.

The next morning they began a leisurely drive towards Flagstaff. At one spot in Oak Creek Canyon Frank noticed a high butte which stood alone about a half-mile from the road. He pointed it out to Sandra who admired it so much that she asked Frank to stop so she could get a better look. It was the very same butte that had been revered by Angela's husband.

It was late Wednesday afternoon when they arrived in Flagstaff. Frank had no problem in locating Ham's house. Star was her usual self once again and she insisted on preparing an early dinner for all of them. She said she wanted to make a good impression on the newcomers because she had not yet had a chance to become really acquainted with them as had the others on the trip to Mount Devine.

She had heard so much good about Sandra and she was anxious to please her. And she did. She had prepared a meal which everyone said was the best they had ever had. Star was happy to be of use again and cleaned up the dinner table while softly singing her *Happiness Song* to herself.

After the supper dishes were cleaned and put away, they all went into the back yard to sit and talk. It was so pleasant outdoors, and it was really the first night in a long time that they had nothing to do except enjoy each others company. For a few minutes, each was lost in their own thoughts.

Then in the pleasant silence, Ham cocked an ear to a familiar sound. "Someone's knocking on our front door. I'll go see who it is."

Ham opened the front door and saw four men in dark suits standing there. A heavy set man showed a shiny badge and said, "My name is O'Brien, with the FBI. Is your name Hamilton Gardner?"

"Yes, it is. I am Ham Gardner. If you don't mind, may I please see your identification cards? All four of them fished out their official I.D. cards and Ham looked at each one. Two of these men were from the FBI, and two were from the President's own National Security Agency. He was impressed.

Ham handed the identification cards back to the men and asked, "What can I do for you?"

A second man, obviously impatient, said "My name is Allen Gregory, National Security Agency. We're trying to locate Angela Beaver and Jay Storm Cloud. Do you know where we can find them?"

Ham answered, "I know the people you're looking for, so can I ask why you want to see them?"

Gregory said, "The President has asked that we talk to them about what happened in Phoenix the other day and he's interested in knowing more about the nuclear problem they talked about."

O'Brien looked at the other men, then said, "We're in a real hurry to find them," O'Brien said, "so if you can tell us where we can find these people, we will appreciate it. The Indian people are in no trouble, *yet*."

Ham thought quickly about the consequences if he refused their request. Then, he realized it would be of great help to their cause if the President himself could be convinced of the dangers. He threw caution to the winds.

"Well, gentlemen. It just so happens that Angela Beaver, Jay Storm Cloud, and others in her team are in my back yard right this minute. Come on and I'll take you to meet them."

Ham led the group into the back yard then let the agents identify themselves. Everyone looked up, surprised at the appearance of this stern looking group. Ham introduced each of them to the newcomers. Whistler had flown to a tree top to watch, and when Ham told the agents that Whistler was one of their team, the men looked at each other in disbelief. Angela and her group then sat silent, waiting to see what these men would do.

O'Brien smiled, trying to put them at ease. "We've been trying to catch up with you people for a week. By the time we flew into Tucson you were gone. We're going to be brief. You're not in any trouble. The President only wants to know more about this problem you have with his nuclear program. He's asked us to get a briefing from you so he can know better what it is that the country is facing. He knows from the media reports that a serious problem exists, and now for the good of the country the situation has to be evaluated. Will you help us?"

Gregory joined in. "Obviously we can't compel you to cooperate with us, but let me tell you that the President is on your side. He's told me to tell you that if the threat to the country is real, you'll have his full cooperation. He only needs to know that this is not just another false alarm. We do have to give him our report as soon as possible. Can we please talk with all of you people tonight? It's imperative. I hope you can understand why the President can't act without some facts."

Ham said, "Angela Beaver is our leader, and along with Jay Storm Cloud, Star, and Fawn, they represent the Indian people's interest in this whole matter. There is one other person who is very important to us, in terms of the spiritual and religious viewpoints of the Indian people as a whole. That is Amos Turkey. He's not here now, but we could put in a call to him and he might possibly be here in an hour. What do you say, Angela?"

Angela called Jay to one side and spoke in a whisper to him. "Tell these men that we need a few minutes alone to talk about this. We can contact Amos and see what he thinks."

"Okay," Jay said. "You're right. We should get his opinion on this."

Jay returned and spoke directly to Gregory. "We want to talk this over for a few minutes alone, if you don't mind, Mr. Gregory. There's coffee on the stove inside if you gentlemen would go in there. We'll call you when we're ready to give you our answer. That'll also give us a chance to get in touch with Amos. I promise you we won't leave. As the government always says, *trust us*."

Mr. Gregory laughed at that and appreciated the irony. He said, "Alright Jay. We have no problem with that. We'll just go inside and make ourselves at home. Thanks for the coffee."

When they were once again alone, Whistler rejoined them. Jay said, "This should speed up our decision-making. Let's quickly get two or three alternatives on how much to tell the President, then see if we can get any help from him to set up our headquarters and get more publicity. We need to first ask him to postpone their tests, otherwise we would have to act immediately on our own."

Angela turned to Whistler. "Let's go into the trees and call Amos. After he hears this new turn of events he may want to be here. In the meantime Jay, you and the others lay out some options for how we can convince the President of the dangers facing the country. We'll be back as soon as we finish talking to Amos."

Fifteen minutes went by and Angela hadn't returned yet, so Jay sent Ham in to tell the federal agents that they needed more time. Another five minutes went by, then out of the darkness came Angela, Whistler, and Amos. They all greeted him warmly then they sat on the two tree logs.

Angela said, "I've already told Amos about the men inside the house, so Jay, let's hear our options first," Angela said. "Then Amos can tell us his thoughts."

"Well, we've agreed on two action plans. We have the President's attention now, due in part to the goat man's appearance in Phoenix, and in part to the killing of Fuzzy Williams. We should tell these men only just enough to convince them that the President has to see for himself what we're saying is true. We think it's important that we convince him to come out West and see the whole scenario for himself."

"That means he has to see us and listen to all of our facts and stories. This would include an appearance by Whistler's father, the tribal shamans, and the geologist rock scientists. In short, a condensed version of the program in Phoenix, except for the goat man, of course. If we can convince him, it saves a lot of time."

"Our request to be carried to him by Mr. Gregory, would be that first, he postpone the H-bomb tests at least until after our talk, and secondly, that he arrange for the meeting with us to be held here in the West at a secret spot of our own choosing."

"That's our first option. Our second option assumes that he will not meet with us, or even if he does meet with us, he will refuse to abandon the tests. In order that we not lose any precious time, we should immediately set up our headquarters in Las Vegas, and begin recruiting thousands of people to come join us at a camp site close to the Test Site. We may want to do this anyway to show the government that we are committed to going all the way. That's as far as we've gone in making a plan. In any case, we have to do whatever is necessary."

"What do you think, Amos?"

He said, "I think you should realize that Satan does not keep promises. Regardless of what he said at Mount Devine he will send goat men to your meeting if it's held in the West. This should not stop your plans, but be aware that they will come. In the meantime, Satan may try to seduce those who have the power to stop the explosions. If so, some of you are included. Anyone could be the object of his seduction, even the president."

"You have made a good plan. I encourage you to carry it out and make corrections as you go along. But you cannot stay here after tonight. Here, the forest surrounds you and there is no protection from the goat men.. You must select a safer place."

"Jay, you know how these men think. Tell them only what they need to know. They can't commit the president to anything. They can only listen and carry our message back to him, so focus on the consequences of exploding the bombs. Don't mention the Council of Eagles, the tribal shamans, or the goat men unless they ask direct questions about them. If they ask, tell them the president can see and hear the Council and shamans only if he agrees to a meeting. You *must* make him *want* to meet with us. If you can do that you will have succeeded in carrying out the most difficult part of your goals. How you do that is up to all of you."

"Now lets invite them to talk with us here, outside, on our terms."

Ham went to ask the men to come outside. Amos sat alongside Whistler in the dark behind the others. A log was rolled into place where the visitors could sit facing them. Star had quickly made a small fire and it was now crackling nicely, giving some light and a fragrant pine aroma to the night air. It would have been an idyllic scene if not for the serious business to be discussed.

Ham soon returned with the president's men in tow. They were in good spirits after having had their coffee. They had found the people they were after, and now they were confident that the truth would come out. The entire episode in Phoenix had been cleverly staged, and they would be able to expose a fraud. Tomorrow the president could return to business as usual.

As a group, they had always dealt with cold, hard facts. Even the cleverest of spies, terrorists, and conspiracy nuts were reduced to quivering liars in a short time by their methods. This time, with these Indians, it would be no different.

"Let's get this over with so we can go home," Mr. Gregory said to the others. They followed Ham into the dim light of the backyard. They all wore their grimmest and most official looks as they sat down on the log and prepared to expose these people.

Jay had correctly figured out what the attitude of these men would be. As a member of Washington's press corps he had witnessed agents like these in action. Now he was the spokesman at one of the most important meetings in his young life. He decided that the best way to proceed was to immediately put them on the defensive so they would be forced to listen intently.

He looked at the men now seated on the log in front of him.

"Gentlemen," he began. "We contacted Amos Turkey, and he was able to come here on short notice to be with us. Amos is the liaison for the Indian shamans and what is called the Council of Eagles."

O'Brien looked at Gregory, wondering if he would take the lead. Jay pretended not to notice as Gregory cleared his throat to speak.

Jay didn't let him get started. He quickly continued, "If you're surprised at how quickly Amos was able to get here, I'll explain that to you later, but first I think you need to meet Whistler, who is the son of Teek-awis, the leader of the Council of Eagles. He will speak with you and answer questions you might have to clear your minds of any doubts or suspicions of magic tricks, and I will assure you now that none of us are magicians. Whistler, please greet these representatives of the President of the United States."

Whistler extended his great wing span, then folded his wings while walking forward.

"I'm pleased to meet all of you. I'm impressed that the president has sent you to hear us. On behalf of my father and the Council, I welcome you and hope that the president will meet with us soon. Very soon, for there is little time left for him to act."

Still very much unbelieving, Gregory stood and went up to Whistler, whipped out a flashlight and looked for any evidence of a trick. He was sure the voice was coming from a radio transmitter on the huge bird.

"Please, examine me closely and touch me if you want. There really are no strings on me," Whistler said.

He obligingly raised his wings and spread them to their full eight-foot span and allowed Gregory and O'Brien to shine their flashlights on him. O'Brien brushed a hand all round the eagle. He found no wires, strings, or radio. Puzzled, and still in doubt, he said, "He's clean. There's nothing on him, and he's real."

"Of course I'm real," Whistler said to O'Brien. "If you won't believe your own eyes and your own hands, I pity you."

"All right, I don't know who I'm talking to, but I'll get to the bottom of this before we leave," the agent replied.

Gregory merely grunted "Huh," and returned to his seat on the log. During his fourteen year stint in the Central Intelligence Agency and four years in the National Security Agency he had witnessed many strange things, unexplainable things, in countries dominated by native cultures and religions. He was not ready to dismiss this action as a hoax. The two men returned to their seats and faced Jay.

Jay realized that Gregory was open minded, and he was the man who would make a recommendation to the president, so he studied Gregory's expression for a minute. He saw nothing to be cautious of, so he began his talk. For another hour and a half the group repeated what had been said in Phoenix for the benefit of the federal agents. Jay expanded on various events, but left out any reference to what had happened at Mt. Devine. Angela explained her involvement and then let Fawn and Star tell their own stories. Gregory's facial expression did not change, but O'Brien left no doubts of what he was thinking.

When Diane, Ham, and then Sandra told of their interest in what was happening, the attitude of the agents changed obviously. It was an involuntary change. Jay and Angela saw this, but said nothing. If this was what mattered to them, so be it. The result would be more important than their prejudice. Amos merely shook his head in disapproval, and Whistler moved around nervously.

After all their stories were told, the questioning began. O'Brien cautioned them that the FBI would check into their backgrounds and keep an eye on their activities. "Any threats to the security of the United States and to the safety of the public will be grounds for arrest," he told them.

Jay reacted to his statement. "Mr. O'Brien, we're not going to make any threats against anyone or anything. If you listened to what was said here, the threat to all of us is coming from the government's planned nuclear explosions in Nevada. We only want to stop those tests until a full investigation can be done by an impartial and knowledgeable group. We're telling you what we have already learned. We're willing to do whatever is necessary to help everyone understand the danger to all of us."

Gregory said, "I'm sure you know that stories like yours are initially hard to take seriously. We deal with facts, not make believe, so I would like to have at least one thing, one little actual fact, that I can show or tell the president why he should meet with you. I want to believe you, and the president wants to act if there is a real and verifiable danger to the country. Can you help me here?"

"Mr. Gregory," Jay said, "After all you've heard here tonight do you still not believe us? Think. What if we're right in what is going to happen? If we're wrong, nothing changes, and nobody is hurt except our credibility. The president would only be doing his job of protecting the country by conducting an investigation."

"If this catastrophe is allowed to take place, all of you will have earned a place in Hell, believe me. All of us here tonight have recently seen the face of the Devil and soon it may be your turn to see them. Only the faith and power of Indian holy men has brought us through that terrible experience. You will have no such protection."

Sandra spoke up. "Mr. Gregory, Mr. O'Brien. Frank and myself were both hardnosed members of the Phoenix Police Department until we met these people. What we heard and saw at the Phoenix meeting, and later in Tucson, was proof positive that what our friends have told you is absolutely true. I can guarantee you that if you had stood there with us over the past two weeks, you would be sitting alongside us on this log tonight."

"We are all facing a catastrophe if we can't convince the president to listen. Isn't it worth a short delay in the tests to save millions of human lives? I will further guarantee you that you will not want to be personally responsible for withholding such information from our president. Your conscience would never be at peace."

Jay let that sink in for a moment, then said, "Here's our proposal. We want to meet with the president, at which time we'll give him proof positive of everything we've said. We'll show him all he needs to know."

"But we will not agree to the meeting until the president assures us he will halt the testing immediately until an investigation can be made of underground rock formations in the test site area. Our only other condition is that the meeting take place at some remote and safe place here in the West. The president can choose the location if he wishes. Mr. Gregory, will you advise the President to do this?"

Gregory looked directly at each of them before answering. "I want to do that, but I still haven't seen that one piece of proof that would make me want to see or hear more. Believe me, Jay, if you can't interest me in this, then you have no chance of convincing the president of anything. I know him well, and he trusts me."

"I believe you are all sincere in what you've told me, but the reason I'm even here tonight is so I can honestly and sincerely tell him whether he should, or should not, meet with you. There must be something you can show me besides the eagle there. I know he's real, but it doesn't prove anything."

Amos cleared his throat and stood up, waiting for recognition. After a short time Jay nodded to him.

Amos said, "Mr. Gregory, do you consider yourself to be a sane and reasonable man?"

Gregory looked surprised at the question. "Why yes, of course. I'm a well educated and well trained federal agent. I've made a career out of providing advice for presidents and other government officials. I've had to prove myself sane and reasonable."

"Then would you consent to coming with me for an hour or so? If you will, I can show you what you want to see. You must come alone. Your friends can wait here for you."

"I'll go with you. I need to see things for myself," Gregory said. Then to O'Brien, "If I'm not back within two hours, take everyone into custody until you find out what happened to me."

Jay then led the others into the house, leaving Amos alone with Mr. Gregory. Jay had an idea of what Amos was planning and he hoped it would do the job.

Approximately an hour later, Gregory opened the back door of the house and walked in. He was visibly shaken. He looked at Angela and Jay and said, "I'll recommend that the president meet with you. We'll let you know when and where."

Then to O'Brien, he brusquely said, "Take me to the airport. I have to get back to Washington as soon as possible."

He was quiet and didn't speak to O'Brien of what he had seen.

Amos had shown him exactly what Amos himself had seen when the Spirit had taken him on the worldwide tour that night six months ago. Gregory knew he could only speak of what he had seen to the president himself. There was no time to be lost.

After the federal agents were gone the group was jubilant. Hugging each other and laughing, they told each other, "We did it, we did it. We have a meeting with the president."

They all knew they had only prepared the way for Amos to convince Mr. Gregory. They had won this round, and Amos was exhausted from his second night vision trip so he returned to his own home for a well deserved rest.

After the excitement had died down Angela said, "We can't just sit around and do nothing while waiting for the president to call us. If he doesn't call, or if he tells us he won't meet with us, we will have lost valuable time. I propose we go along with Frank's suggestion that he and Sandra go on to Las Vegas to meet with Abner and get started with our headquarters."

Hearing no objections, Angela continued, "All right, let's do it that way. Frank, call Abner in St. George and arrange to meet him someplace. Jay and Diane can go with you so Jay can start his work with the media. The rest of us will stay here until we hear from Washington. If we don't hear from the president by the Sunday night deadline, we'll call you and then be on our way to join you."

Chapter Twenty-Four

The next morning, Frank was driving west on Route 66. Jay was in the front passenger seat enjoying the grandeur of the clear blue skies and the pine nut and juniper tree-covered rolling hills of western Arizona.

They reached the small town of Needles, California just past noon. The Mojave Indian Reservation bordered the northern city limits.

Needles was an old railroad hub and stopover point for travelers. They stopped at the Santa Fe Railroad Depot for lunch in the restaurant of the well-known Harvey House hotel. Jay called Milford at his office on the reservation to tell him they had arrived.

"We're at the Harvey House," Jay said. "Come have lunch with us and we'll bring you up to date on what's happening."

"I'm on my way. Be there in fifteen minutes," Milford said.

Jay wanted to ask him to organize Indian people from throughout the country. Then later, thousands of them would be asked to join others at the Nevada Test Site.

When he explained the plan to Milford he was enthused. "After what happened in Phoenix, and last week at Mount Devine, everybody should want to get involved."

Jay left him the press releases from Phoenix and Tucson, and a cleaned up story of what happened at Mount Devine. They agreed on a plan on how to get people to the test site, then they were on their way again to the city that gambling had built.

They reached the city just after five o'clock. Frank followed the road signs easily to the main road leading out of the city to the west.

When they located the Desert Sage Motel, Abner was waiting. By Las Vegas standards it was a small motel with only 100 rooms, but there were other motels nearby.

"It's on the main highway to the test site," Abner explained. "There's a building nearby that's just fine for our headquarters. There's open land around it too for those who camp out. If you'd like we can go look at it this evening."

Jay said, "That's fine with us. Let's leave in a half-hour. I want to call Angela and tell her where we are and how to reach us." They all went to their rooms.

He made the call and Ham answered.

"Ham, we're in Las Vegas and we're going to look at a building tonight. Abner's not wasting any time in getting started." Then he gave him the motel's address and telephone number.

"Angela's been on the phone all day," Ham said. "She's talking to people all over the country, urging them to organize protest groups in their own communities. The big papers are all featuring the sensational parts of the Phoenix and Tucson meetings just to sell more newspapers. She's afraid people may think we staged a show for their entertainment."

"When you talk to her later I suggest you address this point. She's keeping one phone set aside for the call from the president. Mr. Gregory has already called today to tell her they're discussing the matter now. As soon as we hear from them we'll let you know right away."

"Good. We're going to look at the building, then have dinner. We should be back here in about three hours. Tell her to call then."

"Will do, Jay. Good luck."

Chapter Twenty-Five

Allen Gregory arrived at Andrews Air Force Base in Maryland. Last night, an Air Force plane had taken him from Flagstaff to Phoenix, where one of the Air Force's newest four-engined planes, a Lockheed Constellation, was waiting for him. After one refueling stop in Dallas, he arrived shortly after nine a.m.

At his apartment on Capitol Hill, he began preparing his written report for the president.

It was two o'clock before the president could see him, and now he was on his way to the White House. He was still tired and sleepy, and for the first time in his career he felt uncomfortable in delivering a report. He had a vague feeling of trepidation which he just couldn't shake. The memory of what Amos had shown him was still sharp in his mind.

He asked the driver to let him out on the curb of Lafayette Park, directly across from the White House. He walked slowly through the park trying to sort out and identify his strange feelings. Ten minutes later, he walked across the street to meet the president.

The president had blocked out two hours for this meeting. He told his personal secretary, "No phone calls and no visitors."

The only other person present was Monsignor James O'Connell, president of the local Catholic University. The monsignor had known the president since his boyhood days as an altar boy.

President Kenneally frequently asked his advice. He was troubled by calls to halt the nuclear tests and the reports of a supernatural monster running amuck, and he wanted the monsignor to hear Gregory's report.

The president welcomed Allen Gregory, then waved towards the monsignor.

"Allen, you know Monsignor O'Connell. Because of the nature of what we've heard so far, I've asked him to sit with me while you tell me what you've learned. I trust you have the information I need, so let's get on with it, please."

With a quick sideways glance at the monsignor, Gregory began.

"Mr. President, after what I've been told, and what I've seen with my own eyes, I believe this may be the most important briefing I have ever, and may ever, give you. I urge you to keep an open mind on what I am going to tell you."

The president's eyes narrowed as he studied Gregory's expression. This was not the same Allen Gregory he had known for twenty years.

"I interviewed hundreds of eyewitnesses to the Phoenix event, and looked at hours of unedited television film, and in no case, not one, did the film footage differ from or contradict the verbal reports. It only confirmed what I had been told. I'm convinced that what we both saw on television actually happened. Late last night I met with the principals who began this whole chain of events. At the start, I had considered them to be just another bunch of religious kooks who appear periodically to announce the end of the world."

"Mr. President, these people are not kooks, and they are not preaching repentance or the end of the world. I believe their message has sufficient scientific logic behind it to warrant, at the very least, a temporary halt to the nuclear tests. Their message is so authentic that even I, the unshakeable agnostic, have been shaken off my marble pillar."

"Last night, Angela Beaver, the Indian lady who leads the group, told me that all they ask of you is to meet with them very soon so you might see and hear for yourself what the consequences will be of continued nuclear tests. One interesting thing is, although they generally oppose nuclear technology on environmental grounds, the only thing they're insisting on is the termination of the underground tests. They are prepared to launch an immediate nationwide campaign against those tests if you refuse to meet with them. They didn't issue a demand as other groups have, but it was phrased in a simple way as a warning of what will come."

The creature they call *goat man*, is real, according to those who saw it. The Indians claim that many of these creatures have been sent by the Devil. None of the eye witnesses would say that it was faked."

"Apparently there was a secret meeting somewhere in the desert between what was called the Council of Eagles, Angela Beaver's group, and several hundred Indian shamans and tribal leaders. They gathered for the express purpose of striking a bargain with Satan himself to call off his goat men until after Angela meets with you. If you refuse to stop the tests the Devil will release them in greater numbers."

"We first heard this story when our agents ran across an Indian leader who was so upset with what he had seen that he was drinking heavily in a Tucson hotel bar. He swore that he actually saw the Devil when the bargain was struck. This account was later vouched for by another man, Amos Turkey, who spoke to the Devil and hammered out the deal with him. There is a way to verify the meeting's location, and perhaps to verify the story. Our agents are on their way now to the purported location where they hope to find the buried remains of several hundred of these goat men. I may have a report by tomorrow evening."

Gregory paused, waiting for a reaction. There was none. The monsignor had been listening with his eyes closed, while holding a crucifix. He crossed himself and muttered a prayer. The president nodded and said, "Go on."

"As you saw on the television screen, they claim to have solid reason to believe that the tremendous power of the H-bombs, when exploded deep underground, will produce a catastrophe of unbelievable proportions. Preliminary reports from the USGS indicate this may be a real possibility. I talked this morning with Interior Secretary Jennings and he is now waiting for a final report from a geological field team which is due back in town on Saturday. The balance of my report to you will be on what I actually saw and heard."

For another hour Allen Gregory described and explained every detail of his five-day western visit. Finally, he ended with, "Their only request is that you meet with them alone at a secure spot somewhere in the west. No advisers or aides to be in the meeting room with you. No press notices. Just you and them."

"Mr. President, my sincere recommendation is that within the next 72 hours you notify them of your willingness to meet within a reasonable time, and that you should halt plans for the underground tests at the Nevada Test Site."

"I was instructed to tell you that unless Angela Beaver hears from you by ten p.m. Sunday, Arizona time, they and thousands, perhaps millions of citizens from around the country will descend on the Nevada Test Site with the goal of preventing the explosions. With that many people actually on ground zero, you could not possibly explode the bombs."

"I recommend you agree to the meeting. It could possibly be held within the security of Area 51, which is adjacent to the test site. For your safety, two of our men and myself should be in the meeting room with you."

"Lastly Mr. President, I have to tell you that I was taken on a strange trip, a spiritual trip, by this Amos Turkey. He is an older Indian man who apparently has a highly developed power to see things the rest of us cannot." At this, the monsignor's eyes snapped open, and he looked at Allen as if he himself had seen the Devil.

Gregory noticed, but ignored the obvious look of disgust. He went on to describe his tour with Amos and the terrible things he was shown.

The president was surprised at Gregory's tone of voice and facial expressions, which alternated from fear to wonderment, horror to hope, then to admiration for the Native American principles. He was impressed. He had never known Gregory to be anything but hard-nosed and mean. Maybe there was something to this message, at least enough to justify a meeting.

I'll talk it over with Monsignor O'Connell before I decide if I should bring others in on this, he thought to himself.

Then to Allen Gregory he said, "Well, Allen, I'll take your recommendations under consideration and get back to you first thing tomorrow. I do suggest that you get a good nights rest and be ready to tell us more if I decide to meet with the Security Council. Thanks for coming in."

He was concerned that maybe Allen was exhausted from his trip or maybe under the influence of something other than good sense. If so, rest and sleep would give him time to recover.

The monsignor said not a word to Allen. He only looked closely to see if he could see any sign of dementia or any other abnormality.

When Allen was gone, the monsignor waited for the president to speak. The president and the monsignor were good friends and golf partners. Both trusted each other, and neither had reason to question the other's sincerity. The president made some notes, sat back in his leather chair for a few moments, and stared at the ornate ceiling.

"Jim," the president said. "I have the feeling that I've just read a second-rate science fiction book. Know what I mean?" The monsignor only nodded his head.

"I'd like to know your impression of Allen's report. It would be helpful."

The monsignor was still silent. Then he cleared his throat. He looked over the president's head to the outdoor summer sky where the Washington Monument stood guard over the beauty of the nation's capital city.

"Mr. President, everything I believe is at risk if I allow myself to consider that what Allen said is true. Our faith extends to believing in the existence of the Devil, but as far as we know there has not been a physical manifestation of him in modern times. He does his work invisibly through the morally corrupt and the corruptible. I am willing to concede that Satan does exist."

"But to ask a reasonable person to believe there exists a talking and thinking Council of Eagles that works for God, whom they call the Creator, is to mock God's word in a blasphemous way. If God has a message for mankind He would certainly deliver it through the church. The account of a confrontation between the old Indian man and Satan is also too much to believe, and it smacks of irrational hysteria. I think Mr. Gregory's story is fully suspect."

"You may be right," the president said. "In any case I have other pressing affairs to take care of now. I'll have to say goodbye, but I appreciate your coming over. Call me tomorrow if you have more to offer."

The two old friends shook hands, and the monsignor left the White House. What would the monsignor have said if he had known that the Council of Eagles said that God had personally selected Angela to carry out His work? Allen had deliberately left that out of his report.

As soon as the door to the Oval Office closed, the president leaned back in his chair deep in thought. Monsignor O'Connell had shown him what to expect from the general public if the religious aspects of this story were emphasized in any way. For political reasons, if he was to stop the nuclear tests, it would have to be on sound scientific reasons, and not because God was telling him to stop. He needed to know more about the geology of the area, quickly.

He called his secretary.

"Mildred, get me the Secretary of Interior, pronto. In fact, call all cabinet secretaries and tell them not to leave town this week-end. We've got to have phone numbers where they can be reached at all times. That includes the Joint Chiefs and the NSC. Then get the chairman of the Atomic Energy Commission on the telephone. I need to talk to him right away."

He pulled out a yellow legal pad, and began feverishly making notes for a plan of action. Once again, he was planning a mission just as he had twenty years earlier when he had a squadron of twelve torpedo boats under his command. He was excited.

Seven minutes later Mildred buzzed him. "Secretary Jennings is on line two," she said. The president immediately picked up the phone.

"Hugh, I'm glad we caught you before you left the office. Listen, Allen Gregory is back from his trip out west. We have to meet, so don't leave town. Let Mildred know where you can be reached. What I need right away is a report from your geologists about Yucca Flat. I want that report one way or the other by early tomorrow morning. Get on this, Hugh. Call me as soon as you get the information. Goodbye."

The president deliberately hung up before Secretary Jennings could make any excuse.

The intercom buzzed. "AEC Chairman Straub is holding on line three," Mildred said.

He punched the Line 3 button.

"Henry, how are you? Great. Listen, things are moving ahead real quick on this test site thing. What I need are the numbers on the explosive yield of the two H-bombs you're getting ready to explode. Be precise on this. I understand the estimates of the first A-bomb yields were way off. Now with hydrogen and tritium being used to increase the explosive power, our own people are saying that you don't really know what the yield will be. Get me those numbers quick as you can and we'll put those rumors to rest. I'll be available until about eleven tonight, so please, call me if you know anything by then. All right?" Again, he hung up quickly.

He instructed his military aide to assemble the Joint Chiefs of Staff in their Pentagon briefing room within a half-hour. The aide immediately ordered a helicopter to transport the president to the Pentagon. The president was still jotting notes in the yellow pad when he heard the *thump-thump* of the 'copter blades as it prepared to land.

Two Secret Service agents led the way to the South Lawn where the chopper was waiting. Within minutes it rose to a height of five-hundred feet and veered west across the Potomac River to the Pentagon's landing pad.

The Joint Chiefs were waiting in Conference Room A for him.

"Good evening, gentlemen," the president said. "I'm going to be brief. The reason I'm here is that I have an important question for all of you. My question is, if our nuclear weapons development program were temporarily suspended tomorrow, would it affect your national defense capabilities and combat readiness? Don't elaborate too much in your answers. While the question is an important one I don't have the luxury of time. So keep it simple."

He knew that if he had given them time to prepare their answers, their rivalry for a larger share of the defense budget would have produced a much different response. He listened intently as each military branch head answered the question straight-forward and to the best of their knowledge. The consensus was that there would be no effect, unless the tests were permanently halted.

An hour later he was on his way back to the White House. He was looking out the window deep in thought. He was suddenly struck by the early evening beauty of the city. He instructed the pilot to circle around the Jefferson, Lincoln, and Washington Memorials. He wondered what these great men would do in his situation.

He said in a whisper, "Thomas, George, and Abe, you had it easy."

ANGELA'S BATTLE

Mildred was still at her desk when he arrived back in his office. It was almost nine p.m. "Mildred, get me the Secretary of Defense on the phone, then you can go on home." Then as an afterthought, "And Mildred, thanks for everything."

Mildred smiled broadly. It was good to be appreciated.

The intercom buzzed. "Secretary MacAdams is on line one,...and goodnight, sir."

The president picked up the phone. "George. Thanks for being available. In regards to this thing that's happened out west we may have to use this secret site of yours, Area 51. Can it be used for a high-level meeting? There'd be maybe two dozen people at the meeting. It would be a top secret affair and we'd need full security on all fronts. If there's things you don't want anyone to see you could put it under wraps somehow. I need to know how soon it would be available."

MacAdams asked, "Will this secret meeting definitely take place?"

"No, it isn't definite yet. It may depend on what you tell me, George. I need that information by tomorrow morning. Got me? Fine. Come see me then. Don't be late. Goodnight."

Later, as he lay in bed waiting to fall asleep, his last thoughts were that he now knew what he should do about the nuclear tests, and it would be up to others to convince him that he was wrong. It would be difficult to change his mind. The ball was in *their* court. It was now *their* problem, not his. His mind was at ease, and the president rested well.

Chapter Twenty-Six

President Kenneally woke shortly after six o'clock. While he ate breakfast he skimmed the front pages of the New York Times and the Washington Post. Both papers had gone to press at eleven last night. The headlines were old news to him, yet in common they were all criticizing him for not taking quick and strong action to reassure the American people that what happened in Phoenix was faked, and that their country's nuclear program was a safe project.

Well, let them rant and rave. What they don't know won't hurt them, he thought.

By seven-thirty he was in his office putting his notes together in preparation for his meeting with the cabinet. Shortly after eight an aide reported that Interior Secretary Jennings was on line two.

"Hugh, good morning. Do you have the information I wanted?"

"Mr. President. On the contrary, I have extremely bad news for you. Last night about eleven p.m., eastern time, our principle field team of geological experts, including a Dr. Charles Lyell, of the University of California at Berkeley, were all found dead in a canyon at the foot of Yucca Mountain in Nevada. They were finishing the study of a newly discovered ground fault where none was supposed to exist. Now they're all dead before they could give us a report of their findings."

"It's eerie, though. All six of them had their necks broken and twisted so their heads were facing backwards. Just like that newspaper editor and his wife who were killed near Tucson. Some local Indians were on a pilgrimage to an ancient shrine nearby and found the bodies scattered among the rocks. Two of them ran twenty miles to find help. It's very strange. The *Post* and the *Star* are going to do a special edition that will hit the street in about an hour."

"My God, Hugh. Are you telling me they were killed by the same monsters to prevent them from finding out the truth about the geology of the area? We were assuming those monsters were faked."

"We don't have a report yet on how they were killed or who did it. But we suspect it was some group that wants to postpone the bomb tests."

"Hugh, get your butt in gear and find out if they had notes or draft reports that will tell us what they found before they were killed. Call MacAdams right away and ask him to have the military police examine their camp, then fly any written material here as soon as possible. Damn. Things are getting worse rather than better. You have twenty-four hours to get that stuff here. Now get busy." He slammed the phone down and sat back to think.

He had to act quickly before the public got too excited about these new deaths. He called the press office. "Get me a copy of this mornings special edition of the *Post* and the *Star*. Send a police car for it if you have to, but I want it here in fifteen minutes." It wasn't eight o'clock yet and he was already hot and bothered.

Allen Gregory had hardly slept at all last night. He had read a file on the development of the atomic bomb, then another on the means used to increase their explosive power. He saw that the atomic bomb was now completely obsolete. A new generation of nuclear destruction had been born.

At 2:30 a.m. he managed to reach one of the nuclear physicists now working on the H-bomb. R.J. Williams lived nearby in Bethesda, Maryland, and he was not too happy at being called at this hour. At 73, Williams figured he had earned a good nights sleep.

He growled, "Who is it, and whatcha want?"

"R.J., it's Allen Gregory at NSA. There's trouble brewing and I need some help. I'd like to meet with you right away. It's urgent, and I promise that anything you tell me will be strictly confidential. Can you help me?"

R.J. was suspicious of government agents especially from the secret security agencies. Several of his colleagues had been hounded into oblivion after publicly coming out against further development of nuclear weapons of war.

"What do you want to know?" he cautiously asked.

Gregory was also careful. "I want to have a private talk with you. It's very important, and no one is to know I called you or that we talked. If you agree to that I'll be candid with my remarks. Okay? Will you do that? Please, I'm desperate."

R.J. was impressed. Gregory was almost pleading with him.

"Well, okay. There's an all-night restaurant in Bethesda, near the corner of East West Boulevard and 16th Street. I'll be there at 3:30 a.m. sharp. If you're not there, I'm gone. I won't wait for you."

R.J. had a brief sense of power by being the one to set the rules. He got dressed without waking his wife, but he did leave her a note, just in case, detailing who he was going to meet and where.

He drove by the restaurant and saw that the late Thursday night crowd had thinned to less than a dozen persons. He went around the block once looking for signs of surveillance. Seeing none he parked on a side street and walked in.

Gregory was sitting in a booth alone. He shook his hand and sat down. A waitress came, and he ordered coffee and a cinnamon roll. "Okay, Allen. You can start anytime you want. I'm interested in why I'm here."

Gregory began by telling R.J. of the accusations that nuclear scientists had no way of measuring the explosive yield of their H-bombs. He told him of the happenings in Phoenix and the ultimatums of the Indian coalition in the west. He spoke clearly and slowly so as not to leave any important points unsaid.

"Good God, this is incredible," R.J. said. In his business he had witnessed many strange things. He still believed in God, and who knew when God would decide to stick his finger in the nuclear pie. This man Amos, who Gregory talked about, could very well be a divine representative.

After more than a half-hour, Allen Gregory reached his bottom line. "R.J., I have to know. *Is it, or is it not possible to know the exact explosive yield of a hydrogen bomb that is enhanced by a tritium trigger?*"

There was a long silence as R.J. studied the bubbles in his coffee cup. Finally he looked at Gregory with squinted eyes. "How can I be assured of anonymity if I answer that question?"

Gregory said, "I can only give you the assurance of my reputation as a professional and as an honest man. I can assure you that no one will ever learn about your involvement, from me."

R.J. wrung his hands, then looked down at his coffee and spoke softly. "What I'm about to tell you could get me killed if the wrong people knew I told you this. *There is no way yet for us to even guess at the explosive yield of those two bombs that will be exploded at Yucca Flat.*"

He had an agonized look on his face. "The primary reason is that tritium is a comparatively short-lived radionuclide, so each month of its life its explosive effect is lessened. Our stockpile of tritium is already old. There is a plan to produce a new batch of tritium and rush it to the test site then insert it into the bomb just hours before it is exploded. No one can accurately predict what that yield might be. It could be equal to as little as five megatons of TNT or it might be as much as a million megatons."

He wrung his hands. "The shame is that we've gone ahead with production and testing without waiting to find out the correct yield formula when using hydrogen and tritium."

"Son-of-a-dog," Gregory said slowly. Then he asked, "Is there anything else I should know?"

"Yes. Right after the thing in Phoenix and the president had his first meeting with Mr. Straub, Straub secretly ordered the explosions to be moved up to exactly ten days from today. He wants to make sure any stop order from the president will come too late to stop the test. Do you understand now why this could get me killed? Remember what they did to Dr. Oppenheimer fifteen years ago? He was hounded into oblivion. Anyone who opposes the nuclear industrial and military complex is in danger."

"I'm not in favor of what Straub is doing, but I don't want to get killed either. I hope somebody stops him."

"R.J., you may have just saved us all. Thank you. Now I have to go figure out how to stop Straub." He raced home to make his plans. The eastern sky was just beginning to show the light of a new day when he sat down at his typewriter.

Chapter Twenty-Seven

This was going to be a busy day for Washington. President Kenneally was outlining his day when a military aide knocked on the door..

"Mr. President, Sir, Interior Secretary Jennings is here to see you. He says it is very important."

"Send the bastard in, son. He's only about a week late," the president said.

"Yes sir," the aide said, stifling a smile. He went to show *the bastard* in.

The door opened.

"Hugh. To what do I owe this pleasure?"

Secretary Jennings was wearing a sick smile.

"I rushed right over when this memorandum was delivered to me. It's a preliminary report from Judd Martin, who headed our study team out west. Let me read it to you."

The president interrupted him sharply.

"Just give it to me. I'll read it myself, thank you."

He leaned back and studied the memorandum. When he reached the final paragraph, his eyes opened wide, and there was a concerned look on his face.

It read, "It appears almost certain that a strong shock or a major earthquake could cause water to reach the tuff, thereby softening it and weakening the geologic layers which were previously thought to be of hard rock. Although this is a preliminary finding it is within reason that the catastrophic event foreseen by the Indians and Dr. Lyell is entirely possible. More factual information will be forwarded soon."

The president lowered the memorandum and looked sternly at the secretary who quickly tried to explain.

"Martin sent this report to USGS headquarters where its been sitting for three days. Staff thought it was unimportant until they heard of his death."

The president's face now had an angry expression. He looked up at Jennings.

"I think you had better leave, and don't come back until I send for you. For two years I've stood by you in spite of all your mistakes, and I don't like the way you're repaying me. Get out."

When he was alone he tore out the note page he had been writing and threw it into a shredder basket. Without talking to Allen Gregory first, the agenda couldn't be completed.

He buzzed the aide then smiled when Mildred answered, "Yes, Mr.

President?"

"Good morning, Mildred. Would you get me some coffee, then get Allen Gregory in here. Send him in as soon as he arrives. Call AEC Chairman Straub and tell him to be here at eleven for a private meeting. I want to meet with the NSC at two p.m., then with the cabinet secretaries at five."

Thirty minutes later, Allen Gregory arrived looking red-eyed and unkempt.

"Good morning, Mr. President. Forgive my appearance, but I've been up all night preparing my latest report for you. I'm tired as hell, but I've never felt better. I have some information that will shake the AEC to its roots, and....." The president interrupted him.

"Hold it Allen, maybe we'd better put this on the record. Is that okay with you?"

Allen said, "Certainly, Mr. President. I would prefer that."

The president pushed the intercom button.

"Mildred, please get the on-duty stenographer in here fast."

Within two minutes the door opened, and an efficient looking woman came in with pad and pencil. She took a seat to one side of the desk. When she indicated she was ready, the president said, "Allen would you please start over again?"

For the next forty-five minutes Allen Gregory related all he had discovered over the past 24 hours. When he finished he waited for a reaction.

The president nodded to the stenographer and said, "That's all, Miss Dodd. Thank you, and please have that typed and ready for me within an hour."

He then told Allen of his own suspicions which Gregory's news seemed to confirm. "I've got your group scheduled for a meeting at two o'clock, but I'd like you to be here when I talk with Mr. Straub at eleven. That'll give you time to go home and get cleaned up. No offense meant."

"No offense taken, Mr. President, but I have to tell you something else in complete confidence if you don't mind."

Gregory leaned close and said, "We've got a real science fiction mystery on our hands. Our team in Tucson went to the site where the Indians supposedly met Satan. They found signs of a large gathering, but they also discovered a large number of bodies buried in a shallow grave and covered with rocks. What little we know fits in with what we've been told. Two of the bodies are being flown to the FBI lab in Oklahoma City for forensic exams. By Monday we'll know more about how they died."

"The strangest thing is that our men talked with the local sheriff who said one of his deputies was actually at that meeting. Apparently the deputy was so shaken by what he saw that he took his family out of town for two weeks. We're trying to locate him now."

Then he drew his chair even closer.

In a whisper he said, "Sir, I suspect that you or I, or anyone else who knows what we know, is in extreme danger. First, our agents learned that right after you left the Joint Chiefs yesterday, there was a flurry of phone calls from their offices to two of the biggest nuclear defense contractors. Since eight o'clock last night my office has been flooded with calls from these contractors who wanted to talk to me right away. I have not talked with any of them."

"There were also calls from the Pentagon to Mr. Straub at his home. No less than 14 calls between the Pentagon and Straub were logged up until one a.m. I believe Straub is going to ask you to hold off for at least two weeks before making any decision about the bomb test. By then the bombs will already have been exploded. But, that's not all."

"The man who told me about the tests being moved up was R.J. Williams. He's been with the nuclear project for almost twenty years. Very early this morning, he told me that if anyone found out he had talked to me, he might be killed."

"I left him in good health at 4:30 this morning. His wife called me at eight, and said he never came home. It seems he had a collision with a diesel truck and trailer at an intersection in Rockville, five miles past where he lives in Bethesda."

"He must have known he was being followed, and tried to run away from the truck. Later, someone called R.J.'s house, and asked if R.J. was home. His wife was worried and told the man he had not come home after meeting me. I may be next on their list."

"One of our agents inside Dyna-Nuclear, the largest contractor, said that a few days ago there were rumors that a clandestine crew was being sent out west to stop the USGS team. They were told they could use any means necessary to make sure there was no report made."

"When I confronted Hugh Jennings with what I knew, he told me that he had known about the hit team, but didn't think they were going to kill anyone. He said he received a memo from his chief geologist last Monday and told Dyna-Nuclear about it. The team is on its way back from Las Vegas and we're going to arrest them when they get off their plane."

"I know it's hard to believe, but there seems to be a dangerous conspiracy to keep the nuclear explosions from being stopped. You should be very careful from now on. I've arranged for a meeting with the Secret Service to brief them on what they need to know."

The president said, "Secretary Jennings was here earlier this morning to tell me about his USGS team being found dead. He admitted having the memo, but blamed his staff for keeping it from him. He should have known he couldn't keep a secret like that. After we talk with Straub, we'll hold them both in custody until your NSC meets. We'll figure out a way to have them resign and disappear. What a mess they've made."

"Allen, talk with FBI Director Henley and have him take custody of the hit men. Have him here when Straub comes and they can pick him up too, along with Jennings. Take them all to Quantico and hold them incommunicado until we figure out this whole mess. Unless something comes up to change my mind before tomorrow, we're going to meet with Angela Beaver's group very soon. We'll call her tomorrow, how does that sound to you?"

Allen smiled. "I think that sounds great, sir. I just wish the nuclear industry hadn't got so desperate. There's a lot of money involved in their contracts. Billions. We don't know yet who else is involved in the conspiracy so we've got to move carefully. The CEO of Dyna-Nuclear should be questioned. Armand Hemminger would have a lot to lose if the project was stopped. But I'll call Henley first and tell him what's going on. I trust him."

"So do I," President Kenneally said, "but the fewer know about this, the better it will be for the time being."

"Yes, sir. I agree."

On his way out, Mildred told Allen, "A woman named Angela called and left a message for you. She said to tell you she's leaving for Las Vegas right away and left a phone number where you can reach her tonight."

"Thanks Mildred, I'll be in my office in the Old Executive Office Building until the eleven o'clock meeting with Mr. Straub."

When leaving Mildred's small office, he noticed a tall man wearing an expensive looking dark suit sitting in the waiting room. He said, "I thought the president didn't have any appointments today."

Mildred answered, "He doesn't. That man came in, said he was waiting to see the president, then sat down. I assumed the Secret Service brought him in. I'll call

an agent to check it out."
    When she got off the phone a little later, he was gone.

Chapter Twenty-Eight

The telephone in Room 231 of the Desert Sage Motel was ringing urgently. Jay opened an eye and looked at the clock. It was four-thirty. He answered sleepily, "Hello, this is Jay."

"Jay, wake up. Something's happened." Jay came fully awake. His first thought was *something's happened to Angela*. "What is it Ham, what's wrong?"

"Jay, you need to turn on the television news quick. It looks like the goat men have killed the geologists who were in Nevada checking out our story."

"What? How do you know?" Jay asked.

"I couldn't sleep so I turned on the TV set, and there were pictures of the bodies of six men laying dead among the rocks with their necks broken, just like your editor, Fuzzy Williams. Angela said we're leaving for Las Vegas just as soon as we can. The women are packing up now. Whistler is alerting scouts in nearby states to begin moving towards Yucca Mountain. He says there has been no sign of the goat men anywhere."

"We'll be waiting for you. Be careful," Jay said.

He called the others and asked them to come to his room. Soon there was a knock on the door. Sandra said, "Here we are. What's so important?"

"I'll let the television set tell you," he said. He turned the set on and motioned the others to find a spot to sit down. Diane was so nervous that she continued standing.

An announcer was telling of "Mysterious killings of six government geologists in the mountains northwest of Las Vegas." The bodies were shown close up as the announcer said, "The FBI is speculating that they were killed by Indian people who are opposed to the country's nuclear program."

They decided to find a newspaper to get more details.

They piled into Abner's car and drove to the nearest restaurant. They were silent as they dropped coins into the newspaper vending box. Then they filed into the restaurant to read.

Ten minutes later Sandra put her paper down and announced, "Indians didn't do it and neither did the goat men."

The others put down their paper and listened.

"Somebody didn't want them to discover what we already knew. Whoever did this wanted the goat men to be blamed for it. Only the federal government or the nuclear industry would have a reason to do this. We've got to find out who killed these men. If we don't, it could hurt our plans. What do you think?"

Frank said, "The placement of the bodies is too neat. It didn't look like what those demons would leave behind. They didn't do this."

"Alright," Jay said.

"Sandra, I believe you're right, but we should get our headquarters set up before we do anything else. Angela will be here tonight, then we'll make a plan. Abner, you're the key man today. Rent the building, get it cleaned up, and have a dozen or more telephones put in and working soon as you can. Diane and Frank can help you for now."

"Sandra and I will make plans for a big press conference first thing Monday morning. Thousands of people will be coming in and they've got to have a place to stay and something to eat. Let's eat our breakfast, then go to work. We don't have any time to waste."

While they were having breakfast, in Washington Henry Straub was nervously sitting outside the president's office waiting to be called. He had no idea that his secret was known. He had met earlier in the morning with top officials of Dyna-Nuclear, and they had bluntly told him what they expected of him.

"Your future depends on this," they had said.

He knew he would have no future if he failed.

After a short wait, a military aide came to escort him inside. He felt uneasy because he had never been escorted in by a military aide. His uneasiness was justified when he walked in. There were four men in dark suits standing along one wall. FBI Director George Henley, and NSA Director Allen Gregory sat facing the president. He quickly realized where his future really lay.

The president wasted no time.

"Henry, we've discovered the unpleasant news that you're involved in a conspiracy against the United States government. We're going to put you away for a while."

He nodded, and director Henley rose and said, "Henry Straub, you are under federal arrest for crimes committed against the government. We will detain you incommunicado for at least seventy-two hours. As of this moment you are a federal prisoner. You will now accompany these men."

Straub looked at the president pleadingly.

"Mr. President, I didn't mean....." He was cut off immediately.

"Shut up, you miserable fool," the president said.

Straub was escorted out the side door to the South Lawn where a Marine helicopter was sitting with rotor blades slowly turning. There were three armed Marines stationed at the chopper's door. His hands were swiftly handcuffed behind his back, then he was pushed up the steps into the Huey.

Inside, Straub was surprised to see *former* Secretary of Interior Hugh Jennings sitting between two guards, handcuffed like a criminal.

The loud *whump whump* of the blades turning faster and faster made any talk impossible. When they reached Quantico Marine Base, Jennings and Straub had no chance to exchange any words before they were put into separate cells. Their careers were officially finished.

A few hours earlier, Secretary Jennings had left his palatial home just outside of Middleburg, Virginia to have breakfast in the village. Middleburg was in the center of Virginia's horse and fox hunt country. Only the rich and famous could afford the requisite mansions.

He was having breakfast at the Coach Stop restaurant and talking local politics with Brian, the owner, when two dark sedans drove up. Four men got out. They came into the Coach Stop and told him he was under arrest. Other Middleburg residents were shocked when they saw their friend, Hugh, handcuffed and pushed roughly into one of the dark sedans.

He was taken directly to the H-street Secret Service office in Washington. Allen Gregory and George Henley asked him to sign an already prepared letter of resignation.

Director Henley said, "Mr. Jennings, if you refuse to sign this letter, we are ready to charge you with high crimes, any of which will land you in prison for many years."

He signed the letter, then was taken to the South Lawn of the White House to wait for the Marine helicopter. He was going to jail wearing his boots, jodhpurs, and riding club shirt. Allen and the president were considering their next move. The president said, "The only other person we need to speak with now is Defense Secretary MacAdams, and only then to get his cooperation for the use of Area 51. As for what to do with the Joint Chiefs, that can keep until after our meeting. When we have the evidence we'll let their own service court martial them."

"Allen, we're on the verge of a guaranteed safety-before-use nuclear policy and it all hinges on our being able to get all the facts known."

Things were moving fast, both in the western and eastern parts of the country.

Chapter Twenty-Nine

Abner proved to be the answer to most of Jay's logistical needs. He called the owner of the building and worked out a rental plan. Within two hours he had a work crew there to clean the building from front to back, and late in the afternoon trucks arrived with office furniture. Working from a hastily drawn floor plan Frank began placing desks and tables in designated spots.

Twenty telephones and twenty typewriters were soon in place. Abner had also provided Sandra with names and telephone numbers of environmental organizations in nearby states. She began calling them.

"Be here no later than 6 a.m. on Monday morning," she told them. "Charter a bus if you have to, and we'll help pay for it. We need to show the country that we're serious about shutting down the nuclear tests."

At the end of the day, she estimated that five hundred thousand people would be here by the time of the press conference.

Jay was able to get good newspaper coverage, and appeared on local and national TV news spots. Response was quick. The managers of two large casino hotels volunteered their kitchens to turn out soup, salads, and sandwiches each day for 5,000 people. The casinos had no particular axe to grind, but they knew that any accident at the test site would be bad news for their business.

Just before five o'clock, a phone rang. Jay answered. It was Angela calling from the motel office. "We're here," she said. "We can't wait to see all of you. We're coming right over."

A few minutes later, Ham drove up. Star and Fawn were the first out of the truck. It had only been four days since they had seen each other yet it seemed much longer and they were happy to be together again. After hugs were exchanged Ham said, "Let's take a look at our headquarters."

The newcomers marveled at what had been done in such a short time. Angela acknowledged Abner's help.

"Abner, I believe you've been sent by God to help us. This is all so wonderful. Amos will be here later tonight. I think he'll want to go to Yucca Mountain to see what we can learn. Whistler is already on his way there to meet with the scouts to brief them on the job ahead. We'll examine the area where the men were killed for any signs of who might have killed them. We're going back to the motel now and get washed. Then we'll have dinner, I hope."

By the time she returned to the motel, a message was waiting for her.

ANGELA'S BATTLE

The desk clerk told Angela, "A man who said his name was Gregory called. He said he would call back at six sharp. That's only ten minutes from now."

Angela rushed to tell everyone, "Everybody come to my room in five minutes," she said. "This may be the call we're waiting for."

Just before six, everybody was getting comfortable on the floor of Angela's room. They were on edge and excited by speculation of what the call might be about.

They waited for the seconds to tick by. For minutes, the room was as silent as a cat at a mouse hole. The telephone rang and everybody jumped. Angela let it ring twice then picked it up.

"Hello, this is Angela," she said calmly.

The voice on the other end said, "Angela. This is Allen Gregory."

Angela replied, "It's good to hear from you. I hope you have good news for us."

"Angela, we've made a lot of progress here in Washington in several ways, and now President Kenneally wants to talk to you himself. I think you'll like what he has to say. Here he is."

Angela whispered to the others, "It's the president."

Their excitement grew. Abner said, "I can't believe it. The president himself. This is great."

The president had a friendly voice.

"Angela, I've heard so much about you and your friends. It's a real pleasure to finally get to speak to you. Here with me tonight are Allen Gregory and George Henley, the FBI director. I want to talk with you about what is going to happen after tonight. You can say anything you like to me in strict confidence."

"First, I'm going to meet with you and your people sometime within the next three weeks. That is a promise. Within three days Allen will let you know exactly where and when. Angela, we don't know yet who killed the geologists. I can only tell you the killings were done in an effort to keep me from stopping the tests. For now, I am only going to delay the tests until after we meet. Depending on what we learn then, we might stop the tests altogether."

"My decision will depend on what you can convince us of when we meet. I hope you can believe me when I say I'm sympathetic, but I will only stop the bomb tests if I know it's *in the best interest of the entire country*. I hope you understand that." He emphasized those words for her benefit.

Then he asked, "Do you have anything to say to me?"

Angela spoke firmly. "Yes, I do, Mr. President. The fact that you represent the United States in this whole matter is a reason for us to be careful. When you were a senator you learned about Indian affairs. I remember that in 1952 you joined others in trying to terminate the Indian relationship with the federal government."

"You know the history of the mistreatment of Indians by the government, so I hope you forgive me for being skeptical. I don't blindly place my trust in the federal government, as other Indians before me did. I want more than words and promises. Good deeds are more important than either of these."

"The government has gone ahead with nuclear tests regardless of the deliberate, and sometimes accidental harm done to innocent civilians. So until the matter is settled to our satisfaction we're going ahead with our plans to stop the the explosions. We have much more to lose than you do. When the flooding takes place we'll be here, and you'll be safe in your part of the country. I like and appreciate your words, but it will take more than just words this time."

Then she spoke slowly and firmly.

"We know that it was some of your own people who did the killings, and they made it appear as if it was done by others. We think you know this also, but you haven't acknowledged that publicly yet."

"We have a press conference scheduled for Monday morning and we'll be forced to tell the country who really had those men killed, and why, if you don't do it yourself."

There was a short pause before the president spoke again. He looked at Allen questioningly. Allen motioned him to continue.

"I understand. I'll consider it. As for our meeting, someone will call you soon and tell you what the answer is. I'll probably meet with you, but be warned, I'll not let you dictate the terms. I've said all I'm going to say for tonight. Angela, whatever else you may think of me, I am completely honest when I say I am sympathetic to your cause. I hope you'll find reason to believe me. Goodnight."

There was a click from the telephone, and it was over. There was wonder in Angela's eyes as she put down the phone.

"I never thought that this simple Paiute woman would one day be talking tough to the President of the United States. I don't know where the words came from. It was as if the words were put in my mouth. Let's hope we don't get arrested or shot for what I said to him."

ANGELA'S BATTLE

Sandra laughed. "You were wonderful. We're proud of you." Everyone echoed the sentiments. When they were finished, Angela said, "Sit down, all of you, and I'll tell you what the president said to me."

They sat down to listen. When she was finished, she suggested that they all get some sleep. There was a lot to be done.

After she reached her room the first thing Angela did was to call her sister in Albuquerque. By that afternoon her two daughters would be on their way to Las Vegas by passenger train.

When Angela went downstairs in the morning, she found Amos waiting in the lobby. It was so good to see him. She quickly brought him up to date on what was happening.

Then Amos told said, "What I want to do today is to go the site of the killings and see if we can learn anything that will help you in your talks with the government. Whistler and his scouts are already there waiting for us. Let's leave as soon as we can, and we can talk on the way."

"Good. I just knew you'd want to go there," Angela said, "and so do we. Let's go to our headquarters and tell the others where we're going. Jay and Sandra are planning a big press conference for Monday morning and they need to stay here today."

Ham came forward to greet them, and when Angela told him she wanted to talk with the others, he stepped towards a new speaker system which had just been installed for the press conference and called them all.

"That's how we do it now," he said. "The system is loaned to us by one of the big casinos, believe it or not. This system will also work off a truck battery."

It was only a few minutes before they were all together again, plus two. Abner and Milford had been added to the core group.

Amos was impressed with the efficiency shown by each of them. After being assured by Abner and Milford that they were prepared for the thousands of people who would be here this week, Jay reported that at nine o'clock on Monday morning they would hold their first press conference.

Amos told them, "Today, Angela and I are going to Yucca Mountain to visit the spot where those men were killed on Thursday night. Ham and Star will go with us. We want to be convinced that the goat men were not involved. Our strategy from then on will depend on knowing exactly who did this terrible thing. Whistler and his scouts have been patrolling the perimeters of Yucca Flat watching for any unusual activity. Our visit to Yucca Mountain will be very important because until we know exactly who our enemy is we can't focus our energy on them. We hope to be back by sundown. We'll know a lot more by that time."

Chapter Thirty

After topping off the gas tanks they headed north on U.S. 95. An hour later they reached the little town of Mercury, the gateway to the Nevada Test Site. Just outside of town, a road split off and turned northeast. A hundred yards further, the road was blocked with strong iron gates and there was a large sign which read, **U.S. Government Property - Keep Out - Deadly Force Authorized**. There were three buildings here where employees were screened for radiation. If their tags showed any radiation at all they had to remove all clothing and go through a scrubbing process.

Today, there were no employees to be seen. Even the gate guards were gone. The gates were chained closed, so Ham cut the chain with bolt cutters from the truck's tool box. They were now in forbidden territory. This was almost too easy.

Twelve miles further on they came over the crest of a hill and saw red lights flashing in the distance. It was a manned checkpoint. Ham pulled out his binoculars.

"There's another gate blocking the road. If they see us they'll report us by radio and we'll soon have company. We can drive off the road into one of the side canyons and slowly make our way towards Yucca Mountain, which is off to the left."

A shadow passed over the truck. Whistler was there. Amos explained the problem to him. Whistler agreed with Ham's plan and said, "Get in your truck and back up so you'll be below the ridge and out of sight, then follow me."

Whistler led Ham into a gully running between two small hills. Once out of sight of the guard post, he led them up onto a plateau which was almost a perfect highway to their goal.

About 15 miles further the plateau suddenly disappeared and they were descended into a rough looking canyon which was strangely strewn with large boulders unlike others nearby. In the distance, a high flat ridge stretched perhaps twenty miles in an east-west direction. It rose from the desert floor about twenty miles directly ahead of them.

Ham exclaimed, "I know where we're at now. I've been here before some forty years ago. That high mountain ahead with the flat ridge is Yucca Mountain."

The canyon was without the usual desert vegetation, and most of the larger rocks and boulders seemed to be strewn in a rough line on the eastern side of the little canyon. There was a rock cliff on the western side of the canyon. They traveled another mile, dodging boulders as big as their truck. Then Whistler dropped down to halt them. Everyone got out of the truck, and Ham passed around one of the wet, cool canvas water bags.

Amos mopped his sweaty brow with a faded blue bandana, then said, "Folks, this canyon is known to the Indian people as The Place of Ghost Talk. The Sho-shoni people once called this land *Oyer'ungun*, their ancestral homeland. They and the Paiute people have been coming here for centuries because they say the ghosts of their ancestors speak to them here. *Wowoka*, the Paiute holy man who in the 1880s took the so-called Ghost Dance religion to the Midwest tribes, had his vision and inspiration here."

"Indians travel here to listen to their ancestors. At night, when the world is quiet, they say they can feel the spirits approaching. The ground shakes first, then they hear sounds coming from the other world. It sounds much like groans, cries, and whispered words which only the shamans can interpret. Our friend Ham has been here before and can perhaps give us a modern version of what's happening down below, and how this will tie in with our own efforts."

"Sure thing,"Ham said. "A long time ago my wife and I camped down on the plain near the mouth of the canyon. On our first night here, my wife woke me, saying that she could hear people talking. I listened and it did sound vaguely like far away voices. I walked a short way into the canyon, but no one was nearby."

"I came back in the daylight and examined the terrain, and even put my ear to the ground to hear what might be going on below. The strange sounds are caused, I believe, by the movement of many smaller faults criss-crossing this area. If the catastrophe happens, the entire underground solid rock of the Yucca Mountain range will slice upwards like a knife through dozens of yet undiscovered north-south faults like this one, making it easier for the deep western plate to rise suddenly, then fall back below sea level, allowing the flooding to take place. That is the belief I shared with Professor Lyell. I believe that the geologists were killed here for the purpose of stopping their study."

Amos was impressed. "Thank you, Ham. I have no doubt that what you say is true. Let's find the spot where they were killed and see what we can learn. Whistler, have your scouts look around and make sure there is no human activity nearby."

The truck began a slow trek towards the mouth of the canyon. Where the canyon ended there was a flood plain which sloped slightly upwards towards the rock called Yucca Mountain. It was apparent that Ghost Talk Fault ended where the giant rock began.

At the spot where the bodies had been found, there was no evidence of a camp fire. All signs of a camp seemed to be deliberately removed. Not a scrap of paper, coffee grounds, or piece of burnt wood remained to say that someone had recently camped on this spot.

Then Fawn exclaimed, "Here. This where they had their campfire." There was a faint trace of discoloration on a sandy spot that only an experienced eye could see.

"Yes," Amos said. "This is where they were when the killers found them."

The surrounding sand was completely covered with footprints of the police and the media, and of course those of the killers. Nowhere to be found was there any evidence of goat-like hoof prints.

"We need to spread out to find tracks or anything that will tell us from what direction the killers came," Amos said.

Whistler suddenly appeared and told them, "The scouts have located a spot to the east where it appears two helicopters landed. From there booted footprints come this way. Let's go see the place. I'll lead the way."

Whistler led them east about a mile to a place where scouts were circling above. They stopped the truck, then walked to a spot directly below the eagles. On close inspection, there were two circles about fifty feet in diameter on the desert floor where sand and small pebbles were swept clean by the downward wind from the helicopter rotors. In the center of the circles were deep impressions from landing gear.

Ho-go-ton spoke. "The scouts have seen helicopters make these identical marks many times before. Within a few days the desert winds will make the marks disappear, so we know that these marks here are very recent. The footprint trail is easier to see from above, but if you look closely you can see a narrow path where booted feet went in single file towards the white campers. If you look closer there is a broad path made by the same men coming back. They were less careful because they were in a hurry."

Amos gathered everyone around him. "I'm convinced that the goat men were not here. There's no reason to believe they did this thing. Everything points to the military. Now that we know that, we can get ready for our own offensive."

Then they headed back to Las Vegas using the fastest route. They bounced over desert terrain until they reached the paved road, turned right, and 45 minutes later they were waved through the guard post they had avoided before. The guard's orders were to stop anyone coming in, not going out.

On the way back, Angela told Amos she had sent for her two daughters. Amos was delighted. "I'm happy that I'll get to see them again. When will they arrive?"

"They'll be into Las Vegas at six tomorrow morning. I'll have to pick them up sometime before breakfast."

"I'll go with you," Amos said.

They were back at their headquarters building. The time was almost 5:30 p.m. The number of automobiles, trucks, and campers had grown surprisingly in the few hours they had been gone. Jay was not around.

Diane said that both Jay and Sandra had gone into the city to see newspaper editors at their homes.

"He said to tell you that they would be back by six, so you have time to get cleaned up. You're all dusty. And, Angela, there's a message waiting for you. Someone in Washington wants you to call them back as soon as you can."

This Saturday evening was like no other Angela had ever known. Everywhere she looked, thousands of people were busy. As soon as they had greeted Ned and others who had recently arrived, she and Amos went to the motel to review what they had learned.

Chapter Thirty-One

After a quick shower and a change of clothes, Angela called the Washington number given her by the desk clerk.

"Hello," a familiar voice said. It was Allen Gregory. "Angela, I'm so glad you called. Where have you been?"

Angela reminded herself to be cautious of what she said. For one thing, the president had said they knew Indians had not killed the geologists, but he didn't say who they suspected. They might still try to blame the goat men. And, they still hadn't told her anything that would prove they were really going to delay the tests. Everything the eagles had told her indicated preparations were still being made.

"Some of us were out seeing the countryside. Do you have news for me?" she asked.

"Yes, I do," Gregory said. "The president has agreed to meet with you on Saturday, September first. That's only three weeks away. It will take that long to make necessary arrangements. For reasons that I can't tell you, this has to be a super secret meeting. We're asking your assurance that you will tell no one outside of the nine members of your core group of the date and place of the meeting. If you agree, he is willing to delay the tests for an indefinite time."

Angela's mind was busy trying to assess the consequences of what Allen Gregory was proposing. "Give me a few moments, please," she said.

She wished Jay was here. He was familiar with the ways of politicians. Something Amos had said came to mind. "Trust your instincts."

She cleared her throat, buying a little time to think.

"Mr. Gregory," she said. "Hundreds of thousands of people who are opposed to your nuclear program will be here by midnight, and hundreds of thousands more will be here within a few days. We are no longer a fringe group. We are a national movement for change and we'll soon make our move. Now, I want to know the truth. Do you know who killed the geologists?"

Gregory hesitated, then said, "No, we don't. We're still trying to track them down."

If this was true, it confirmed her thinking.

Angela was suspicious of keeping both the date and place secret. It would be too easy for the government to kidnap her group without a trace and no one would know where they had gone. With them out of the way the president could easily resume the tests.

If Allen Gregory was truthful, the fact that the government didn't know who the killers were meant there was a secret third party involved which was powerful enough to oppose the federal government. She could be in more danger from this unseen enemy than from the goat men.

She decided that if there was to be a meeting at all, it would have to be on her terms. The federal government had many resources at its command, and it had years of experience in secret operations. Openness would be her best protection. She felt justified in taking a stronger position.

She played what Earl used to call a *hole card*.

She said, "If the country finds out who really did the killings, and why, it will be a national scandal and there will be hell to pay."

She knew she had struck a nerve when Allen Gregory gasped sharply.

"As for your super secret meeting," she continued, "things have changed drastically. The president has to issue an Executive Order stopping the tests before we agree to any meeting. Then we want the meeting date moved up to August 24th. We will agree to the location being kept secret, but we insist the date and the purpose be made public knowledge."

"The president told us that whatever he decides, it will be *in the interest of the entire country*. Nothing is more important to all our futures than the issue of nuclear destruction. We're firm on that. No compromises. Remember. Executive Order first, then we'll talk about a meeting."

Diane had told her that an Executive Order would be their best protection. When signed it became law until rescinded by a subsequent president. It was against her nature to be so rude, but she knew she had to force him to act swiftly. Too many lives were at stake.

Chapter Thirty-Two

Saturday In Washington seemed to be just another serene summer day. Hot, with the humidity in the 90 percent range. But a small inner circle of Washingtonians knew it wasn't a typical day.

At the Pentagon, the four Joint Chiefs of the military forces had came to their offices in civilian clothes at an early hour. Not long after, high ranking corporate officers of the largest defense contractors entered through doors on the opposite side of the Pentagon. They hoped no one took notice of them.

In the halls and corridors of Washington, there are those who are paid to look for the unusual. An experienced Washington-watcher could easily see something was definitely *up* on this day.

In the Pentagon, a sharp-eyed electrical maintenance foreman, who had been alerted by an equally sharp-eyed cleaning woman, went to an out of the way telephone. A phone rang somewhere in the District, and a man answered. The maintenance foreman said, "Sam. Something big is happening. The Joint Chiefs are here in civvies, meeting with the three-piece suits, and they're trying to keep it secret."

Sam was on his second cup of coffee, trying to come fully awake.

Just twelve minutes earlier, Sam Robertson, who was the White House news correspondent for one of the largest national television networks, had received his first call of the day from a White House intern who called to say things were unusual this morning.

The caller said, "The Secret Service is thick today. National Security Council people have been arriving for some kind of special briefing. There's a rumor that the president had a member of his cabinet and AEC chairman Straub arrested. This info came from a friend of a friend who is a Marine chopper pilot stationed at Quantico Marine Barracks. That's where they're being held. No visitors, no telephones."

Sam was stunned. If this was true, things were really serious. Sam called the White House press office to see if any special news conferences were in the making.

He was told by a spokesman that nothing was planned until after Labor Day. "Everybody will be leaving town soon, and everything is just as quiet and peaceful as a duck floating in a pond. See you later, Sam."

Sam hung up.

"Yeah, quiet and peaceful, just like a duck, but if you look underwater, this

Washington duck is paddling like hell." Sam had a nose for news, and instincts to match. He knew something big was going to happen. But what?

He called three free lance reporters, stringers he could trust. They served as his eyes, ears, and legs for flushing out important stories, especially those involving government secrets. He told each one what little he already knew, then turned them loose on the town, on Quantico, and on the Pentagon. He wanted a scoop ready for the seven a.m. newscast from the front lawn of the White House on Monday morning.

Sam sat down at his antique cherry-wood desk and pulled out his notes on recent White House involvements in political events. The Cuban fiasco was over and done with, but the CIA, the Soviets, the Cuban rebels, and Fidel Castro, and even the Mafia were all mad at the president. That was old news. Who *wasn't* mad at him?

He ran across a scribbled note from his White House intern contact. Sam remembered the note had been slipped into his coat pocket two days ago. When he first read it he had dismissed it as unimportant. He hadn't believed any part of the story which came out of Phoenix .

The note read, "*NSC involved in investigation of weird killings in Arizona. Allen Gregory to meet with Indians, including reporter Jay Storm Cloud, DC office Tucson Advocate. This is tied to thermonuclear H-bomb tests at Yucca Flat.*" The note went on for two more paragraphs.

As he re-read the note, the reference to nuclear H-bomb tests jumped out at him. The Indians were trying to stop the nuclear tests by telling some nutty story of hellfire and damnation. A name was mentioned. Earl Jemison, head of the Nuclear Institute. He was a close friend of Henry Straub, chairman of the AEC, and now Straub was missing and rumored to have been arrested. Sam's nose for news was twitching furiously.

The phone rang again. A voice said, "Guess what, Sam. The missing cabinet member is Interior Secretary Jennings. His wife hasn't seen him and no one knows where he is. And listen to this. A top scientist of the AEC was killed at four-thirty a.m. yesterday morning in a car and truck accident. His wife said it's the first time he's ever gone out at night. She said he met with Allen Gregory at two a.m. The strange thing is there's no police report of the accident and no sign of the truck that crushed his car. Check with you later."

"Thanks, Tim. Be careful. Look for surveillance as you move around. It could be dangerous. Call me tonight and we'll meet somewhere. Don't make any written notes yet. You can give me a verbal report." He knew that a high level hush-hush story could affect one's health in a big way.

At the Pentagon meeting with the Joint Chiefs, the consortium of nuclear contractors wanted to know if President Kenneally intended to stop the nuclear tests.

Armand Hemminger, the President of Dyna-Nuclear International, told the Joint Chiefs, "Without confirmation, we'll have to assume the president will try to stop the test explosions. Our corporate future and bottom line depends on those tests. Just remember, your futures are now closely tied to that of Dyna-Nuclear."

Hemminger had made his fortune and reputation by quick decisions and quick actions. He behaved no differently at this meeting. He bullied them into approving a decision to disregard the president and to go ahead with an acceleration of the nuclear test preparations. The explosions would take place on Monday, August 19. The Joint Chiefs were so deeply involved in the conspiracy that they had no choice but to agree. The explosions were only a week away.

When the meeting broke up the corporate fat cats were whisked away as fast as they exited the building. Not one of them was smiling. They knew that Straub had been called to the Oval Office and had not been seen or heard from since.

Later, Armand Hemminger tried to call Hugh Jennings to see if he knew what the president had in mind. Hemminger was alarmed when Mrs. Jennings said she hadn't seen Hugh since he had got dressed for a ride on his favorite horse, then went to breakfast in Middleburg. She had already reported him missing to the local county sheriff.

Straub and Jennings had disappeared at about the same time. Hemminger put two and two together, then decided to put his own plan into action.

Chapter Thirty-Three

At five a.m. Sunday morning, Angela and Amos drove into Las Vegas to meet the train carrying her two daughters. When the girls stepped down from the coach car they saw their mother, and ran towards her. They dropped their little suitcases, and hugged her tightly. They had enough of being separated from her and seemed to be trying to make up for lost time. Amos picked up the suitcases and carried them to the truck.

The older girl said, "Mama, we've been following your work by reading the newspapers and seeing the television news. We want to be with you and help you however we can. Can we do that?"

Angela replied, "That's why I called you, honey. All of us, the elders and the young men and women have to get involved and work together. I'm glad you've volunteered. I'm going to let you work with Star and Fawn. You've never met them, but you will love them, I'm sure."

When they got back to the building, she drew Fawn and Star aside and told them she would like to place Angela and Mina in their care. The older women were surprised and happy.

Star said, "There is much an Indian woman must know, and we will be glad to teach them about the Indian way."

It was done. They immediately liked each other, and by afternoon they were like old friends.

Shortly before four p.m. Whistler came to Angela. Another eagle was with him. "Angela, this is Swift Wing. He's just arrived with important news. I've sent for Amos." They went into a larger room. When Amos came in, Angela said, "Tell us what's happened."

Whistler asked Swift Wing to give his report.

Swift Wing said, "The scouts say there has been no sign of military aircraft flying in or out for two days. Large airplanes carrying many men have been arriving at the test site air strip all day. They are not military planes. There are now a lot of men there wearing dark clothes which have this patch on them. One of the men dropped this one."

Angela saw that it was a shoulder patch. She read a name out loud, *"Hunsaker Security Corporation."*

Diane exclaimed. "Hunsaker Security is the armed security contractor for almost all federal and commercial defense installations in the country. Hunsaker guards have federal authorization to shoot to kill. There's been many stories of them killing local people, but that's never been proven. Protestors and trespassers are found dead and there's no sign of the killers. They must have been hired by the government to keep us away."

Whistler spoke again. "Angela. There is more bad news to tell."

Swift Wing resumed his report. "Just over two hours ago, a helicopter landed next to a building. One other circled the area as if on lookout. Six men got out, went into the building and tried to force men who had white clothes on, like doctor's clothes, into the helicopter. An older man drew them all into a tight group and urged them to resist getting into the helicopter."

"The ones in black clothes began beating the men. The elder man tried to stop them and was shot. When the old man was shot, Tondo ordered our battle group to attack the men on the ground. We were able to rip the guns from their hands, but two others came out of the helicopter with machine guns and fired on us. Two of our young eagles are dead. Tondo withdrew us to re-group because they were now firing on us from the circling helicopter."

"Tondo took us behind a hill where he told us to each pick up the heaviest rock we could carry. Then he took us high above the circling helicopter. We dove at it and released our rocks on the whirling blades. The helicopter crashed and only one man came out of it. He was lying nearby and appeared badly injured. A short time later, men in a truck came and carried the injured one away."

"By this time Ho-go-ton arrived. He took us high again for safety, and said it was important to follow and see where the men in white were taken. Tondo's patrol followed the helicopter towards what Amos had called Area 51. Then Ho-go-ton instructed me to bring you this report."

Angela looked around her. Everyone had an angry look on their face. Sandra spoke. "It's clear now that the president has lied to us. For all we know, the government may have killed those geologists, and now he's brought in hired guns to stop us. We're going to fight back. We're going to whip those bastards. Damn, damn, damn them."

Diane looked thoughtful, then said, "But it's possible that the nuclear industry is doing this without the knowledge of the president. That may be why Allen Gregory seems to be as much in the dark as we are. The nuclear contractors will do anything to protect their gold mine. I'll bet that's it."

Angela said, "I think you're right. We have to assume the nuclear industry wants to make sure the explosions take place. Why else would they go to such lengths to deceive the public? I have to reach the president or Allen Gregory immediately. If our suspicions are correct, the president could be in grave danger."

She had no way of knowing that the president already knew this.

She went into one of the offices and closed the door. She dialed the private number that Allen Gregory had given her. There was no answer. Almost frantic now, she called the White House. She was told, "The president is not available. Do you want to talk to his someone else?"

"No. Please tell him this is Angela Beaver and this call is very important," she said.

Haughtily, the telephone receptionist said, "Why, of course it is, dear. I'll send the message along to him. I'm *sure* he'll return your call immediately." Angela pretended not to notice.

Visibly upset, she went back into the other room and told the others, "I think we have to move our schedule up. We've got to reach ground zero quickly. Even if the president returns my call it may too late. We can't let the explosion take place."

"Jay, Sandra, tell the media that in one hour we're going to announce something very important to the American people. Tell them we've learned the bombs are going to be exploded soon. I can't believe the president is willing to sacrifice people *for the good of the country*. What did he mean when he said he cared about us?"

"After you make your announcement, come on back and help us write a statement. Jay do you think you could get a local television station to carry the press conference on their national network?"

"Good idea," Jay said. "I'll call somebody right now."

He called the local TV station and asked them to track down the station manager quickly, and if possible, a network official. The manager called back within two minutes. He was not pleased. "We already have a crew there. What more do you want?" he asked.

Jay didn't want to make him angry. He said, "I'll call you later." Then he went to the station's local reporter who was setting up equipment near the new platform. He knew he'd have to impress this reporter if he was going to succeed.

He took him aside. "Something very important has happened and we've moved the press conference up to five p.m today. Believe me, it's block buster news. We want to go live on the network. Will you help us do that?"

The reporter expressed some doubt. " Call my office," he said.

"I've done that," Jay said. "I'm sure you recognize big news when you see it. How about talking to Angela about this?"

He agreed and Angela briefed him on the new events, then added, "If you want to, you can interview the eagle who was there at this morning's fight."

The reporter took advantage of the offer. He spent five minutes with Whistler and Swift Wing and came out of the room highly excited. "Holy Cow. This is big news. Let me call the station manager. We've got to do this." Within ten minutes the manager called back.

"The network stations are being alerted now," he said. "We're switching to network at one minute to five, Pacific time. It means a lot to us to get this scoop. Thanks."

Jay hollered out to the others, "We're going live on national television." A loud cheer answered him.

Angela again called the White House. A different voice answered her call. "This is Angela Beaver. Tell the president to watch the NTC network station at eight p.m. your time. It's very important. He may be in danger."

"Ma'am," the telephone voice said. "Please repeat the message. Are you threatening the president?" She had already pushed a button to alert the Secret Service and to begin a recording. Angela replied, "No. But he is being threatened by someone else. Just tell him to watch NTC-TV. Goodbye."

If nothing else, the telephone call raised the White House's level of Secret Service activity and interest. The president, who was conferring with Allen Gregory was notified. Allen immediately called the TV network and was told of the nationwide coverage.

Chapter Thirty-Four

An emergency meeting had taken place in Washington between the president and the Secretary of Defense. After briefing congressional leaders and assuring them there was good reason for the arrest of some officials and detaining others, the president and Allen Gregory went to the Pentagon.

Secretary MacAdams told the president that an investigation had revealed the Secretaries of the Army and the Air Force had removed all military personnel out of the test site, as well as from Nellis Air Base without authorization. They were now scattered among several military bases in Utah and northern California. Base commanders were told they should evacuate their Nevada bases until after the nuclear tests because they might be needed for rescue operations if the predictions of a catastrophe proved to be true. The Secretaries of the Army and the Air Force were arrested by the FBI for conspiracy to overthrow the U.S. government.

MacAdams said the Defense Intelligence Agency had determined that the two secretaries and the Joint Chiefs were in collusion with the AEC to carry out Dyna-Nuclear's aim to explode the bombs. Armand Hemminger, the CEO of Dyna-Nuclear, could not be found.

"At the first sign of discovery, Dyna-Nuclear and Hunsaker Security had begun moving half of their 10,000-man security force from around the world into the Nevada desert to take over the Yucca Flats and Area 51 complex. The first contingents were due to arrive at about eight a.m. this morning," MacAdams said.

"FAA radar reports indicate a large transport plane arriving at Area 51 and Yucca Flats every thirty minutes. They are, without a doubt, fortifying the area now and if the civilians get too close to either the test site or to Area 51, they will surely be fired upon. At this point the conspirators are very dangerous and must be considered as enemies of the state."

"We've got to move against them," the president said. "You were a unit commander during the Anzio Beach campaign, what would you suggest, Colonel?"

The secretary smiled. "Thank you for asking, Mr. President."

Then without hesitation, he added, "At this time it would be difficult to estimate how far down the chain of command the influence of the conspirators has reached. We don't know who we can trust right now, and we don't have time to find out. We need commanders who can be depended on to follow your orders."

"My advice is this. Because we want to localize and limit any ground fighting to hand-to-hand fighting, we should have General Dooley bring in a regiment of

Marine Infantry from Camp Lejeune to neutralize any opposition from Hunsaker's forces and gain control of the area. An armored strike force from Camp Pendleton should assist them."

"At the same time, you should mobilize the National Guard in New Mexico and Arizona for logistical support and occupational duties. Those states have good Air Wings which would be helpful in transporting men and supplies once Yucca Flats is secure."

"Very good, colonel. I wonder if General Dooley is up to leading the effort. I know he was asking to be retired soon."

"Why don't you ask him yourself, Mr. President." MacAdams pushed a button and a buzzer sounded in the next room.

"Butch," he said into the intercom. "Come in, will you please.?"

The door swung open and a rugged-faced man in Marine-green officers uniform came in and stood at attention.

The president said, "Stand easy, General. It's good to see you again. Please sit down."

General Dennis "Butch" Dooley had served with distinction in both World War II and in the Korean conflict. Desk work was not to his liking and he was considering retirement.

"Butch, the president wants to know if you'd do one more job before you retire. You know, the job we talked about last night. Do you still have the plan and maps you showed me?"

"They're in the next room, right where we left them," Butch Dooley said.

The president said, "You knew all along I'd want you, General. If you would take charge, it sure would be appreciated. We're in a hurry here and things need to happen right away. The lives of many civilians are in danger."

"I'm at your service, sir. I can have my Marines in the air tomorrow afternoon. If you can mobilize the Guard immediately and place them at my command, I'll call them in to occupy the area and we'll proceed from there. I can have it secure within 24 hours of Zero Hour."

"Do what you have to do, and good luck, General. I'll issue your authorization. Just get it done quickly."

Allen Gregory listened with some fear. He knew it was possible that as soon as Hunsaker's men realized they were being attacked, Angela or any of her people could be used as shields. If this didn't stop the Marines, they would probably be

ANGELA'S BATTLE

killed.

The president tried and was unable to reach Angela. She knew nothing of his plans and could be moving into a danger zone.

In the White House, an intern was making another phone call to Sam Robertson who was at home preparing for tomorrow morning's telecast. NTC-TV was Sam's employer. When Sam was told the news that General Dooley was being briefed before moving into Nevada, he quickly arranged for a special report to be telecast at nine p.m. He also called his boss to cancel tomorrow's report and asked for permission to charter a plane to fly him and his camera crew to Las Vegas. His nose was *itchin'* and *twitchin'*.

The president tried one last time to reach Angela. Her phone at the motel went unanswered. Then all telephone lines at their headquarters were suddenly cut. Jay didn't want any calls to be made before Angela made her announcement.

At two minutes to the hour, television sets in Washington, and the nation, were switched on and dials clicked to NTC-TV's local channel. Across the country, network stations had been interrupting regular programs every five minutes to announce the live coverage from Las Vegas.

At one minute to five p.m. the network control shifted to the Las Vegas station as the live coverage began.

Allen Gregory was seated on a couch in the president's living room, trying to calm him. He said, "How could they possibly know any more of where those technicians are than we do? They couldn't know who's behind the killings. Relax. They're just trying to speed up your Executive Order so they'll have more time."

"Allen," the president said, "I've got a strong hunch I may regret not acting sooner. As soon as you told me about the Joint Chiefs I should have had them and Armand Hemminger arrested, along with Straub and Jennings. Now we have the Joint Chiefs, but where is Hemminger? He's the man we really want. We've got to find Hemminger and Hunsaker. As long as they're loose I could be their next target. Somehow Angela knew this."

"I'd like you to get word to Angela and the media that my Executive Order stopping the nuclear tests will be issued at seven p.m., Las Vegas time." Then he called his Chief of Staff.

"I want an E.O. issued right away to stop all underground nuclear tests in the continental U. S., effective immediately. Have it brought to my office. I'll sign it immediately."

230

As the president watched the television screen there was a lot of talk by the news anchor about what might be said today. The camera panned outward and President Kenneally saw thousands of cars, trucks, trailers, tents, and tepees, all lined up as if carefully placed. The size of the crowd is what made him catch his breath.

"There must be over a million people there, Allen. There would be no way to control them if they were angry people. It's simply amazing what this Indian lady has done. It's quite an accomplishment."

Finally, Angela was introduced. The crowd had been waiting for her and thunderous applause and shouts of *"An-gel-a, An-gel-a,"* rolled out over the warm desert lands. When she came to the microphone the TV audience heard cheers and applause from a million people. When Angela began speaking, the crowd quieted. The Indian woman who just a few short months ago was unsure if she could assume the role handed down to her by the Creator, now took control of the largest civilian army ever seen in this country.

She began, "Friends, our government is trying to stop us from telling the truth. The truth is that the men who were killed the other night were not killed by monster goat men. They were not killed by Indian people. They were killed by agents of a federal contractor."

She paused a few seconds, then, "The reason why they were killed is very important."

President Kenneally's knuckles were sickly white as he gripped the arms of his chair. "Here it comes, Allen. I'm afraid they know more than we thought."

Allen Gregory quietly sipped his coffee.

Angela paused again, then resumed. "The geologists were killed because they were on the verge of proving that what we have been saying about the nuclear bombs causing a catastrophe is true."

The huge crowd became hushed.

"Yesterday, five of us went to a place called Ghost Talk Fault and we found proof that government contractors killed those men!"

"As I speak to you, U.S. military personnel have been pulled out of Yucca Flats and it has been taken over by armed agents of the notorious Hunsaker Security Corporation. Protest groups and environmentalists already know of Hunsaker's violence and their willingness to protect the nuclear industry at all costs. Our government has turned the nuclear test site over to them and they have kidnaped the bomb technicians. Their own technicians will no doubt be used to explode the bombs. It is our belief that the president plans to go ahead with the explosions very soon."

"I have been in touch several times with the president himself, and he would not commit to a meeting with us. He admitted to me that he knew the geologists were killed to keep him from stopping the tests."

Turning towards the network cameras, she looked directly into the lens and shook a finger at it. "Mr. President, if you knew these things, *why haven't you taken actions to stop the tests?*"

Instinctively, the president drew back from the screen. The crowd roared in support of her questions.

She then told of her talks with Allan Gregory beginning with the night he spoke with them in Flagstaff, and about all their subsequent telephone conversations. She held nothing back. She knew if she was to force the president to act swiftly she would have to embarrass him enough to make him move decisively.

"Last night Mr. Gregory said the president offered to meet with my small group on September 1st, at a secret location. He said the tests would be stopped only if it was *in the best interest of the country.*"

"I submit to the president, and to the American people, that *saving the lives of 20 million American people and the southwestern part of the country is in the best interest of the entire world!* Mr. President, you should have already issued your Executive Order."

The crowd roared in agreement.

"We think it's a real possibility that plans are being made to explode the bombs very soon, maybe tomorrow. There may not be time to have a meeting with the president. We can't afford to let them explode the bombs without a strong effort to stop them."

"There is also the very strong chance that the situation is now entirely out of the president's control. The hired guns of the nuclear industry are in complete control of the entire area, and we now have proof that armed thugs from Hunsaker Security are the real killers."

"By making all of these facts known we hope the president will wake up and realize that he himself is in danger from these thugs. The president may already be powerless to stop the nuclear explosions. Even if he signed the Executive Order today, the plans to explode the bombs would go ahead. We---you and I, together, have to act for him and for the country. We must occupy the Test Site. We must hope that the bomb will not be exploded if we are there. We must act in defense of all Americans. *Are you ready?"*

The crowd set up a roar heard across the country. Angela turned once more to the network camera and asked the nationwide television audience, *"Will you join us?"*

Throughout the country, millions of citizens were wondering if it was true that the nuclear industry was wrongfully going ahead with plans to explode the bombs, and was it true that their president was indeed powerless in the matter?

Typical of the 175 million concerned Americans were Claude and Sarah Sorenson in upper Minnesota, near Red Lake. After a few minutes of shocked silence, Claude said, "Well, Sarah, we'll just give old Hubert a call. He's always on top of things in Washington." Hubert was a local man, and their U. S. Senator.

Within ten minutes of the end of the televised gathering in Nevada, telephone lines were overloaded with calls to congressional offices in Washington, D.C. and to the White House. When 175 million citizens couldn't get through to their congressmen, anxiety and nervousness began to spread across the country.

Chapter Thirty-Five

Shortly after Angela's talk ended, a small army of Marine infantry from Camp Lejeune, North Carolina was in the air flying towards Nevada where they would rendezvous with battalions from Camp Pendleton in Southern California. The rapid-response battalions were scheduled to leave from March Air Base near Riverside at ten p.m. They would link up with infantrymen at Nellis Air base near Las Vegas at midnight.

General Dennis "Butch" Dooley, USMC, was in command. He had already decided that his fast-moving armored cars would move into Yucca Flat's test site compound at daybreak. He had told the president that "Yucca Flat will be secure in its entirety by sundown." He had been made aware of the possibility of the technicians being held hostage somewhere within the complex and their safe release would be a priority.

Sam Robertson was doing a special report to the nation from the front lawn of the White House. In a large way, he was corroborating Angela's charge that the president was floundering.

He began, "Good evening. NTC has confirmed that all of the military Joint Chiefs of Staff in the Pentagon have been placed under house arrest by their commander-in-chief, and we have also confirmed that Henry Straub, head of the Atomic Energy Commission, and Interior Secretary Hugh Jennings were arrested early Saturday morning and are now being held at the Quantico Marine Base. The charges against the two federal officials has not yet been revealed."

Over the next ten minutes, he reported everything that had happened in Washington which actually fit in with Angela's descriptions. "So many questions are unanswered," he said, "but the White House is not ready to talk."

"In the meantime, the death of nuclear scientist R.J. Williams early last Friday morning, shortly after meeting with Allen Gregory, head of the National Security Council, is still a mystery. There has been no motive established, but it may be that he talked too much to the wrong person. The mystery is heightened by the fact that it was only a few hours after Mr. William's death that Henry Straub was arrested by the FBI while inside the White House."

"We had reported to you earlier, that National Security Director Allen Gregory had ordered an investigation into incidents in Phoenix, Arizona. We are now told that Mr. Gregory personally visited with Angela Beaver and her companions in Flagstaff, Arizona just one week ago."

"Tonight the president will issue an Executive Order declaring a national emergency and this effectively places all nuclear testing under his direct control. In addition, all military installations and their commanders are now under his direct order to mobilize themselves and wait for further orders. It appears something big, something big enough to threaten our government, is taking place and as soon as we discover more we will bring that news to you."

Sam Robertson continued, "Angela Beaver was very close to the real truth in her remarks today. The president has no choice but to do something, anything, to show he's still in charge. If he does not move quickly now to resolve the situation to the satisfaction of the American people, we may be seeing the end of his political life."

"Sam Robertson reporting live from Washington."

The special report ended.

Sam quickly gathered his crew around him. "Look guys. We've got a chartered plane to catch at eleven. Be at National's corporate hangar on time. Don't be late or we'll leave you."

Angela had decided that they now had to move fast. The first thing to be done would be to send the eagles out on a night mission to see if there were any new developments near the test site. Frank was asked to brief them on security methods they might encounter. "Your first danger will be radar. To avoid their radar, don't fly higher than 50 feet above the ground and if you see anyone, you should move away. In each patrol, scouts can be sent in to begin the search, while the main body of eagles can wait nearby in case of trouble. Remember, you don't have a defense against their machine guns. Good luck."

"May the Creator keep you safe," Angela said. Then Whistler and Swift Wing were off into the starlit sky.

Angela outlined a basic plan. "We should move towards the test site no later than two a.m. Abner, get the buses and trucks here by midnight, and line them up alongside the highway where it'll be easier to load them and get them on the road. Frank, you and Ham should lead the way and begin assembling everyone as close as we can get to the turn off to the ground zero spot. We will hope that by then Whistler will have a report for us, and we just might have to split into two groups. Wait for us at that turn off."

"Abner, I'm sorry to have to ask you to stay here, but we need someone here to make sure everyone moves out on time. Milford, please work with Abner and

ANGELA'S BATTLE

keep as many of your people here as he needs to help. After the people are all on the road, you can leave someone else in charge here and come join us. We're also going to need the two-way radios to keep in touch. Ham, you take one, and Abner can keep the other."

"Jay, you and Sandra please make an announcement of what's going to take place so the people can get ready for the trip. The first units will leave at two a.m."

Angela went to her motel room for a short rest. She sat for a few minutes with her daughters and held them close. She was suddenly tired from the days of non-stop activity. She closed her eyes and found herself wishing they were back in their Utah mountain home. It had been so peaceful then.

She enjoyed the memory for a short time, then she remembered why she was here. The squirrels, birds, and deer had abandoned the area and the forests were turning brown. That's why she was here. She had a job to do.

The phone rang. It was Allen Gregory. "Angela. I've tried to reach you several times, before and after your television report."

"Well, obviously we've had a lot of reaction to what was said, so we've been very busy," she said. At this point she didn't know who to trust.

Gregory went on. "Listen, if you go into the test site, you will be in great danger. Please believe me. The president has a job to do, but he is sincerely concerned for you and the other citizens, as I am. I'm on your side, and I do have a conscience in spite of the work I do."

"I have to tell you that early tomorrow morning the test site and its airport is going to be a dangerous place to be. I hope you have no plans to be there. Just stay away, please, at least for another day. Will you do that?"

Angela was silent. She couldn't believe what she was hearing. Her mind was working furiously. *They're planning on exploding the bombs tomorrow*, she thought. *That's why they want us to stay away. We can't let them do that or all we've worked for will have been in vain.* Her anger was building up.

She told Gregory sternly, "I warn you not to explode the bombs or even try to. I'm so mad at you and your kind of government, and if you did harm to any of us here, I would make it my business to have my revenge. You can't do this and still say you have a conscience. Damn you!" She slammed the phone down.

Meanwhile, in a complex built deep underneath a small airport in backwoods Arkansas, Armand Hemminger was contemplating his next move. He had watched the televised report from Las Vegas, and as he swirled an ice cube in a now empty glass, he convinced himself that he had done all he could to develop the new bomb. His plan was being carried out.

His company had built this airport for the CIA during the Cuban missile crisis, and while under construction he had conveniently had his crews build underground living quarters equipped with modern communications devices. It had been paved over by the runways and the entrance hidden inside a warehouse in the surrounding woods.

A day earlier, when his informants had told him of the actions taken by the president against the Joint Chiefs, he had immediately fled in his private plane to this obscure airport near Mena, Arkansas. No one ever questioned the arrival or departure of any planes here, because there were always armed guards at the perimeters of the airport and large signs reading, **Danger-Trespassers Will Be Shot**, were posted all along a 10-foot-high steel fence.

Hemminger had ordered the nuclear explosions to take place as soon as possible, and everything necessary was now being moved to the test site. He had removed the AEC scientists and replaced them with those of his own company. When he received information that the president was sending in troops to take over the test site, he had decided to leave for another hidden location in the jungles of Guatemala until after the explosions took place. If they were successful, he would return. If not, he would disappear until it was safe to emerge with another identity.

After destroying all paper records, he flew out of the country to await developments. Ironically, after reaching a cruising altitude of 28,000 feet, his pilot reported there were military transports flying 2,000 feet above them and heading west.

Like the proverbial ships that pass in the night, Armand Hemminger crossed paths with the very Marines who would move against his private army.

In the lead plane, General Dooley suddenly experienced a strange sensation, and his neck hairs stood up. He looked out the window and saw a plane crossing his path far below. He had no way of knowing that in the plane, Armand Hemminger was sipping, unconcerned, on his second Martini.

Chapter Thirty-Six

At two a.m. Angela's vehicle took the lead and pulled onto Highway 95, heading towards the southwestern edge of the test site. Following close behind was a long caravan of vans, campers, buses and trucks. More would follow as soon as they could get packed. Abner and Milford had begun making calls to get the buses and trucks ready as soon as possible and then as quickly as they were loaded they got on the road. Food and water trucks would follow soon after. The civilian army was on the move.

Angela's caravan was nearing the little desert community of Mercury. The steel gates which blocked the road to Yucca Flats and the nuclear test site were once again chained shut, and the guard shack was empty.

There was no one around to stop them. Ham cut the new chain and swung the gates open. Again, they were into forbidden territory. Amos studied a map of the local area. Once inside, they drove at a slower speed in order to not miss forks and turnoffs, and to not lose any of those behind them. It was a very dark night. Angela moved ahead slowly. One by one, the trucks and campers turned and followed the lead trucks driven by Frank and Ham.

They had gone no more than twenty miles and the first morning breeze, pushed by the warming air far to the east, was just beginning to be felt when there was a sudden series of bright flashes to the east. Flares by the dozens could be seen floating in the air. Angela stopped to look.

Ham told them, "The preparations may be starting. We'll have to move faster."

Ham called Abner on the radio and asked him to send the food and water trucks as soon as the last vehicle started out. "When we get to the turn off to test site, we're going to set up a supply camp near there. We'll park most of the vehicles and begin our march towards ground zero. Someone will be at every turn to direct people where to go and what to do. Abner, there are lot of flares off to the east, so we think the preparations to set off the bombs have begun. Wish us luck."

Abner said, "I wish you a lot of luck, my good friend, and I wish I was with you. May God bless you, and be careful."

Angela's caravan resumed their slow drive through the early morning darkness. Frank was now leading. Jay and Diane were in the front seat with him. Jay had almost forgotten how calming the desert nights could be. While during the day the sun could turn the desert into a broiling oven, at night the heat quickly dissipated and the surface temperature could drop as much as 50 to 60 degrees, requiring a sweater or light jacket. It was a beautiful and mysterious place full of Nature's creations, animal, bird, plant, and Man's imagination.

Overhead, the stars shone like diamonds every night and the desert was one of the few places where the Milky Way could be clearly seen. This night was no different. Jay loved the desert.

Occasionally, a desert creature would start to cross the road, then stop, blinded by the headlights, and would move only when frightened by the engine's roar. Now and then, they would see a silver ribbon move towards the road's edge when caught by the light. This was a cold-blooded rattlesnake who had been enjoying the warmth of the roadway. The snake's white scales and underside shone like silver when hit by the light.

An occasional owl, its hunt disturbed by these intruders, would cross the headlights. A gray fox, curious about the night travelers ran alongside for about fifty feet then veered off into the more familiar darkness when the pungent odor of a skunk, hit by a vehicle sometime during the day, spoiled the smell of sweet desert sage and mesquite.

Nature's creatures often were seen near roadways because the asphalt paving was much warmer than the surrounding sand, and it attracted the smaller creatures of the food chain as well as the predators. For them it was a ready-made super market.

A half-hour later, Angela asked Frank to stop. "Amos, please call Whistler. Ask him to send Ho-go-ton and 50 scouts. It'll be light soon and we're going to need them to make sure we're not running into an ambush or some kind of trap. As soon as we can see better we'll have to go faster. Let's send someone back to pass the word that everyone can get out and stretch then we'll be moving in about ten minutes as soon as the eagles get here."

"Amos, where are we at now on the map?" she asked.

"Here," Amos answered, "about 15 miles from Shoshone Peak." He pointed to a spot on the map. 'Ground zero is about 50 miles east of that rocky peak. About twenty more miles, we'll turn off to the northeast."

Sixty miles to the southeast, General Dooley's Marines were massing their armored vehicles for a swift run at the administrative buildings and laboratories of the AEC Test Site headquarters, located about ten miles southwest of ground zero.

Headquarters was a small village complete with laboratories, warehouses, hangars, and housing for staff and technical support groups.

There was also an airport which had long runways to accommodate large aircraft. There was no way of knowing how many armed men Hunsaker Security had guarding the perimeter or were available to fight any invaders. It was estimated that there could be as many as 10,000 men.

At 0430 the attack was to begin. Mobile radar units were already in place on the flanks of the attack column. Once inside the perimeter of the air base the armored personnel carriers would take the advance units across the three main runways, then the troops would be on their own to make their way in to secure each building one by one. Their orders were to not fire unless fired upon. The taking of live prisoners was preferred to dead bodies. They were to be on the lookout for a group of AEC technicians who were being held against their will.

Hours earlier, just after midnight, the plane carrying Sam Robertson and his NTC-TV news film crew flew over Lake Meade, crossed the Nevada state line, then descended into an approach to McCarran Airport in Las Vegas.

The control tower contacted them with an advisory, "There's a lot of traffic above you, so be careful. We've got military traffic descending into Nellis."

When the pilot told Sam what was going on he almost swallowed his bubble gum. He always chewed gum just before landings to keep his ears from hurting, but now his nose began to twitch. Something big was happening down there. He couldn't wait to get on the ground.

As soon as they had collected their equipment and loaded it into their rented van and stake bed truck, he set out for Nellis Air Base, just outside the northern city limits of Las Vegas. When he saw the air field all lit up and dozens of transports unloading, he knew he had hit pay dirt.

Sam Robertson had the scoop he had been looking for when right under the nose of General Dooley, Sam set up two cameras in the back of his stake-bed truck, covered them with a tarpaulin, then took a round-about cross-country route and followed the infantry units to their objective. He had placed his truck nearby the supply trucks, and when the attack began he had raced in along with the invading Marines. He parked the truck on an air strip and he was filming the Marines as they exited the carriers and stormed into the buildings.

He had decided to stay in full view because the hundreds of magnesium flares lit up the place like daylight, and there was really no place to hide so he just acted like he belonged here. Marines debarking from the armored carriers saw the cameras and immediately became more gung-ho, and young officers bellowed orders and waived their arms dramatically.

Here and there, shots were being fired, but Sam couldn't see what was happening so he tried to get closer to the action. An officer finally noticed that the truck had no insignia and reported his presence to the command post. The officer returned and told Sam, "Get the hell out of here or you'll be shot."

Sam had always believed in preparedness, and this time was no exception. He had already mapped out an escape route. His instincts had been honed by covering numerous battles in WW II and in Korea. He told his driver, "Head to the end of the runway and turn right past the row of buildings and we'll go back the way we came in, only slower this time."

To the two cameramen he said, "Pull off the tarp and keep those things rolling. Get a close-up of any officers you see." An officer in the command post waved at them as Sam went by and ordered the truck and its occupants to be detained and their film confiscated, but Sam was long gone.

Once back on the main highway he headed for a restaurant to get an early breakfast, then on to Angela's headquarters. Now he wanted a view of this war from Angela Beaver's standpoint. As he savored his coffee, he told his crew, "It's good to be back in a war. Feels like old times."

After Abner had received Ham's message, he met briefly with Milford Haynes and others to tell them of the new activity near ground zero Over the loud speakers, Abner brought everyone up to date on what was happening. Then he found 24 volunteers who would be the last to leave and would have the responsibility of arranging for shipments of more food and water beginning tomorrow morning. Then he and Milford made plans to move out. They wanted to be there when the caravan reached ground zero.

A white van and a stake bed truck drove up. A man jumped out of one of the vans with a TV camera and began filming the vehicles leaving. Abner was reminding a driver that Angela suspected the government was going to try to go ahead with the nuclear explosion. Sam heard him and threw his cup of coffee away and ran towards Abner, shouting at his cameraman, "C'mon. This is the big news we were waiting for. Someone in the White House has flipped their lid if they're going to explode a bomb underneath a million citizens."

Sam turned the cameras off and asked Abner where they had got their information. Abner refused to tell of Angela's late night call from Allen Gregory and only said, "She got it straight from the horse's mouth. Now every person in our million-man army is on their way to stop the explosion by putting their bodies at risk. Their safety is in the president's hands, and the people of the United States can't let him kill our people."

Sam said, "Abner, my name is Sam Robertson of NTC-TV. I can get this story on national television right away. You've got to tell this story to the nation. It may the only way to save your friends and all those other people. Look, I was there this morning when this....this invasion started and it's a full-scale military operation. Everyone out on that desert is in real danger. Sure, I want the story, but this is part of the people's right to know about these things. The public can be more powerful than the president if you get them mad enough."

Abner was convinced. He didn't want to think of what would happen if the bomb was exploded. No one here would live to see another day. "Alright. Let's do this and we'll get on with our work." After a ten minute interview Sam called his Washington office and they arranged a national showing of the interview at 2 p.m. Washington time. Sam called the local network TV station and asked them to come pick up the tape for transmission to Washington. His next move was to find a way to get out to the site without getting bogged down in the caravan traffic. He reached for his map. He had learned to never be without a map while in the field.

Just as the eastern sky began to turn blue-green-pink, Tondo flew overhead with at least two hundred eagles in a formation. Tondo landed on the hood of Angela's truck and greeted everyone.

"Whistler sent me," he said. "He is at Area 51, and he said he would join you soon. In the meantime, many huge airplanes arrived earlier at Nellis air base. There are thousands of soldiers gathering there and one of the scouts heard them say they would be going into the test site. They have already begun an attack."

Angela was puzzled for only a moment. "Amos, that may be what Allen Gregory meant when he asked us to stay away from there. He didn't want us to get caught in the fight. Let's look at your map." Amos laid the map on the warm paved road.

She said, "Okay. Here we are." Then moving her finger a little, "We should reach the final fork in the road in about another half-hour. Then we'll stop and set up a rest camp and form into a march towards ground zero. Let's get rolling." One by one the trucks and vans moved forward.

Frank was driving and Jay was "riding shotgun" for him with an eye on the near horizon and both sides of the road. Their orders were to stop immediately when something, anything, was spotted. Daybreak had silently come and the sun was now threatening to show over the mountains to the east. Behind them were a long line of trucks and vans filled with people, some of them children, who were placing their faith and trust in Angela's leadership. High above a dozen eagles kept a watch over them.

Chapter Thirty-Seven

They were only a few miles from the turnoff when Whistler appeared. After greetings were made, Whistler told them, "As you know by now, U.S. troops are attacking the test site, and there's now a lot of firing from both sides. It's mostly hand-to-hand fighting and as yet there are no aircraft involved nor are there any big guns. Tondo has seen these big guns, called artillery, used on targets at Fort Wingate and he said that apparently the U.S. does not want to destroy the buildings."

"Swift Wing said that before an underground explosion, a lot of men would gather at one particular building a few hours before the explosion. Last night many people gathered there just after dark and they are still there. At the spot called ground zero there is unusual activity. Last night, several large trucks arrived there from Area 51. This morning the big trucks were gone, but two pickup trucks are still there. The men are apparently still underground."

Amos spoke. "They're preparing to explode a bomb. And even if the troops are able to capture the building, we don't know for sure that the U.S. won't want to go ahead with the explosion themselves. We can't wait if we're to have any chance of stopping an explosion, by accident or on purpose. Let's get to the last turnoff and begin parking the vans and trucks. We have to form the march just as quick as we can."

In Washington there was a war, of sorts, going on at the highest level. When President Kenneally came to work early Monday morning, he was surprised to find a man sitting in the Oval Office waiting for him. His first thought was to call a Secret Service agent, but his mind suddenly went dizzy and he had to sit down quickly. He immediately felt better, and asked the stranger, "What is it you want me to do?"

"Nothing," the tall man wearing a dark suit said. "I'm here to help you. Didn't I hear you say last night that you'd sell your soul if you could solve your nuclear bomb problem? So let's talk, okay?" Kenneally said weakly, "Okay," and they talked for thirty minutes.

At nine a.m. Secretary MacAdams had called Allen Gregory at home. MacAdams was worried. "Allen, I'm glad I caught you in. Listen, I may be cutting my own throat here, but I have to tell you, I've never been gung-ho on this test explosion in Nevada. Why couldn't we test at Bikini, Kwajalein, or Eniwetok again, instead of at Yucca Flats here in our own backyard? Allen, I just can't get over all of the problems, big problems, we've created for ourselves with this damn H-bomb thing."

Allen Gregory was short on patience. Ever since NTC-TV had begun live coverage of what was supposed to be a secret operation he had been in a bad mood. What had started as a secret military action was turning into an embarrassing exposé of governmental corruption. No, Allen Gregory was not happy.

He asked, "What can I do for you today, George?"

"Don't be so snippity, Allen. I'm on your side today. I've discovered I too have a conscience. I want to tell you something that's important to you and your Indian friend, Angela."

"I got a call an hour ago from the president telling me to assemble a team of nuclear technicians capable of taking over test site procedures for the explosion. The team will leave Andrews in just two hours and will be in Nevada by two p.m. local time. As soon as General Dooley secures the administrative buildings and laboratories the president's team will move in and complete the preparations for the explosion. It worries my soul that he would do this knowing that Angela Beaver and her million-strong army is moving towards Yucca Flats."

"Worse, he's ordered the National Guard in to stop Angela cold. Paratroopers will hit the ground about three p.m. local time, and they have orders to seal the perimeters of the test site. Worse, they're authorized to use deadly force on all trespassers. Allen, I'm completely disillusioned. What kind of a government do we have when it makes war on its own people? I'm going to tell Kenneally that I'm considering resigning, and I'll go to the press if he refuses to listen to me."

Now, an hour later, Secretary MacAdams and Allen Gregory were in the White House, but President Kenneally refused to see them and they were talking to him over the intercom. Marine guards at the door would discourage anyone barging in uninvited.

"I'm very busy, gentlemen. Unless its very urgent I can't see you until late tonight," the president said.

"Mr. President," MacAdams said, "You can't keep me in the dark in this operation."

"Yes, I can," was the president's only reply.

"This is Allen, Mr. President. This *is* an urgent matter. Please see us now. It's about the Nevada problem."

"I'm sorry, Allen. I just don't have time right now. Call me in the morning, first thing." Then the intercom went dead.

"I'm sorry, gentlemen," Mildred said as they left.

MacAdams and Allen left the White House, crossed Pennsylvania Avenue and went to have a late breakfast at the Adams Hotel restaurant and discovered they had both lost their appetites.

Allen ordered coffee, then asked, "Are we really on the same side, you and me?"

"If you mean do I not like what the president is doing, the answer is yes, I don't like it. Do you have a suggestion?"

"I surely do. If you can get us one of the fastest planes the DoD has, I suggest we both go out to Las Vegas right away. We've got to save the president from himself, and the lives of a million people while we're at it. Do you want to go with me?"

"I'm still the Secretary of Defense. I can get whatever plane I need. How big a plane do we need. How many will be going?"

"Just you and me. That's all we need, but we have to go before the president finds out and fires us both."

"Damn. You're right. If we lose our status we'll have no authority. I forgot one thing, Allen. We can't take a military plane. The Pentagon will want to know where we're going. Let's take my own private plane. It's a four-seater and has two big engines. It's at the Leesburg airport. Take Route 7 to Leesburg then look for the airport sign. We'll make good time in that baby, and all I have to do is to file a flight plan with the local airport office and they don't touch base with Andrews or the Pentagon."

"I'm going to run home and get a change of clothes. You'd better put on some desert-trekking clothes, too. I'll order coffee and sandwiches to take along. The plane will be fueled and ready by the time you get there. Jeez, I feel better already, thanks to you."

Two-and-a-half hours later they were in the air, crossing over the Shenandoah Valley only minutes from the Ohio River, and heading west at 250 knots per hour. Their ETA was 1:45 p.m. local time.

Chapter Thirty-Eight

Amos' eyes were closed and Angela was studying the map when Frank slowed, then suddenly shouted, "Here we are!" They had topped a small hill and ahead of them Frank saw a well paved side road running to the northeast.

Angela gave a yell, "This is the turnoff to Yucca Flats and ground zero."

They made the turn, and then stopped when they reached a wide, flat spot on both sides of the road. From here it was only ten miles to ground zero. On foot, they could reach it in about an hour. Jay glanced at his wristwatch. It was almost 10:30.

Whistler flew down to talk with Angela. "One of Tondo's scouts reports that a small force of Marines are moving towards you across the desert. I suggest you hurry to get as far as you can before they reach you."

Angela had planned to park all vehicles here, then form a column of marchers. She changed her mind at the news of approaching Marines. She said, "Everyone start your engines and let's move ahead quickly. We have no time to waste now."

Angela's truck again took the lead. Frank was driving as fast as he safely could. They had gone no more than two miles, when a large dust cloud covered the highway ahead of them. When the dust cleared, they could see a dozen jeeps blocking their road. Several trucks were unloading Marines who immediately formed in front of the jeeps. They were all armed and dressed in battle gear.

Frank drove to within 500 feet of the Marines and stopped. Angela quickly realized that they would have to form their column here. She again instructed the others to begin parking the vehicles off the road to make room for the huge crowd which would be arriving soon.

While the vans and trucks were being parked, Angela asked Amos to come with her. She walked to within a hundred feet of the Marines.

An officer came forward and said, "Ma'am. I order you to turn around and leave the area. This is U.S. government property and you must leave now. If you proceed you may be shot."

Angela told the officer, "There are 200,000 people directly behind me and a million more on their way. Our objective is to stop the explosion of H-bombs. The lives we are trying to save includes yours. So please, let us go forward."

"Ma'am. Our orders are to use deadly force if you refuse to leave."

He gave an order and the Marines leveled their rifles on Angela and Amos.

"I will give you thirty minutes to turn around and begin leaving. This is my final warning."

ANGELA'S BATTLE

Angela called for a scout. She wrote a note for whoever was left at their headquarters. "The Marines have stopped us two miles from the turnoff. Come as fast as you can. Inform the people that we have to make a stand here. We need everyone here to impress them with our numbers. Hurry."

She quickly explained the situation to those with her, then she sent others back to tell people to begin forming into a huge column. As fast as the vehicles could be parked, people came running up front. Soon there were several hundred thousand people facing the outnumbered Marines. The Marine officer reported this by radio to his command post.

Five minutes later, the radio on the Marine captain's jeep crackled, "Jumpers are on their way. ETA five minutes. Move back 4,000 yards and observe."

Angela was surprised to see the Marines get in their vehicles and move back on the road. A loud cheer went up. They thought they had won.

Angela shouted, "Let's move out." The huge crowd began moving towards the retreating Marines and closer to ground zero.

They had gone no more than a quarter-mile when Whistler dropped down. Whistler said excitedly, "Angela. Amos. Airplanes are dropping men by parachute all around the test site and some are coming here. They will be here very soon."

Ham grabbed his binoculars and stood on top of the truck looking to the south and east where he saw parachutes by the dozens floating down to the desert floor. Soon there was the sound of approaching aircraft engines, then paratroops were dropping from the sky directly in front of them.

Quite by accident and his pure good luck, Sam's camera crew was also coming towards them driving north on an unmapped dirt road when they stumbled on the scene. He stopped his vehicles to one side of the huge column, and the crew began filming what was happening. Sam climbed out of the van and began to work his way towards Angela's position.

The first paratroopers to hit the ground began running towards the paved road and formed themselves into a line facing Angela's marchers with weapons at the ready. Every other trooper in line dropped to one knee and others quickly filled the empty gaps. Farther up the road, huge Boeing Chinook helicopters were unloading jeeps, which were quickly driven towards the roadblock.

Angela asked the people to spread out in a wide column on both sides of the roadway to face the armed men in front of them. She wanted to make room for more people. She estimated there were a half-million people here now and with each passing minute a thousand more were arriving to take their stand against the armed troopers.

She placed the larger stake trucks in a single line on the paved road, just in case they needed the trucks to clear a path for the crowd as they moved forward. Hand-made signs began to appear with names of states from where the bearer was from. Every state in the union and many foreign countries were represented here today. The new arrivals joined the others in moving closer to the line of khaki-clad soldiers. The crackle of radio static was occasionally broken by a voice reporting what was happening.

Sam decided to mingle in the crowd and report what was happening using his battery-operated recorder. He felt the excitement building in the crowd, and he sensed that if the crowd was to challenge the soldiers, they would overwhelm them. The cameras would catch all the action from the back of the truck.

A jeep drove up with an officer who was apparently in command of the troops. He got out of the jeep and swaggered into a position directly in the middle of the road, facing the people. He spoke into a bullhorn.

"Listen up, you people," he said. "I am Major Westmoreland, Nevada National Guard, operating under the command of the President of the United States. Which of you is the leader of your group?"

Without hesitation Angela moved to the middle of the road and faced the major.

"I'm Angela Beaver, and I am the leader of this citizens army. We are unarmed. We're here to save the country from nuclear destruction. We ask that you, as an American patriot, move aside and let us do our duty."

The major ignored her and announced, "I inform you that all of you are disobeying a lawful order of the President of the United States. You are ordered to disburse and return to your homes, wherever that may be. If you do not disburse, and you attempt to move forward you risk being shot. We have orders to use deadly force if necessary. You are warned, and you must leave immediately."

Angela returned the threat and declared, "I demand that you move your troops out of our way. If you do not, we will all die when the nuclear H-bomb is exploded. If you do not clear the way we will march over you."

For a moment, the Major was shaken. He had not been told of an imminent nuclear explosion, and privately, it was something he feared. Shortly after the

ANGELA'S BATTLE

Hiroshima and Nagasaki blasts in 1945 he had commanded troops at both locations. He had never forgotten the devastation and human suffering he had seen there.

Angela looked at her watch, then turned smartly and came back to stand alongside Amos and her two daughters. She said, "Ham, are the speakers in your truck?"

"They sure are, and we brought batteries to operate them. Do you want me to set them up?"

"Yes, I do. Bring a big truck over here and we'll mount the speakers on it. One facing forward and the others back towards the crowd. I want to be able to speak to our people as well as to the troopers. Quick, we have little time now."

Sam was now close enough to hear what was going on, and he immediately went to introduce himself to Angela and offered the use of his rented truck to her. She accepted, and Sam waved to his driver to come over.

The truck was positioned in front, between the two columns, much to the delight of Sam. His luck was holding up. Here he was, in the thick of the action.

Angela looked back at the huge crowd. "Look at them, Amos. There must be half a million people here and they're still coming. Jay, run back and get all the Indian drums up here quick. We need them and the singers. Bring them right up front. Hurry."

The crowd was growing tremendously in size. Amos said, "We must move now. It's getting late."

"Alright," Angela said. "Let's get started."

Amos motioned to the Blackfeet Elder, *Old Person*. Old Person came forward and placed a feathered war bonnet on Angela's head. Eagle feathers trailed down from the bonnet, almost reaching the ground. Another man brought an ancient staff to her, from which hung several eagle feathers. The staff was one which had already been tested in battle more than a century ago when the first European settlers invaded the Great Plains of the mid-West.

Ham handed a microphone to Angela. "Listen to me, everyone," she announced. The crowd quieted in expectation. "We are here today to ensure that there will be a safe world for our seventh generation and for their seventh generation."

"What happens today will be of little significance if we don't succeed in our mission. You and I are now in the front lines of a battle for the future. In front of us are a few misguided military men who are willing to obey the orders of the government, regardless of the consequences. We are going to roll over them if they do not see the error of their ways. Are we ready?"

The roar of three-quarter million determined voices rolled over the dry hillsides of the Nevada desert.

"This fight was begun by Indian people, therefore we may be the first to fall in this battle. It is our duty. If we fall, it is then your duty to pick up our staff and move ahead. If we die, we will die with honor. If we win, it will be a glorious victory for all of us as caring human beings, the children of our Creator, our God. We are now ready to step forward into history. Amos Turkey, and I, Angela Beaver, will lead the way. Follow us."

Again, almost a million voices roared in approval. What would be, would be.

Angela took the decorated staff and lifted it high above her head. Its feathers were fluttering and shaking like aspen leaves in a strong breeze, yet there was no breeze. She turned and looked at her two daughters standing proudly by her side. Fawn and Star had changed into their tribal dress. Storm Cloud, with Diane by his side, was to the right side of the line standing with a large group of Quechan warriors who had brought their families with them to join the fight.

All along the long front line, there stood the most diverse group of Indian people ever seen. The Mojave, Chemehuevi, Quechan, and Cocopah, all from the Colorado River valley, the Navajo, and Rocky Mountain Utes, stood alongside Arizona mountain Apaches. A group of the Cahuilla people from California stood alongside the Sho-sho-ni who once owned all of the area now called the Great American Desert.

Great Lakes Anishinabe and forest-dwelling Chippewa stood with Choctaws, Creeks, and Cherokees. The Maidu from the northern California mountains, Pueblos from New Mexico, who were descended from the Anasazi, stood with the Tonto Apache, Tohono O'dham and Pima from Arizona desert country.

Ned and others from Angela's Paiute reservation stood close by, along with people from four hundred other Indian nations who were represented in the line of battle, dressed for war. The Indian people were finally united as never before in their long history. Nearly a million non-Indians were directly behind them. The crowd was increasing by the minute.

A drum carried by four Comanche singers began to thump a cadence from the left side of the column. Angela looked to the front, to the brown line of National Guard troopers, then she lifted the decorated staff above her head, and without a word she moved forward with Amos by her side. A million Americans moved forward with her, not knowing what would happen, but with full faith in their cause, knowing only that what they were doing was necessary if they were to have a seventh generation after them.

Sam looked at Angela proudly wearing her feathered bonnet. He admired the way she was leading the people against tremendous odds. Who could hope to win a battle against the armed might of the United States? Yet Sam found himself wanting to join with her.

She looked heroic, like a Joan of Arc. That's it, he thought. That's how he would describe her to his television audience, a modern-day Indian Joan of Arc, a heroine leading her people to a victory that she herself might not live to see.

He spoke into his recorder, "*Faith and determination may decide the outcome of this historic and unprecedented battle for this land which was once the domain of Angela's forefathers.*"

The leading edge of the huge crowd moved to within one hundred yards of the troops, and an order was shouted. "Fix bayonets."

Amos heard the order. A thousand soldiers unsnapped their bayonets from their belts and clicked them into place on their rifles. The sight would have stopped weaker people.

Angela turned and waved the staff towards one end of the front line to the other. Amos shouted, "*Teton La-ko-ta.*"

Immediately six Lakota warriors came running to the front center, two of them holding a kettle-shaped drum between them. They formed a small circle around the drum, and then a high falsetto voice, quivering with pride, began singing a Great Plains Teton warrior's song. All along the front line, other Indians joined in. When the song was done, there was a series of war whoops up and down the line.

Angela shouted "Let's go," and again stepped forward.

The crowd moved with her, heads high and shoulders back. What would be, would be. Angela thought she had never felt better. Yes, this was a good day to fight and a good day to die, if necessary.

Chapter Thirty-Nine

Angela was now a mere 100 feet away from the troops, many of whom were now fidgeting nervously. Publicly, they were called "Week-end Warriors" and had not been trained to shoot American civilians.

Another order was clearly heard, "Prepare to fire one volley only on my order. Prepare for skirmish."

At fifty feet they were almost eye to eye when underfoot there was a sudden sharp jolt, so short that those who felt it weren't sure if they had felt something or not. Angela's first thought was that "We're too late. A bomb has been exploded." But she continued moving forward.

At the time, Ham had been looking for eagles in the sky through his binoculars. The jolt was so sharp that his glasses bumped against his cheek bones. Startled, he looked towards Amos and Angela. She raised her right arm in a signal to stop the advance.

Angela called, "Fawn, come with me." She reached over and took a microphone from Ham.

Together, the two moved towards the troops. When no more than ten feet from their line Angela stopped. The huge speakers boomed out her voice, "Bring us your commanding officer."

An officer stood up in a Jeep from behind the line and his startled voice said, "I'm Colonel Bingaman. I order you to disperse these people and stop your march immediately or....."

Amos waved his hand at the colonel and he suddenly lost his voice.

Angela said, "It is we, citizens of the United States, who tell you to move aside. Disperse your soldiers and let us through or else you will be destroyed by your own actions. You are our friends and brothers. We do not wish to hurt you, but our mission is to stop the nuclear explosions. You men are proud soldiers and have defended our country bravely in many battles. But so have we. You cannot allow the explosions to take place or we will all be destroyed."

The Colonel was still standing, but was now clutching his throat unable to utter a sound. Strangely, Major Westmoreland seemed to have suffered a loss of voice too.

The Colonel was a good soldier. Finding himself without a voice, he motioned towards a sergeant who was standing to one side with a platoon of men who were holding rifles capable of lobbing gas grenades a distance of 100 yards.

ANGELA'S BATTLE

The sergeant gave an order, "Fire grenades." Immediately two dozen gas grenades were lobbed into the air towards the civilians. The crowd gasped, not knowing what to do.

Angela quickly announced, "Everyone. Close your eyes and stand still. Do not move."

Amos shouted to Whistler, "Now is the time. Bring in the entire group of scouts."

Whistler rose into the air and flapped his huge wings, staying stationary in the air. Immediately from above came a huge formation of eagles. Even as they drew near, the grenades hit the ground in front of the marchers and released their eye burning, throat choking gas. Five hundred eagles came to join Whistler in hovering a short distance from the spewing clouds of gas.

Then the force of a thousand and two eagle wings flapping mightily created a tremendously strong wind which forced the gas back into the faces of the soldiers. Out of nowhere a dozen "whirlwinds" appeared and wandered through the soldier's ranks, creating panic among them.

Unluckily for them, a command to put on their masks had not come in time. Blinded and choking from the fumes, they dropped their weapons and fumbled with their masks, but it was too late. Men ran forward and threw gas canisters back at the troops. Their commanders had been completely unprepared for such a counterattack.

The colonel's jeep driver, now blinded, tried to drive the colonel to safety, but the jeep left the road and ran unchecked through the desert rock and sand. The sight of the eagles opposing him completely unhinged the major and he ran screaming and stumbling into the hot desert.

Angela announced, "We've won the first skirmish. Now we have to move on if we want to win the war. Will volunteers please gather up the weapons dropped by the soldiers and pile them beside the highway. We will remain unarmed."

The roadway was quickly cleared, then the march resumed.

No one was more amazed at what had happened than was Sam, the hard-nosed reporter. The simpleness of the defense was unbelievable.

"The most primitive of weapons have won this time. An eagles wing, a dash of wind, and a ton of courage. This is the recipe with which Angela has routed our modern army," he said into his recorder.

He was overjoyed to find that his cameras had filmed the entire sequence. Pulitzer stuff, for sure, he thought.

About two miles ahead of them, the Marine unit was trying to find out why the soldiers were all running towards them.

A Marine captain radioed his command post, "All hell seems to be breaking loose. The guard troops released gas, and now they're retreating. They appear to have lost their weapons. Apparently the civilians are well-armed. Sir, do we fire on them?"

"Negative," came the reply. "Form a rear guard for the troops, then lead them back to our command post. Command wants to mount an attack by armored. Rejoin your unit."

The captain persisted, "Sir, you should know there appears to be many tens of thousands of them. They appear to stretch in a column two hundred yards wide and back as far as we can see. They're like a huge army of ants. Don't forget, sir, these are U.S. citizens." His last sentence was ignored.

As word of the victory filtered back to the rear of the column there was renewed spirit in the ranks, and as they again moved forward they felt assured that their cause was a just one.

They were marching into the area recently vacated by the Marines. Abner and Milford joined them, saying they had recruited volunteers to stay at the turnoff and set up the supply trucks which would soon be along.

Ahead of them the ground seemed to slope upwards slightly. She mentioned this and Ham told her, "The explosions here on Yucca Flats over the past few years has probably little by little pushed up the underground layers of rock and sand around ground zero. There's no doubt a huge domed cavern down there just waiting to collapse from the right amount of pressure from above or below."

Earlier in the day, General Dooley's Marines had been able to move faster than anticipated towards the test site's administrative village. The airport and ancillary buildings had been cleared of small pockets of resistance from Hunsaker's security force. One of them told an officer that they had not been told they would be facing a military force, that they were to only keep civilians out of the area. Most of them had surrendered on seeing the armored force descending on them.

The Marines had easily moved into the administrative buildings and laboratories and removed every person found there. Gen. Dooley received a message from the Pentagon that the hand-picked nuclear technicians would arrive at Nellis Air Base at approximately three p.m. They were to be met by military police and immediately escorted to the test site laboratories where they would determine how close the Dyna-Nuclear people were to being ready for a test explosion. Gen. Dooley was told they would *disconnect* the bomb detonators.

But the technicians had other secret orders. They were to prepare the bomb for detonation at eight p.m.

A problem for Gen. Dooley was the fact that no Dyna-Nuclear scientists had been found at the labs. After some heavy questioning, a technician had admitted that some time after midnight final components for the bomb had arrived by truck from Area 51. They were delivered to elevators at ground zero which descended to the 5,000 foot level below ground. The components were transferred to another elevator which was built to descend to the 10,000 foot level where the bomb, once the detonators were installed, would be ready to be exploded.

The explosion itself was to be set off by a remote control panel which was contained in a mobile laboratory. When last seen, the mobile lab had been at ground zero for final adjustments and coordination with the bombs components.

There was a good chance, he said, that when the Marines had attacked, the scientists may have advanced the hour of explosion. His guess was that the explosion could be ready as soon as six p.m. Detonation would be dependent on the technicians getting to the remote control laboratory. If they could not, the bomb could still be detonated from a local panel not far from the bomb, but the technician would die in the explosion.

General Dooley looked at his watch. It was 2 p.m. That's when he had ordered the paratroopers in to keep all civilians away and out of danger. He sent a detachment to ground zero to check below ground. Their orders were to arrest everyone found there and bring them to the surface. They had no way of knowing that when the Dyna-Nuclear scientists had finished the critical work, they had left a single technician there to finish the panel hookup.

The Marine detachment found the thick steel doors leading underground at ground zero closed and locked, and the elevators were inoperative. They could not locate the electrical switches which opened the door or controlled the elevators. In spite of all General Dooley could do, the explosion could happen at any time. Now he had reports of a million civilians moving towards ground zero.

Lord, he said to himself, *I sure picked a hell of an assignment for my farewell party.*

ANGELA'S BATTLE

By four p.m., the Military Police delivered the president's hand-picked technicians to the administration's laboratory. They were told that a hold had been placed on their project. With the steel doors to the underground bomb chamber locked, the explosion couldn't be prevented. They had to find a way to get into the bomb chamber. As far as General Dooley knew, the preparations for the explosion were either complete, or being completed. Anyone within five miles of ground zero was in mortal danger.

Then he received a report of what had happened at the roadblock set up by the National Guard troops. He decided to try and turn the civilians back one last time. General Dooley looked at his wrist watch. It was a quarter past five. The civilians were now just about five and one-half miles from ground zero. He ordered two more companies to reinforce the three companies of Marines already there. They were to stop them by force, if necessary.

He tried once to call Secretary MacAdams and no one in the Pentagon knew where he was. He slammed the phone down. "Damn, am I the only one working today?"

Meanwhile, MacAdams and Allen were having their own hard times. Nellis Air Base denied them permission to land because they were flying a private plane. When they were finally able to land at McCarran Municipal Airport they found every available car and truck had been rented by the huge group of civilians who had arrived for the march to the nuclear test site. A rental car attendant suggested they take a taxi to the headquarters of the protest group. "It's out on west Highway 95. All taxi drivers know where it is. The TV news has been saying that there are buses and trucks taking people out to the test site," he told them.

An hour later, they were in the back end of a truck which was carrying food and bottled water out to the people. The driver said it might take four hours to get out there because of the huge crowd so they settled down for a long, hot ride.

As the marchers crossed over Yucca Flats and drew nearer to ground zero, the hot desert sand and rocks were throwing heat up into their faces. Late afternoon always seemed to be the warmest part of the afternoon. After storing heat all day, the sand and rocks were only too glad to give it up in the form of radiation as the air cooled slowly. Everyone was drenched in sweat so Angela halted and announced a fifteen-minute rest.

Ham climbed on top of his truck and looked over the few remaining miles to go, he saw that the sandy hills were formed like ripples radiating outward from the center point of ground zero. The several previous explosions had shaken the desert so hard that the looser topsoil, without vegetation to hold it in place, had taken on an appearance similar to that of ripples in a pond. Yet in one place there was a depression running outward from ground zero as if a giant finger had drawn a line through the ripples of sand. Strangely, the giant finger had stopped slightly to the left, and a short distance ahead of them. He studied the anomaly. What did this mean to a geologist?

For a few minutes Ham drew on his knowledge and experiences of forty years. He had never seen anything like this. He suddenly jumped up and shouted at the others. "Angela, gather the others quick. I've discovered something."

When they circled around, he used a twig to draw what he had seen on the sand. "What this is telling us is that the rock plate below is already fractured along this line here," indicating the finger line. It was probably fractured by the first bomb explosion, and since that time the upper level of desert sand and gravel has been gradually sifting through that crack in the rock layer."

"Now, I think the reason that this crack stops here, is that there is a large fault running at right angles to the crack and this stopped it from going any further. My theory is based only on what I can see. Back a few miles I felt a sharp jolt and I think it came from this fault. What this means to us is that if there's any further movement of the fault, the roof of the dome which is already cracked, could collapse at any time."

"Because of the responsibility we have for the people, I recommend that we make our stand right here where we are now. If we go farther, and the dome collapses, everything and everybody on top of it could drop down several thousand feet. I know it sounds far-fetched, but I suggest we should be better safe than sorry."

Angela said, "We're almost there. We can accomplish more by getting closer. It's always been our intent to use our bodies to force the government to stop the explosion. They would not want to kill innocent and unarmed civilians in front of television cameras. We have to go all the way. We may also find some way to disconnect electrical wiring or disable pumps, fans, transformers or other equipment. We can't do that from here. So we'll go ahead and camp right on top of ground zero."

Before the march could be resumed, Whistler dropped from the sky. "Angela. We may be in deep trouble. A large force of U.S. Marines are on their way with armored cars, machine guns, and a lot of other things. I've sent for the rest of the eagles to come in a hurry."

The situation had suddenly changed. Angela grabbed the microphone and explained the news that Whistler brought. She told the two columns to broaden out to allow more people behind them to move up closer. "It looks like this may be the place where we have to make our stand, so leave the vans and trucks where they are and make room for the other people who are coming up to join us on the front lines."

The huge crowd began to slowly shift and move into place.

"When the Marines form in front of us, I want those farther back to swing to the right and left of them and gradually walk around them. I want to make it impossible for them to stop one million people. So crowd up as far as you can, then when someone gives you the word, begin slowly walking around them. Until they get here, how about a volunteer to lead us in a song?"

This would take their mind off this serious turn of events and also give Angela more time to think this through.

A woman in the crowd said loudly, "I'll do it."

When she got to the microphone she explained to Angela and Sandra that her name was Melissa Glenn, a singer with the Metropolitan Opera Company in New York City.

"I believe in your cause, Angela, and it's a pleasure to be here with you," she said.

The dust raised by the approaching Marines was beginning to reach them. Melissa Glenn was leading the crowd in singing *The Battle Hymn of the Republic*, and the front lines were getting larger and larger. While the singing was going on, Amos and Angela were discussing strategy with Ham, Frank, and Jay.

The tension was growing. For the third time within a few hours they were being confronted with military opposition. Angela thought that the media could be used to prevent the Marines from using violence. "Ham, send Abner to the rear and have him use some of the buses to bring the media reporters up here fast. We need them."

Chapter Forty

This time, instead of the simple roadblock as before, fast moving armored vehicles were moving up the road towards them. They halted 100 yards away, spilling ten fully armed men out of each one. They set up ten lines across the road, fifty men in each, and the rest numbering another 500, split up into two groups, one on each side of the road, standing in reserve.

Angela stood directly in the middle of the road facing the Marines. Amos was beside her. Angela called for all of the Indian people to join her.

The 50 armored vehicles withdrew and formed a half circle around the Marines. When they were all in place, an officer in Marine battle dress, came forward and addressed the crowd.

"I'm Lieutenant Colonel Burgess, United States Marine Corps. Then looking at Angela, he said, "You must be Angela Beaver, the group's leader. And you, sir, are Amos Turkey?"

"Yes," both answered.

"It's a pleasure to meet you both," the officer said. "I've heard much about your talents. Can we discuss our situation here?"

"Of course we can," Angela said. "But you have to be brief. We don't have time to waste."

"I see," Lt. Colonel Burgess said.

"Tell me. What are you trying to accomplish? You know, this is restricted federal land and even without the Marines being here, it would be a very dangerous place. In short, you have no lawful right to be here. You have no business here, do you?"

Angela was impatient. *This man talks too much*, she thought. She whispered to Sandra, "Pass the word to tell the marchers to begin their move to go around them."

While Sandra was doing that, Angela spoke to the officer. "The answer to your question is, Yes. We do have legitimate business here. We have no quarrel with you or your men as persons. It's just that we dislike what the government, which you represent, is doing to the citizens of this country. I'm going to assume that you don't have any idea of why you're here, except to force us off this land. Let me educate you for just a moment."

"Your Marines are in mortal danger. In a short time your government plans to explode a nuclear hydrogen bomb right underneath where you and your men are now standing. Do you want to be here when they do that? I would think not."

"Your government has been warned several times that if the nuclear bomb is exploded, millions upon millions of people will die as a result. Now, I'm not going to argue with you, I told you I don't have much time, and neither do you if you want to save yourselves. I'm only telling you this to warn you to leave and let us pass so we can stop the explosion. We are unarmed and cannot harm you, but you would die all the same, buried in nuclear waste."

The Colonel couldn't think of an immediate reply. He hadn't heard of any plan to explode a bomb.

During the lull, Tondo arrived and flew down to speak with Whistler. The colonel was taken back at this unusual sight. While the colonel waited, Tondo gave an astounding report to Angela.

"There is a strange vehicle at a place in Area 51. It is like a van, only much larger, and is hidden in the trees. Whirl Wind flew down to look at it close and he heard two men talking. They said one man had been left deep underground at ground zero to make final adjustments to the nuclear bomb. From what was said, they intend to explode it at eight o'clock."

Angela asked, "Sandra, what time is it now?"

"It's six-fifteen."

"Then we have no time to waste. Sandra, tell the people to hurry in getting around the Marines. We have to move soon. I'll try the truth with this colonel. If he won't listen we'll have to run over them." With that, she turned her attention back to the Marine colonel.

"Colonel, I've just received word that the situation is more urgent than ever. There is one man below ground at ground zero making the final preparations for the explosion of the nuclear bomb. There is also a van hidden nearby which has the means to explode the bomb when it's ready. They plan to explode it at eight o'clock. We have to stop them. Will you let us through?"

"Ma'am, I can't do that," the colonel said. "My orders are to stop you or to turn you back. You must leave now or my men will begin an advance on your position. You have five minutes to begin your retreat."

Angela turned towards *her* army. In the distance she could see two buses coming slowly towards them. They soon got close and stopped. Photographers and reporters quickly exited and came forward to see what was going on. The Marine colonel saw them and ordered them to leave. They did not. They also stood and held their ground.

Because of the colonels refusal to listen, and his threat of force, Angela realized that it was here that their final battle would take place. They had to get by these Marines to be able to stop the man underground from finishing his job. They would win or lose by eight o'clock.

"Sandra, please get on the speakers again and explain what we now know. The people need to know the truth."

After Sandra finished telling her story, Angela resumed her efforts to convince the Marine colonel to let them through.

"Colonel," Angela said firmly. "I've been honest with you and I've told you exactly what we know. Now it's my turn to tell you that unless you decide within two minutes to let us through, to save your lives and ours, we will advance on *your* position. This is my final word to you. You must let us through within two minutes or we will move through you. It's now your decision to make, not mine. I will say no more."

A lieutenant came and reported to Colonel Burgess. "Sir, the people are walking around us on both flanks. Shall we stop them?"

Colonel Burgess was shaken. In his thirty years in the Corps, he had never had anything like this happen. Without an answer, the lieutenant had no choice but to watch as the marchers moved around them.

The colonel turned on his heel and went to his armored vehicle and told the radio operator to "Get General Dooley on the horn."

General Dooley was having his own set of problems. He couldn't get any more information out of the technician who had told them about the mobile control panel. Neither could they find out how to get below ground to the bomb chamber.

As a last resort he had released the government's hand-picked technicians and questioned them one more time. He had to get them below to start disassembling the bomb. He was under the assumption that he still had eight hours left to do the job.

The Chief Nuclear Technician finally admitted they knew how to get into the shaft at ground zero. "Give us a truck and we'll go over there, find the bomb, and disarm it. We'll leave the rest up to you. We should be back by nine o'clock if everything goes well. All we have to do is remove the tritium trigger and disconnect some circuits, then its all yours, General. We'll just follow the president's orders."

Of course, Gen. Dooley didn't know the president had ordered an explosion.

Dooley said, "Okay, gentlemen. I'll let you do that, but I'm sending ten men with you. I have to tell you that there's a lot of civilians trying to get to ground zero to stop an explosion. They don't know our orders are to disconnect it. We're going to turn them back by force if necessary, so you guys can do your work undisturbed. Now get going. I'd like to have this whole thing secure by nine o'clock. The president is waiting for me to report."

It was 7 p.m. before they reached the steel doors leading to the elevators which would take them down to the bomb. They located three hidden switches which would open the doors. One man inserted a special key and the steel covers rolled back from the doors.

When Colonel Burgess couldn't reach General Dooley, he sent one of the armored vehicles to the command post in the laboratory building with a message of what Angela had told him about the mobile control panel. The message had reached General Dooley after the technicians had left for the bomb site. He dismissed the information as *scuttlebutt*, the Marine's word for *rumor*. He tried to reach Colonel Burgess, but there was no reply.

He told a lieutenant to get an armored vehicle for his use. "I'm going out to Colonel Burgess' position and make sure he's sending those Indians back to their reservations."

In the underground chamber which held the control panel for the bomb, a technician inside was making final tests of the remote control circuits in the bomb's main control panel. Everything looked good. The lone technician put down his hand tools, exited the chamber and closed its steel doors behind him. Then he pushed hidden buttons which locked the doors in place. Then he headed for the elevator for the slow ride up to the surface.

The Marine guards seized the lone bomb technician when he suddenly exited the elevator. He refused to tell them who he was, and what he had been doing down below, so they took him back to the command post for questioning. The hand-picked technicians decided to take the elevator down to being their work of getting the detonation system working.

At 6:30 p.m. Angela had become nervous and impatient about the loss of time talking with Colonel Burgess. The marchers bypassing the Marine roadblock were only a trickle of what they would need at ground zero. Time was now of the essence. She looked at Amos with a question in her eyes. Amos said simply, "It's time to go."

Angela turned to the line formed by her closest friends, and went to hug each one. She said, "Star, pray for us," and hugged her tightly. "Fawn. You are a fine woman, a credit to the Navajo. Diane, I'm so happy to know you." Diane kissed her cheek. "Sandra, I'm glad I met you." Sandra squeezed her hand tenderly. "Frank, thank you for your loyalty. We Indians have to stick together. Ham, you're a real champion. Thanks for everything. Jay, without you we couldn't have begun this fight, or came this far."

Jay replied, "We'll win."

Then last, "Amos, my dear friend. We've come a long way in such a short time. I hope it continues."

Amos smiled and touched her cheek with his forefinger. "It will, Angela. Just trust the Great One," he said.

From his backpack, Amos took out a roll of velvet holding two magnificent tail feathers which Sharp Eye had given to them as a special gift. He tied them on to Angela's staff.

The two minutes were up.

She wiped a tear from her eye, then took the microphone and told the marchers, "We're going to move ahead now. I thank each and everyone of you for being here with me. I want each of you to be brave. Do not use unnecessary violence. Just try to force your way through"

"While we move forward I would like Melissa Glenn to again lead us in singing, and I want the Teton Lakota and Blackfeet drums to set our cadence."

Then, facing the Marines, she said, "Colonel Burgess, please move your men out of our way. We are coming through."

The line moved ahead as the drums gave a steady cadence. Amos and Angela were again in the lead. Colonel Burgess immediately brought his Marines to attention, then barked orders to his Company Commanders. He then went to his armored vehicle to observe.

When Angela was approximately 50 yards from the Marines, a captain barked another order and the front row of troops made a half-turn into a firing position with rifles firmly planted on their shoulders.

Angela took time to bring young Angela and Mina close, and they held hands as they pressed forward. Star moved to walk beside young Mina.

ANGELA'S BATTLE

Behind her, the words *"Glory, glory, hallelujah...."* rang out loud and clear as Melissa Glenn sang into the microphone.

Ten yards further, the Marines fired a volley over the heads of the marchers. The captain then ordered them to stop.

"You must stop now. The next volley will be fired at you. I beg you, stop. Please."

His words were not heard in the din of the drums and the singing. Whistler and the 500 eagles watched from above, confident that the Marines would not fire on their own people.

Sam watched, horrified, but confident no one would be shot.

Ten more yards and rifle sights were lowered chest high. The singers had just sang, *"Our God is marching on,"* when the captain ordered, "One round. Fire."

The shots echoed like cannon.

Twenty people in the front rows fell, some without a sound, and some with a loud scream. There was no alarm or general confusion from the crowd. Many were just stunned, not believing that U.S. bullets would be fired at them. They paused while the bodies were quickly picked up and carried to the roadside. Many others were wounded and were rushed to rear for treatment.

Suddenly a man rushed out towards the Marines shouting, "Put down your guns, you sons of bitches. What are you doing? You're shooting at United States citizens. Damn you. Put your damn guns down. You no good bastards, these people are trying to save your lives, and you're shooting them?"

It was Sam Robertson, hard-boiled news correspondent, who had seen death all over the world. What he had just witnessed was too much for him. He lost his head and charged the shooters.

In full view of his own cameras, and the nation's media, he attacked the armed Marines with fists clenched and swinging wildly. The captain tried to stop him, but a punch caught him just below the chin and sent him sprawling. A rifle butt slammed Sam's head backwards, then a bayonet stabbed into his chest and his heart burst from the puncture. He fell, blood flowing from his mouth.

One of his own cameramen ran to him, while the other cameraman continued to film what was happening. The faces of Marines closest to Sam were caught close-up. From experience he knew such pictures were helpful in proving criminal activity.

ANGELA'S BATTLE

Angela looked around and quickly counted faces. Ham, who had been standing to her left side was missing. Star, who had been to her right was also missing.

"You men are murderers," she shouted at the well-trained Marines who fidgeted nervously, but held their ground and their firing positions.

Sandra quickly got to the microphone and asked people to stop the march for a few minutes. Then she described what had just happened. Loud roars of anger were heard and men were seen to be rushing to the front.

Allen Gregory and George MacAdams rode in the truck to the ground zero turnoff, then began running towards the mass of humanity moving ahead of them. They hurried, forcing their way through the huge crowd. When the singing began they were about 200 feet behind Angela. When the first shot was fired they increased their speed. The second volley sent bullets ricocheting through the crowd and they could actually hear the sounds as the bullets hit the flesh of one person and tore through clothing of another.

"Holy Smoke, they're shooting at these poor people. We've got to stop them," Allen shouted.

They reached the front of the columns, and MacAdams threw up his arms and pleaded to he Marines. "Stop this shooting. I order you to stop. My name is George MacAdams and I'm the United States Secretary of Defense. Stop, I tell you."

The Marine captain's larynx was smashed from Sam's punch, so he was replaced by a young gung-ho lieutenant. He shouted, "Prepare to fire."

Then he addressed the two men who were shouting at them.

"Sirs, stop where you are or you will be shot."

He leveled a .45 caliber automatic pistol at MacAdams. "Stop, sir," he repeated.

MacAdams was seconds away from death.

A booming voice rang out, "Lieutenant, drop your pistol. Drop it I say."

It was General Butch Dooley, who had just rode up on the Marine's left flank and saw what had happened. The lieutenant recognized his commanding officer and holstered his weapon. "Sir," he said.

"Lieutenant, unload the ammunition from your weapons, then bring your men to parade rest. Where is Colonel Burgess?"

"Sir, he is to our rear trying to reach you, sir."

"Go tell him to come up here. We're going to talk."

266

Allen Gregory turned and recognized Angela and Amos. He rushed over and asked, "What the hell happened here? How did this turn violent? I told you to stay away from here today."

Angry, Angela turned away from him and asked Frank to check on the condition of Ham and Star. Frank returned and reported, "Ham and Star are both dead. Ham was shot in the chest and Star was shot in the neck. I'm sure they both died instantly, without pain."

Angela was furious. She shouted, "How could they do this to innocent people? It just shows what we're up against. A government determined to get their way regardless of who they have to sacrifice. I think we've misjudged the government. They're heartless. They haven't changed a bit from their massacres of the 1860s. They would kill us all for the sake of their damn nuclear bomb. They've killed our friends so now we can do whatever we have to do to get our job done."

Chapter Forty-One

Allen and MacAdams were in a huddle with General Dooley. Dooley listened while MacAdams explained why they were here.

"The bottom line is that the president seems to have flipped his lid, Butch. He sent the AEC technicians here with orders to explode the bomb."

"He came to me with a sob story of how he knew the Indians were right about the earthquakes and flooding, and how he didn't know how to stop Hemminger in time to prevent the catastrophe. I fell for his story and that's why I called you, Butch. I knew you were the best man for the job and he knew all along that you'd be able to throw Hemminger and his Hunsaker thugs out of here and clear the way for his own plan."

"As soon as we found out, Allen tried to warn the people to stay away without telling them about the bomb, because we knew you'd be able to stop it without a lot of bloodshed and there would be no chance of a catastrophe. It appears that Angela knew all along that it was going to be exploded. I don't know how the president knew, but he knew the Indians were the only ones that could stop him. That's why he ordered you to keep them out by any means necessary."

"It wasn't Indians or monsters that killed Interior's geologists. It was Armand Hemminger's men from Dyna-Nuclear. The Indians were handy and got the blame. Hemminger is in hiding somewhere, and he left his men here with orders to explode the bomb as soon as they could. I only hope we're in time to stop the AEC technicians. Where are they now?"

General Dooley hung his head in genuine grief. "What a mess I've made by trusting in the president, but that's what we're supposed to do, right? He's the Commander-In-Chief, right? He's my boss, for Chrissakes. Now he's used me to do his damned dirty work, and I've screwed up royally."

"My men have killed innocent civilians here tonight, and I've delivered the AEC people right down to the bomb chamber. They're down there now probably getting it ready to explode. They told me their orders were to take it apart so it couldn't be exploded. I believed them, and why not? We're all supposed to be loyal Americans, and now whatever happened and will happen, is all my fault. Sweet Jesus, forgive me."

"Butch, it's not your fault. We were scammed by the president too, but we can't just let it end this way. We need to fix our screw-up. We need to get down there as soon as possible and stop them," Allen said.

"You don't understand, but then how could you. See, I sent those technicians, and a few Marines to protect them, over to the explosion site. The Marines found one Dyna-Nuclear technician coming up from below. They brought him to our command post for questioning and after awhile, not twenty minutes ago, he said the bomb was behind locked steel doors and it was ready to be set off. He claimed that at eight o'clock it would be exploded by remote control from a mobile lab hidden somewhere nearby. A half-hour from now we may all be dead."

Angela had made sure Ham and Star were laid side by side and covered with a blanket to protect them from the insects which would soon be coming out from hiding. She had Sam's body brought over and laid beside Ham. In her mind, they were all heroes who had been willing to die for their belief in what was right. After Fawn performed a cleansing ceremony for them to release their souls, she had their bodies put into the pickup truck.

Then she turned her attention back to the problem which had brought them all here. Her anger had turned cold and she had a steely look of determination in her coal-black eyes. She was going to get this job done regardless of whatever or whoever stood in her way.

She asked Whistler to send an eagle to their headquarters and tell them what had happened. Some one should call every newspaper, radio, and television station in Las Vegas to let them know of Sam's death. She knew that Ham's or Star's names would mean little to them, but when the news of Sam Robertson's death at the hands of the Marines got out, there would be hell to pay for the president and Sam's killers. Jay said they could count on a full-scale congressional investigation into the entire affair.

Angela convened a council back away from the front line. She wanted nothing to do with Allen or the other fellow, and certainly did not want to discuss anything at all with the funny-looking general who she believed had ordered his Marines to shoot. She glanced at her watch. It was almost 7:35. The sun was about to disappear behind Shoshone Peak and Yucca Mountain, then there would be less than an hour of light left. They had to move quickly. There was only 25 minutes left to accomplish a miracle.

She laid out a plan. She knew the only way they could stop the explosion now would be to destroy the remote control panel hidden in Area 51.

She told them, "The only way to get there in time is for the eagles to carry hand grenades to the hidden van and blow it up. The only place we can get the grenades is from these Marines who are in front of us. There is no doubt more in the armored vehicles. We are going to have to attack these Marines, not for revenge, but to get the means to save this land."

The men standing around her looked at each other. She sensed they were itching for a chance to get back at them.

"The general has ordered them to unload their weapons. We can be on them before they can reload. That means a physical fight with them. When we re-form our line in a few minutes I want men who will volunteer, to be up front with Amos and I. The women and children will move to the back. I think we can move closer without a problem. When we get close enough for a charge the men will rush in and disarm them all. Their bayonets will be dangerous so be careful. Tie their hands with whatever is available, then strip the grenades from their belts. The Marines in the rear will not shoot for fear of hitting their own men, so all you have to do is move swiftly. Do it quick, time is short and the eagles are ready. Pass the word along."

"That's it. It's a simple plan, but it's all we have left to us. Our huge mass of humanity, one-million strong, and the spirits of our ancestors, will bring us victory. Let's go then. Brave hearts to the front."

In the history of the western world, there should never again be such a sight as the two groups facing each other on this evening. One group sworn to follow orders, right or wrong. The other willing to act and face death, just because it was the right thing to do. The beauty of this desert sunset setting belied the danger and threat of death all around.

The desert was bathed in the almost pink glow of a sunset that was reflected off of high clouds. In other times it would be called a beautiful evening. Flights of unsuspecting sparrows flew overhead thinking that these humans might drop morsels of food for them. In the distance a hawk circled, sensing excitement that might mean rodents were ready to scamper over the sands.

Suddenly, it sensed a great danger to itself. It wheeled around to face the danger. The largest flight of eagles it had ever seen was swiftly approaching, flying low to the ground. Tonight they were not interested in hawk for dinner.

Angela was standing with Amos in front of the huge mass of humanity. The crowd behind her had changed in appearance. Now it was an all-male crowd. Staff in hand, she walked towards the Marines who were still standing at parade rest. She noticed that the bayonets had been removed from the rifle barrels. She was thankful for that.

When she was a mere twenty feet from the gung-ho lieutenant, she stopped and firmly planted the staff on the pavement and made a demand. "I want to speak to Allen Gregory and the other man from Washington. The general who commands these men here," she gestured towards the Marines, "should also come forward, if he dares."

From Angela's right side the three men were walking towards her. The two civilians had a sheepish appearance as they shuffled forward while General Dooley marched as if he was in a review parade. They came and stood in front of her. Allen attempted to begin the conversation.

Angela raised one hand, and said firmly, "Quiet. *We* want to talk this time. We've listened to you too many times. Now it's our turn."

MacAdams took a chance and spoke.

"My name is George MacAdams, the Secretary of Defense. This is General Dennis Dooley personally appointed by the president to come here. We'll listen to what you have to say. Of course, we owe you that much."

"Good," Angela replied. She turned toward Allen Gregory who had been their contact with the president ever since that night in Flagstaff.

"Allen, we've talked many times and you always seemed to say the right thing. But it has been all lies coming from your mouth just as lies have come from the mouth of the government for many years. I will not speak falsely to you, as you have done to us. I will tell you the truth, then it will be your decision to help us or to oppose us."

"We know that the nuclear bomb is scheduled to explode in less than fifteen minutes from now. We also know it can be prevented. We know where the mobile remote control panel is hidden. It is far enough away that we are the only ones who can destroy it."

As she spoke she slowly moved closer to the Marines. The others slowly followed.

"Your men have killed two of my dearest friends and a nationally known television news reporter, Sam Robertson, with your cursed military force." Allen's mouth dropped open. He knew Sam personally.

"You have also wounded twenty others, including a famous opera singer from the New York Metropolitan Opera Company. Do you think your president and your men can escape the anger of the nation for what you've done? I think not."

"We don't seek revenge for those you have killed. We will leave that to your system of justice. All we want is to keep this land from being destroyed, as we know it will be if the nuclear bomb is exploded. We have come this far because of the things we know, so you must believe us now. You know about the remote control panel, but you don't know where it is, and there is no time for you to find it. Our eagles can be there in ten minutes."

She pointed to the sky, where directly overhead, a huge cloud of 500 eagles slowly circled.

"To destroy it we need your hand grenades. We will drop them on the remote control panel then the bomb cannot be exploded. Your scientists will then have all the time they want to dismantle the bomb. Will you give us the grenades? We need your answer quickly. The time is now 7:39. I will give you one minute."

General Dooley spoke. "This is nonsense, lady. Those grenades are U.S. Government property. We can't give them to you."

MacAdams motioned to Allen and the General. They began a hushed discussion. Allen's arms would occasionally wave around as he talked. MacAdams listened, and the General stood firm on his answer. As one, they turned to Angela.

Allen Gregory said, "I'm sorry, Angela. We just can't give you the grenades. What you have to do is tell us where this mobile control panel is and we can have the Air Force bomb it out of existence. For your own good tell us where it is."

"And how long will it take to get a plane to Shoshone Peak?" she asked.

General Dooley said, "Well, to get a plane armed with bombs and in the air will take at least 15 minutes, and probably seven or eight more minutes to locate the target and drop the bombs."

Angela laughed derisively. "General, you should brush up on your arithmetic. That adds up to at least 22 minutes. By then, you, and all of us, will be swimming in the Pacific Ocean. I'm sorry, but we can't wait any longer."

By now she and the men were less than 15 feet away from the first line of Marines. She very deliberately raised the staff, held it up for a moment, and again, the feathers on the staff waved excitedly. Then suddenly she dropped it.

"Now," she shouted.

ANGELA'S BATTLE

On both sides of Angela, eager men were charging into the line of Marines. General Dooley, Allen, and MacAdams, were buried and lost in the sea of men running over them. Excitement was running high as 100, then 1,000, then 2,000, then 5,000 men descended on the confused Marines. Even more were coming to help if needed. The mass of humanity would be enough to frighten a brave man.

There were so many people that the Marines lost sight of each other. They were overwhelmed. Frank and Jay were directing part of the crowd to get the Marines between the armored vehicles and themselves to prevent them from firing into the crowd. One flight of eagles dropped down, ready to rip the rifle away from any marine who raised it against the people.

Angela looked at her wrist watch, and reached for the microphone. It was ten minutes to eight. Time was dangerously short. A flight of eagles was hovering overhead, waiting for the grenades.

She shouted, "Jay, Frank, Abner. Get the grenades. We've got to get moving."

In the crush of bodies it was hard to find the grenades. Frank found four and he took one in each hand and tried to get them to Angela. It seemed hopeless, so he raised them in the air, one in each hand.

Tondo was the first to reach for a grenade. He grabbed a grenade in one large claw leaving the other free to pull the pin out. Then he rose up and began a swift flight to the oasis. He was rising swiftly, flying north in a direct line to the oasis. There was a cheer from the crowd.

Then, several shots rang out from the rear line of Marines. There was an explosion of feathers, and Tondo came tumbling out of the sky. There were screams of horror and loud groans.

Whistler quickly dropped down, took a grenade from Frank, then with his strong wings flapping mightily he flew low just over the heads of the crowd then headed towards the oasis at a tremendous speed. Swift Wing grabbed another grenade and keeping low to the ground followed Whistler in their race to beat the clock.

The sound of two more shots were heard, and everyone looked fearfully towards Whistler and Swift Wing. Fish Beak, a young eagle newly called to duty, swooped down and ripped the rifle from the shooters hands. Cheers went up again as they saw Whistler and Swift Wing streaking away to the north.

When Ho-go-ton saw his friend Tondo fall, he had quickly ordered his scouts to hit anyone showing a rifle. The air was now full of eagles circling and watching

ANGELA'S BATTLE

for any sign of a gun. Two more eagles dropped down and each picked up a grenade. They too flew off, low to the ground. No more shots were heard. The fighting stopped. The two sides separated and assessed their casualties and injuries. General Dooley retreated with Allen and MacAdams to consult with Colonel Burgess.

Chapter Forty-Two

Fearfully, Angela looked at the time. She told Amos, "It's too late. There's only three minutes left. He'll never make it in time."

She whispered the bad news to Sandra and asked Sandra to make an announcement. Angela wanted to tell the crowd to begin moving away from ground zero. Whistler might not have time enough to stop the explosion.

"Attention civilians. Listen. The eagles are on their way with the grenades. Please untie the Marines, then move back behind our front line." Sandra repeated the message twice.

As everyone began to move back, Angela instinctively looked for the unseen line where Ham had said there was a deep fault in the underground rock plate. She encouraged everyone to move behind that line. She didn't know why, but for some reason she wanted people to come back over that line.

Ho-go-ton sent several eagles to pick up Tondo's broken body. They brought him back and Fawn laid him in the truck, alongside Ham and Star.

Meanwhile, Whistler was straining to make more speed. He still had to get over the high ridge surrounding Area 51. Now there were less than two minutes left, and he still had not crossed over the ridge. He was pushing with every ounce of his strength. Pushing, pushing, pushing.

At thirty seconds to eight o'clock there was a single hard, sharp, earth shock. One very severe jolt. Everyone stiffened, expecting more, thinking that the bomb had exploded.

At ground zero, just outside the bomb chamber 10,000 feet below the surface, the technicians were still waiting for help to open the steel doors. The initial sharp jolt was much stronger at this level. It knocked them down, then a strange acidic, foul odor seeped upward from the floor of the room.

"Earthquake," one of them screamed. They noticed that the rock walls were beginning to get damp.

Five seconds after the first shock, a second jolt hit, much harder than the first. Then another, and another, five shocks in all, each one stronger than the one before. The whole valley was shaking, and clouds of dust rose up from the desert floor. Frightened birds flew up and away, and small animals ran for their lives.

For a full thirty seconds, an earthquake of a magnitude greater than 8.0 on the Richter scale, shook the floor of the Great American Desert, literally knocking people off their feet in Las Vegas as well as in other cities and towns within a 200-mile radius of Yucca Flats.

No one, including Angela and her million-person army, had at first doubted that the bomb had been exploded. They waited expectantly for the final shift upwards of the rock fault, and the flood to come afterwards. This was how their lives would end, they thought. They sat and waited as the dust gradually cleared.

Amos sat calmly alongside Angela and her daughters. He patted her shoulder and told her, "Don't worry. The Great One is on our side. Everything will be all right."

They were sitting just a few yards from the invisible line which Ham had described. As she looked, the line was now visible in the form of a crack in the earth about six inches wide. If Ham was right, the dome underneath would collapse soon.

She went to the microphone and urged the frightened Marines to get across the line as fast as they could. General Dooley got off the ground, dusted himself off, and ordered the Marines to get across the line in *double time*, the military equivalent of *run like hell*. The general reached down and helped MacAdams and Allen to their feet, then they did their own version of double time.

The first to feel the deadly effect of the quake were the AEC technicians who were trapped below ground with the nuclear bomb. A crack in the rock wall quickly became a major break, and the entire area was immediately filled with putrid water. Inside the locked bomb chamber the bomb was shaken off its perch, effectively breaking all electrical wiring and communication with the remote-control electrical panel. The technicians died along with the bomb. A few seconds later the entire room was flooded.

The entire area called Yucca Flats began to sink as the underground rock absorbed water and began to crumble.

The entire mass of people, including the U.S. Marines and their commanding general, watched in disbelief as the desert floor to the east of the line envisioned by Ham, began to slowly sink in fits and starts as the hollow dome deep underground began to fall.

Within a half-hour the surface in the center had sunk almost 1,000 feet, then someone shouted, "Look, it's starting to fill with water."

Chapter Forty-Three

The dust was still settling over Yucca Flat when Whistler and the other eagles returned and told of how it had been unnecessary to use the grenades on the mobile control panel.

Just as Whistler cleared the ridge the big shocks turned the van on its side. A diesel generator which had been supplying electricity for the control panel was knocked off its platform. There were electrical flashes and smoke coming from inside the van, and soon four men had staggered out, apparently unhurt. The eagles had pulled the pins of the three grenades and dropped them near the four men, who were running towards a row of buildings. Apparently the men were killed by the force of the grenades.

In addition, Whistler said, "The earthquake also destroyed and flattened most of the buildings of Area 51. By the time we left, water was flowing into the crater from the eastern end. The way it was going it won't be long until there's a lake up there."

General Dooley had withdrawn his Marines and returned to the Test Site headquarters. Before he left, he told Angela that he and the others would be back to see her in the morning and they would talk about what had happened here.

Angela announced to the huge crowd that the earthquake had saved them. There had been no nuclear explosion and the country had been saved by an act of the Creator. They would camp where they were tonight, since they had both food and water. She urged them to say prayers of thanks before going to sleep.

It was well after dark before Angela could be alone with her close friends.

Fawn had built a fire and began making a light supper and fresh coffee. Her two daughters sat close to Angela. She wondered about Ham and Star. She was told that because the deaths occurred on federal land, the bodies had all been taken to a mortuary in Las Vegas, where they would stay until released by the F.B.I.

They reminisced and talked of Ham and Star. They grieved for both of them, and shed tears while they remembered what they had been through together. It was decided that they were the closest to them, almost their next of kin, so they would plan later where they would be buried.

They talked until eleven o'clock. The fire had died down, and Angela happened to look up to the southern sky. A new moon was beginning to show. "Look everyone," she said. "A new moon. All good things should be started at the time of the new moon. That's a good sign for us."

ANGELA'S BATTLE

The new day dawned bright and clear. Fawn was up before daybreak, making coffee and biscuits. She had slept very little last night. She missed Star very much. She had been like her very own sister, and they had depended on each other. She had decided that after Star was buried, she would go back to Kla-begatho's house and spend the rest of her life in his service. In the meantime, she had to keep busy in order to keep from falling apart. She knew biscuits and honey was something Amos really liked, so she busied herself, while inside, she was crying.

Amos awoke and joined others who looked to the east to greet the sun, and to give thanks to the Great One, the Creator, for the favors granted to them. The rising sun had revealed a shimmering blue lake, where before there had been desert sand polluted by several generations of nuclear explosions.

Ducks and other water birds, puzzled by the sudden appearance of the lake, criss-crossed the water and explored the shore line for future feeding expeditions. Fish and other creatures would soon discover this place and come to make their home here. This would provide a necessity for continued life: a food chain. They marveled at this beautiful gift from the Creator.

As they ate their breakfast, they made plans for a dedication of this new lake to the memory of all who had given their lives here. Amos would speak on behalf of everyone. This would be the first of many annual meetings to be held here and it would serve as a reminder of their commitment to continue their efforts to stop any form of nuclear power for purposes of war or for uncontrolled commercial uses.

At seven a.m. an announcement was made that everyone should gather beside the new lake in one hour for the dedication ceremonies. Soon, cars, trucks, and buses began to move, and it was apparent that people wanted to be as close to the new lake as possible. An hour later, the lake was almost completely encircled by a sea of humanity.

When all seemed ready, Angela called on the combined drums of the many native people represented here on this day to begin their honoring song. The slow, steady thump of the rawhide-covered drums rose up to the heavens. Then, without a signal or a conductor's downbeat, ten thousand Indian voices rose up in unison in a song of thanksgiving which was as old as the surrounding hills and mountains. The cool morning air carried their song over the water to the farthest corners of Yucca Flats. The Creator heard and was pleased.

From the mountains to the east, huge flocks of birds of all kinds, led by the king of birds, the eagle, came flying straight out of the sun and circled the newly-created lake. As the song continued in a crescendo, the bird species took turns in flying over the lake to deposit plant seeds and fertilizer into the water and onto the banks. It was their contribution to a new life for Yucca Flats. By next spring, plants of many kinds would begin to flourish as food for fish and fowl. Then as suddenly as they had appeared, they flew back to whence they had come. As if on an unseen signal, the song faded away to silence.

When all was serene again, Angela began by saying, "Thank you, all of you, for having the faith and courage to join in this important battle. All of you being here made it possible to stop the nuclear explosions from taking place. We did all we humanly could, and because of your courage and the sacrifice made by our friends, our Creator saw fit to intervene and cause the earthquake which prevented the explosions. Your victory is one of the greatest victories ever accomplished in the name of the people. You may all be very proud of what you have done in the name of your seventh generation. I congratulate you."

"We dedicate this gift from our Creator to the memory of those who gave their lives so that we might succeed. Their names are Hamilton Gardner, a Hopi woman named Star, and a television newsman, Sam Robertson. Although Sam was not with us at the start, he saw what was really happening and acted on our behalf. Among our eagle friends Sharp Eye, Stone, and Tondo gave their lives for us."

"By this time next year we will erect a monument to commemorate what all of you have done here, and with special mention of those killed during our struggle. We will all meet here on this spot exactly one year from now, and every year thereafter. Is that alright with all of you?"

Loud roars of "Yes. Yes." rolled over the desert and the lake.

"So be it, then," Angela said. "One year from now, we'll meet you here for three days of remembering and celebration." Then she waited for cheers and the honking of many horns to die down.

"We're only going to have one speaker this morning. Amos Turkey will be that speaker."

Angela took the microphone and gave it to Amos. He confirmed to them that the Creator had made the earthquake happen to prevent the killing of innocent people, but had wanted the people to do as much as they could for themselves, even if it meant losing some of them.

"Only by sacrifice, would the victory have a deep meaning to the rest of us. It has been thus for thousands of years. Our sacrifices makes us stronger," he said.

"As you can see, ground zero and all it contained has been destroyed. In its place there is this sparkling blue lake fed by an underground river which the Sho-sho-ni revered. Their legend had predicted that the river would one day save their lives, and it has. This desert will no longer be suitable for nuclear test explosions, but contamination has taken place over the years, and this river will help cleanse the earth by sending that contamination downstream to where it will eventually reach the mighty oceans where it will no longer be dangerous to humans. Everything else you know."

Then it was time for Angela to close the meeting and to say goodbye to them all. She was near exhaustion and tears. Her daughters came to stand with her.

"I ask the Creator to bless each and every one of you. You have given of yourselves so unselfishly. So bravely. Goodbye, until we meet again."

Then the desert listened as a million voices sang,

> *"Oh Lord, my God, when I in awesome wonder*
> *consider all the worlds Thy hands have made;*
> *I see the stars, I hear the rolling thunder: Thy*
> *power throughout the universe displayed.*
> *Then sings my soul, my saviour God, to thee:*
> *how great thou art, how great thou art........."*

The voices rolled over the water and eventually echoed off the rocks and far hills. It was a moving and spiritual experience for them all.

The many vans, trucks, and buses formed into their final caravan and drove slowly past the spot where Angela and her small group were camped. They all waved goodbye and said a final farewell as they passed. The caravan drove along the lake's shoreline a short distance then reluctantly headed back the way they had come only 24 hours ago. It was 24 hours that none of them would ever forget. Everyone of them agreed, it had all been worth the effort.

Chapter Forty-Four

Angela's group was quietly drinking their coffee and munching on more of Fawn's freshly made biscuits when Allen Gregory and George MacAdams drove up with General Dooley.

Sandra was sitting next to Whistler, brushing his back feathers with her hand. Whistler was having no coffee or honey, but he was enjoying life. MacAdams and the general were surprised at seeing an eagle in their midst. Allen had said nothing about Whistler to them.

Allen said, "Good morning, everyone. Good morning, Whistler."

Whistler replied, "Hello, Allen."

The general and MacAdams had a look of astonishment on their faces.

"Impossible," the general thought. "I must be hearing things."

Angela was not yet ready to be friends with these men who had helped to kill Ham and precious Star. She sat without a word of greeting to the men.

Amos spoke for the others. "What is it you want with us? The nuclear bomb was not exploded, and the western country is still in place. No thanks to your people. Things could have been much worse this morning."

MacAdams seemed uneasy.

He said, "Well, there are some things none of us know yet, and we cannot speak for the president, but on our own behalf, we are extremely sorry that this incident was allowed to go as far as it did."

"We don't yet know if the bomb exploded or not. We are not convinced that it was an earthquake that happened last night. Our geologists tell us there has not been an earthquake of this magnitude here in at least forty or fifty thousand years, so until our scientists test for radiation we have to assume the nuclear bomb was exploded, and the catastrophe forecast by you people did not happen."

"We have come a long way in understanding nuclear explosions. It is only by such tests that we learn more, and we believe we understand these things better than you possibly could. Even our most learned scientists admit they have only scratched the surface of understanding nuclear fission."

"But first, we would like your civilian army, as you call it, to leave today. There may be dangerous radiation or other poisons in the waters of this new lake. In any event, we think it is in your best interests to leave as soon as possible. Then too, until we hear otherwise from the president, General Dooley is still under orders to remove you by any means necessary. We need to talk about an agreement to stay away from this area."

Angela heard and looked at the others. Frank's face was twisted with anger, his coffee cup shaking in his hand. Sandra's face was flushed and her fists were clenched. She was having trouble keeping her mouth closed. Diane likewise. Jay had heard this kind of talk before. He listened with a smirk on his face.

What Sandra had experienced just within the past twelve hours had awakened long-forgotten teachings from her Methodist upbringing. She was certain now that regardless of skin color, or ethnic origin, everyone was worshiping the same Creator, the same God. It mattered only that they believe, if they were ever to win their battle for peace and justice. Her anger subsided a bit, and she addressed the men from Washington.

She began, "God has chosen us to be here today. Angela has challenged evil and has won. There may be another battle yet to come, and if it comes, we will again do what we have to do, this time without fear. The wisdom of the ages has told us that, 'If God is with us, who can be against us?' What happened only yesterday was proof of that."

"Yesterday, each of us, as frightened as we were, was willing to give our lives for our fellow man and for those yet unborn. There can be no greater sacrifice than to do so. We are blessed by being a witness to what happened yesterday. God has brought forth the waters and has blessed it by fish and fowl. But once again, we are reminded that we are responsible. God once made humans the stewards for all that lives and grows on this earth. This can be our own beginning for a nuclear-free world. God is calling on each of you to be responsible stewards. I pray you will listen."

The three men said nothing.

Allen Gregory said, "We would like to talk with you and get some kind of agreement as when you will leave, and then make arrangements for any future visits you may be planning."

Amos said, "Yes, we can talk, but we will make no promises yet."

MacAdams showed his ignorance once more, while Allen Gregory winced.

"Do we have to light a pipe or something before we talk about an agreement?" He thought he was recognizing protocol.

ANGELA'S BATTLE

Amos challenged his faux pas. "Should we resurrect General Custer? You've seen too many Hollywood movies, Mr. MacAdams. Just sit on the ground there and I'll talk while you listen," Amos said.

After the three were squatted on the dirt, Fawn offered them coffee, and young Angela and Mina served it to them. The nicety was not lost on General Dooley.

Amos began, "I'll first tell you about your most recent problem, then I'll tell you how we know about such things, if you want to listen. Let me give you the bad news first."

"Your president had an interesting visitor about five days ago. He was a handsome-looking tall man who wore shiny black leather boots. The man wore a hat which he refused to take off. Allen, you saw him waiting outside the Oval Office as you were leaving on Friday morning."

Allen nodded.

"The man was an emissary of Satan. He eventually made a pact with your president in which he promised that if the president would explode the bomb, the nation's economy and its future would be bright for many years."

"Our Creator had to act, because as you should already know, the devil never keeps his word. If the presidents plan was carried out, we would all be dead now. The devil was depending on the destruction, otherwise he would not have had to corrupt your president."

"The president had decided to stop the work of Dyna-Nuclear. This is what forced Armand Hemminger to act swiftly on his own. In fact, General, you crossed paths with him on your flight from Camp Lejeune. Remember when you looked out the window and saw another plane crossing below you? That was Armand Hemminger on his way to Guatemala."

General Dooley remembered and shivered again. How could this old man have known?

"When you return to Washington, you will find that the president will remember nothing of what happened over the past two days. He will ask, and what will you tell him? His future will depend on this. The Congress will ask why a million people were put at risk. You don't have the answer. The American people are going to ask, why was Sam Robertson killed? What will you say?"

"So the fact that the explosion did not take place does not end your problems, or ours. Angela has won this battle, but if the Congress, and future presidents continue a reckless nuclear policy we may meet again as adversaries."

"Your friend, Allen Gregory, is the only other living person besides myself who has actually seen close-up, the past and the future to come if the government continues on its road of nuclear destruction. The president was not impressed with Allen's description. I tell you now that nuclear devices for warfare are the devil's own tools. You have to rise above things to see the whole picture as Allen has seen it. If you continue, your country will become infested with nuclear waste with nowhere to safely store it. As once predicted, you will have fouled your own bed."

"In a few years, the cumulative radioactivity and other chemicals set loose in the water you drink, in the air you breath, and even in the food you eat, will cause hideous diseases, deformed children, and painful lingering deaths. Do you want your seventh generation to curse your stupidity?"

"General, I want to call you Dennis, your Christian name, because you really are human and not a military robot, and someday you will realize this. You are skeptical about our explanation for what happened here yesterday, and you don't believe eagles can communicate with us. It is understandable. You are unenlightened. Your father and grandfather were military men, so you are a product of the mentality of 'follow orders, right or wrong.' But to not believe the truth when placed in front of you is pure egocentricity."

"Dennis, I would like some day to spend time with you and share with you our belief about the creation of this world, and yes, even talk about its end. I think you would find we're much closer in philosophy and spiritual beliefs than you might think. The peace you secretly wish for is right here in your back yard."

General Dooley acknowledged the personal invitation with a nod of his head.

"My talk is ended now. We will leave you as friends. Perhaps our paths will cross again, and if so, let it be in peace instead of confrontation. I sincerely hope you will remember my invitation to each of you to visit us and discuss the art of living. Goodbye. Our meeting is ended. A-ho."

General Dooley went to shake the hand of each of the Indians. On reaching Amos, he said, "I would like to continue this conversation. Please contact me and tell me where I can reach you."

"Angela, you are a brave woman, and I have much respect for you and your beliefs. To your credit, you have won this battle. I will pray it is the last battle in this war, but wars are a series of battles until one side wins. I hope you win all of your battles. Goodbye, until we meet once more."

The trio left as insecure as when they had arrived. They would have much to contemplate over the coming weeks. The three men got in the general's car and were soon gone. It would be a long time before they would see any of them again.

Chapter Forty-Five

After all the cars and trucks were gone, Angela suddenly felt a great emptiness, a loneliness that descended on her like a cloud, obscuring her vision of the world. She felt tired, almost exhausted. Angela asked to be left alone with her thoughts. Angela walked along the bank of the lake remembering all the work, sacrifices, and lives, it had taken to get to this day.

Maybe Amos would be able to help raise the curtain from her insight, and remove the troubling cloud. She wanted to know why she couldn't accept her victory and be happy for what the one million civilians had accomplished.

She sat on a rock near the water and called to Amos. "Amos, please join me."

Before joining Angela, Amos stopped to get something from his bedroll. He walked to where she sat. Angela had a look of despair about her, something that Amos had never seen before. Her shoulders drooped, and her head was lowered enough to signal that despair.

Amos squatted on the ground in front of her, saying not a word. He started a small fire with twigs, then sprinkled on a mixture of sweet grass from the mountains of Utah, Colorado, and New Mexico, native tobacco picked from the banks of the "red river," and sage from the deserts of Chihuahua, Sonora, Arizona, and Nevada.

A thin wisp of smoke found its way towards Angela and slowly covered her like a shawl. Her eyes closed. In her mind's eye she saw Ham and Star together, holding hands and laughing. Aaron too, was there. She wondered, "Why do I feel so badly, when they look so happy?"

Star reached out and touched her. Star looked so healthy, and happy. "We are so glad that we got to know you, Angela," she said. "Don't grieve for us. We are the lucky ones, and we cherish the time we spent with you. You are a wonderful person. You must know we are all happy here among our friends and relatives. Remember us while you are there, and believe that we will be together again some day. Give our love to your fine daughters."

Then the vision was gone. Still Amos sat, not saying a word.

Angela next saw Earl. He smiled at her. "Angela, it's just like you to worry about someone else. You always did take better care of others than yourself. Now you're feeling some guilt for the deaths of those who died. They were there because they chose to be there. Even knowing the risks, they chose to be with you, and to stand up for everything you and they believed in. Knowing that, there is no room for guilt to spoil your victory. Get rid of it now."

"Let me tell you, Angela, you owe thanks to Star for the life of young Mina. In the final seconds of her life, as the troops fired on you she chose to move in front of Mina to shield her from the bullet she knew would come. At a proper time, you might consider giving Mina the new name of *Star*. Star would consider it an honor, although she would never suggest it herself."

"I will not be visiting you again. I am told I will be journeying to the Lake of Souls soon. Until we meet again, I wish you all the best of good fortune. Thank you for loving me." Then Earl was gone.

Angela sat for a while longer with eyes closed. The wisp of smoke still wound itself around her from toe to head top. A beautiful lake surrounded by green shrubbery, green willow and cottonwood trees came into view. Flowering jacaranda trees grew here and there. Mud hens, ducks, and small animals could be seen enjoying the oasis where before, none had existed. It seemed so peaceful here she didn't want to open her eyes. When she did, the fire was out, and Amos was gone.

She looked back to their camp where Jay, Frank, Diane, Sandra, and Abner were still waving goodbye to those in the caravan passing by. Fawn was helping Amos to gather their things in preparation for their leaving. Angela remained quiet for awhile, thinking.

The funeral held a week later for Ham and Star, in Flagstaff, was simple and private. Amos had informed the tribal shaman's, and all twelve of them were there, as was the Council of Eagles. Kla-begatho officiated at the burial ceremony. Diane and Jay shared the eulogies, and the two coffins were laid side by side in the grave. Then it was over. Goodbyes were said, and everyone, except Angela and Amos left town. Fawn had gone back to Kaibito with Kla-begatho.

When Ham's death had been announced in the *Flagstaff Courier,* a town lawyer pulled his file labeled Gardner, Hamilton, out of a cabinet. After the funeral, he went to the house and spoke to Angela. Ham had left all he owned to Angela.

The lawyer handed her an envelope. In it was a letter written by Ham before they had gone to Las Vegas. When she was alone she read:

Dear Angela,
The fact that you are reading this letter means that I have gone on to my reward, whatever it is. I am leaving you all my worldly goods in the hope that it will help you to carry on the work against our country's obsession with deadly nuclear radioactivity.

I enjoyed working so closely with you and your friends, and I leave this world happy in the knowledge that you have opened the eyes of the world so that others will now join your campaign. I love all of you and I will always remember you with great fondness, wherever I am.
Sincerely, with much love,

Ham

The pent up emotions and stored tears of the past three weeks finally welled up in Angela. They flowed freely in the darkness, and she cried herself to sleep. She hadn't cried this hard since Earl had died. Now she was able to sleep peacefully.

She couldn't have known, though, that the ripple effect of what she had done would reach into the bowels of official Washington and change the face of politics for years to come. Citizens would begin to question political motives and new national policies would affect the world.

Afterword

Satan, thwarted by Angela and her civilian army, decided he would begin a new plan. He saw a change in political thinking, so he would change with the times. He would bring up his own apprentice who would one day be President of the United States. He would be the most powerful man in the world. Everything he touched would turn to gold, and the results would serve Satan's purposes.

In the future he would make nuclear weapons into a political weapon. Just the threat of a nuclear hell would keep the U.S. as the world's super-power. Small wars between small countries, fed by oppression sanctioned by U.S. policies, would be ready markets for the U.S. merchants of weapons needed to fight those small wars. Satan's hand would be hidden behind a curtain of economic growth and profit making. In the resulting turmoil, his goat men would have little problem gathering souls.

In October, 1963, the U.S. Senate began an official investigation into the whole matter of the nuclear development program. The following year was an election year, so hearings, studies, and investigations were bogged down in a political morass. No one was ever held responsible for the killings of the three civilians by the military at Yucca Flats. Acting under orders from their Commander-in-Chief, it was said, the military had no choice but to shoot the *dissidents*.

In November, the president was in Seattle, Washington for a meeting with the AFL-CIO labor unions. In a motor cavalcade to the meeting site, a number of shots were fired from a building along the parade route. President Kenneally was killed instantly from a rifle bullet to his head. It was apparent someone held a grudge against the president, but who? There were so many possible enemies. His killing would never be solved.

The vice-president was sworn in as president within a few hours of the president's death. Within a month, President Kenneally's Executive Order halting the underground testing of nuclear bombs was withdrawn and the new Nuclear Regulatory Commission immediately made plans to resume testing.

Armand Hemminger suddenly reappeared in his executive offices and took control of Dyna-Nuclear International. No element of blame ever touched him for what happened at Yucca Flats. Things returned to nearly normal in the nuclear industry.

An important thing did happen which would have an effect on the face of politics and nuclear policy. U.S. politicians committed the United States to a war in southern Europe, and thousands of American young men were called to fight a war where the United States had no real interests.

A young man appeared from nowhere to take a leading role in protesting the war and he encouraged American youths to resist being made to fight what he called "a politician's war."

By the time the war ended, the youth had grown into a man, and entered state politics where he made a name for himself as a forceful and knowledgeable state governor. His goal was to be the President of the United States, where he could manipulate political situations to create more wars and unrest worldwide.

Amos and Angela returned to Canyon de Chelly together, where they were living a life of peaceful bliss along the banks of the little stream where willows grew, and mourning doves nested. Allen Gregory contacted Angela through her address in Flagstaff. He and ex-General Dooley, now a private citizen, arranged to visit them at their canyon home. Both experienced a spiritual awakening there, and they returned to Washington to offer their help and expertise to Jay and Diane Storm Cloud, who had formed a national non-profit organization dedicated to opposing the production of nuclear materials, and to the safe storage of the growing piles of nuclear waste.

Frank and Sandra Hayes divided their time between helping Jay and Diane, and running their own non-profit organization which helped victims of nuclear radiation worldwide. Abner was invited to join them, and he became their Executive Director.

They had fought the good fight, and won. They had lived to fight another day.

The End?